Outstanding praise for Tessa Harris and her
Dr. Thomas Silkstone Mysteries!

The Devil's Breath

"Excellent . . . Both literally and figuratively atmospheric, this
will appeal to fans of Imogen Robertson's series during
the same period."
—*Publishers Weekly* (starred review)

The Dead Shall Not Rest

"Highly recommended."
—*Historical Novel Society*

"Outstanding . . . well-rounded characters, cleverly concealed
evidence and an assured prose style point to a long run for
this historical series."
—*Publishers Weekly* (starred review)

"Populated with real historical characters and admirably
researched, Harris's novel features a complex and engrossing
plot. A touch of romance makes this sophomore outing even
more enticing. Savvy readers will also recall Hilary Mantel's
The Giant, O'Brien."
—*Library Journal*

"Tessa Harris takes us on a fascinating journey into the
shadowy world of anatomist Thomas Silkstone, a place
where death holds no mystery and all things are revealed."
—Victoria Thompson, author of *Murder on Sisters' Row*

Books by Tessa Harris

THE ANATOMIST'S APPRENTICE

THE DEAD SHALL NOT REST

THE DEVIL'S BREATH

THE LAZARUS CURSE

Published by Kensington Publishing Corporation

The
LAZARUS CURSE

A DR. THOMAS SILKSTONE MYSTERY

TESSA HARRIS

KENSINGTON BOOKS
www.kensingtonbooks.com

To Katy, with thanks

Author's Notes and Acknowledgments

The story of black people in Britain did not, contrary to popular belief, begin with the docking of the *Empire Windrush* in 1948. The ship's arrival from Jamaica, bringing 492 passengers to settle in the country, is widely seen as a landmark in the history of modern Britain. Yet almost two hundred years earlier there were an estimated 20,000 black people out of a population of 676,250 living in London alone. Most of these were living as free men and women. Their number was swelled in 1783 by Black Loyalists, those slaves who, in return for their freedom, had sided with the British in the American Revolutionary War and been given passage to British shores.

Unsurprisingly when I decided that the story of these displaced Africans should form the backdrop of my fourth Dr. Thomas Silkstone mystery, I found research material quite hard to come by. While there were a few prominent black people in eighteenth-century England—the concert violinist George Bridgetower and Francis Williams, who studied at Cambridge University, for example—there were hundreds more who lived as servants or beggars. One of the most famous manservants of the day was Francis Barber, who was in the employ of none other than Dr. Samuel Johnson, the great lexicographer.

The British attitude to those of color has been far from exemplary. As far back as 1731 the Lord Mayor of London issued an edict forbidding "negroes" to learn a trade, thus effectively sentencing them to servitude and poverty. Look hard enough and you will see these people everywhere, in the paintings of Hogarth and of Reynolds, in the caricatures of Rawlings and Gillray, and in poems and plays of the period. As Gretchen Gerzina put it in her excellent book *Black England,* eighteenth-century Africans occupied "a parallel world . . . working and living alongside the English."

My own foray into this parallel plane was prompted by the remarkable story of a young African slave by the name of Jonathan Strong. Cruelly beaten by his master and left for dead on the street, he was found by a kind surgeon, William Sharp, who nursed him back to health. Two years later, however, Strong was recaptured by his master, who promptly sold him back into slavery. He was due to return to the slave plantations of Barbados when, in a last-ditch attempt to evade his terrible fate, he appealed to the surgeon's brother, the abolitionist Granville Sharp, for help and was eventually freed. In 1772, Sharp was instrumental in securing the famous ruling by Lord Chief Justice William Mansfield that reluctantly concluded that slaves could not legally be forced to return to the colonies by their owners once they were in Britain. The judgment was widely seen as abolishing slavery in Britain, although the law was not necessarily practiced by all citizens. Nevertheless, the case elevated Granville Sharp to his rightful place as one of the most influential men in the British abolition movement.

Crossing the Atlantic to the West Indies, a number of fascinating but disturbing accounts of life in the colonies threw up more background material for this novel. A compelling collection of original documents was drawn together in an online project edited by Dr. Katherine Hann, called *Slavery and the Natural World,* and carried out at the Natural History Museum, London, between 2006 and 2008. The information is based on documents held in the museum's libraries, and explores the links between nature (especially the knowledge, and transfer, of plants), people with an interest in natural history (mainly European writers from the sixteenth to eighteenth centuries), and the history and legacies of the transatlantic slave trade.

Firsthand accounts from slave owners and overseers as well as botanists, naturalists, and physicians painted pictures of life with devastating and often brutal clarity that shock and appall our twenty-first-century sensibilities and, indeed, went some way to helping the abolitionist cause at the time. William Blake's barbaric image of a woman being whipped, *Flagellation of a Female Samboe Slave, 1796,* had a huge impact on public opinion in Britain.

When calling African slaves "Negroes" I am using the terminology that was employed widely in contemporary accounts from the eighteenth century. While the backdrop to this novel is based on fact, all the characters are fictitious apart from Granville Sharp and Thomas Clarkson.

In my research I am indebted to the Natural History Museum, London, The Old Operating Theatre, Southwark, and to The Museum of London, Docklands. For her medical expertise I must thank Dr. Kate Dyerson. As ever I am also grateful to my agent, Melissa Jeglinski, my editor, John Scognamiglio, and to the rest of the team at Kensington, to John and Alicia Makin, and to Katy Eachus and Liz Fisher. Last but not least, my thanks go to my family, without whose love and support I could not write these novels.

—England 2014

Chapter 1

The Elizabeth, *somewhere in the English Channel*
November in the Year of Our Lord 1783

As he lay in his hammock, the young man dreamed he was back on the island. In the black of a jungle night the drums began. Low and throbbing, they drowned out the sound of his heartbeat. The rhythm was slow and steady at first, like the relentless turn of a rack wheel. Each beat was a footstep in the darkness, each pause a breath held fast.

In his mind's eye he saw himself and the rest of the party make their way toward the sound, slashing through the thick stems and waxy leaves, as the beat grew louder and louder. Reaching the clearing, they saw them: a circle of Negroes and at their centre a man gyrating madly, his head ablaze with bird plumes, dancing around a fire. In his hand he grasped a long bone at its heft, shaking it as he pranced wildly in the ring.

The victim, little more than a child, was brought to him struggling, flanked on either side by men. They held him in the centre of the circle, his cries for mercy drowned out by the sound of the drums.

The onlookers were shouting, cheering on the priest, as he whirled 'round like a demented dog. From time to time he would take a pipe made from hollowed-out sugar cane and blow a cloud of powder into the face of his victim. The drumbeats gathered momentum and the cries and caterwauls grew louder.

Someone in the crowd handed the magic man a skull; it looked like a human's. It was lined and filled with some sort of potion. To a great roar, he thrust it up to the victim's lips, forcing him to drink the contents. Seconds later the hapless boy was being whirled 'round rapidly like a spinning top until he finally lost his senses and fell to the ground, clutching his belly in agony.

As the victim writhed in the dirt, the sorcerer also began to judder violently. While the youth's body convulsed and shuddered, the magic man mirrored his actions as if the very ground beneath him were quaking. Then, when the boy's juddering lessened, so, too, did the priest's until he stopped as suddenly as he had started. The crowd was hushed, and watched as he examined the motionless victim until, with a triumphant whoop, he raised his arms aloft and pronounced him dead.

In his hammock, the young man, his dark brows knitted across his forehead, sat upright. His heart was pounding as violently as the jungle drums and his hands were clammy with fear. He looked down at the skeletal frame he hardly recognized as his own. He was safe on board the ship. Glancing to his left, he made out a circle of inky sky that was visible through the porthole. Dark clouds scudded across the moon, making the stars blink. He shivered with cold, but sighed with relief. It was the finest cold that had ever pricked his skin. It was English cold and after the steaming jungles of the West Indies it felt as sweet and as thrilling as the touch of a maiden.

There had been three of them on the expedition. It had been their mission to gather specimens of flora and fauna of potential interest to the medical fraternity. Dr. Frederick Welton, his assistant, Dr. John Perrick, and himself, Matthew Bartlett, were accompanied by ten porters and a guide. Battling through swamps and under endless attack from vicious mosquitoes, it had taken them two days to reach the Maroon encampment. Their reception was hostile at first. Indeed, they had feared for their lives, but, after much negotiation, they had managed to convince the priest, or obeah-man, and the rest of the elders that they meant no harm; that they were not spies. They were there to observe and learn. In return they gave them clothes and trinkets, beads and mirrors. Through smiles and slow gestures, the initial suspicion turned to mutual respect. They were fed and watered and in exchange the doctors were able to use iodine or sundry physic to treat some minor infections that native medicine had not been able to ease. Indeed, Dr. Welton managed to win the Negroes' confidence to such an extent that the priest allowed his myal men to show them how they treated various ailments with bark and sap from the plants of the forest.

Even though several days had passed since they set sail for England, the fear of what he had seen lingered. In his nightmares Matthew Bartlett relived his experience during his time in Jamaica a thousand times. The memories would stay with him forever. He dreaded closing his eyes for fear of seeing the horror replayed once more.

This time he remembered seeing the child lifted into a nearby hut, an open-sided shelter made of cut palm leaves, and laid on a reed mat. The women—there were four of them as he recalled—sat by the dead boy. They murmured low chants throughout the night, calling upon the spirits of their ancestors to help him.

At sunrise the following morning, the whole of the village was summoned by the blowing of a conch shell to watch once more. The boy's body was placed in the circle and the men began dancing around it, their feet stamping in time to the drumbeat. The mad priest's throaty bawl began again and so, too, did his dance, punctuated by obscene gestures and a frantic scrabbling around in the dirt. After what must have been an hour at least, someone handed him a bunch of herbs. The leaves were large and flat and he called for the boy's lips to be opened. Standing over the corpse he squeezed some juice into the child's open mouth and anointed his eyes and stained his fingertips. All the while the men sang and chanted around him in a circle.

It did not happen quickly. Another hour, maybe two, elapsed until it came to pass. And when it did, the crowd watched in stunned silence as slowly the boy's eyes opened. Another few moments and his fingers moved, then his toes, until finally the priest took his hand and he rose from his reed mat. The youth had been raised from the dead by the magic man.

"Like Lazarus," muttered Dr. Perrick, his eyes wide in awe.

"Fascinating," said Dr. Welton, looking up from his journal. He was recording everything he saw in detail, his pencil moving furiously across the page. Turning to the young man at his side he asked, "Mr. Bartlett, you have a sketch of this remarkable plant?"

Matthew Bartlett recalled nodding. He was a botanical artist and for the past two days he had been making detailed sketches of all the various plants that the obeah-men used in their medicine that appeared particularly efficacious in the treatment of native disorders and ailments. But this plant, the plant used by the sorcerer to raise the youth from the dead, was special, unique. It was the real reason for their mission.

Dr. Welton had been allowed to examine the victim the next time the ritual was performed, this occasion on a woman. He was able to confirm that there was no pulse, no breath, no heartbeat; that she was, medically, dead. And yet the following day she had been revived. She had stood up and walked, but there was something strange in the way she moved. He was allowed to check her vital signs once more and in her eyes he saw a faraway look. When he had inquired of the obeah-man whether she could speak, the priest smiled and shook his head. Pointing to his own head, he told the doctor that the woman's mind had been altered so that she would now obey her husband. Apparently her sin had been that of idleness. From now on, the obeah-man assured Dr. Welton, she would do whatever her husband told her, without question.

Now easing himself up on his elbows, the young artist shook the memory from his head. He needed to reassure himself that the expedition was over; that he and Dr. Welton and Dr. Perrick and the others were safe once more. But then reality hit him like a round of shot and he recalled that the doctors were not with him on the return voyage. Their legacy was on his shoulders.

Everything they had seen and heard, learned and discovered in those few momentous weeks in Jamaica now rested with him.

He surveyed the deck. They were still there, the precious treasures; more than two hundred plants, insects, reptiles, and small mammals had been collected and stored in a variety of pots, jars, barrels, and crates.

Of all of the plants, however, the branched calalue bush, the Lazarus herb, as Dr. Welton dubbed it after Dr. Perrick's remark, was most prized. Hundreds of cuttings had been taken and bedded in pots that were regularly watered. The *Elizabeth*'s captain, a Scotsman by the name of McCoy, had even vacated his cabin for the containers so that the tender shoots would receive the correct amount of sunlight. Yet just as the bloody flux had wreaked havoc among the sailors on the outward voyage, so too did pestilence and flies and salty sea spray cause the plants to wither and die. Finding himself in sole charge of the cuttings, the young man had tried his best to nurture them, protecting them from intense heat when the mercury rose or fixing them down in the storms. Yet despite his efforts, out of the scores of plant specimens, only a few survived.

Yet as important as the plants were, the real prize was Dr. Welton's journal, containing the formula for the extraordinary narcotic. And that was safe. Of that he could be sure. He patted the leather satchel emblazoned with the crest of the Royal Society that lay next to him in the hammock, containing his sketchbook and pencils.

The *Elizabeth* must now be in the Channel, he reassured himself. A few more hours and she would dock in London. The thought of treading on dry land brought a smile to the face of a young man who had had very little to smile about for the past three months. He settled back in his hammock, the very hammock that could so easily have become his shroud. Too often on the voyage they had wrapped a seaman's corpse in his own rectangle of canvas, pierced his nose with a darning needle to make sure he was dead, then with a few glib words had lowered him over the side. Why he had been spared the ravages of disease he did not know. Mercifully the flux had not returned with them. Yellow fever, too, had wrought havoc among the white men on the island, but had chosen to stay ashore. The seamen who died on the homeward journey had been taken by other ills or accidents.

The drumbeats in his nightmare soon turned into the jangle of the spars as they flayed the ship's masts frantically in the prevailing westerly. They were rising and falling in the swell, cresting waves with ease in the lee of the land. The salt tang of the spray filled his mouth and nostrils and up above he heard a lone gull cry. Closing his eyes, he felt the rhythm of the water rock him like a babe in his hammock and he willed the wind to strengthen, the quicker to blow them ashore, the quicker to dispel his lingering terror and further his purpose.

Chapter 2

The knife men were assembled at the operating theatre at the anatomy school in London's Brewer Street. Before the sheet was pulled back, they had gathered 'round the table. The soles of their shoes rasped across the sand scattered on the floor to soak up the blood and other bodily fluids. The large window in the roof allowed the light to flood in, bathing the covered corpse in a bright halo. The men set their features appropriately, nonchalant yet sufficiently sombre as befitted the occasion. All of them had seen more corpses than a plague pit in an epidemic. They were hardened, self-assured. Somewhere in the cavernous room, a fly buzzed; its high-pitched drone a minor irritation that chaffed at the composure of the moment.

The men were all there at the invitation of Mr. Hubert Izzard, an eminent figure of the chirurgical establishment with a stature that matched his lofty ambition. Those minded to be cruel, and there were many, said he had the face of a prize fighter. His nose had been broken when he was young and it was flattened and skewed to the left.

At Izzard's sign, the beadle whipped away a cloth with all the flourish of a fairground conjuror to reveal the face that lay beneath on the table. The spectacle solicited the desired effect. In an instant, the men's expressions changed. Gone was the blasé air, the quiet cynicism, and in its place veneration. Like shepherds 'round the holy manger, they stared at the woman full of amazement.

Dr. Thomas Silkstone, a Philadelphian anatomist and surgeon, was among them. He had no particular regard for the men
around him. He had even crossed swords, or rather scalpels,
with some of them and his dealings with others in the medical
profession left a bitter taste in his mouth. Most of the practi-
tioners were old enough to be his grandfather. Most were set in
their ways, convinced that bloodletting was a cure-all and that
the possession of healthy bowels was the key to longevity. He,
on the other hand, had different ideas and found his respect for
his fellow anatomists and surgeons regularly tested. This, he
feared, would be another such occasion.

After a moment's awe-filled silence, one of the surgeons
standing next to Mr. Izzard managed to express the thoughts of
the others.

"But how did you lay your hands on such a one?" he asked in
wonderment.

Izzard's large mouth widened into a smirk. "Apparently the
blacks are more prone to chills. They come to our inclement clime
from the plantations, take cold and fever and die," he informed
them, adding cheerfully: "Their great misfortune is our gain,
gentlemen." A ripple of polite amusement circulated around the
room like a gentle breeze.

The anatomist's eyes dwelt on the woman and he touched her
head lightly, almost reverentially. "Is she not magnificent?" he
said in a hushed tone, neither expecting nor receiving a reply.

The woman's beauty was beyond question. There was a
Madonna-like serenity in her attitude, thought Thomas. She
was clearly of African origin, her skin black as ebony and her
features fulsome, yet angular. Her hair was cropped close
against her skull and her lips were slightly parted, so that she
gave the appearance of being merely asleep. Indeed, several of
those gathered did secretly think that she might open her eye
lids at any moment, so uncorrupted and perfect did she appear.

"But wait! There is more." Mr. Izzard raised up a long finger
in the air and again the beadle rushed forward. With even
greater theatrical flair he pulled back the sheet that covered the
woman's torso. A collective gasp arose. She had been pregnant

and her belly was as rounded as a whale. Glistening in the sunlight thanks to an application of teak oil, the sacred mound encasing an infant drew admiration from every quarter.

"Full term, gentlemen," announced Izzard over the din. The anatomists quietened down to listen. "She was fully dilated."

Walking over to a nearby table, he pointed to a large, leatherbound atlas. "You will all be familiar with the late, lamented Dr. William Hunter's epic work *The Gravid Uterus*," he said in a reverential tone. A murmur of acknowledgement rippled around the theatre. "And I know that a few of our older brethren will have witnessed Monsieur Desnoues's most extraordinary waxwork of a woman who died in labor with the child's head pushing through the cervix." One or two more senior members nodded. "But I aim to venture even further into the field of obstetrics and I can guarantee that you have not seen anything of this quality and this"—he fumbled for a word—"this freshness." Heads were shaken in agreement.

"What I propose to do today, gentlemen, is to dissect the abdomen, but initially leave the uterus intact," he announced. There was a chorus of approval.

Izzard, confident he had his audience enthralled, strolled back to the operating table with the air of a man on a Sunday promenade. The corpse now lay fully exposed. Thomas felt uncomfortable, not because of the public dissection that was about to take place, but because of the nature of the cadaver. Corpses were so rarely available these days that the motley specimens that made their way into the theatre were very often on the turn. It was usually obvious, too, how they had met their end, from some fatal injury or debilitating disease. It was also usually obvious that they had been interred for several days before being landed on the dissecting table, courtesy of unscrupulous grave robbers. Thomas had even been offered bodies where the sack-'em-up men had not even bothered to clean the soil from their skin. The cadavers were either very young or very old. Pregnant women were a rarity and, by the very nature of their circumstance, often very poor and always alone.

Edging his way toward the corpse, and seeing his fellow

anatomists' attention taken by Mr. Izzard, Thomas studied the body more closely. It was then that he saw it: a raised silver scar on the top of the left breast in the shape of two letters, possibly a B and a C, although tissue had grown around it, making it harder to decipher. He put out a hand to touch the woman's skin. It was cold, but not as cold as one might expect. He pushed the flesh lightly with the tips of his fingers. There was still a telltale elasticity in it that deepened his concern. It was also clear from the way her arm rested on the table that rigor mortis had not yet set in. Quickly he felt her fingers for signs of stiffening. They were still malleable. He estimated she had not been dead three hours.

"Ah, Dr. Silkstone!" called Izzard. All eyes turned on Thomas. "I see you cannot wait to get your hands on my corpse!" he said with a laugh.

Thomas, embarrassed that his surreptitious prodding had been uncovered, gave a polite bow. "It is, indeed, a magnificent specimen, sir," he replied. His heart was beating fast, but he knew he had to make his point. "You obviously have a new supplier, sir," he said with an assurance that belied his nervousness.

The smile that had been hovering around Izzard's lips all morning suddenly disappeared. He pulled back his shoulders in shock. "A new and most discreet supplier, sir," he retorted, obviously insulted by Thomas's insinuation.

"I expect they drive a hard bargain," he persisted.

The color rose in Izzard's cheeks. "I pay a good price, but," he said, looking around him at his peers for support, "I believe it is entirely worth it."

Some of the others in the room shouted, "Hear! Hear!" A few glared at Thomas, dismayed that anyone, especially a youngster from the Colonies, would dare to question the great Hubert Izzard.

The disapproving gathering parted as Izzard made his way toward the young anatomist who remained near the dissecting table. On another small table at the side, an array of surgical instruments was laid out on an oiled cloth. Izzard gazed upon them, then picked out a scalpel. Walking up to Thomas, he presented him with the sharp blade.

"In that case, Dr. Silkstone," he said with a smile tight as a tourniquet, "I am sure you would be honored to make the first cut."

Thomas could not leave the stifling atmosphere of the operating theatre soon enough. Usually his eagerness to quit such a place was caused by the sickly sweet smell of corruption as the dead flesh started to putrefy. But the Negro woman's corpse he had just been compelled to dissect was far too new for that. Had the outside temperature not been so cold, he would have taken off his shoes and shaken the sand from them as he departed Hubert Izzard's anatomy school.

Ridding himself of the company he could not abide, Thomas took a lungful of air. The late afternoon grew colder, wreathing him in his own breath as he walked. He plunged his hands into his pockets and quickened his pace. Past a chestnut seller he went, where three or four unfortunates huddled simply to keep warm, the brazier glowing red like a beacon in the street. Some shopkeepers were already locking up for the day. A peascod hawker cried forlornly, her breath catching on the icy chill.

Thomas was just passing a coffeehouse, its pungent aroma wafting from its open door, when a man appeared. In his hand he held a large poster and he started hammering it onto a noticeboard outside. Stopping a few feet away, the doctor registered that a reward was being offered for the return of a runaway slave.

His thoughts flashed to the dead Negro woman and the brand on her breast. If, as he suspected, she was enslaved, then her baby would have been born the property of another. Little wonder that pregnant slave women so often resorted to drinking concoctions that forced their menstrua and aborted their unborns. Rather that than let their children enter the world bound to white masters. He paused for a moment, still gazing at the poster and trying to recall the words of Rousseau, the French philosopher. *Man is born free, and everywhere he is in chains.* Even he, that very afternoon, had been forced by convention into carrying out a postmortem that he found distasteful. And yet he had felt bound to do so. His profession demanded it. He turned away from the poster and shook his head before continuing on his way back home to Hollen Street.

So preoccupied had he been that he did not notice a young man slipping into the back entrance of the anatomy school. He was pushing a handcart with a load covered in sacking. There was no reason to mark him out as being anything other than an ordinary lackey running an errand, save for one thing: anyone who drew near could clearly have seen a black toe sticking out from beneath the hessian.

Chapter 3

The Negro girl picked her way through the dank streets toward the river. It was the end of a day that had not seen light and the lamps had been lit awhile. With a shawl covering her head, she threaded in and out of alleys and under arches as easily as black silk through cotton. Her eyes were kept to the ground, not so much as to sidestep the slushy ruts or frozen pools of waste, but to avoid eye contact. She had no wish to be noticed, no desire to be singled out.

A sudden squall blew up as she ventured down one of the side streets off the Strand. It sent the trade signs creaking on their hinges. The few citizens who were abroad hurried to shelter in shop doorways from the sudden icy rain. The street women on the corners feared they were in for a lean night, a night when the sleet would douse all but the most fervent ardor. Still the girl carried on, all the while clutching a small drawstring bag under her shawl.

It was almost nine o'clock when she reached the tavern near the waterside. The windowpanes were frosted over, but she could see the warm glow of lanterns from within. It was as cold a November as anyone could remember and it was not yet the time Christian men called Advent. Even she, who'd only heard stories of English winters from the older household slaves, knew that this weather was out of the ordinary.

She paused for a moment, nervously fingering the silver collar about her neck while listening to the music coming from inside the tavern. There were voices raised in a sad song, an old lament from the plantations. A lone baritone made a sound as rich as hot chocolate. He was answered by a chorus of notes as sweet as sugarcane itself. The girl smiled, not through happiness or nostalgia, but to reaffirm her resolve. She patted the bag and as soon as the voices had died down and given way to applause, she entered the inn.

The place was full of her own kind: Gold Coast Negroes, Coromantees, sold to the white traders by the Ashanti at the great slave market at Mansu. They were the best sort, the noblest, prized above others for their superior physique and courage. These were the men and women who had been wrenched away from their African homeland and doomed to a life in chains. Under their thick frockcoats or their shifts most of them still carried the scars of the lashes or the marks where the manacles cut their flesh. Some still walked with the stoop of slaves kept in a yoke so long that their spines bowed.

On benches and pews, they sat around tables drinking rum and ale and listening to the songs. Tobacco smoke curled in the air; tobacco from the very plants that profited their white masters. A parrot, its feathers red and gold and blue, perched on one man's shoulder as a girl fed it scraps. And there was a man sporting a hat modeled on a ship. These were the fortunate ones, the ones who had bought their own freedom or fought for King George against America in the war and been given passage to London to forge new lives for themselves. They could not learn a trade—a Lord Mayor's edict had put paid to that fifty years before—but at least those present had all broken their slave bonds. She could join them. She could run away. But not tonight.

In this strange country that was colder than stone, slavery was not permitted. All Englishmen were free and yet because she was only staying a short while, she still had to wear her collar. Her master regarded her as little more than a trinket and certainly of less value than his thoroughbred horse. So, for now, she would content herself with slipping out of his mansion after dark, unseen.

Amid the cheering that night, as the singers returned to their seats, nobody noticed the girl, no one apart from the landlord at the pump, a mulatto, a large hoop piercing his ear lobe and a gold front tooth in his mouth. She caught his eye and, with a wordless greeting, he gestured her to a low door at the back of the bar. She felt a flutter in her stomach when it opened, as if a trapped bird was stirring inside her. The room was dimly lit with a single lantern dangling from the ceiling. The shutters were closed and the smell was earthy and damp. In the darkness she could make out bunches of dried herbs hanging from the beams. She narrowed her eyes and shivered, not with cold but fear. There were other objects, too; what looked like a snake was draped around a rafter and something round and white, a small skull, perhaps, sat next to it. On one wall there were shelves crammed with an assortment of oddities; lumps of coral, twisted animal horns, and jars of teeth.

From over in one corner came an odd cackling sound, then a sudden flurry. Startled, she let out a faint cry as her eyes followed the movement. In the darkness she could make out two white cockerels pecking among the rushes on the floor.

An old man sat at a table in the centre of the room, his head bowed. Around his bony shoulders he wore a goatskin, and a necklace of sharp teeth hung from his neck. His hair was grizzled and gray as pumice stone, but when he lifted his gaze a faint yelp escaped from her lips. Even in the half light she could make out his twisted features. She had heard this obeah-man was hideous, that his face looked as though it had been mauled by a lion—but still she could not hide her shock. One of his eyes was completely closed and where his nose should have been there was a small hole encrusted with pus. She had seen men like him before, blighted by the yaws. The disease had eaten into his flesh. He would have been banished from the plantation so that he could not infect the other slaves.

He lifted his hand—she noticed it was crabbed—and gestured to the chair in front of him. A strange grunt issued from his mouth. Part of his lips had been eaten away, too, so that the black stumps of his teeth showed. He seemed unable to form words properly, as if the disease had eaten into his soft palate, making his tongue flap loosely in his mouth.

Taking a piece of flint and a spill, he lit a candle in front of him. It cast a sickly light across the table. The girl sat down, but kept her eyes away from his face. They darted up to the rafters, or along the shelves, anywhere but on the old man's grotesque features.

Sensing her unease he sought to allay her fears. He knew he was a hideous sight. For many years now he had been reviled. In his makeshift hut on the edge of the cane fields he had managed as best he could, fending for himself, grubbing for worms in the red earth, living on plantains and coconuts. Even the fierce Maroons who dwelt in the mountains and raided the plantations carrying off women and livestock had left him alone. They feared he would bring misfortune on them. He would have died alone in the humid heat, his own flesh becoming food for the leeches and mosquitoes, had not the great snake god, Ob, looked kindly upon him. One day news came that he had been sold, along with all the other slaves on the estate, and he was eventually given his freedom. In London, just as in Jamaica, he was forced to hide himself away. But his power had not faded with the strength of the sun. It may be cold and gray and damp in the white man's land, but his special gifts had not deserted him.

The expressions of horror that his disfigured face prompted were the same, too, but he took no pleasure in frightening the young and vulnerable.

"You want?" he asked her, lifting up the bottle of rum from the table. There were two cups next to it. He filled one and pushed it toward her but she shook her head.

"Have na fear," he said in a hoarse whisper. If he had been able to smile, he would have done so, but he could not, relying on his red-rimmed eye to reassure the girl. He guessed she was no more than fourteen full suns old and she was as nervous as a bride. They always were, those who sought him out. He downed his rum in one.

"You come for obeah?" he asked, his eye resting on the collar around her neck that bore her slave name, Phibbah.

Still unable to bring herself to look at the man's face, the girl nodded. "Yes," she replied, twisting her shawl between her fingers.

"Who has wronged you, child? Your massa?"

"My missa," she hissed, a look of contempt tugging the corners of her mouth.

She shifted on her chair and straightened her back. As she did so, a silver scar above her right breast glinted like a fish in the candlelight. He could make out the letters of a white man's brand: S. C.

"What she do? She hurt you?" They always did, he thought to himself. In England most Africans were no longer slaves in name, but many were treated as if they were still in shackles.

Slowly the girl turned, as if steeling herself to look at him. Her eyes lifted to meet his. "She kill my child."

The obeah-man nodded sagely, as if he already knew what pained her. "She beat it out your womb?"

The girl's gaze was steady now and he saw her eyes were weeping like juice from fresh-cut cane. "She was mad at me and threw a jug and I fell down de stairs." Her breath juddered into a sob. "That night I was taken bad and de baby came away."

The obeah-man paused a moment. It was a story he had heard before. "It was your massa's child?"

She nodded, feeling the blood rushing to her face. The obeah-man understood. Not a month went by without he had a visit from a girl with a similar sad tale to tell. They all overcame their revulsion of him as their stories unfolded.

He tapped the table with his wizened hand. "You got money?" His tone seemed to bring her back from her dark place.

"Yes. Yes," she replied. Delving into her apron pocket, she brought out two sixpences she had stolen, together with the drawstring bag.

The obeah-man swooped on the coins like an eagle and scooped them across the table and into a drawer. Satisfied he could do business with the girl, he poured rum into the other glass. This time she did not refuse it, but drank it in one gulp. Leaning back in his chair he watched her cough and splutter for a moment before eyeing the bag. It was made of sacking and was the width of a man's foot. He lifted a gnarled finger and pointed at it.

"Your obeah?"

She stretched the neck of the bag and put her hand inside. First she brought out a small square of paper and unfolded it to reveal three or four fingernail clippings. The obeah-man inspected them, lightly touching the half-moon fragments with his own grubby stumps.

"Good," he said. But it was the next object that seemed to lift his wizened face. From the bag the girl pulled out a length of kersey, a coarse woollen band of cloth stained dark brown with blood. Slowly she pushed it across the table and the obeah-man gave her a knowing look as he opened out the folds.

"You have done well," he nodded.

The girl turned her head away, unable to look at the bloodied rag.

The man folded the linen, but laid his hand upon it.

"So, you want it quick or slow?" he asked. His words were rasping, as if his mouth were full of ashes, but he spoke with all the confidence of a priest.

She, however, was unable to answer. Her voice had deserted her, choked by her tears. Her hands flew up to her face and her shoulders heaved in sobs.

The obeah-man drew the cloth closer and nodded. "Either way," he told her, "your missa be dead afore winter is out."

Chapter 4

Thomas felt a mounting sense of excitement as his carriage swept into the great courtyard at Somerset House. It was an emotion that he rarely experienced. By nature he was a calm and reasoned man, not prone to mood swings. He liked to think that he handled the blows that life dealt him in a logical and ordered way and that if fortune smiled on him, he would be equally sanguine. Indeed, it seemed that after several months of hardship, providence might be a little more inclined to favor him. The Great Fogg that had covered the eastern half of the country over the summer had loosened its grip. The foul air had, however, been replaced by icy blasts that could prove almost as deadly to the poor and those of a weak constitution. His mentor, Dr. William Carruthers, had returned to rude health after a nasty bout of bronchitis brought on by the noxious haze, and then there was Lydia. Despite their enforced separation, they remained in touch.

Lady Lydia Farrell wrote to him twice a week, detailing her routine with her newfound young son. The child had been rescued from a terrible fate and found to have a crippled arm. Yet, under Thomas's supervision, his muscles had strengthened and now seemed fully restored. At Boughton Hall, the Cricks' country seat in Oxfordshire, each day brought a new discovery or achievement: "Richard tied a bow today" or "Richard went riding," Lydia would write. Her mother's pride was evident in every phrase. There were words for him, of course. She told him she loved him and missed him and her sweetness buoyed his spirits, but they were poor compensation for her absence. By making Lydia's son a ward of court, the law had forbidden their longed-for marriage on the grounds that Thomas, as an American citizen, was a foreign enemy. His countrymen had triumphed in the revolutionary war, and hostilities had long ceased, but, until the Treaty of Paris was ratified, he would technically remain so.

Never one to wallow in his own misfortune, however, Thomas Silkstone had thrown himself into his work, teaching anatomy to eager students and operating on patients for whom surgery was the very last resort. All the while, however, he had been anticipating a call, a summons that would give his career a new impetus and his intellect a new challenge. That call had come the day before yesterday from the lips of one of the most revered living scientists and adventurers, Sir Joseph Banks.

The great man, who had accompanied Captain Cook on his famous voyages to the Pacific Ocean, was now president of the Royal Society. The aim of the august body was to push the limits of scientific knowledge and last year they had funded an expedition to the West Indies. Its aim was to collect flora and fauna and to catalogue it. There would undoubtedly be some specimens that would have medicinal uses. Tragically, the expedition's leader, Dr. Frederick Welton, had been struck down by yellow fever and died two days before his ship, the *Elizabeth,* set sail for England. The expedition's second in command, Dr. John Perrick, had succumbed the following day. Of the original scientific team of three, only the botanical artist, Matthew Bartlett, remained alive.

In the absence of any senior scientists to continue the team's important work, the Royal Society needed to enlist the expertise of someone knowledgeable and reliable, someone who would work diligently and without conceit, someone committed and well-respected. There were many who put their names forward: after all, the work carried with it a generous fee, not to mention the prestige and a possible membership, subject to the usual terms, of the Royal Society itself. It was Sir Joseph himself who put forward Thomas's name. And that is how the young American anatomist, surgeon, physician, and pioneer in the field of science came to be alighting from a rather grand carriage, helped down by a liveried footman and escorted by a clerk, into the inner sanctum of the Royal Society.

The room, vast and wood paneled, smelled of linseed oil. On its walls hung portraits of the great and the good, members of the Royal Society both alive and dead. Newton, Herschel, Pepys, and Sloane glared down at the young American from their gilded frames. Thomas noted there was no likeness of Benjamin Franklin, who had demonstrated the electrical nature of lightning using a kite and key some thirty years before. Perhaps, he considered, the Society felt it impolitic, at this delicate time before the ratification of the Treaty of Paris, to include a portrait of a former enemy.

Sir Joseph sat alone behind a large desk. He rose when Thomas was ushered in. Tall, trim, and wigless, he exuded an air of calm authority. He held out a hand. Thomas shook it. The two men looked each other in the eye. The handshake was firm.

"I have heard good reports about you, Silkstone," said Sir Joseph, motioning Thomas to a chair. "Sir Tobias Charlesworth and Sir Peregrine Crisp both spoke highly of you. God rest their souls."

There was a brief pause as both men acknowledged that Thomas's supporters had been taken in untimely ways.

"I am most grateful for their confidence in me, sir," replied the young doctor. He was feeling slightly less anxious, but nonetheless he remained on edge. As Thomas sat down, Sir Joseph walked over to a window where a large globe stood on a stand. He spun it playfully.

"The world is a vast place, Silkstone," he mused. "And it is growing with every expedition on which we embark."

"Thanks to men such as yourself, sir," replied Thomas quickly, only to cringe immediately at his own sycophancy.

Sir Joseph brushed his remark aside with a smile. "I have been fortunate," he said, gazing out of the window and onto the River Thames. "There are many who have sacrificed their lives in the pursuit of knowledge. Good men. Men of great intellect and determination," he said. He switched his gaze to Thomas. "Men such as yourself, Silkstone."

The young doctor shifted in his chair, uncomfortable with such praise, but before he could reply, Sir Joseph continued. "I'll be plain with you. There were those in the Society who were a little reluctant to employ an American in the light of recent"— he searched for an appropriate word—"er . . . circumstances. However, I don't hold with such stuff and nonsense. Knowledge needs to be shared. It has no borders or boundaries; no politics or prejudice. And we need the best men. That is why I have decided"—he paused briefly to correct himself—"the Royal Society has decided, to ask you, Dr. Silkstone, to take charge of cataloguing the manifest of the West Indies expedition."

Thomas had, unconsciously, been holding his breath as he listened to Sir Joseph. Now he breathed deeply with relief and his face broke into a smile.

"You honor me, sir."

"It was not easy, mind." Sir Joseph wagged his finger. "The applicants were falling over themselves for the post. But I believe you show such promise." He nodded his head, as if to reassure himself as much as Thomas that he had made the right decision, before he went on. "There are many great discoveries to be made," he said. "The expedition's collections will no doubt contain treasures beyond compare; new flora, new fauna, new cures, new treatments."

Thomas pictured the array of exotic specimens in his mind's eye as the *Elizabeth* breasted the waves on her homeward voyage, a sort of Noah's Ark of all the weird and wonderful creations that the Lord had bestowed upon the islands of the Caribbean Sea. It would be his task to classify them all, from the tiniest seed to the tallest tree fern, from the humblest insect to the most magnificent reptile. He was well aware that Sir Joseph and the late botanist Daniel Solander had invented a new method of plant classification while on the *Endeavour* expedition with Captain Cook. The learning curve would not merely be steep, but strewn with many unexpected hazards. There would be unavoidable errors, misidentifications, and false dawns. His face betrayed his anxiety at the enormity of the venture.

"I see you have doubts, Dr. Silkstone," remarked Sir Joseph, settling back behind his desk.

"I . . ." Thomas found himself fumbling awkwardly. "I am sure your trust in me will not be misplaced, sir."

Sir Joseph's dark brows dipped slightly. "Your humility is a good thing. I cannot abide arrogance in a man, but you are right to feel burdened by the weight we are placing on your shoulders."

Thomas frowned. He anticipated there was more.

Sir Joseph's lips curled into a smile. "Have no fear, Silkstone. I have arranged assistance."

A look of puzzlement slid across Thomas's face.

"Mr. Bartlett will be helping you," continued the great man. "He is the excellent botanical artist who accompanied the expedition. I trained him personally in the new method of classification. He will be invaluable to you."

Thomas nodded. "I am most grateful to you, sir."

"It is Mr. Bartlett who is deserving of your gratitude," came the reply. "He has endured great torments in the name of science. In the last dispatch I had from Dr. Welton before he died, he informed me they spent an uncomfortable few days in the company of the Maroons."

Thomas was unfamiliar with the term. He frowned.

"Runaway slaves," explained Sir Joseph. "At one point the expedition members feared for their lives; however, by some means they managed to befriend the natives and, I believe, became privy to some of their cures. The Maroons even assisted them in their collection. As a result almost two hundred specimens were gathered." He was nodding enthusiastically as he spoke. "Welton instructed Bartlett in how they should be drawn and which parts were to be depicted. He knew it was imperative to capture the plants' forms while they were still fresh, so Bartlett made brief outline drawings, coloring specific areas so they could be finished later." Sir Joseph's long fingers held an imaginary paintbrush which he flourished in the air.

Thomas recalled the botanical drawings of Sydney Parkinson from the *Endeavour*. He had fallen prey to the bloody flux on the return voyage, but his superbly detailed sketches were as brilliant in their execution as Leonardo's anatomical images. He managed a nervous smile across the desk.

"Then, sir, I accept your gracious commission," Thomas replied.

Sir Joseph leaned forward, slapping the palms of both his hands on the desk. "I know you will not disappoint, Silkstone."

Thomas gave an elegant nod. "And when does the *Elizabeth* arrive?"

"She was spotted five days ago off The Lizard, so by the latest accounts she should be here on tomorrow's afternoon tide."

The young doctor had not expected such an early arrival. There was so much to do to prepare to take delivery of the hundreds of specimens. But as if Sir Joseph had read his mind he interjected, "I have arranged for the storage of the items at kew, so that you can work on them in batches in your own premises."

Thomas felt immense relief. "I am most grateful, sir," he replied as Sir Joseph rose.

"I know you are the man for the job, Silkstone," he said, extending his hand. "I have great faith in you. Play your cards right and you will go far."

Thomas smiled, broadly this time, as he shook the great man's hand. "I will not disappoint, Sir Joseph."

Chapter 5

Mistress Cordelia Carfax shivered and gathered her silk shawl about her shoulders. The fire was lit but the heat that emanated did little to warm the air of her fashionable London drawing room. She could not decide which she loathed more: the languid Jamaican humidity or the insidious English cold. A small short-haired dog lay sprawled in front of the hearth, toasting its back. As soon as she reached for the bell, the animal sprang up and leapt onto her knee in a single bound, looking into her face with large brown eyes. She smiled. It was not something she did often. Whereas most women of her age bore the marks of expression at the corner of their lids, her temples were perfectly smooth. It was the space between her eyes that was furrowed with two parallel frown lines so deep that they were clearly planted by hatred and contempt. These lines creased a skin that was almost unnaturally pale. It was certainly very white for a woman who had spent the last thirty years of her life on a sugar plantation ten miles inland from Kingston. It was not that she painted her face with lead, as was the fashion, but that she steadfastly refused to allow the sun to touch her face, a slave shading her with a parasol every time she ventured outdoors.

Any shows of affection Mistress Carfax did display were usually reserved for her pedigree pug. In the absence of children, the dog was a substitute. She patted the creature's head lovingly.

"Hello, Fino, my dear, sweet Fino."

Phibbah, who came rushing to answer the bell, received no such welcome. Her sullen-faced mistress pointed to the fire as it blazed brightly.

"More coal. More logs. Anything!" she ordered. "I shall freeze to death before this winter's out!"

Phibbah bobbed a curtsy and, looking slightly bemused, hurried over to the grate. Picking up the poker, she prodded the embers. They flared for a moment, then settled back into their steady blaze.

"More coal!" cried Mistress Carfax, only this time louder. The dog, sensing its mistress's anger, jumped off her lap and sat at her feet.

The slave reached for the fire tongs and, opening them wide, grasped a large lump of coal from the scuttle. Quickly she dropped it onto the flames, followed by another black nugget and another. All the time she was being watched by her mistress, who was drumming her fingers impatiently on the arm of her chair. The flames were now leaping higher and the room grew brighter with the intense white light, but still Mistress Carfax was not content.

"More!" This time she screamed and, in her frustration, she reached out and grabbed the poker, bringing it down with a crack on the slave's back.

Taken by surprise the girl was knocked off balance. Stumbling, she let out a yelp. Mistress Carfax jumped up from her seat, still clutching the poker, and hurried over to where she lay, crumpled in a heap by the hearth. As she did so, there was a loud hiss from the grate and a starburst of sparks. A shard of coal whizzed through the air like a bullet and pierced her voluminous skirts. In an instant the smell of scorched silk filled the room and, looking down, Mistress Carfax saw that her hem was on fire. She screamed and flung the poker to the floor. The pug began to bark.

"Fire! Fire!" she cried, rushing away from the hearth, but the flames pursued her. She flapped her shawl in the air like a crazed bird and whirled 'round as if she was dancing, knocking a china vase to the ground as she did so.

Hearing the commotion, another slave arrived on the scene and, thinking hastily, decanted an arrangement of evergreens and threw the remaining water over her mistress's skirt. The silk made a noise like retreating snakes and the flames disappeared in a puff of acrid smoke.

"You all right, missa?" inquired the slave who had put out the fire.

Mistress Carfax, leaning against a high-backed chair, composed herself. She wiped her forehead with the back of her hand.

"Yes. Yes, Patience," she replied breathlessly. Then, looking down to inspect her damaged skirts, she added: "Although I will need to change my gown." She eyed the brown circle of scorched silk, then lifted her gaze across the room to where Phibbah remained crouching, terrified, by the hearth.

"This is your doing," she snarled, spittle flecking her lips.

The girl shook her head, her eyes wide with fear.

"I could have been killed and 'tis your fault. I shall see to it that you are punished soundly. Now get up." The girl began to whimper softly. "Get up, I say," shouted Mistress Carfax.

This time the slave did as she was told. Her back still burned from the crack of the poker and she rose slowly, wiping the tears away from her cheeks. And as she did so, her own features loosened so that her pained expression disappeared. Her mistress must not see her anguish, nor delight in her humiliation. It was time for her obeah to give her a secret strength. As she drew herself to her full, yet still diminutive, height, the light from the fire that now burned more brightly than ever caught the scar on her right breast and flashed silver.

Chapter 6

Lady Lydia Farrell sat in her study at Boughton Hall, next to her son Richard, Lord Crick. His name had been changed from Farrell by order of the Court of Chancery. He was drawing two long lines and several short ones splaying from the top of the paper. His hand was shaky and awkward and his tongue protruded from his lips as he drew, concentrating wholeheartedly on his artistic efforts.

When he had finished what he proposed to do, he leaned back and looked up at his mother, awaiting her reaction. Lydia beamed with pride.

"A tree! Richard, you have drawn a tree," she squealed excitedly, as if he were the first child in the world to do such a thing. "Look, Nurse Pring." She seized the paper and held it up in front of the demure woman, of middling years, who sat opposite her, sewing.

"Yes, your ladyship," she replied, laying down her needle. She leaned forward, smiling with a more measured enthusiasm.

Lydia drew the child close and kissed his forehead.

"My clever son," she told him. She then reached out her hand and stroked his brown curls. "How did I live without you?" she murmured under her breath.

Six years of enforced separation, during most of which she thought him dead, had left her wanting to cherish every moment with him. Each minute was to be savored, lived to the full. But the child pulled away, objecting to her fussing fingers. He was more used to angry blows than loving caresses. Any physical contact he still regarded as a potential threat rather than a gesture of affection.

Lydia checked herself. She looked at Nurse Pring; wise, caring Nurse Pring, who had seen her through her darkest days when she lay in a coma after attempting to take her own life. Practical, sensible Nurse Pring, who had proved so invaluable at the caves in West Wycombe when so many were being struck down by the Great Fogg. A slight expression of reproof crossed the matron's face and it was enough for Lydia to know that she must not rush to reestablish maternal bonds. They must grow naturally, organically, not be forced like greenhouse flowers, but nurtured slowly and lovingly.

"I am sure you must be hungry after your efforts, my sweet," she told Richard, then to Nurse Pring she said, "Perhaps you could see what Mistress Claddingbowl has in the pantry? I am sure there will be jam tarts."

The nurse nodded and was about to open the study door when there came a knock. Howard, the butler, stood on the threshold and side stepped to allow Nurse Pring and her charge to leave the room.

"Yes, Howard?" said Lydia.

The butler, a heavy man with a gravelly voice, bowed. "A Mr. Lupton is here to see you, my lady."

Momentarily forgetting herself, Lydia rolled her eyes. She had completely forgotten her appointment with the candidate for the position of estate manager. Richard took up so much of her time these days that all other demands seemed trifling. Yet a replacement for the late Gabriel Lawson was vital to the future prosperity of Boughton.

She rose from her desk and, smoothing her skirts unthinkingly, she told Howard she would receive her visitor in the drawing room. It was especially at times like these that she wished Thomas could be at her side. After her husband's death she had been handed a mantle of responsibility that did not sit easily on her slight shoulders. For a few blissful days that summer, Dr. Silkstone had helped her bear her burden, talking through problems that presented themselves, suggesting solutions. They had shared the running of the estate, but now she had been robbed of that comfort by an Act of Chancery and so had lost his reassuring presence and unquestioning devotion.

Lydia's first glimpse of Mr. Nicholas Lupton was of his rear as he stood, his feet planted squarely and his hands behind his back. His hair was sun-bleached, so that darker roots showed beneath the blond. He appeared quite stocky of build and his neck seemed to sink into his broad shoulders. Wearing a riding coat and boots, he was gazing out of the window and onto the lawns. He turned swiftly when he heard Howard announce her ladyship.

"Mr. Lupton," greeted Lydia courteously, walking toward him, her hand outstretched. Had she not assumed that, as an estate manager, he was of middling rank, she would say from his bearing that he was a man of good breeding. When he drew nearer, his aquiline nose and his high cheekbones made her think he would be more at home dispensing orders rather than ensuring they were carried out.

Lupton ducked a bow and kissed Lydia's proffered hand. His smile was easy and ready and, after the usual formalities, they both sat down to tea.

"I see you rode here, Mr. Lupton," remarked Lydia, glancing at her guest's attire. She warmed the silver teapot with water from the kettle of boiling water that Howard had left.

Lupton shifted in his chair and smiled. "Yes, your ladyship. I stayed the night at the Three Tuns in Brandwick."

Lydia nodded as she spooned tea leaves into the pot and let it brew. "So you have seen a little of the area? That is good. Boughton Estate runs on either side of the road from the village."

Lupton smiled. "So I believe."

Lydia arched a brow. "You have been making inquiries?" She was partly intrigued, partly piqued by his answer. She poured the tea and handed him a dish.

As he reached for it, Lydia noticed his hands were those of a gentleman, and his nails were manicured.

"I would be failing in my duty to both myself and to you, my lady, if I did not familiarize myself with some rudimentary knowledge of Boughton's affairs," he replied disarmingly.

Lydia nodded. She would have preferred it had he come directly to her with his questions, rather than gathering up any rumors and insinuations that were blowing like chaff on the wind, but she forbore. "So, do tell me what you have discovered, Mr. Lupton."

He took a deep breath and tilted his head slightly. "I heard that your ladyship is a widow, but that you manage your affairs most diligently and your care for your tenants is unparalleled."

Lydia did not feel comforted by the remarks, even though she knew they were designed to flatter. She was all too accustomed to being told what idle tongues were saying about her. Nevertheless she felt compelled to listen.

"Go on," she said.

Lupton resumed. "I heard that you have a good herd of Cotswolds, although their numbers have been much depleted by the recent fog, and that your barley and wheat yields were reasonable before, but could be improved."

Lydia's back stiffened. She was not certain that it was seemly to listen to her father's life's work summed up in a couple of perfunctory sentences, even though she privately acknowledged their accuracy.

"Interesting," was all she would say before parrying his cutting remarks with a flourish of her own. "And what of yourself, Mr. Lupton? As I recall it is you who are applying for the position of estate manager. Perhaps you might like to summarize yourself."

Lupton jolted slightly at the upbraid before his face broke into a smile. "Forgive me, your ladyship. You must think me forward. It is my habit."

"And how might you have come by that?" interjected Lydia, suspecting that there was more to Mr. Lupton than he had told her.

He acknowledged her comment with a nod. "I fear that you

have seen through me, your ladyship," he said. "I come from a family whose interests lay in Virginia."

"In America?" Intrigued, Lydia leaned forward.

"Yes, your ladyship. Now that we have lost the war, so have we lost our fortune. Our English home and lands all need be sold to pay our debts and so it is time for me to seek gainful employment."

Lydia reached for the letter she had received the previous week from a gentleman of means who vouched for him. A business associate of his father, he spoke of Lupton in glowing terms, calling him "resourceful and of the utmost integrity."

Integrity was a quality that Lydia had come to prize most in a man. In all her dealings with the opposite sex she had found it the attribute most lacking. She thought of her cheating husband, the duplicitous lawyer Lavington, her treacherous cousin Francis. Integrity was a foreign word to them; something that was not in their vocabulary. And as for principles, they were merely trifles, targets to be shot down at will. Only Thomas remained true to his ideals; never wavering from his purpose to help those in need and uncovering the truth in all things.

"I admire a man of principle," she said finally, looking up from the letter. "I think we should take a ride around the estate."

With Lydia at the reins, they toured 'round Boughton in a dogcart, first taking the track that led up to the pavilion. Lydia drove past her husband's grave without remarking upon it. She had no wish for pity, or to draw more attention to her widowed status.

At the pavilion they paused to take in the view. The sky was gray and the fields were sombre in their winter garb, all checkered shades of brown, punctuated now and again by clumps of evergreen bushes or hedges that were black against the dormant landscape. The spire of the chapel, so long obscured by the Great Fogg, was now clearly visible and, beyond that, the tower of St. Swithin's on the edge of Brandwick.

"The estate stretches as far as you can see," said Lydia, with a gentle sweep of her hand. "Five thousand acres of arable and pasture land, commons and woodlands, too."

Lupton surveyed the view in silence at first, as if drinking in every detail, then nodded his head. "A fine estate, Lady Farrell," he acknowledged with a smile.

Lydia felt a kernel of pride within. His appreciation seemed genuine, unembellished, and, although there was no need, she felt grateful for it.

"Thank you," she replied unthinkingly.

They returned to the dogcart and drove back down the hill. Passing through the woods, they joined the track that led to Plover's Lake and the cottage that had been home to Gabriel Lawson. The noise of the horse's hooves sent three or four geese squawking across the water. Two mallards took flight.

"This is where the new estate manager would live," said Lydia, pointing to the house and its compact grounds.

Lupton smiled. "A handsome abode," he remarked diplomatically.

"I am afraid it is probably much more humble than that to which you are accustomed," replied Lydia. "But you would have a housekeeper." She suddenly checked herself. "The estate manager, whoever fills the position, is given a housekeeper." The truth was that apart from a clearly unsuitable applicant who wrote a ten-page diatribe on the virtues of the feudal system, there were no other candidates for the post.

Out of feigned guile or politeness Lupton should have let the faux pas pass unremarked, but he felt confident enough to draw attention to it.

"I am sure the arrangement would be most satisfactory," he replied, "whoever takes the position." He gave Lydia a sideways glance and she allowed a smile to flit across her face. She found his manner affable, if a little forthright, but she liked his approach. There were several similarities between his father's small estate in Yorkshire and Boughton, he told her. He had worked with his own estate manager to turn 'round falling yields and made the tenants more productive by fostering a community spirit. Raising rents was always a risky move when times were hard, he'd found. Yes, he was a man of principle and integrity. She liked that. She liked him. She would offer him the job.

By the time they arrived back at the hall, it was growing dark. The November light was fading fast.

"I must away before dark or I might lose my way back to the inn," said Lupton, stepping down from the dogcart. Will Lovelock, the groom, had been sent to fetch his horse.

"But you must be hungry, Mr. Lupton," said Lydia suddenly, remaining seated in the cart. "Why do you not eat here? The cottage is not aired but you are most welcome to stay in the house, tonight."

Lupton paused. If he had expected an impromptu invitation, he did not show it.

"I could not prevail upon your ladyship's hospitality so," he replied, shaking his blond head.

"Nonsense!" replied Lydia. "You are part of Boughton now. Part of the estate. We can talk of the fine details over dinner and there will be no need to rush." She surprised herself with her own enthusiasm. She hoped it was not too obvious that she craved adult company. The prospect of an agreeable companion at dinner greatly appealed.

"You are most kind," said Lupton, suddenly acquiescing.

Lydia smiled triumphantly. "Then it is settled. I shall have the servants prepare a room."

Chapter 7

The large round fish floated serenely in the jar with unseeing eyes, its spikes a warning that it was not to be trifled with. Next to it on the shelf sat a large chunk of red coral, which, according to its label, was said to be efficacious in the treatment of the bloody flux. Thomas recognized Dr. Carruthers's handwriting. Next to that was a case containing an array of small birds with bright plumages.

Clouds of dust billowed as soon as Thomas began to remove them. The shelves had been their home since Dr. Carruthers brought them back from his own trip to Jamaica, almost fifty years ago. Now they needed to be moved to make way for new and potentially even more curious Caribbean residents. Thomas was expecting scores of them, not just small mammals and insects, but shellfish and other sea creatures, as well as dozens of plants. He was about to take delivery of a treasure chest of exotica. It would be his mission to order them, label them, and subsequently work on them. It would be his job to help unlock the mysteries that these treasures held. He had heard of corals that stemmed hemorrhages, of plants whose sap soothed burns. Just what other miracles might be waiting to be uncovered was almost unimaginable.

Unable to sleep he had entered the laboratory early that morning. Such was his excitement and apprehension at being entrusted with the important task that he had worked by candlelight. He had cleared the shelves of their old inhabitants and had placed them carefully, according to their classification, into sturdy crates, ready for transportation to the cellar.

Despite so many distractions, the words of Sir Joseph Banks kept ringing in Thomas's ears.

"I have great faith in you, Silkstone. Play your cards right and you will go far." He had winked as he said the last sentence, as if he were delivering an understanding between gentlemen. *"Play your cards right."* What could he mean, Thomas asked himself as he wiped the shelves with a damp cloth.

Sir Joseph had been most helpful, answering his many and varied questions. How many specimens were there? Of what nature? Where would they be stored before they were catalogued? And afterward? How much time did he have for study? Would there be regular meetings to discuss his progress? All these pressing questions were answered to his satisfaction. It was just this peculiar phrase that niggled him. He understood there was a protocol for such research; certain scientific rules and procedures that must be followed strictly. And yet he was under the impression that Sir Joseph's words were almost a warning. It was as if the president of the Royal Society was taking a personal risk on this young American, as if he were an untried and an untested maverick on whom Sir Joseph was staking his own, very considerable, reputation. It was as if Thomas were being told that he had to conform to establishment thinking or suffer the consequences—ironically, he mused, as if he were in chains.

He thought of the poster advertising a reward for the return of the runaway slave and felt the bile rise in his throat. He had heard talk in the coffeehouses about the treatment of slaves in the Caribbean colonies, but he had dismissed them as businessmen's bravado, tales told by merchants wanting to impress their fellows. Sugar was a necessary luxury. The foundations of all of London's fine new buildings were bedded in the white gold of the West Indies. But someone needed to plant the cane, someone needed to cut it in the scorching sun, someone needed to drag it to the cane sheds and boil it in the great vats that bubbled and spat like the infernos of hell itself. It was the devil's work, too hard for white men; make the Negroes do it under threat of the lash and when they buckled and died under such a treacherous yoke, there would be more plundered from Africa. Like wax softened in the heat, it seemed white men melted easily into barbarous practices and customs, thought Thomas. Perhaps he should have paid more attention to such stories, but he chose to dismiss them. A profound feeling of shame seeped through his veins and he had almost surrendered himself to melancholy when he heard the familiar tap of Dr. Carruthers's stick on the flagstones.

"Good morning, sir," he greeted the elderly gentleman as he entered the room. The first shards of daylight were cutting through the window high up in the wall.

"I thought I would find you here already," replied William Carruthers. The anatomist was Thomas's mentor and friend. The young doctor had spent the last ten years with him since his arrival in England as a student from his native Philadelphia. Four years ago the old man had been dealt a cruel blow when he lost his sight. Thomas had become his eyes and the bond between them had grown even stronger. Carruthers was his professional rock—not a mere sounding board for new ideas and hypotheses, but a fount of knowledge and expertise upon which Thomas frequently drew. His health may have been failing and his joints stiffening, but his brain was most certainly as sharp as a surgeon's knife. Thomas greatly valued his knowledge and his judgment and sought his advice on many weighty matters.

The old anatomist sniffed at the dusty air.

"So you have been clearing the shelves?"

Thomas smiled. Nothing managed to get past his mentor, whose other senses seemed to have sharpened since he had been deprived of his sight.

"Indeed, sir," he replied, clamping the lid on yet another crate. "Most of the specimens are to be stored at the Royal Society, but Sir Joseph says that I may work on the ones of particular interest to me here, so I have made room for them."

Carruthers nodded his head. "Oh, that I could see them," he murmured forlornly.

Thomas sensed his sadness and frustration. "But we shall

work on them together, sir." There had been several occasions when his mentor's sense of smell had proved vital in solving scientific quandaries and his eagerness to engage him in the important work was genuine.

"I would like that very much," he replied, smiling and easing himself onto a high stool at the workbench.

Lifting a jar full of a dark-colored bark, Thomas nodded. "Your knowledge of Jamaica will be invaluable," he said.

The old anatomist looked thoughtful; his filmy eyes were fixed into the distance. " 'Tis many years ago, now, and 'twas a time I would rather forget."

Thomas knew that his mentor's experience of the island had been a harrowing one. He had assisted a physician who advised on the purchase of slaves at the dockside. It was clear from his manner that he cared not to talk of it and Thomas knew he still bore the mental scars of it. He had seen men separated from their women, mothers from their children, floggings and unspeakable tortures. Even so, he anticipated Dr. Carruthers's understanding of the climate, culture, and diseases of the godless colony would be indispensable during his work.

No sooner had the old anatomist settled himself down, however, than more footsteps could be heard on the flagstones. Mistress Finesilver, the pinched-faced housekeeper, appeared at the open door. It usually took a dose of laudanum to solicit a smile from her and this morning was no exception. She handed Thomas a message as if it were a soiled bandage.

"This just came for you, Dr. Silkstone."

Thomas thanked her and read the letter. He glanced up. "The *Elizabeth* has been sighted in the Thames and will dock on the morrow. I am to meet her," he said, his voice rising in his excitement.

Dr. Carruthers tapped the floor with his stick and nodded. "This is, indeed, the start of a great adventure, young fellow," he declared.

Chapter 8

Lydia found dinner agreeable enough. Nicholas Lupton's trunk had been fetched from the Three Tuns in the village and he had quickly settled into his room at Boughton. He had presented himself sporting a gray wig and wearing a green frockcoat. A faint whiff of sandalwood swathed him. Seated at the opposite end of the long table he and Lydia had dined on pork from the estate's finest Gloucester Old Spots and a good blackberry tart.

Conversation had centred on Boughton and the problems that it faced. It emerged that Mr. Lupton had been in Yorkshire during the time of the Great Fogg, and had not been badly affected, so Lydia had informed him of the havoc it had wrought to man, beast and vegetation. She told him how there was much work to do to remedy the devastation it had left in its wake.

Lupton had listened attentively, asking pertinent questions when deemed necessary. He seemed sensitive to the welfare of tenants, asking about their conditions and terms of tenure.

"I hope you won't think me impolite if I say it was clear from the way they regarded you this afternoon that your workers have much affection for you, your ladyship," he said, pushing his empty dessert plate away from him.

Lydia hoped that in the candle glow her guest could not see her blush. She glanced at Howard, who was hovering attentively by the sideboard.

"My father instilled in me the fact that we are mere custodians of this land. We are looking after it for future generations and must treat those who assist in that task with due respect," she replied.

Lupton nodded his approval of the sentiment.

"So will you be joined by Mistress Lupton in the cottage?" she asked as Howard and another manservant cleared their plates.

At this question, however, the new steward looked grave. "I am afraid my wife is deceased," he replied.

Lydia felt awkward. "I am sorry. I did not mean . . ." The color rose in her cheeks once more.

Lupton shook his head. " 'Tis my fault, your ladyship. I should have made my state plain. My wife died in childbirth less than a year ago."

"My condolences," said Lydia solemnly.

Lupton gave a tight smile, as if remembering his late wife. "She was giving birth to our first child, a boy." He paused, then added: "I lost them both."

In the candlelight, Lydia thought she saw Mr. Lupton's eyes moisten. She averted her gaze for a moment to allow him to compose himself.

"It is hard, being on one's own," she said gently. Her tone sounded knowledgeable, and he recognized she spoke from experience.

Lupton took a deep, juddering breath. "That it is, your ladyship." His large shoulders heaved, as if he was trying to shrug off a great sadness. "But you have your son, I believe." His mood lightened.

Lydia nodded and played with the stem of her wineglass. Howard filled it without being asked. "Indeed, I do, and a great comfort he is to me."

Lupton smiled as Howard filled his glass. "I am looking forward to meeting him. Perhaps he would come for a ride, with your permission, your ladyship." His bewigged head gave a slight reverential bow.

"I am sure Richard would like that very much," she replied, smiling.

An hour later they had both retired to their separate chambers. Lydia lingered a little longer than normal and did not call for Eliza, her maid, until after eleven o'clock. The girl unlaced Lydia's stays, helped her off with her gown, then brushed her long chestnut hair. She noted her mistress was smiling at her reflection in the mirror.

" 'Tis good to see you looking cheery, your ladyship," she said, speaking out of turn, then realizing her mistake to her own embarrassment.

Lydia nodded. "I spent a pleasant evening," she replied, adding: "I have engaged Mr. Lupton as the new steward."

Eliza continued brushing her mistress's hair unthinkingly. " 'Twill be good to have a man around again."

Lydia arched a brow and shot back at her maid, "Mr. Lupton is a steward, not a suitor, Eliza."

The girl curtsied awkwardly. "Begging your pardon, my lady. I did not mean . . ." The hairbrush flapped in her hand.

A smile crossed Lydia's lips. "You are right, Eliza. It will be good to have the support of a man who knows what he is about and understands business."

There was an awkward silence as both women's thoughts turned to the man who they knew should be rightfully heading the household by now. It was Lydia who spoke her mind.

"I am sure Dr. Silkstone will agree with my choice," she said, as if seeking approval for making the engagement.

Eliza looked slightly taken aback, as if her mistress deemed it necessary to emphasize her unwritten commitment to Thomas. Nevertheless she nodded. "I am sure, your ladyship," she replied.

Chapter 9

Phibbah slipped out of the house as night fell, her heart pounding in her chest. The cook, Mistress Bradshaw, was more kindly than the usual English woman. She had heard her talk with some of the other white servants in the household, saying it was not right for the blacks to be enslaved and that every man and woman in England should be free to come and go as they pleased. But the others had laughed at her and told her it was none of her business and that as long as the Negroes were around they wouldn't have to do as many dirty jobs like take out the slops, so they would not complain. She had shrugged her shoulders and tutted, but she had still shown a little kindness, although if she guessed the reason for her excursion, Phibbah knew Mistress Bradshaw would not be so forgiving.

The slave girl had still not fully recovered from yesterday's punishment. Twenty lashes, the mistress had ordered, and Mr. Roberts, the footman, had relished delivering every stroke. Each crack of the whip was music to his ears. Each yelp, each sob, each cry of pain was a symphony to him. Patience had rubbed ointment on the wounds last night, but the cuts still wept and her back would remain raw as butcher's meat for the next few days. In Jamaica, in the sun, the welts attracted the flies. Here, in London, she was forced to cover them with coarse clothes that chafed at her skin just like the manacles 'round her ankles on board the ship all those years ago.

She steadied herself by the back gate. Her head was light and sometimes her sight blurred. Ghosts would appear from nowhere, swimming across her vision, shrieking in her ears. They were the spirits of her ancestors, the ones who had not been buried according to tradition, the ones who had lived and died under the white man's rules and not been accorded the right and proper ritual. They would roam this earth forever.

She unlatched the gate and slid through it, then slipped down the lane. High brick walls rose on either side, overhung by leafless trees. She did not like English trees in winter. Their black branches were arms, their spindly twigs fingers. A carriage passed. She kept her head down and quickened her pace. Not far now.

At the end of the lane she turned left. A church bell tolled nearby. Almost there. She rounded the corner and came to the lych-gate. Passing through it she found herself in the graveyard, an Englishman's churchyard, with its cold mossy stones and its fine statues of women with wings. How strange, she thought, to honor the dead in this way. She had heard they were buried without their cooking pots and their jewelry. How would they eat? Did they not want to look their best when they rejoined their ancestors? Worse still, their graves were often sealed, so that robbers could not take their corpses. She had heard that the churchmen might sometimes set spring guns to ward off the sack-'em-up men. Sometimes they put cages over the graves and locked them with padlocks as big as coconuts. So how would the dead eat? How would they find their way home? It was all a puzzle to her. These places were strange and baffling and frightening. She would not loiter.

A lone woman stood praying by a new grave. She wore a black veil that covered her face. Hurrying over to the wall of the churchyard, where thick thorn bushes grew, their berries red as blood, Phibbah crouched low to watch her. The shadows were melding into the blackness as the first stars appeared in the sky. The widow would be gone soon. Only the evil ones would stay in a place like this after dark, she told herself.

Sure enough, after one or two minutes Phibbah saw the woman's head bow reverentially and she retreated through the lych-gate and into the encroaching darkness. Now she was alone, apart from the hundreds of spirits that surrounded her. Scurrying forward, she reached the grave where the earth had been newly smoothed and saw worms writhing blindly in the soil. A garland of holly and ivy had been placed on the mound.

Quickly she took out her bag, knelt down, and began to scoop up handfuls of the damp dirt. It came up easily, in sticky clumps, clawing 'round her fingernails. She was doing well; a few more handfuls and she would have enough. Just then a bird swooped overhead. It was huge and called to her with a voice that was shrill and trembling. She looked up. An ancestor, she thought, but then something caught her eye in the far corner of the churchyard. A man in a long black robe was approaching her. He was waving a stick. Now he was shouting. She must go. What was it the obeah-man said? Enough to fill a goat's horn. She looked at her bag, whose sides now bulged. What she had was sufficient. Scrambling to her feet, she headed for the lych-gate. The man was coming closer. She broke into a run. She winced with pain as the cuts on her back reopened.

"You! Stop!" cried the man. But from his gait she could tell he was old and from his robes a priest, perhaps. He thought she was disturbing the dead. He did not understand that they were all around; that they never stayed in the ground, unless their burial chambers were locked or sealed.

She ran on until she joined the path leading to the lych-gate, but just as she slowed down at the entrance, her foot caught a jagged stone and she tripped, dropping her bag and spilling some soil. A gasp escaped her lips as the man approached. She turned her back to him. He must not see the color of her skin. Grabbing at the bag, she made off once more, down the path, through the gate and out onto the lane.

Running as fast as if Mr. Roberts himself were in pursuit with his whip, she soon reached the end of the lane and turned left to the road that would take her back to the big house. It was only then that she stopped momentarily to look inside her bag. Almost half its contents had spilled out when she fell, but there should still be enough for her obeah-bag—still enough grave dirt for the curse to work.

Chapter 10

Sir Theodisius Pettigrew had embraced the game of golf with great enthusiasm if not skill. The Oxfordshire coroner had found that since taking to the sport only a few months ago, he might even have shed a few pounds from his not inconsiderable midriff. Of course he could not play a whole round without recourse to his hamper, carried alongside his clubs by his caddy. But suitably sustained by the frequent consumption of chicken legs, sausage rolls, and the occasional plover's egg, he found the new pastime an excellent way to spend his leisure hours.

After the frightful weeks spent in the grip of the Great Fogg, he had promised his dear wife, Harriet, that he would take her to London so that she could shop in Oxford Street. While there he could combine her pleasure with his own business. He had a few small interests that required his attention and had been delighted when an invitation had come from Hubert Izzard, an acquaintance of many years' standing, to join a party to play golf at Blackheath Club.

It was a crisp, clear morning when the four gentlemen set off for the first hole on the heath course. The purple heather carpeted the rough and the views of the Thames below were quite breathtaking. Hundreds of ships, large and small, could be seen plying up and down the river, or stationary in dock, forming a forest of masts in the water.

"A sight for sore eyes, eh, Sir Theodisius?" declared the ruddy-faced gentleman who strode out toward the first tee, taking in the view. The coroner and Mr. Izzard had been joined by Mr. Samuel Carfax and his associate Mr. Josiah Dalrymple, accompanied by his Negro slave Jeremiah Taylor. Both merchants were vaguely known to Sir Theodisius as being involved in shipping and, more particularly, slaving and the sugar trade, although how Izzard knew them was beyond his ken.

Dalrymple was handsome enough, but clearly not a real gentleman. There was something slightly studied in his mannerisms, thought Sir Theodisius. Each one of his gestures appeared to be a flourish rather than a mere practicality. The way he brandished his club, or waved his kerchief, rankled, as if he had learned the affectations rather than been born to them. His manner with his slave was also overbearing and harsh. The Oxfordshire coroner took an instant dislike to him.

"London's great wealth is built on those ships," butted in Dalrymple.

"Or more particularly on their cargo!" corrected Mr. Carfax, raising a stubby finger in the air. He was squat and pigeon-chested and his short neck caused his large head to disappear between the humps of his broad shoulders. Word had it that he had his eye on a rotten borough in next year's elections and was in town to garner support. His manner was bluff, but jolly, no doubt helped by the regular swigs of rum he took from a hip flask.

"Yes, those slaves are black gold to London," he said, letting out a hearty laugh.

Dalrymple shot a sideways glance to Izzard. "How true," he agreed.

Izzard snorted. "Be careful, sir. Your slave has a club in his hand." He nodded at Jeremiah, who was supplying his master with the appropriate irons for the shot. "I certainly would not trust one. Bludgeon you to death as soon as look at you!" he quipped.

The round was enjoyable enough. None of the players produced great shots and Sir Theodisius, coming the latest to the game, was not made to feel woefully inept. His willingness to share his sausage rolls seemed to more than compensate for his awkward swing and slow gait in his companions' eyes.

The casual talk centred on the price of sugar and tobacco and the recent slave revolts in Jamaica, where the men owned plantations.

"Dreadful business over at Melrose's estate," commented Carfax, shaking his head. He paused thoughtfully before adding: "What those savages did to the overseer!"

Sir Theodisius was aware of the incident, one of a growing number, where slaves were rising up against their masters on the island.

Dalrymple smirked. "Trouble is Melrose was too soft. He started treating them too well. Regular floggings, that's what they understand. What, Jeremiah?!" He let out a contemptuous laugh as the slave remained impassive at his master's side, then swung at the ball and hit it hard into the distance. "No mercy!" he said, smiling, as he watched the ball drop just a few feet away from the intended hole.

Sir Theodisius raised a brow and Carfax caught his look of approbation.

"We must not bore our guests with merchants' small talk," he upbraided his friend. He took another swig of rum from his hip flask, but Dalrymple would not be put off.

"The next thing you know, the do-gooders will be calling for abolition and then where would we be, gentlemen?" he asked, shaking his head. His conjecture was met with laughter from both Carfax and Izzard.

"Just wait until I get my seat in Parliament, old chap!" chuckled Carfax. "I'll see their sort get no quarter!"

The banter continued, although Sir Theodisius began to tire a little of the men's talk and thought instead of the mutton pie Cook would have waiting for him on his return home.

At last they reached the fifteenth and final tee. Just after he had taken his shot, however, the coroner noticed that Samuel Carfax seemed to be experiencing pain of some sort. He had lately spied him wincing as he took aim. Could his resort to the rum be designed to ease his discomfort? he wondered. He waited until the other fellows were occupied before broaching the subject.

"My dear sir, forgive me for the intrusion, but I have noticed you seem to be having difficulty with your arm." He pointed at Carfax's coat.

"Ah, nothing escapes the coroner's notice!" he replied with a smile, then, easing back his sleeve, he revealed a bandage of gauze with a large yellow stain at its centre just above his wrist. "Some sort of bite, I believe. Getting worse, too." He groaned a little as he pulled down his cuff.

Sir Theodisius sucked in his flaccid cheeks and clicked his tongue. "You have seen a physician?"

Carfax shook his head. He had been back in England less than a week and the demands of business had taken priority over his own health.

"Can you recommend one? 'Tis too trifling a matter for Iz-zard, yet I fear a quack who thinks a good bleeding is a cure-all."

The coroner's jowls wobbled as he nodded and thought of Thomas Silkstone, a physician and surgeon whose dislike of ve-nesection was as well known as his distaste for pomposity and show.

"Indeed, I can recommend a most excellent chap," he said, before helping himself to another sausage roll.

Chapter 11

The foreshore leading to the Legal Quays was so packed with people and handcarts that the carriage was obliged to drop Thomas a quarter of a mile away in Thames Street. Clutching his case tightly to his side, he battled through the melee. He knew he was headed in the right direction. Up above him in the distance he could see the masts of the ships, rising skyward like the great giant pine trees of his homeland. On either side were workshops and warehouses. Men hammered rims on barrels, or forged iron chains, the clatter of their heavy hammers barely audible above the din of the street. Others barged past him, crates or sacks on their shoulders, their heads angled with the weight of their burdens.

Sir Joseph had impressed upon Thomas the need to oversee the unloading of the cargo. The quays in the Pool of London were a notorious hunting ground for gangs of thieves who roamed the shore looking for opportunities to steal. He'd heard of the Scuffle-Hunters and the River Pirates and did not want to trifle with them. Just what they would make of the *Elizabeth*'s cargo was open to conjecture, but he did not want to give them the chance to lay their grubby hands on the priceless consignment that could be worth more to medicine than any amount of French brandy and fine cheese.

Finally he reached the quayside. Rarely had he beheld such a scene of mayhem. It was as if the Thames had brought in on its tide the flotsam and jetsam of humanity and deposited it on the shore. Merchants mingled with fishwives and costermongers, and sun-beaten sailors rubbed shoulders with porters, their eyes wild from months away at sea. A hapless preacher, perched on an upturned crate, struggled to be heard above the curses and oaths below. Whores hawked for business alongside ginger-bread sellers, while in among them cutpurses and pickpockets plied their trade largely unchallenged.

Beyond the chaos Thomas's eyes were drawn to the vast masts that rose from the river. Flags flapped like leaves in the gathering gusts and the ropes that hung from them reminded him of giant vines. Somewhere in that tangle of wood and rope and spars and ladders lay the *Elizabeth*.

He craned his neck above the crowd and spied the Customs House a few yards up ahead. Sir Joseph Banks had already sent a letter to take to the chief customs officer, explaining the nature of the *Elizabeth*'s cargo. There should be no duty to pay. The tide waiter, taken on board at Gravesend, would be able to confirm that.

The imposing building itself was also teeming with people, mainly merchants and captains, anxious to register their cargo. There seemed to be no orderly queue and Thomas found himself being buffeted by elbows and his toes trodden upon by eager feet. At the far end of a large hall, four men sat behind desks on a raised dais. He guessed they were the officials and he, too, joined the fracas, edging his way slowly, and not without considerable discomfort, to the front.

The officer to whom he eventually delivered the letter deliberated for a moment, then frowned. He rose, consulted with a colleague, and returned to deliver the news. Looking down his nose through spectacles, the official told Thomas that the *Elizabeth* had been directed to a sufferance wharf.

"This ship is not here, sir," he informed Thomas, "but downriver. You'll need to take a ferry." He clamped a piece of paper into his hand. On it was written the name of the wharf.

The young doctor could not hide his frustration and groaned at the news. This new world of customs and excise was completely foreign to him. Even the language that was spoken on the quayside with its strange vocabulary may as well have been ancient Greek. He would have to reenter the fray and take to the water in search of the *Elizabeth*.

Steeling himself for the onward journey, Thomas left the Customs House and ventured once more onto the wharf. A lighter had just berthed at the quayside and the gangplank had been lowered. Two seamen were the first to disembark, but instead of walking away from the ship, they stationed themselves on the quay, as if waiting for something. Thomas did not have to watch for long to find out what cargo they had been carrying. From the deck below a Negro man emerged, followed by another and another. He counted about two dozen in all, and three women. The men wore the red coats of the British Army. Some were limping and were supported by their fellows. Others were clearly wounded, their arms in slings or their heads bandaged. The women bundled themselves in thin shawls and looked anxious.

Most of them kept their eyes to the ground, as if they were still wearing the slave yokes from the auctions. They were bloodied and they were bowed. But there was one man who stood prouder than the rest. He was looking about him, taking in the detail of this cold and drab place where he now found himself, and as he looked about him, his eyes latched on to Thomas. Their gazes met fleetingly and it was as if their two worlds came together for a split second and each understood the other, before they were lost in the melee once more.

A crowd had gathered to watch the arrival of these strange visitors. A horse-drawn tumbrel pulled up and the seamen began shepherding them on board. One woman spat at a Negro man as he passed her. Fists were raised, insults hurled. "Monkey men!" shouted a sailor, who proceeded to jabber and swing his arms, much to the amusement of the mob.

Thomas felt his blood course through his veins at the sight. He knew these people to be Black Loyalists. They had fought for King George against his fellow Americans and in return they had been granted their freedom. He felt no animosity toward them. Any man would have done the same. Yet it was clear that although they were no longer in chains, the taunts and jeers of the white men and women who stood on the quayside with their fists raised were as cruel as any plantation overseer with a bull-whip. Thomas suddenly felt a great sorrow wash over his anger. Despite their newfound freedom, he knew their color would enslave these people in England.

In the attic room of the Carfaxes' villa, the houseboy's head rolled on the bare ticking. His forehead was dotted with beads of sweat and his skin was as hot as a branding iron, yet his teeth chattered with the cold. It was Phibbah who found Ebele collapsed on the floor in the hallway. His slave name was Sambo, but she refused to call him that. His mother was an Igbo. His name meant mercy and that is what she prayed her weakling son would be shown when she had handed him over at the plantation to be seasoned. Phibbah dragged him out of sight before the mistress saw him and Cato carried him upstairs to the attic room where the male slaves slept.

There they had removed the ridiculous silk turban he was forced to wear on his head. If anything he should have worn a fine headdress of carved wood and antelope horn, the mark of a brave warrior people, not the costume of the very Arab traders who had sold his mother into slavery in the first place. Not content to rob him of his freedom, they had stolen his identity, too.

Phibbah tucked a coarse blanket under his chin, but it was so cold in the room that her own breath whirled around her head every time she spoke. Taking out a rag from her pocket, she began to dab his wet forehead. He was much younger than she, but she did not know how old. What she did know was that he had been a sickly child and it was a wonder that he had survived infancy. After he had been seasoned and bled for the cane fields, he had grown even weaker and was often unfit for work. That was why they had set him to domestic duties rather than on the plantations. He had a pretty face and a beguiling smile that seemed to endear him to white ladies. They cooed over him in his bright red turban and his baggy silk pants. "How charming," they would say when he offered them their dish of tea.

They spoke of him as they spoke of the mistress's pug dog. He was a plaything. A pet. And now he lay fighting for his life.

"You told Venus?" Phibbah asked Cato, as she knelt by the boy's side.

The great bear of a man nodded. He was a Coromantee, too, fierce and proud. Tilting his head toward the landing, he replied, "She come now."

Seconds later Venus, the housekeeper, appeared in the room and glided over to where the child lay. She was a mulatto woman, her skin the color of milky coffee, and she wore her black hair piled on top of her head the white woman's way. From a belt around her small waist hung a bunch of keys, the keys that locked the doors at night so that the slaves could not run away. In effect she was their jailer, even though she, too, was denied her freedom, but she was kind enough. Rumor was that she had been born into the Carfax household, the result of a union between one of the master's nephews and an Ashanti woman. There was a poise in her manner and an elegance in her gait that set her apart. She did not carry herself like a slave, always looking low, afraid to let her eyes roam freely. Her gaze was always steady and now it settled on the boy.

"How long has he been like this?" she asked, leaning over the palliasse.

"I found him downstairs. He had fainted away," replied Phibbah. "He very bad."

"I can see that," Venus replied, calmly looking down her long, thin nose at the child, whose breathing had become labored. She thought for a moment. "He needs medicine."

Cato nodded. "I fetch white doctor?"

"No," the housekeeper replied firmly. Her reproving gaze slid sideways. "You know the mistress will not let you call one. They cost too much." Cato looked crestfallen, but a smirk crept over Venus's lips. "I have something much better than white man's medicine," she said.

Delving into the pocket in her skirt, she pulled out a small glass bottle and held it up to the square of light from the window. Inside was a pale liquid.

"This was given to me by a myal man before we left Jamaica. He say, if you are troubled by any white man's disease, this will make it better." She nodded her head as her eyes flitted between Phibbah and Cato. They both seemed heartened by her words. They knew the myal medicine to work.

"Hold his head," Venus instructed as she uncorked the bottle.

Kneeling down Phibbah slid one arm under Ebele's neck, so that his body was forced up. His head tilted back limply, but Cato held it steady as the girl opened his lips with her free hand. Venus edged forward and poured the bottle's contents into the boy's mouth. He spluttered and jerked his body, but the housekeeper clamped his lips shut until she was sure he had swallowed the liquid. Taking a step back, she watched as the boy's breathing relaxed almost immediately.

"There!" she said triumphantly. "By tomorrow he will be back to work."

Phibbah and Cato glanced at each other and smiled. They both knew the myal men on Mr. Carfax's estate had great powers. They could ward off the duppies with their dances and drumming. They possessed healing magic. Their potions did good. Ebele's ancestors would watch over him as he slept and he would soon be restored.

"Now you must leave him and get back to your work, too," Venus told them, clapping her hands quickly to hurry them along. "Do not trouble yourselves about Sambo."

Chapter 12

It was after midday when Thomas finally arrived at the quay where the *Elizabeth* was berthed. She had docked with the afternoon tide. The ferry had dropped him at the King's Stairs a few hundred yards away and he had cut his path through the throng to the berth where he had been directed. The wharf was still busy, but not too busy. There was room to turn about and peer, even though one still had to weave around the handcarts and trolleys that plied up and down.

The tang of smoke from the braziers mingled with the smell of salt fish and rotting vegetables. There were no French perfumes or other luxury goods here. Or if there were, they were packed under cod or sacks of coal to escape the customs officers' eagle eyes. Ships that berthed at this wharf were there "under sufferance." They did not have to pay a high duty, if any at all, on their cargoes. The *Elizabeth* was exempt and the papers to prove it were already lodged with His Majesty's Customs.

Thomas could see she was indeed a fine ship, dainty and well preserved. He spotted a gentleman he assumed to be an officer standing on the quarterdeck. He appeared to be supervising the ticket porters who were unloading barrels and crates from the vessel. He seemed to be checking boxes against a long manifest in his hand.

Up above the great jib was in full swing. Seamen were fixing a devilish-looking hook to the roped crates. At a signal they rose from the deck and swung through the air to be deposited on the quayside. Below, men were stacking the crates onto waiting wagons. Thomas scanned the crowd looking for someone in authority: someone who was supervising the whole operation. Of the artist Matthew Bartlett there seemed no sign.

He paused for a moment as the large box swung over the deck and onto a waiting wagon with a loud thud. The horses that were hitched to the cart shifted a little, nodding their heads violently as if in protest. Watching to see if anyone might chastise the dockers, or inspect any damage that might have been done, Thomas found himself unable to discover who might be in charge. Disappointed, he decided to intervene himself.

"Gently, men," he cried, striding forward to the cart to check on the crate.

His protests met with surly grunts from the men, who carried on regardless, seemingly unsupervised.

Cupping his hands around his mouth, Thomas hollered to a sailor on deck.

"I wish to speak with your captain," he shouted.

The mariner looked at him suspiciously, then climbed up to alert the officer on the quarterdeck. A moment later Thomas found himself on board the *Elizabeth,* being shown below deck into the captain's cabin.

Bobbing low through the doorway, he could see the captain's table, covered with maps and charts. Most of the remaining floor space was, however, set aside for a large number of pots that contained plants.

"Dr. Silkstone, welcome aboard," greeted the florid-faced man, who rose behind the table. He wore the sea-weary expression of a sailor newly returned from a punishing voyage. His leathery skin was pulled taut across his cheekbones, his brows were unruly, and his lips were flaking.

"At your service, sir," replied Thomas. "I am sent by Sir Joseph Banks."

The captain's face broke into a smile. "Then you are even more welcome aboard the *Elizabeth,* sir," he said in an affable Scottish brogue. He gestured to a seat.

"I see you have returned with a large cargo," said Thomas. He surveyed the smaller crates and barrels piled up in every available space.

The captain shrugged. "Och, our children, we call them, Dr. Silkstone," he said with a grin. "These are the delicate things; small mammals, insects, that sort of creature."

"You have clearly done an excellent job in very tragic circumstances," said Thomas, thinking of the dead doctors Welton and Perrick. He, himself, had seen many a man die of the yellow fever on his own voyage from Philadelphia to London all those years ago, and the memory of it would never leave him.

A forlorn look scudded across the captain's well-worn face.

"They were good men," he replied thoughtfully.

"And only one remains, I am told."

The captain looked Thomas in the eye.

"The artist. A Mr. Bartlett, I believe."

"You are correct, sir."

"I am to liaise with him regarding the specimens. Is he not on board?"

The captain sat back in his chair and shook his head.

"I am afraid you have just missed him, Dr. Silkstone."

Thomas looked puzzled and waited to be enlightened.

The captain's expression hardened. "There was an issue with some of the cargo, I believe, and an officer asked if Mr. Bartlett would accompany him to the Customs House. He'll be back presently."

"But papers were sent by Sir Joseph Banks himself," said Thomas. A note of anxiety crept into his tone.

Seeing his concerned reaction, the Scotsman's face split into a smile again and he shook his head. He was clearly unfazed by the artist's absence.

"Dunni worry yoursen, Dr. Silkstone. He'll turn up soon enough and in the meantime your precious specimens of flora and fauna will be unloaded safely."

The plan was to store most of the cargo in the Royal Society's own warehouses, and the plants at Kew Gardens.

Thomas nodded in reply. This Mr. Bartlett was, by all accounts as Sir Joseph had indicated, someone who took his duties most seriously. If there was a problem with His Majesty's Customs, then he would know to contact the great man directly.

"Thank you, Captain," he said. "I am sure you are right."

McCoy slapped the desk as he rose, as if trying to draw a line under the slight hitch.

"I expect you would like to inspect the cargo, Dr. Silkstone," he said as he began fastening the buttons on his jacket. It seemed rather too big for him after his voyage.

Thomas nodded. "Naturally I must take receipt of Dr. Welton's papers, too. I need them before I can start to catalogue the specimens."

The captain stopped by the low cabin door. "I have possession of most of them. They are in my chest."

"Most of them?" queried Thomas.

Still hovering on the threshold, the captain nodded. "All except for Dr. Welton's private journal. That is in the safekeeping of Mr. Bartlett. He was most insistent that he should take charge of it. He told me he swore on his own life, as the doctor lay dying, that he would see it was delivered into Sir Joseph's hands himself, so you've no need to worry on that score, either," added McCoy.

Thomas's concern was aroused. He wished he could have as much confidence in this Mr. Bartlett as his superiors seemed to.

"So the journal is on his person?" Thomas tried to hide the disquiet he was feeling.

"Aye. In his satchel. Carries it with him everywhere," came the captain's reassurance.

Thomas remained concerned, although he tried to mask his feelings with a smile and allowed the captain the last word.

"He'll be here soon, or with Sir Joseph. Either way, Dr. Silkstone, Mr. Bartlett is a most dependable young man."

Chapter 13

Cordelia Carfax's small eyes followed her husband as he flopped into a chair by the fire. His normally ruddy face was rendered even ruddier by a day spent in the biting wind on the golf course. She could tell by his expression that all was not well and she suspected it was not his game that had put him in a sour humor.

"Your arm is worse?" she inquired tersely as Cato, looking resplendent in a fine lace ruff and scarlet waistcoat, removed his master's boots.

Her husband nodded. "The devil it is!" His reply was unequivocal, but he turned his face away from her, signifying he did not wish to dwell on his discomfort. She clicked her tongue and sat down opposite him, smoothing her skirts as she did so, ready to receive the dog that waited eagerly at her feet.

"You will call a physician?"

Carfax propped his right arm on a cushion. "I will have to," he replied with a resigned sigh.

His wife rolled her eyes. "We all need a physician in this English winter," she countered peevishly. She held out her thin hands toward the fire. "It escapes me why this visit could not have waited until spring," she added, her thin lips curling in a sneer.

Carfax, who normally parried such jibes with avuncular ease, was in no mood for an argument. "You did not have to come with me, my dear," he countered, knowing that the prospect of new gowns was too much for her to resist. "You were aware my business was pressing."

Cato, meanwhile, had poured his master a glass of rum and now presented it to him on a tray. Despite the fact that the slave bent down low, the effort of reaching for it clearly pained Carfax and he was forced to take it in his left hand.

Ignoring her husband's obvious distress, Cordelia Carfax continued: "The slaves are falling like flies in this cold." The dog was now on her lap and she was stroking him.

Carfax shrugged his broad shoulders. "Still fewer than those lost on the estates in as many days, I'll wager." He smirked, knowing the number insignificant compared with that on the sugar plantations, where slaves died daily, due to illness or brutality or both.

His wife's back stiffened. "You know as well as I do, Samuel, that domestics live longer as a rule."

Her husband sipped his rum thoughtfully. "Perhaps we should give them warmer clothing while they are here?" he ventured.

Cordelia Carfax blinked and looked askance. "You would waste our money on such trifles?" The very thought of kitting out her slaves in warmer clothing to suit the English climate was clearly an anathema to her.

Carfax gulped down the rest of his rum. " 'Tis up to you, my dear, but can we afford to let them die of cold? A trained one can fetch upward of twenty-five pounds, but you won't find many for sale in London."

His wife nodded, as if acknowledging the notion that it was better to return to Jamaica with slaves that were already accustomed to the tropical climate and a planter's strict regimens.

"And we can always rely on the servants here," added her husband, leaning his head against the back of his chair. The Carfaxes' London household employed a skeleton staff of white servants to maintain the property in their master's absence. There was Mason, the butler, Mistress Bradshaw, the cook, three housemaids, two footmen, and a gardener and general factotum, Mr. Roberts. Their housekeeper, Venus, always traveled with them, on the master's insistence, together with half a dozen slaves from the Jamaican estate.

Just then, one of the white maids by the name of Bateson entered carrying a kettle of hot water. She set it down on the table nearest her mistress, next to the open tea caddy. Mistress Carfax, however, seemed slightly agitated and craned her neck toward the door. "But where is Sambo?" she asked indignantly. She liked the boy to bring her the hot water for her afternoon tea.

The maid bobbed a curtsy. "Begging your pardon, madam, but he is very ill."

Her mistress sucked in her cheeks and took a deep breath. "What did I tell you, Samuel?" she said sharply. "The blacks are falling like flies! It is most inconvenient."

Carfax shot her an exasperated look and shifted in his chair but the movement obviously pained him. He winced and bit his lip. "Most inconvenient," he replied unenthusiastically, as he reached into his waistcoat pocket.

"What are you doing, Samuel?" she chided, as she watched him produce a small card and begin waving it in the air.

"Bateson," he called to the maid. His forehead shone with sweat in the fire's glow.

"Sir?"

Handing her the card he said, "Tell Mason to send for this gentleman, will you?"

The girl took the card and curtsied. "Yes, sir."

Clutching his arm, he tried, unsuccessfully, to stifle a cry.

" 'Tis time I saw a physician," he muttered.

A number of small crates and barrels had been left piled high in the middle of the laboratory floor. Thomas was standing by them, a copy of the ship's manifest in his hand, trying to make sense of their contents. Dr. Carruthers sat on a stool nearby. He tapped the floor with his stick impatiently.

"Well?" he chuntered.

Thomas knew the old anatomist was anxious that he open

the crates. He, too, was keen to see what treasures they held, although he knew that without Dr. Welton's papers they would mean little.

Picking up a hammer, he prized the lattice off the lid of the first crate. There were no surprises. Inside it was fitted with shelves and the top layer held six plants in pots.

"And?" pressed the old anatomist.

Thomas sighed. "It is as I thought, sir," he replied, obviously frustrated. "Pots containing green-leaved plants with red flowers. But what they are I cannot say."

One by one, he began unloading them and ranging them on a shelf opposite the high window that caught the direct sunlight.

Dr. Carruthers sniffed the air. "Will you give me a leaf, young fellow?" he asked. Thomas handed him a pot.

"Is it familiar to you, sir?" he asked, watching the old anatomist inhale the scent.

He tilted his bewigged head in thought, as if trying to recall a place or a landscape where the plant might have grown. After a moment he nodded.

"*Hibiscus elatus,* I think you'll find," he said, adding cheerfully, "Also known as Blue Mahoe. But the journal will tell us all."

Thomas smiled in admiration at his mentor's knowledge, but had to agree. "The sooner Mr. Bartlett chooses to present himself with Dr. Welton's journal, the better," he muttered. A note of uncharacteristic annoyance had crept into his tone.

He had returned to the crate and was just about to embark upon unloading the second tier of plants when he noticed that Helen, the housemaid, was standing at the threshold of the laboratory.

"Dr. Silkstone, sir, a carriage has been sent for you to take you to the house of Mr. Samuel Carfax. He is unwell and requests that you attend him, sir," she related, without pausing for breath.

Carruthers arched a brow. "Samuel Carfax?" he repeated. "Does he not own estates in Jamaica?"

Thomas thought for a moment. He recalled having read in *The Gazeteer and New Daily Advertiser* the previous evening that the plantation owner and his entourage had recently arrived in London for a short sojourn. "I do believe you are right, sir."

The old anatomist delivered an odd sort of snort from his nostrils that signified dislike, or disapproval, or both.

"He'll either have caught a good old English cold or brought some tropical ague with him from Jamaica, mark my words," said Carruthers, raising an arthritic finger.

Thomas nodded. "Either way I had best attend him without delay," he replied.

Chapter 14

The Carfax mansion was a fine brick-built villa with a grand portico in Chelsea. It was a fashionable area where the houses overlooked the river. Yet it was not this aspect that caught Thomas's attention, but the crest on the gates as they swung open for his carriage. The image of a Negro man in chains was emblazoned at its centre. This Mr. Carfax was obviously very proud that his fortune was built on the suffering of others, mused Thomas.

As the carriage pulled up outside, a liveried footman let down the steps and the doctor soon found himself standing in a grand hallway. Mason the butler greeted him formally.

"The master is in his study, Dr. Silkstone," he informed him, bowing. "Please follow me."

Thomas was slightly bemused. Carfax was obviously not so ill as to take to his bed. He began to follow the butler, but as he did so, he heard the rustle of silk. A lady, Mistress Carfax, he presumed, was making her way down the stairs. Dressed for dinner in a blue gown, her beady eyes latched on to him.

"You are the physician?" she asked haughtily, negotiating the final steps. She was closely followed by her dog, which descended behind her in a sort of controlled fall.

Thomas bowed his head. "Dr. Thomas Silkstone at your service, m'lady."

She looked at him squarely, although her eyes narrowed slightly.

"My husband claims he is in great pain," she sneered, emphasizing the word "claims." Turning 'round, she picked up her dog from one of the steps and tucked him under her arm. "Personally, I do not think men know the meaning of the word."

Thomas hoped she did not see his wry smile as he proceeded toward the study behind the butler. Samuel Carfax was sitting at an awkward angle in a high-backed chair behind a desk. Despite the coolness of the room he wore no jacket, but a thick blanket had been wrapped around his torso, leaving his shirt sleeves exposed. He was clutching his right arm and grimacing.

"Ah, Silkstone!" he cried even before Mason had time to announce him.

Thomas bowed and moved toward his patient. "Mr. Carfax, sir, I see you are in pain."

Carfax nodded and, as Thomas approached, rolled up his sleeve to reveal the soiled bandage. "An insect bite of some sort, I think," he ventured.

Carefully Thomas began unwinding the dressing to reveal a clean hole the size of a farthing. He called for more light and Mason, who had been hovering in the background, obliged with an oil lamp, enabling a closer inspection.

Taking out his magnifying glass from his bag, Thomas peered at the wound, and noted it was surrounded by swollen and taut tissue. A yellow-colored fluid spilled over the rim of the crater, oozing like a lava flow down the arm. Perhaps this is not a bite, but an abscess, thought Thomas. He was about to reach for a scalpel from his bag so he could enlarge the opening and drain off some of the pus, when he thought he saw something move in the crater. He peered into the hole once more and there it was again. A movement. No, more than a movement. A creature! To his horror Thomas saw two pincers emerge from the hole followed by a stubby gray head.

Carfax, who had been watching Thomas's investigations, let out a cry. "God's wounds!" he exclaimed. "What the deuce is that?"

Armed with the knowledge that his patient had recently arrived from the West Indies, the doctor's reaction was not as dramatic. "I think you may have inadvertently carried a passenger with you from Jamaica, sir," said Thomas.

Both men now looked at the hole, Carfax gawping openmouthed as more of the gray tube emerged, flexing black claws on the top of its head.

"Get that devil out of me!" cried the patient as the creature retreated from view.

Thomas steadied his arm and eyed the decanter on the desk. "A rum for Mr. Carfax, if you please," he instructed Mason.

Taking a pair of forceps from his case, Thomas's hand hovered over the beast's lair. He did not have to wait long before it reemerged and this time the young doctor was prepared. He lunged at it with his forceps and pinched its head. Wriggling and writhing it surfaced from the hole: a grub, covered in tiny hooks that scrambled to keep hold of their moist den.

As his patient wisely gulped down his rum, Thomas fought the vile creature and won. After a few seconds he held its slain carcass up to the candlelight to inspect it.

"Sir, allow me to introduce to you a *Dermatobia hominis*," he said triumphantly.

Carfax's eyes opened wide. "What the . . . ?"

"Also known as the larva of the botfly," continued Thomas, dropping the offending grub into a glass tube for posterity. Dr. Carruthers already had one in his collection. "The fly must have bitten you and laid its eggs in the wound," he explained, adding: "They usually bite cattle, I believe."

Carfax let out a muted laugh. "In my line of business it pays to be thick-skinned, Dr. Silkstone!" he joked.

Thomas secured the dressing. "You deal in sugar, sir, if I am not mistaken?" he said.

His patient eyed him and arched a brow. "You are wellinformed, sir."

Thomas nodded. "In my line of business it pays to know the background of my patients," he countered.

Mistress Carfax entered the room just as Thomas was closing

his medical case. Looking up, her husband beckoned her over with his healthy arm.

"My dear, you'll never believe it! Dr. Silkstone has found the problem! A most disgusting larva had taken up residence in my arm." He spoke almost gleefully.

It was clear to Thomas that he would be asked to show the sour-faced woman the offending grub, but before Carfax could make the request there came a terrible sound like a banshee wail that rent through the house and reverberated down the stairs. It hung in the air, quavering for a few more seconds before it gave way to a lower wail.

"Good god!" exclaimed Carfax. He seemed agitated; then, turning to his wife, he scolded, "Can you not keep them under control, wife?"

Mistress Carfax's normally pale skin had reddened at the noise. Thomas could tell from her furious expression that she knew instantly its source. This was clearly not the first time she had heard the bloodcurdling scream or the cries that followed. He watched the woman ball her fists.

"Those wretches," she hissed though clenched teeth.

"Best get Roberts on them," suggested Carfax, flexing his injured arm. "He'll deal with them."

His wife shook her head. "I will take care of this myself," she cried, by now incandescent with rage. She barged into the hallway and turned down along a back passage before taking to the service stairs, her dog in hot pursuit. Such was her fury that she almost ran up the two flights to the males' attic room from whence the cries were emanating.

There she found Phibbah, her hands outstretched toward Ebele. Venus was struggling to pull her away from the boy, who lay perfectly still on the mattress. The girl was sobbing uncontrollably, flailing her arms, dragging herself toward him.

Mistress Carfax swept into the room like a tropical storm. Even Phibbah's sobs were drowned for a moment. Venus had let go her grip and the young girl was kneeling over the child once more, rocking backward and forward, touching his head, pulling at his hands. He remained still as stone.

Mistress Carfax took a deep breath. "What is the meaning of this?" she barked. Her hot breath billowed into the cold air.

Venus's full lips trembled as she curtsied. "Sambo is dead, missa," she told her. She pointed to the boy lying below, his eyes closed, as if he were asleep.

Her mistress darted a cursory glance in the boy's direction. "I can see that," she replied coldly. "But this noise! This screaming! I will not have it, you hear!" She had turned to Phibbah and cuffed the side of her head.

"Get Roberts to deal with her," she instructed Venus. The housekeeper's body tensed as if braced against the storm of harsh words that came from her mistress's mouth.

"Tell him to put her in the bridle. That'll quiet her crying."

At these words, Phibbah's eyes widened with terror.

"No, missa. No, please!" she pleaded, shuffling on her knees toward Mistress Carfax. She pawed at the hem of her gown, just like the small dog that sniffed at the corpse as his mistress ranted. This time a heavier blow was dealt to the top of her head, as if the girl were a troublesome fly to be swatted. "And another twenty lashes," she snarled, as Phibbah collapsed sobbing at her feet.

Venus remained expressionless and nodded slowly. "Yes, ma'am," she replied without enthusiasm. Her voice was carefully neutral.

"And see he is"—she pointed at the child—"disposed of."

With these words, she turned and called Fino, who by now was licking the child's face. She tucked the dog under her arm and headed out of the room. Before she could reach the narrow stairs, however, Thomas appeared, blocking her exit.

Fearing his professional skills might be needed, he had followed the woman up the service stairs.

"Do you need my assistance, madam?" he asked her.

Mistress Carfax, her anger still not fully abated, shook her head and tried to make light of the situation. " 'Tis nothing." She let out a self-conscious laugh and patted the dog in her arms. "A Negro boy is dead. He took a chill. 'Tis all."

Thomas edged forward on the small landing. "Then I shall

certify the death," he said, looking toward the open door of the attic room.

Mistress Carfax's back stiffened. "Is that really necessary, Dr. Silkstone? He was only a . . ." She broke off as she read Thomas's disapproving expression.

"A slave, ma'am?" He finished her sentence for her.

There was little room to maneuver on the cramped landing and only a few inches separated them. The woman's breaths came in short, sharp pants. She nodded and stuck out her chin defiantly, stiff-faced, as if her cheeks and lips had been starched. "Yes," she said finally. "A slave."

Thomas leaned closer to her and lowered his gaze to meet hers. Her eyes were as cold and unseeing as those of the fish in his laboratory. Flattening his lips in a smile, he began to shake his head. "The law may be ambiguous as to whether a slave is an animal or a human, but I would be failing in my duty as a physician if I did not examine the child." He let his words linger on the air until the woman blinked and agreed with a sullen nod.

"Very well, Dr. Silkstone," she muttered, letting Thomas pass into the room.

He walked in to find Venus comforting Phibbah, trying to still her sobs. Her long thin arms were wrapped 'round the girl, whose head was nestled on her shoulder.

"I am a physician," he told her, walking toward the boy. As Venus nodded, Phibbah pulled away. She eyed Thomas suspiciously as he knelt down, took the child's emaciated wrist, and felt for his pulse. There was none. Lifting his lids, Thomas looked at the boy's pupils. They were fully dilated. He was satisfied that his short life had ebbed away.

"The fever?" he asked, lifting his gaze and looking at Venus. She simply nodded.

Pulling back the coarse sheet, he looked at the boy's torso. His ribs showed through his brown skin like the veins of a leaf. He was evidently malnourished, thought Thomas, so that his guard was already down before the fever struck.

Mistress Carfax returned to the room, without the dog, and walked over to Thomas, fixing cold eyes on the corpse.

"I shall write out a certificate," Thomas told her, even though he knew the death would probably not be registered. The child's body would, in all honesty, be dumped in an unmarked grave.

"Thank you, doctor," she replied, not bothering to lift her gaze from the boy's face. It was the first time she had displayed a modicum of civility.

Standing upright, Thomas waited until it was obvious Mistress Carfax was ready to return downstairs. On the landing he paused and faced her squarely as she lifted her skirts to descend.

"Mistress Carfax," he began.

Surprised, she turned. "Yes?"

"Perhaps next time one of your slaves is seriously ill, you might think to call me," he told her, adding: "I will not charge to see them."

She digested his words as if they were bitter pills and nodded slowly before heading downstairs to join her husband.

Left alone in the attic room, the housekeeper and the slave stood motionless, staring at the dead child. The cruel taunts of the fever were nowhere to be seen on his face. In its place was a peace and a contentment that neither of them had seen while he was alive. Perhaps he had been reunited with his mother. Perhaps he was running wild and free in his homeland, thought Phibbah.

It was Venus who broke the silence. "Sleep well, child," she whispered. She straightened her long neck and switched her gaze to the girl, slight and hunched, at her side. The look Venus gave Phibbah dragged her from her mourning and she shivered as if suddenly recalling the fate that awaited her downstairs. Both of them knew what had to happen next.

Chapter 15

Thomas returned to the quay the following day to meet with Mr. Bartlett. As soon as Captain McCoy appeared, however, he did not need to be told that the young artist had not returned from the Customs House. He could read the captain's sober expression as he met him on deck. The nonchalance he had shown before had all but disappeared to be replaced with apprehension.

" 'Tis most out of character," said McCoy, shaking his head.

"And you have checked with the Customs House?" pressed Thomas, clutching for any grain of information.

The captain, a man whose skin was chapped by the wind and burned by the sun, hesitated, then said, "They denied sending any official to board us, Dr. Silkstone."

Thomas balked. "Then who . . . ?"

"I fear I have no idea," replied McCoy, shaking his head.

The doctor thought for a moment. "And you say he had Dr. Welton's journal about his person?"

"Aye. I believe so. In a large satchel." Thomas's insinuation suddenly seemed to register and the captain's brows lifted. "Surely it could not be that anyone would wish to steal the doctor's diary?" he asked.

Thomas felt a mounting sense of frustration. "If, as it seems, this customs official was an imposter, can you think of any other reason for Mr. Bartlett's disappearance?"

The captain faltered and he shook his head, as if recalling a conversation.

"I remember Mr. Bartlett said that the information was of great value and for Sir Joseph's eyes only," he said.

Thomas could not hide his surprise. As the man charged with cataloguing the expedition's specimens he felt entitled to be privy to all its findings. Sir Joseph had made no mention of any momentous discoveries, or indeed anything of material value. Unlike Captain Cook's expedition, where the primary goal was to discover the transit of Venus, Sir Joseph had not spoken of any specific goal. As far as he had been briefed, the expedition was purely to gather specimens of potential medicinal interest. Thomas felt slightly aggrieved.

"Why should that be?" he asked curtly.

"I cannot say," shrugged the captain. " 'Tis all I know."

"I will inquire if Mr. Bartlett has been in touch with Sir Joseph," said Thomas finally.

"A good idea, Dr. Silkstone," acknowledged McCoy. "In the meantime, you'd best take these." He handed Thomas a sheaf of Matthew Bartlett's sketches and several folios of Dr. Welton's notes.

Thomas glanced through them. "These will be of great help," he said.

And with that the two men bade each other a good day, neither, it seemed, any the wiser as to the whereabouts of the one man upon whose shoulders the success or failure of the Jamaican expedition now rested.

As soon as he climbed into the carriage that was to return him to Hollen Street, Thomas began to read Dr. Welton's notes. Scrawled in a haphazard manner across several sheets of paper, they were secured by a thin ribbon. A cursory look told him they appeared quite perfunctory. They were notes and observations, rather than the detailed scientific reports that he was anticipating. He supposed the doctor had reserved his most important findings for his journal. And that, of course, he had yet to see.

This collection seemed to be arranged in no particular order, as if the pages had been thrown together without great care and in haste. Nevertheless from the very first line of the text, Thomas was drawn in.

Kingston, May 6, 1783

Some Negroes fervently believe they will return to the Country of their origin when they die in Jamaica. They therefore have little regard for their own deaths, so convinced are they that they shall be free from the white man's shackles once more. To enable this to pass, I have heard many cut their own throats. Whether they die by their own hand, or naturally, their kindred people make a great show of lamentations, mournings, and howlings.

Thomas looked up from the page and felt his own breath judder. He thought of the Carfaxes' dead child slave, thousands of miles away from his native land. No one would be attending his grave.

Chapter 16

Boughton Hall
Brandwick
Oxfordshire
November 1, 1783

My Dearest Thomas,

As I write to you the first snows of winter have fallen early. We have endured frosts for many days but we awoke this morning to find the hills and vales covered in a thick carpet of white. From my study window the chapel spire looks like a needle piercing through a crisp linen sheet and the twigs on the trees are draped in lace. I wish you could be here to share the view with me, my love.

Lydia looked up from the piece of paper on her desk and glanced toward the fire blazing in the grate. Richard was lying on his stomach on the hearth rug, his legs bent upward, waving restlessly in the air. He was playing with some tin soldiers Howard had found in the attic. They had once belonged to her late brother, Edward. But she knew their novelty would wear off in a few minutes and her son would seek some new adventure. She took up her pen once more.

Richard continues to prosper. His arm grows
stronger by the day, thanks to the exercises you
showed him. I am teaching him to read and write
and to count, although he is not a very willing
pupil. He would much rather be outside on the
estate.

She was about to write *riding with Mr. Lupton,* but checked
herself.

When Richard had woken that morning and looked out onto
the snow-covered landscape, his first reaction was one of wonder
and delight. This was not the first snow he had ever seen, but
such was his joy that it took all of Nurse Pring's strength to stop
him from rushing downstairs and out of doors in his nightshirt.

Over breakfast Lydia had promised to venture out with him
herself, although she was worried that the icy air would harm
his already delicate lungs. So now, almost every ten minutes or
so, he asked her the same question. When could they go out into
the snow? And when she replied, as she always did, that she
would take him out after she had finished writing her letter to Dr.
Silkstone, he sulked and moaned and knocked down the soldiers
in a display of temper that she found understandable but un-
seemly. And here it came again. Her son shifted himself up onto
one elbow. Only this time his question was more strategic in its
phrasing. It showed the military tactics worthy of a good general.

"Can Mr. Lupton take me out in the snow?"

Her pen hovered over the paper. Lupton. For some reason she
had not thought to mention the new estate manager in her last
letter to Thomas. She felt he was settling in well. He had been in
post for just over a week and was getting to grips with the day
to day management of Boughton. Richard also seemed to have
taken to him. Ever since they had ridden out together, her son
had continually asked if he could accompany Lupton in his duties. Not a day had gone by when Richard had not stood by the
front door in his riding boots, waiting to saddle up with his new
friend, only to be told he could not.

"Mr. Lupton is a very busy man, my sweet," Lydia would say, adding: "Besides, you have your letters to learn." That riposte was never well received and the child would whine and trail his feet into the study to sit sullenly while his mother taught him his alphabet. She knew full well that Richard needed male company, a man he could look up to, someone dependable, who would always be there for him. And the worm of doubt that had crept into her brain ever since Thomas had returned to London almost two months ago began to reemerge.

Now she found herself beginning to lose her patience, but she bit her tongue. "No, Richard. He cannot take you out," was her curt response.

Taking a deep breath, she poised her nib once more, but before she could resume her letter, Howard appeared at the door.

"Mr. Lupton is here to see you, m'lady."

Lydia arched a brow. Their daily meeting was not scheduled until the afternoon. She put down her pen. "Very well," she replied.

Nicholas Lupton marched in wearing a thick coat and a muffler about his neck that obscured his chin, but not his mouth. His face was wreathed in a broad smile.

"Good morning, your ladyship," he greeted her, jovially. He made a shallow bow, but his movement was severely restricted by the fact that he carried something large and wooden under his arm.

"Good morning, Mr. Lupton," replied Lydia, somewhat bemused by the object that her estate manager was holding.

By this time Richard, on seeing Lupton, had scrambled to his feet and was dancing around him, tugging eagerly at his coat.

"Richard, please!" scolded his mother. "Leave Mr. Lupton alone or I shall have to send you upstairs." She found herself raising her voice to the child, something she was doing with increasing regularity, and she disliked herself for it. She looked at the object of her son's excitement. "I do apologize, Mr. Lupton," she said.

The estate manager merely laughed. Waving dismissively with his free hand, he bent low to greet the young earl, who immediately began inspecting the strange object tucked under his new friend's arm.

"What is it?" inquired the boy.

Lupton beamed again. "Why, this"—he announced with all the flair of a showman—"is a sledge."

Lydia was shocked. Her son looked puzzled. The estate manager was holding what appeared to be a small wooden table with curved runners attached to its legs.

"A sledge. What is a sledge?" asked Richard, forming the unfamiliar word carefully.

Lupton eyed Lydia, trying to gauge her reaction. Had he overstepped the mark? She returned his gaze for a moment, before she, too, began to smile.

"A sledge is like a carriage for the snow," she told her son.

The estate manager crouched down and planted the sleigh on the floor. "You sit on it, see?" he said, pointing at the planks, "and then I will whirl you 'round and 'round on the ice till you're dizzy as a gadfly." There was an infectious enthusiasm in his tone.

The boy laughed and plonked himself on the seat, then brought both his short legs up at right angles and tried to shuffle as if to make the strange contraption move.

"You have taken to it naturally, sir," Lupton told him, patting the child on the back.

"Can we go now, Mamma? Please? Can we go on the ice?" Richard looked at his mother with large, pleading eyes and melted her resolve.

"Very well," she relented. "But we must wrap up warm!"

And so the small party, Lydia, Richard, and Nicholas Lupton, boarded the dogcart and headed off on the track toward Plover's Lake. The brilliant blue sky was cloudless and the sun was bright, but the air was freezing and their breath billowed about them like steam as the horses trotted along. Lydia was swathed in a fur stole and hat and her hands were tucked into a muff. She had made sure that Richard was equally protected, with woollen stockings, a worsted coat, and stout boots. A thick scarf hugged his neck.

The snow lay three or four inches deep on the road, but on the verges and against the hedges the overnight wind had blown it in drifts. In some places it was as if a giant had spread a bed-sheet over the fields and hedgerows and forgotten to smooth it down. Lydia found herself smiling, despite the fact that her cheeks were tingling with cold.

After twenty minutes or so they arrived at the lake. Its surface was frosted white, like a huge mirror, and the reeds that fringed it were rigid as spears. A few ducks skidded comically on its icy surface as they drew up close by. Lupton offered Lydia his hand and she descended from the cart, her feet crunching into the snow below.

"How do you know the ice is thick enough to walk on?" she asked warily.

"I have measured it, your ladyship. 'Tis four inches thick. Safe as stone," he replied.

The estate manager seemed sure of himself, but he held her gaze until she gave a nod of approval, then clapped his gloved hands gleefully.

"Come, come then, sir!" he chirped.

Richard, already standing up, jumped down into Lupton's arms, then, taking him by the hand, pulled the estate manager, with the sledge in tow, toward the lake. Together they set foot on the ice, edging very slowly at first, keeping close to the bank. Lydia watched anxiously from the shore, but every few seconds Lupton gave her a reassuring smile.

"You're sure the ice will not crack?" called Lydia, nervous as an ill-sitting hen.

"I give you my word, your ladyship," came the unequivocal reply.

Both man and boy had stepped out onto the lake's surface now, the ice taking the full weight of both their bodies. In one hand Lupton carried a stout log and, without warning, he hurled it out into the middle of the frozen plane. It hit the sur-face hard and skidded a few feet before finally coming to rest near the centre, the hollow echo that it made reverberating loudly in the still air.

"You see, your ladyship?" he called. "Frozen solid."

Lydia silently acknowledged this reassuring gesture and tucked her hands back into her fur muff. At least that way, she told herself, no one could see that she was wringing them.

"Now sit yourself down, sir," ordered Lupton, positioning the sledge. Richard eagerly obliged, drawing his legs and elbows inward and clutching the sides.

"Ready?" asked Lupton.

His charge nodded nervously. First threading a long length of rope through a hole in the seat, Lupton walked a few feet away from the sledge.

"Here we go!"

Extending his right arm, he began moving it in a wide arc. The sledge started to slide as if following the sweeping line of an unseen circle. It moved slowly at first but soon gathered speed and Richard squealed with delight as he slid 'round and 'round Lupton, pulled by the rope. Letting out the length, so that the circles made by the sledge grew bigger and bigger, Lupton, too, found himself whirling 'round and 'round. All the while he was laughing along with Richard.

Watching the pair, Lydia, although still fearful, permitted herself to smile. It was wonderful to see her son who, only a few weeks ago was so close to death, enjoying himself as a child should.

Faster and faster Richard went, as Lupton pirouetted on the ice like a ballet dancer. Keeping the rope taut, he let it out even farther until there was at least twenty feet between himself and the sledge, but still he continued to steer it 'round like a boat caught in a whirlpool. It eddied for a few more seconds until, seemingly exhausted, the estate manager jerked on the tether to slow it down. Lydia could tell from the way he lurched drunkenly on the ice that he had made himself giddy. The rope in his hand slackened. Richard called out.

"More!" he yelled. "More!"

Lupton's head was bowed and his body began to pitch and sway like a sea-weary sailor before dropping to his knees on the ice.

"Mr. Lupton!" exclaimed Lydia.

Richard stood up on the sledge and stepped gingerly onto the ice.

"Are you ill, sir?" he asked, skidding toward the estate manager.

"No, Richard!" yelled Lydia. "Get back onto the sledge!"

The little boy jerked his head toward his mother. As he did so he lost his footing and went crashing onto the ice. Lydia screamed, but Lupton shook his head quickly, as if dispelling sleep, and heaving his frame up from the frozen surface, reached out for the boy.

"Here, Richard. Give me your hand." His voice was calm and reassuring and in no time the child was back seated on the sledge and calling for another ride.

Lupton looked over to Lydia and saw her gesturing for them to make for the shore. They obeyed. "You've had quite enough excitement for one day," she told her son as soon as he came within earshot. Richard's face was flushed. The cold and the excitement had combined to turn his complexion bright red. Mr. Lupton's face was also ruddy with his exertions. The child reluctantly disembarked from the sledge and scrambled onto the shore once more, followed by his playmate.

Lydia breathed a deep sigh of relief.

"Can we do that again, Mamma? Can we? Please?" Richard pleaded, his large eyes looking up at his mother's face.

Lydia and Lupton exchanged glances.

"We'll see," she said. "But now, we must return to the warm. You must both be frozen."

Chapter 17

Thomas found himself once more in the grand, wood-paneled room at Somerset House, where only a few days ago he accepted his most prestigious assignment. His ebullient mood had now ebbed and was turning to frustration and anxiety. Sir Joseph clearly shared his concern.

"I have heard nothing, Silkstone," he said, rising from his desk and walking over to his globe. He spun it wistfully.

"It is most unlike Mr. Bartlett," he mused. "So there is no news on this so-called official?"

"Extensive inquiries have been made, sir," replied Thomas, relaying information he had received from Captain McCoy. "It seems the man was an imposter."

Silence filled the cavernous space as the young doctor waited for a reply to an unasked question that hung precariously in their midst. Thomas was hoping that Sir Joseph would lift the veil on a situation that seemed to be beyond his own limited briefing. It was not forthcoming, so he pressed on.

"Were you aware, sir, that Dr. Welton's journal was on Mr. Bartlett's person?"

Sir Joseph looked up from the globe. He did not seem shocked. "I feared as much."

"Presumably he took it for safekeeping, sir," replied Thomas. He had come to the nub of the matter; he could tell as much from Sir Joseph's expression as mounting concern gathered on his features. It was obvious to Thomas that he was aware of the significance of the notebook above and beyond what he had thus far revealed.

"The journal was in a leather satchel that he kept about him at all times," added Thomas, watching for a reaction. It came swiftly and decisively. With a face that had paled by the minute, Sir Joseph Banks paced over to his desk and tugged at the top drawer.

"A leather satchel like this?" he asked, shunting a package wrapped in brown paper across the desk. The reek of river water rose from it.

Thomas felt his hands begin to tremble as he gingerly opened the folds of the sodden parcel. Inside there was a kid leather satchel. The crest of the Royal Society was emblazoned on the front. He felt his stomach lurch.

Sir Joseph knuckled the desk.

"A waterman handed it in this morning, hoping for a reward," he said. He sat down, his elbows on the desk, and tented his long fingers, brushing his lips as he thought. Finally he said, "This journal, do you have any idea of its contents?"

Thomas shook his head. "I only know that it was to act as my guide, sir," he replied. "Surely it would be of no consequence to anyone else."

Sir Joseph shot back, "That is where you are mistaken, Silkstone."

Questions flooded into Thomas's mind, but he held his tongue. He could tell from Sir Joseph's expression that he was struggling to keep a secret from him, weighing up in his own mind whether he should divulge the truth. Doubt hovered in the air until, after an agonizing moment, the great man brought down his hands on the desk without revealing anything.

"This is a worrying development, Dr. Silkstone," he admitted. His tone was measured, as if he were trying to deny the gravity of the discovery in the Thames. "The cutpurses at the docks would not think twice about robbing a man for a few coins," he concluded. "But a journal would be worthless to them. 'Tis probably bobbing on the Thames tide as we speak."

Thomas did not follow his master's logic. He knew that a

common thief would not have tossed the satchel into the river, but would have tried to sell it. He held Sir Joseph's gaze for a moment, as if willing him to act, but he merely stared down at the floor, leaving Thomas with the impression that he was not prepared to divulge any more information. Then, without warning, the great man looked up and slapped the desk.

"I thank you for your help, Silkstone, but now you must leave the matter of Mr. Bartlett with me." He rose and changed his tone. "Instead you must concentrate your considerable expertise on cataloguing all those specimens, eh?"

Walking from behind his desk, he offered Thomas his hand and patted him on the arm. There was a finality in his tone; their conversation was at an end.

"Of course, sir," replied Thomas with an uneasy bow. Sir Joseph's abruptness troubled him and he left the meeting, at which he had sought reassurance, deeply disturbed. Not only was he now more fearful for Matthew Bartlett's safety, he was left wondering what knowledge contained in Dr. Welton's journal was so momentous that a man may have been kidnapped, or even killed, for it.

The pale sun was low in the sky when they arrived back at Boughton Hall. Lupton had taught Richard the chorus of "God Rest Ye Merry Gentlemen" on the return journey and the boy was in high spirits, giving a hearty solo rendition before they reached the steps at the front of the house. Helping Lydia and her son down from the cart, the estate manager was in an equally buoyant mood.

"Thank you for your company today, my lady," he told her, taking her hand and kissing it.

Lydia smiled. "No. It is I who must thank *you*, Mr. Lupton. My son has obviously enjoyed himself enormously."

"And you?" he shot back, somewhat impertinently, Lydia thought.

She paused for a moment, unsure as to how to react. "Yes," she said, nodding finally. "Very much."

The estate manager beamed once more. "I am glad," he

replied, before turning to the young earl and lifting him down from the cart. "And I'll wager you've had a fine time, sir!" he cried.

Richard nodded his tousled head. "Can we do it again tomorrow, Mamma? Can we?" he exclaimed.

Lydia glanced quickly at Lupton. "We shall see, my sweet," she replied. "We shall see." And with that she put her hand on Richard's shoulder and turned to see Howard waiting to greet them at the top of the house steps.

Later that day, when Nurse Pring took Richard to his bed, Lydia found herself at her writing desk once more. She had resumed her letter to Thomas, but still the words did not flow easily. Buoyed by the morning's outing in the snow, she felt lighthearted and cheerful. And yet she did not want her letter to give the impression that she was experiencing happiness without him, less still that the source of her mirth was the new estate manager about whom he knew nothing.

A grain of guilt planted itself into her conscience. Just why, she did not know. Perhaps it had something to do with the fact that Richard, just before he turned to climb the stairs with Nurse Pring, had told her: "This has been the best day of my life." His words washed over her in a great wave of joy and she had rushed forward and hugged him. Now, on reflection, as the candles cast a soft glow over her own script, she realized that her son's happiness had been brought about by a man barely known to either of them. A virtual stranger had burst into their lives like a jester into a king's court, and brought with him fun and laughter. There was an infectious vigor and cheerfulness in Lupton's manner that clearly endeared him to Richard. He was a clown, a playfellow, and—dare she even think it—he was fast becoming like a father. It was a role she had reserved for Thomas. He was the man who should take her son sledging or riding or fishing. He was the one who should make him laugh, or comfort him if he grazed his knees or burned his fingers. But he was not there, nor would he be in the foreseeable future.

Dipping her nib into the inkpot, she sighed deeply before

starting another paragraph of her letter to Thomas. *We have enjoyed a pleasant enough day,* she wrote.

Phibbah sat huddled in the attic room, her legs drawn up to her chest. Tears were flowing freely down her cheeks but the bridle around her head meant that if she cried out the spike would pierce her tongue. The iron collar weighed heavily around her neck and the chain was so short that she could barely move away from the wall.

Mr. Roberts had clamped the cage over her head last night, just after the beating. She had tried to bite him as he forced open her mouth to slip the plate between her teeth, but he only pushed it in harder, cutting her lips. Now the taste of blood and iron melded into one, seasoned with the salt of her tears. Unable to sleep for the pain and the cold, she had been plotting her revenge.

She'd once heard Mr. Roberts tell Cook he always ate well after he'd given a good whipping. He said all that exercise whetted his appetite and the sight of the blood put him in mind of a thick, juicy sirloin. As it was, he was usually happy to settle for a large bowl of Mistress Bradshaw's mutton stew with dumplings. Well, she hoped that he had supped heartily because soon he would be eating his last meal.

Her blurry gaze slid along the cold floorboards to the far corner of the room, beyond her reach. There, hidden from view, pressed into a dark, dank crevice, was her obeah bag, a bag so powerful that not even Mr. Roberts with his callused hands and foul breath, or Missa Carfax with her small eyes and tongue as sharp as a bullwhip, could resist its magic. The nail clippings, the pig's tail, the grave dirt, and the blood from her unborn child—all the special ingredients were there, new-charmed by the obeah-man. Together they were stronger than any chain or manacle. Soon she would put a curse on this house and so terrible would be its power that every white man and woman who entered it would fall on their knees and beg for death.

She was thinking about the bag when the wedge of light that

sliced under the door was suddenly darkened by a shadow. She heard footsteps. Patience, perhaps, bringing her some illicit scraps from the kitchen, or Venus come to check on her. Yes, it was Venus. She recognized the slow glide of her footsteps. But there was another footfall; heavy, masculine, and a voice she did not know. In the landing's glow she saw the two shadows meet.

"You have the boy?" said he.

"Yes," replied Venus.

"They will come at midnight. See that he is ready."

They parted and the footsteps retreated once more, leaving Phibbah alone and confused in the dark.

Chapter 18

Five days had passed since Matthew Bartlett was last seen disembarking from the *Elizabeth* in the company of a customs officer. Unable to wait for more news of him, Thomas had begun the laborious work of single-handedly unpacking and listing the scores of specimens from the expedition. He had left the smaller crates containing the more delicate creatures, the insects and reptiles and small mammals, unopened, concentrating instead on the remaining plants. His progress was such that he had catalogued almost half of those herbs to be included in Sir Joseph's famous herbarium. The great man had donated it to the British Museum after the *Endeavour*'s return from Australia and new additions were always made with each expedition.

Thomas had commissioned a carpenter to make him a large wooden cabinet that held drawers, divided into sixty-four small compartments, to hold preserved leaf specimens. He had been working his way methodically through the ship's manifest and had succeeded in ticking off all of the plants listed, apart, that is, from the final herb on the list: the branched calalue. He searched for a sketch of it among Bartlett's papers. It was there all right, with its smooth-margined leaves and pinkish white flowers, but among the samples he could find no corresponding herb. He recalled Captain McCoy's words: how difficult it had been to keep plants alive on board ship given the terrible conditions. The specimen must have died and been discarded. It was lost and there was an end to it.

*   *   *

In the absence of Dr. Welton's journal, Mr. Bartlett's excellent drawings were proving invaluable. Thomas was also deeply indebted to Dr. Carruthers. His knowledge of the Caribbean islands and their flora was most useful.

"Aloe vera, if I'm not mistaken," he had said, sniffing one of the plants on which Thomas was working. He had sliced its stem and the smell had wafted into the air. "Very useful, with most excellent healing properties," added the old anatomist.

For his own part, Thomas had never ventured into tropical climes before. His experience of humidity and tropical rainfall, of deadly insects and poisonous frogs, was confined to his reading of Captain Cook's journals from the *Endeavour* and of Dr. Grainger's tracts on diseases of the West Indies. His own encounters with spiders as big as dinner plates and snakes as long as a large intestine were limited to those in the jars that surrounded him. His understanding of the very creatures and samples of flora that he had been tasked to catalogue was necessarily narrow because he had not seen them in their natural environment. Bereft of Dr. Welton's journal, organizing and contextualizing these exotic treasures, was, indeed, a tall order. Mr. Bartlett's sketches, with their detailed captions, were most helpful, but they were no substitute for his presence. Try as he might, however, Thomas was unable to put the artist's disappearance behind him.

On that fifth morning in the laboratory, Dr. Carruthers could stand the tension no longer. He sat on his usual stool, alert and ready to give his opinion to Thomas irrespective of whether or not it was requested. The young doctor was preparing to examine a leaf under his microscope and had laid his specimen flat on a glass slide.

In the corner of the room, Franklin, the white rat, named in honor of the great American polymath and kept as the young anatomist's companion, pawed at his cage.

"He wants to be let out," remarked the old anatomist, tilting his head to one side toward the scratching. "He is anxious."

Thomas looked up and walked over to the rat's cage, opened the latch, and allowed Franklin to roam free.

"That is what you should be doing, young fellow," said Carruthers.

Thomas returned to his workbench. "Sir?"

The old anatomist let out a short laugh. "I do not need eyes to see that you are not happy in your work. I can sense it. You should be out and about, sniffing around like that rat of yours. Making a nuisance of yourself."

Thomas sighed. "But Sir Joseph . . ." he protested.

"Tish tosh!" exclaimed Carruthers. "When has the voice of authority ever stopped you from seeking out the truth?" He waved his stick in the air. "You know as well as I do, Thomas, there is something fishy behind this young man's disappearance and you'll not rest until you find out what it is."

Putting down the slide, Thomas nodded. "You are right, as usual, sir," he acknowledged. "I cannot work efficiently while Mr. Bartlett remains missing. I shall pay a visit to the Customs House myself."

It was late afternoon by the time Thomas's carriage arrived in Thames Street, outside the Customs House. Inside, the long room was still hectic, but not as crowded as it had been on the morning of his first visit. It did not take long for him to find an official who would listen to his inquiry.

A bespectacled clerk sat surrounded by scrolls of paper. His manner was brusque.

"Ye . . . e . . . s," he drawled over his lenses.

"I wish to speak to someone regarding the cargo of the *Elizabeth*," Thomas began. "She is berthed in a sufferance wharf."

At his words, however, the clerk raised his hand. "I know exactly where she is berthed, Hope Wharf," he snapped, and his stubby fingers hovered over the scrolls which, to the untrained eye, seemed to be arranged in no particular order. Yet within a second or two he was unrolling the appropriate document and scanning it. "The *Elizabeth*. She . . ." he began, but then stopped abruptly. "Ah!"

"There is a problem?" asked Thomas anxiously.

The clerk looked up, pulling his spectacles down the bridge of his nose. "I am not at liberty to say, sir."

"What do you mean?" Thomas felt himself tense. He craned his neck to look at the document and saw, written in red across the *Elizabeth*'s entry, the Latin words *Graviora manent.*

Thomas eyed the official, who returned his gaze apprehensively. "Heavier things remain?" he mouthed. "What heavier things?"

As the clerk pushed his glasses back up his nose, Thomas noticed it was suddenly shiny with perspiration. "It is obviously a matter for a higher authority," he said, his tone hardening.

"Then I would speak to a higher authority," said Thomas, trying to suppress his rising anger.

The clerk raised his voice. "That is not possible, sir," he said, snapping his fingers. Two uniformed officers were quickly at his side. "I would ask you to leave now, sir," he barked.

The doctor shifted his look to the two officers standing nearby. He did not wish to cause a scene. At least he had uncovered some information about Mr. Bartlett's disappearance. At least now he knew that someone very influential wanted no further investigation to be undertaken by unauthorized persons. And that included himself.

"Very well," he said, outwardly conceding defeat. "I thank you for your time. Good day to you, sirs." Raising his hat to the clerk and the officers, he walked out of the Customs House. Now he was even more determined to find out what had really happened to Matthew Bartlett and the precious journal.

The wherry fought against an icy wind that blew up the river. The waterman tied up the boat at the King's Stairs and Thomas alighted within sight of the *Elizabeth,* her prow looming over all the other smaller craft at the wharf. The quayside was busy, but with the encroaching darkness, stalls were closing, warehouse doors were being pulled to, and shutters were coming down, just as they would have done five days ago.

Deciding to retrace Matthew Bartlett's reported journey with the customs official, Thomas began with a cheerful old waterman who was stationed at the pier by the *Elizabeth*. Pushing back his hat, the old man scratched his forehead with his thumb in thought.

"I see'd him, as I recall," he croaked at the sight of Thomas's sixpence. "He was with a customs man, carrying a box."

"A box, you say?" It was the first time Thomas had heard mention of any box.

"Aye. A small crate." But that was all he could say. "I ain't see'd where they went, sir," he replied meekly when pressed.

Thomas walked on. The shadows were already so long, and his mind so agitated, that he did not see a woman standing at the corner until she shouted at him.

" 'Evening, my dear," she called as she rearranged her bodice. A sailor moved away, still lacing his breeches.

Normally he would have ignored her and she may have either cursed him or blown him a kiss, but on this occasion he stopped in his tracks and doubled back. She was a pretty enough wench, somewhere twixt a girl and a fully grown woman.

"You up for it?" she said with a giggle, giving a provocative shimmy as she spoke.

Thomas smiled benignly at her and walked a few steps closer.

"My, but you're a handsome one," she remarked with a wink as the streetlamp lighted his features. "Just sixpence to you, my pretty."

Drawing up beside her, he smelled the strong liquor on her breath. "Are you here at the same time every day, miss?" he asked.

No one ever called her miss these days; baggage, bunter, slag, whore, or jade, but never miss. Her world-weary eyes opened wide with glee.

"That I am, dearie, regular as clockwork. That's why the cullies have named me Constance." She winked at him. "If you come regular you can call me Connie!" She nudged him, but despite his smile, he knew he was about to dash her hopes of frequent custom.

"On Monday last, about this time of day, did you see a young man carrying a box walk this way with a customs officer?"

The girl's red lips drooped at the realization he was not a punter, then, after a moment, she said, "Come to think of it, I did, but they seemed to have other things on their minds."

"Were they arguing? Did there seem to be a problem?" persisted Thomas.

The woman shook her head. "No. Didn't say a word," she reflected, adjusting her corset.

"Did you see where they went?"

She threw him a saucy smile. "Off that way." With her right hand she pointed toward the lanterns of the main thoroughfare, beyond a line of dilapidated warehouses. She upturned the palm of the same hand and winked at Thomas once more.

"Worth a sixpence?" she asked. He gave her a shilling.

Returning to Hollen Street later that afternoon, Thomas found Dr. Carruthers dozing by a sickly fire in the study, a spool of saliva dribbling from the corner of his open mouth. He woke with a start.

"Thomas? Is that you?" he rasped.

"Have no fear, sir," calmed the doctor, laying a hand on his mentor's shoulder.

Seeing the state of the fire Thomas took charge of the poker and began jabbing the dying embers.

"Shall you read me today's newspaper?" Carruthers asked him.

"I most certainly will," replied Thomas, settling himself by the fire opposite. It had been his custom ever since the old anatomist had lost his sight.

"I'll wager you'll be looking for a report on the Jamaica expedition," ventured Carruthers, as Thomas perused the newssheet. William Carruthers may have been well into his eighth decade, but he was still as sharp as the scalpel he used to wield with such precision.

"It made the front page," Thomas replied, scanning the report. *"The deaths have been announced of Dr. Frederick Welton and Dr. John Perrick, who were engaged by the Royal Society on a scientific expedition to Jamaica. Both succumbed to the yellow fever and died before returning home."*

"No mention of Mr. Bartlett!" barked Dr. Carruthers, almost indignantly. Thomas looked up. The tone of the article sounded very official. He could imagine Sir Joseph Banks dictating the statement to an official reporter in his lofty office. He was wise to make no mention of the missing artist. A whiff of scandal would damage the Royal Society.

"Poor old Welton. He was a good man," mumbled Carruthers.

"What about Perrick? Do you know anything of him, sir?" asked Thomas reflectively.

The old anatomist thought for a moment. "Welton's son-in-law, I believe," he declared. "Rather after my time. Why do you ask?"

Thomas, who had only just sat down, rose once more. "Because I am going to pay my respects to their widows," he said emphatically. "Perhaps they can help me shed light on Mr. Bartlett's whereabouts."

Carruthers shrugged and nodded as he contemplated the proposition.

"Good luck," he shouted as he heard the study door shut.

Chapter 19

The Welton household was in mourning not just for its head, but also for a second member, Dr. John Perrick. Both he and Dr. Welton had lived under the same roof, Perrick having married Welton's only child, Henrietta, two years previously.

The townhouse was a short walk away and Thomas was greeted courteously enough. Shown upstairs into the drawing room, he was asked to wait until the maid had inquired whether her mistress would receive him.

Left alone, Thomas marvelled at a collection of fabulous exotic birds in glass cases. Perched on branches, some had their beaks open as in mid-song, others posed with their heads cocked. They were so lifelike he could imagine them taking flight at the slightest sound.

There were several paintings, too. A particularly striking portrait, Thomas assumed of Dr. Welton, took pride of place over the mantelshelf. In it the late doctor stood tall and regal and his hands rested on a globe. His eyes were a striking blue that lent him an intensity of gaze, and his expression was sage, yet benign.

Nearby another painting caught Thomas's eye. The familiar golden dome of the church at West Wycombe leapt out at him from a small gilded frame. Memories of the fateful day in the caves, and up St. Lawrence's tower that looked over the village, came flooding back and he wondered what significance, if any, the landmark held for the family. He was musing on the picture when he heard the door creak open. Turning 'round, he saw two women enter, one in her later years, the other much younger. Both were dressed soberly in black.

"Dr. Silkstone," the older one addressed him.

"Mistress Welton," he replied, bowing low.

"This is my daughter, Mistress Perrick," she said, gesturing to the younger woman at her side. Thomas gave another bow.

"Madam, I am come to offer my condolences," said Thomas, as Mistress Welton pointed at the sofa. She and her daughter sat opposite.

"We thank you, sir," said the older woman, her face bleached of all color by her intense grief. "My husband would be most heartened to know that his work is now in your hands."

Thomas felt a little awkward. "Although I only knew your husband by reputation, Sir Joseph Banks spoke most highly of him." Looking at the young widow, he corrected himself: "Of both of them," he said reverentially. "They will both be sorely missed," he added.

The women nodded their heads simultaneously. A respectful pause followed before Thomas resumed his mission.

"As you know, I have been tasked by the Royal Society to record and catalogue all the expedition's collections," he told them.

"A great honor," interjected Mistress Perrick. Her voice was refined but self-assured in tone. She was probably of a similar age to himself, Thomas estimated.

"Indeed, yes," replied Thomas. "But a challenging one, made all the more difficult by the fact that Dr. Welton's journal seems to have been mislaid." He did not wish to alarm the ladies with the truth.

As it was Mistress Welton seemed sufficiently perturbed. "Mislaid? But my husband was always most meticulous with his writings. He will have entrusted them to someone when he knew"—she broke off, biting her lip—"when he knew he was dying."

Mistress Perrick put a comforting hand on her mother's lap. "I am sure they will be recovered soon, Mamma," she soothed.

Then, switching her gaze to Thomas, she adopted a sterner tone. "We thank you for your visit, Dr. Silkstone, and wish you well with your work, but as you can see, we are in mourning." She pulled the servant's bell. "We shall see you at the memorial service, perhaps?"

Thomas recalled the invitation had arrived the day before.

"Indeed you shall," he said, rising. He understood that he was being dismissed, albeit in a courteous way.

"I am most grateful for your good wishes, ladies. My sympathies once more," he said, as the maid appeared to show him to the door. He left feeling none the wiser.

Chapter 20

The sound of the key scraping in the lock left Phibbah a prisoner once more. As she sat in the corner of the attic room, a single candle her only comfort, the wind whistled in through the rotting casement. She hugged herself tight, rubbing her own arms to stop her blood from freezing. Again she found herself isolated from the rest of the slaves for a minor misdemeanor. She had been tardy to take out the slops and this was her punishment, yet another evening alone with the cockroaches and her own brooding thoughts.

Now and again a gale of laughter would tear through the house and rise up the narrow stairway. The Carfaxes were entertaining some of their slaver friends, feasting and quaffing while her own belly was sunken and empty. There would be suckling pig and roast goose and fancy sweetmeats and tarts filled with frangipane. There would be French wine and brandy and rum, while all she had eaten all day was a crust of bread and some dripping.

She crossed her arms over her chest in an embrace, letting her fingers feel the strange landscape of her back. The shafts of her ribs and the scabs made by the lash rose like long ridges beneath her scarred skin. She could not wait any longer. She must not. Now was the right time. Sliding over to the far end of the room, she prized up a loose floorboard and delved deep. Groping around in the space below for a few seconds, she smiled to herself as she retrieved the small bag—her obeah bag.

The rest of the slaves were downstairs in the scullery, but Mr. Roberts had ordered her to stay in the freezing attic. Although he had locked her in, Patience had slipped the key under the door. Slowly and carefully she opened it and, with the candle in one hand and the bag in the other, she began her silent descent down the service stairs to Mistress Carfax's bedchamber.

Samuel Carfax was in fine fettle. His face was reddened by rum and his tongue loosened by it. Although his arm was still bandaged, the discomfort he had experienced had almost completely disappeared. Besides, any pain that he had suffered was more than compensated for by the regaling of his extraordinary tale. The telling of it made excellent dinner party conversation, although some of the ladies present found it a little vulgar.

Mistress Cotter, wife of the slaver Benjamin Cotter, pulled a disapproving face as Carfax described how Dr. Silkstone had grabbed the head of the grub with his pincers. Mistress Dalrymple had also tut-tutted when he related how the pus had seeped from a crater in his arm. His wife noticed her guest push away her dish of figs in disgust.

"Perhaps, Mr. Carfax, you should leave this conversation for your port and cigars," she upbraided her husband, in an effort to save her own face as much as his. She turned to her female guests. "The weather is so inclement at the moment 'twill kill more than insects, I fear."

Hearing her hostess's comment, Mistress Cotter chimed in. " 'Tis killing our slaves, more's the pity. We lost one last week and another the week before to distemper. Not to mention one in childbirth."

Carfax nodded. "We had a boy die of fever only a couple of days ago, too. 'Tis a costly business. I'll leave them in Jamaica next time I come to London." He fingered his tumbler, then emptied his glass of rum.

Dalrymple let out a snort. " 'Tis strange how they die in their dozens in Jamaica and yet here when they drop we notice them," he observed wryly, wiping the corners of his mouth with his napkin.

Cotter took up from where his host left off. "Could it be that life is cheaper in the Colonies?" he asked.

"A slave's life is cheap anywhere," Dalrymple cut in. "It is we planters who pay the price for their laziness and incompetence."

Carfax sat back in his chair. "I've always found that if you treat your slaves well, you will earn their loyalty," he said, thoughtfully fingering a spoon. "You beat a dog and it may turn on you one day and bite you. But treat it well, feed it regularly, and it will learn to respect you."

His wife darted him a scornful look, then, turning to her female guests, she fixed her face in a wide grin. "My husband is far too soft at heart," she told them.

Upstairs, Phibbah had entered Cordelia Carfax's chamber. The embers of the fire cast a warm glow about the room as she padded over to the dressing table. The scent of musk and roses hung in the air, but did little to diffuse the smell of damp. Searching among the cologne bottles and the combs, she spied an ivory-backed hairbrush. Seizing it gleefully she clawed her fingers through the bristles so that a ball of loose copper hairs came away. They felt fine in her hand, like spun silk. She sniffed at the hair: apple and cloves, Mistress Carfax's pomade. It was a smell that filled her with fear and dread and loathing and she stuffed the clump in her bag. Now it was complete. Her obeah bag held all that was required: the grave dirt, the pig's tail, the blood of her unborn child, nail clippings: and the hair of the victim.

She began to make her way over to the door but froze halfway. What was that noise? Ragged breathing? A snort? Panic rose in her chest and she held her breath. There it was again. That strange noise. She turned and the light of her candle fell onto the counterpane of the bed. There, asleep on a pile of cushions, was Fino. Her fear juddered out of her with a sigh of relief, but she had to remain quiet. She must not wake the dog else he would bark and alert his mistress.

Continuing on her way to the door, she stopped and picked up a footstool from the hearth rug. She set it down in the doorway and stood on it. Reaching full-stretch, she placed the obeah bag on top of the lintel, then, stepping down from the stool, she walked a few paces back. The sack was not visible. It would remain hidden. It would begin to work its magic as soon as her vile and wicked mistress, her tormentor and the murderer of her child, walked into the room. There would be no escaping its spell. She would be cursed, doomed to die an agonizing death. And as she closed the door behind her, the words of the obeah-man rang in Phibbah's ears: *Your missa be dead afore winter is out.*

Chapter 21

The following morning dawned dull as lime wash over London and the chill on the air grew even sharper. The old waterman stood by the quay, licked his finger, and held it aloft. The wind had changed direction. It was a northerly and that could mean snow. As long as the river did not freeze over as it had done two or three years back, he would manage. If it did, he would be done for. Why take a ferry when you can walk across the frozen ice from bank to bank? There would be no custom. He would starve.

He was contemplating the dire prospect, chuntering to himself, as he negotiated the weed-slimed stairs down to his boat. The familiar stench assailed his nostrils as he plunged down toward the water. There had been a spring tide, much higher than usual. Risk of flooding, they said. But the risk had passed. Now the tide was well into its turn and was leaving a foul stink in its wake. It would go out much farther, exposing larger expanses of the shoreline than usual, so the mud larks were making ready. Stationing themselves on the quayside, they would swoop down just as soon as it was safe to do so, in search of filthy carrion. Scrabbling through the stinking river silt they would look for discarded treasures—clay pipes, bottles, or lumps of coal. They were young ones mainly—all ragged and dirt-coated themselves. Most mornings at least one of them would make a grisly find— a body washed up on the stony beach. Wapping was the worst, or best, place to find a hapless whore who'd thrown herself off Westminster Bridge or a down-on-his-luck gambler who'd lost everything. The currents often carried them there, depositing them near Execution Dock. Then the mud larks would rifle through the corpse's pockets, rob it of any trinkets, sometimes steal boots—shoes usually floated off. The carrion picked over, the scavengers would then leave it once more to the mercy of the river.

On this particular morning, however, it was the old waterman's misfortune, for he never did like it when he came across one, to find a cadaver. This one, however, had not been washed up on the shore, but had been tied, most securely, to the wooden pier at which his boat was moored. What was more, it was without a head.

At first glance the old man thought it a dead animal; a sheep, perhaps. Then, as he drew closer, he realized the dirty white he could see was not wool, but a shirt. As he realized what his eyes were beholding, he turned and retched. Then sheer panic took hold. Clambering back up the steps as fast as his old legs could carry him, he began waving his arms in the air and hollering. When he had attracted the attention of a fellow waterman, he pointed down to the river where the receding tide was revealing more of the gruesome flotsam by the minute.

The other waterman fetched the watchman, who called the customs man. The customs man, unsure of himself, called an officer who informed the Admiralty, who said it was a civilian matter. So the justice of the peace was informed and he, in turn, told the Westminster coroner, Sir Stephen Gandy. Although new in post, following in the illustrious footsteps of Sir Peregrine Crisp, who had died suddenly a few weeks ago, Sir Stephen knew exactly what to do.

"There has been a body found over at Hope Wharf," he told his clerk, handing him a letter. "Please see to it that Dr. Thomas Silkstone receives this," he said. "The deceased will be dispatched to him shortly."

*　*　*

From his upstairs room Thomas surveyed the scene as he dressed. The window frame rattled as a gust of wind blew down the street. He looked up at the sky. It was tinged with a pink glow. There would be snow soon, he knew it. Walking over to his desk, he decided to take advantage of the first rays of winter light to write a letter.

> *34 Hollen Street*
> *Westminster*
> *London*
> *December 4*

My Dearest Lydia,
> *It brought me such happiness to read your letter and to hear that you and Richard are doing well. It is almost three months since I was at Boughton and I can imagine the young earl has grown in both stature and health. I am only sorry that I cannot be there to see him and share with you the joy that he brings.*
> *My love, I write in testing times. As you know I have been tasked by Sir Joseph Banks to catalogue the specimens brought back from an ill-fated expedition to Jamaica that left its leaders dead from disease. My work has, however, been severely disrupted. The journal of the expedition's leader, a Dr. Welton, was to be my primary guide in the cataloguing of almost two hundred specimens of flora and fauna. It was in the care of the last remaining expedition member. He went ashore as soon as his ship arrived in port at London but has not been seen or heard of since. His satchel was subsequently found empty in the Thames.*
> *Just what lies behind these mysterious events can only be left to conjecture at the moment. I*

*worry, however, that there is a link between the
artist's disappearance and the contents of the
expedition leader's journal. My fear is that this
volume could contain knowledge so powerful that
unscrupulous men would kill for it.*

He reread his words, hardly believing himself the gravity of
what he had just written. He had no intention of sending the letter to Lydia. She would go out of her mind with worry if she
thought he was involved in anything so sinister. He grabbed the
letter and screwed it up into a tight ball, venting his own anger
on the piece of paper, before tossing it onto his desk.

His dressing complete, he headed downstairs where, as usual,
breakfast awaited him in the dining room. Dr. Carruthers was
already enjoying a plate of bacon and coddled eggs, a napkin
tucked under his chin to catch any spills.

"So what did you glean from your visit to the docks yesterday, young fellow?" quizzed the old anatomist as soon as
Thomas sat down.

"Very little, I fear," replied Thomas, sipping from a dish of
tea. "And that is exactly what someone intended."

The old anatomist chuckled. "Come, come! You're saying
this is all part of some conspiracy?"

Thomas put down his tea and gazed into the dish. "I can
think of no other explanation," he replied. "Even Sir Joseph
seems reluctant to act and is keen that I should not interfere. I
have even seen words to that effect on the customs documents."

Carruthers's head jerked up. "That is most troubling," he
agreed.

Just as the doctor was about to reach for a slice of comforting
toast, Helen entered the room with a letter on a silver salver. It
bore the familiar seal of the Westminster coroner.

"This just came for you, sir," she said, bobbing a curtsy.

"What news, young fellow?" asked Carruthers, eagerly.

Thomas broke the seal and studied the contents of the letter.
A strange tingling sensation prickled his spine. He looked up.

"I am to conduct a postmortem for the new coroner, sir," he replied.

The old doctor raised a brow. "Anyone interesting?"

Thomas had often been called upon to conduct autopsies for Sir Peregrine Crisp when he was the Westminster coroner. Sir Stephen Gandy, although he had never met Thomas, obviously wished to continue the professional relationship.

"It seems the dead man was murdered," answered Thomas in a voice that was flat with shock.

"A murder, eh?" replied Carruthers enthusiastically, dabbing the bacon grease from his chin with his napkin before recovering his sensibilities. He suddenly realized why Thomas's reaction was so muted. "Not . . . ?"

The doctor took a deep breath. "I do not know the victim's identity, sir," he began. "Only that his body was recovered bound to a pier in the Thames," adding, "without its head."

Dr. Carruthers groaned at the thought. "Someone did not mean their victim to be identified," he said.

Scanning the letter once more, Thomas could only agree. Equally disturbing was the fact that the body was found near the very steps where he had disembarked only yesterday in his search for Matthew Bartlett. He never relished the prospect of conducting a postmortem on a murder victim. He could only pray that this macabre discovery would prove totally unrelated to his quest for the missing artist.

Chapter 22

Lydia went to meet with Nicholas Lupton at the stables as agreed. The morning was crisp and a sharp frost had laced the fields and hedges. There had been a sudden thaw and much of the snow had melted, although the temperature had plummeted again overnight. Nevertheless Lydia was eager to ride. The estate manager had come to her with an idea to drain twenty acres of bog land near Plover's Lake and she had jumped at the chance of fresh air and exercise.

Jacob Lovelock, the head groom, saddled up Lydia's favorite mare, Sheba, and helped her mount. It felt odd being back in the saddle. Three years had passed since she had last ridden and she was as nervous as she had been on her first hunt. But Sheba was a good, placid horse that could be trusted to deliver her safely back. All would be well, she told herself.

"Set fair, m'lady?" asked Lovelock as he finished adjusting Lydia's stirrups.

Lydia nodded. "Thank you, yes," she replied, taking the reins.

The groom patted the horse's neck as the mare nodded her head and clattered her hooves on the cobbles waiting for the off.

"She'll give you no trouble, m'lady," he reassured her.

As the clock struck ten, Lupton rode into the stable courtyard.

"Good morning, your ladyship," he greeted her. "What a fine mount you have."

Lovelock shot him a disapproving look as he let go of the

mare's reins. He did not like this new estate manager. "Far too cocky for his own good," he had told his wife, Hannah.

Lydia merely smiled. "So, to Plover's Lake," she said awkwardly. She could feel the groom's glower as he silently censured the outing. She nudged her horse and tugged gently on the rein, heading it toward the track that skirted the lake. Lupton drew alongside and together they rode out of the courtyard and into the lane.

The talk was of the bog and how it could be drained. Digging ditches at strategic points would lead off surface water into the lake and within a year, Lupton told her, the area could be tilled and turnips sown.

Lydia listened as they rode, asking questions at what she thought were appropriate points. Yet, in truth, she had little interest in dikes and gullies or any other form of engineering that seemed to so enthuse her estate manager. She was simply enjoying being outside and the sense of freedom that came with it. It was wonderful to see the beech woods and the hedgerows dotted with red berries and to hear the crows caw, to see nature in its winter rawness and feel the wind on her face.

Suddenly she flicked her crop on Sheba's flank.

"Come on, girl," she urged.

The mare quickly responded, breaking into a canter. The lane ahead was clear and the ground wet.

"Your ladyship!" exclaimed Lupton, taken by surprise. He followed suit, making up the distance between them and cantering alongside her. They rode at a fast pace for at least three minutes until the lane dipped between trees and a gate loomed before them a few yards ahead.

Lydia tugged at Sheba's reins and the horse slowed to a trot, as did Lupton's mount. She was a little breathless, but smiling. Tears streamed down her cheeks and her normally pale skin was flushed pink by the cold.

"Forgive me," she panted, patting her horse. "I could not help myself."

Lupton smiled as he drew beside her. "Clearly you are an excellent horsewoman, your ladyship," he told her.

"I had not realized how much I missed riding," she replied, lifting her gaze.

"Then you must do it more often," came the quick riposte.

Once again she felt he was crossing over the dividing line between mistress and servant. Yet something told her that it was of no consequence.

She nodded. "You are right, Mr. Lupton."

Leaning down from his mount, he opened the gate and Lydia urged her horse through, waiting for the estate manager on the other side. Beyond lay a wide expanse of open countryside that was folded into gentle hills. A flock of sheep grazed in a nearby hollow. She surveyed the scene and breathed deeply. Behind her she heard the latch of the gate click shut and turned to see Lupton nudging his horse toward her.

Drawing alongside her, he smiled.

"Is it not magnificent, Mr. Lupton?" she asked. She felt glad that she was not alone. Sharing the view gave her even more pleasure.

"It is indeed most beautiful," he replied. As he did so she turned to see that his eyes were not on the vista, but on her. Feeling the color rise in her neck, she urged her horse on, but it suddenly seemed to take fright. Rearing up, it gave out a loud whinny and shot off at a gallop, its ears flat to the wind.

Lydia tugged at the reins, trying to pull up the mare, but she could not control her. Behind her she could hear Lupton's shouts, then the thunder of hooves as he caught up with her. He had just drawn alongside when suddenly the horse's head jerked and it came to an abrupt halt, bucking its hind legs as it did so. Lydia could no longer hold on. She was thrown and sent hurtling to the ground.

"My lady!" cried Lupton, leaping off his horse and rushing to where Lydia lay, dazed and shaken. She had been flung onto a mossy hillock that was springy to the touch. It broke her fall as she landed on her left side. It took her only a few seconds to regain her composure. Propping herself up on her elbow, she shook her head. The mare stood close by, wreathed in the smoke of its own breath.

"Are you hurt, my lady?" asked Lupton, anxiously dropping to his knees beside her on the grass.

Lydia looked down at her own body, held out her arms, and felt her legs as if her limbs belonged to someone else. Her riding habit was caked in mud on her left side, but otherwise she seemed unharmed. "No, I am perhaps a little bruised, but mercifully nothing is broken," she replied a moment later.

"We best get you back to the hall," he told her, giving her his hand so that she could stand upright. "You have had a terrible shock."

Straightening herself, she smoothed her habit and brushed off the wayward flecks of moss. Lupton retrieved her hat that had flown off as the horse galloped wildly.

"Yes," she replied. "A shock."

"You must ride my mount. I will lead yours. The mare cannot be trusted," he said, taking control.

It took a few moments to switch the saddles, so that Lydia could be comfortable on the journey back to the hall. Lupton helped her mount. She felt self-conscious as he cupped his hands for her to ease herself up onto his horse. His face was so close to hers that she smelled his sandalwood cologne.

The return ride took little under an hour, with Lupton leading both horses. The journey was undertaken in almost complete silence, save for Lupton's interjections about how worried he had been and how he hoped she was not in pain. Lydia herself just willed to be back home, seated in front of a roaring fire. She thanked him for his concern and expressed her gratitude for his solicitousness.

The sun was already beginning to set by the time they eventually turned into the stableyard. Jacob Lovelock and his son, Will, were there to greet them. Both rushed forward when they saw that Lupton was on foot leading their mistress's mount, as well as his own.

"What happened, my lady?" asked Jacob, as Lydia pulled up the horse.

"I cannot be sure," she replied.

"The horse bolted," interrupted Lupton. "It threw her lady-ship."

"Are you hurt, my lady?" Jacob was most concerned.

Lydia shook her head. "Thankfully not," she replied, as he eased her out of the saddle and down to the ground. "Mr. Lupton has been most diligent in his care of me."

Will was standing nearby, his face a meld of anxiety and cynicism.

Seeing the stable lad's expression, Lupton's smile vanished. "Take the mare, will you?" he ordered, thrusting the reins into the boy's hands. He fixed him with a scowl. "She's a wild one," he added.

Lydia's muscles had stiffened during the return journey and she found herself limping slightly. Her left leg caused her pain when she put pressure on her foot. Nevertheless she managed to walk inside, accompanied by Lupton, who fussed around her dramatically.

Meanwhile Jacob and Will were left to unsaddle the horses. Flecks of foam dotted Sheba's forelocks and withers. She had galloped hard, there was no mistake. As the groom unbridled her, Will unbuckled the saddle and pulled it off. She winced and jerked her head as a strap caught her spine. As he patted the mare to steady her, Will noticed a dark patch on her back. Standing on the mounting block he inspected the area where the saddle had lain and was shocked to see an open sore on her ridge.

"Look at this," he called to his father.

Lovelock stood on tiptoe. Squinting at the circular wound, he saw it was raw; the blood still congealing 'round a large crater.

Stepping back, he patted the mare's forelock. "You're no bucker," he told her softly, then turning to Will he said, "A bur; that's what did that. Someone put it there and I've a mind just who."

Chapter 23

O vernight the snow was blown south to London. It whirled around like feathers and fell two or three inches thick in some places. It made it more difficult for the coroner's cart, laden with its grim cargo, to struggle through the streets. Nevertheless it pulled up outside 34 Hollen Street, as planned. A plain wooden box was deposited unceremoniously onto the flagstones in Thomas's laboratory and its contents, wrapped in sackcloth, were dumped carelessly onto the dissecting table. Another parcel, containing the victim's clothes, was flung nearby.

Thomas had already lit the fire and scattered sweet-smelling herbs onto it, but nothing could mask the familiar smell, only this time it was mixed with river filth. The coffin bearers gagged and exited as soon as they could, leaving the young doctor and Dr. Carruthers to breathe the unsanitary air alone. Anticipating the sickening stench, the instruments were already prepared. The saw, the scalpel, and an assortment of knives were all laid out and, as the natural light from the window was so dim, the lamps were lit. On a stand nearby sat two filled clay pipes.

"God's wounds, it stinks," declared the old anatomist as soon as Thomas unwrapped the corpse.

"But we are prepared, sir," retorted the doctor, lighting a spill and holding the flame over the bowl of a pipe. Sucking it hard, he soon had smoke curling from it. "You have taught me all I know," he smiled, handing over the pipe to his mentor as the smell of tobacco began to mask the stench of rotting corpse.

Carruthers sucked hard on the stem. "So what have we?" he said finally, pointing toward the reeking body with his pipe.

Thomas took a moment to examine the cadaver by eye. Even to one as experienced as he, it was a most unsavory sight, discolored and bloated.

"A man," he began, "without a head."

"Yes, yes. I know that," came the impatient response. "Young, old? Middle-aged?"

"In his early twenties, I'd say," replied Thomas, assessing the muscle development. "But malnourished," he added.

"After a long voyage?" asked Carruthers.

"It could be," replied Thomas, knowing that men had been known to lose several stone in weight during a lengthy sea trip.

Noting the overall condition of the body, one of the first things that struck him was the fact that the blood had pooled in certain areas. The skin was blackened where this had occurred and it seemed from the dark areas on the buttocks and calves that he had died lying down.

"I am beginning to think that our victim was killed quite a few hours prior to his body being tied to the pier."

"Livor mortis?" asked Carruthers.

"Yes."

"And how long had our friend been in the water?"

Thomas looked at the headless torso—blanched, swollen, and wrinkled—but he knew the answer to his mentor's question probably lay in the skin of the finger pads. He examined them first, then the palms, before inspecting the soles of the feet.

"The water in the Thames is near freezing at the moment," he said, prodding the victim's hands once more. "Putrefaction has begun, but is not very advanced." Again he peered at the fingertips. "The epidermis is still intact, and so are the nails."

Thomas knew that if the body had been in the water some considerable time, the outer layer of skin would have peeled off like a glove.

"So we are talking hours, not days," surmised the old doctor.

"Correct."

The torso, Thomas knew, was bloated, but not to any great

extent, which added weight to his theory that it had not been long in the water. Nor were there many abrasions on the skin, apart from the odd bruise, which could easily have been caused by the body being buffeted, postmortem, against the pier.

"Now I shall begin the examination proper," he announced, his tone becoming more formal. "The head has been severed cleanly. I would say a saw or a cleaver has been used to cut through the second and third cervical vertebrae and . . ." He broke off suddenly.

"What is it?" Carruthers jerked forward.

"It would seem, from the angle of the severance, that the victim was lying on his back when he was decapitated. But . . ."

"Yes?"

"But I would surmise that he was already dead at the time," said Thomas, inspecting the severed spinal column.

"The lungs will reveal more," remarked Carruthers, excitedly.

As he worked Thomas gave a running commentary to the old doctor who sat, head to one side, listening to every incision, every squelch, every slurp of the man's innards, even recognizing some of the sounds as if they were musical notes. Within the next ten minutes, Thomas had cut through the sternum and was studying the victim's lungs. They were empty of the soapy fluid normally associated with a drowning.

"It is clear to me, sir," he said, peering at the dark brown pillows of tissue, "that this man was well and truly dead when he was tied to the pier."

Carruthers nodded. "Thank the Lord for that!" he muttered.

"And, judging by the bloating of the stomach, dead for a good while." Thomas was peering over the corpse's internal organs, reading them as if they were runes to be used in divinations.

"But wait," he said, suddenly.

"What is it?"

"This is interesting," he said, reaching for his magnifying glass.

"What?" Carruthers could not bear such suspense.

"There are some adhesions to the pleural walls, especially in the upper lobe," Thomas told him.

"Cut them open," came the excited command.

Thomas did so to expose a brownish parenchyma. On the surface and in the interior of the pulmonary tissue were small white hard masses, most the size of a peppercorn.

"Interesting," he mused, inspecting the granules. "There seem to be a good deal of calcified tubercles."

"So he was afflicted with phthisis?"

"It seems so, and in quite an advanced state," replied Thomas. "But there's more." Thomas was slicing through the bronchioles that led from the lungs to the trachea. Examining them closely, he could see the inside walls of the airways were swollen and in-flamed. "I'd say this poor chap had a hard time breathing, sir," he said at last.

"So, cause of death?"

Thomas cocked his head to one side. "This was not enough to kill him." He clicked his tongue in frustration. "I cannot be conclusive, sir."

"A blow to the head, perhaps!" suggested Carruthers. "That would do for the poor blighter!"

The truth of the matter was that any postmortem conducted on a headless corpse would, by its very nature, be incomplete.

"So, we do not have a cause of death," said Thomas deject-edly, stitching up a flap of skin to the torso once more.

"But the real mystery remains," pointed out Carruthers. Thomas looked at him bemused. "The chap's identity," he added after a moment. "What of his clothes?"

Thomas had laid them in a pile on the nearby work surface. Rinsing his hands in a bowl of water, he walked over to them and first inspected the breeches. They were made of worsted and the stockings were silk. He wore no shoes.

"And a jacket?" asked the old anatomist.

Thomas shook his head. "No jacket. Just a shirt of good Egyptian cotton," he said, feeling its texture between his fore-finger and thumb. "I'd say he was a gentleman," he mused, still casting a keen eye over the stained shirt. Reaching for his magnifying glass, he peered at the material.

After a short pause, Carruthers could wait no more. "You have found something?" he snapped like an excited terrier.

Thomas leaned away from the workbench and straightened his aching back. "I am afraid I have," replied Thomas. "Our victim's shirt was monogrammed. The shirt bears the initials M. B."

Carruthers's forehead dipped into a frown. "Ah!" was all he managed to say at first.

"It is as I feared," murmured Thomas. "Matthew Bartlett; but as to what killed him, how he died . . . I am at a loss."

Hearing the frustration in his protégé's voice, the old anatomist shrugged. " 'Tis not your place to conjecture, young fellow," he said in a conciliatory tone. "Ours is not to uncover how or why or by whose hand poor wretches die, just what killed them."

"And that I have failed to do!" Thomas protested. He sucked on his pipe as he stared at the headless body. "I can only conclude that he must have died from an injury to the head or a disease of the brain."

Slowly he unfolded a length of winding sheet and began swathing the victim's body, ready for identification. A proper burial would follow. The corpse had given up many of its secrets, but how Matthew Bartlett, if indeed it was the young artist, had died, remained a mystery.

Chapter 24

Thomas had been asked to wait in the small anteroom outside the new Westminster coroner's office. He had decided to deliver his postmortem report to Sir Stephen Gandy in person in the hope that he might introduce himself. The fact that the clerk had asked him to wait was, he considered, a hopeful sign.

The hearth was empty and Thomas shivered as he sat, watching his own breath waft gently about him. He told himself that his shaking was purely due to the cold, but in reality, he knew that his nerves were getting the better of him.

After what seemed to him an age, he was summoned into the office. This time there was a fire in the grate and the room, although only slightly warmer than the antechamber, was of a bearable temperature. Sir Stephen sat at his desk and rose to shake the young anatomist's hand. He was a man in his later years, gray-wigged and with the sort of gravitas one might expect of one in such an important role. Looking into his eyes, Thomas saw the whites were yellow. It was obvious to him that he might have a liver condition. He wondered if he was aware of it.

Seating himself once more, the coroner elbowed his desk and glanced down at the bound sheets of Thomas's autopsy report.

"I thank you for undertaking this task," he said, fingering the papers. His voice was deep and his delivery studied, but his manner was easygoing.

"I am glad to be of service, sir," replied Thomas. His shivers,

or nerves, he could not decide which they were, had all but sub-
sided until Sir Stephen's smile dissolved to be replaced by a
frown. The coroner suddenly became very grave.

Turning the pages of the report, he ventured: "I do not doubt
your professional ability, or your accuracy and observation, Dr.
Silkstone."

Thomas sensed there would soon be a caveat. "Thank you,
sir," he said.

The coroner continued: "You make some interesting points.
The head, for example, possibly removed when the victim was on
his back, you say. And the lungs . . ." He looked up at Thomas.
"Phthisis."

"An advanced state," said Thomas, nodding.

"So are we dealing with a murder or no, Silkstone?" he asked,
a strand of frustration creeping into his voice.

Thomas shook his head. "Obviously someone tied the corpse
to the pier, sir."

As soon as he had said this, he could tell the coroner thought
him impertinent. He shot back: "And why would a murderer do
that, Dr. Silkstone?" His voice took on an imperious tone.

It was a question that had kept Thomas awake the previous
night. Why did this man's murderer not simply throw the corpse
into the Thames and let the tide carry it downriver to be washed
up at Wapping or Deptford, miles away from where the heinous
act was committed?

"I cannot say, sir," he replied meekly. He wanted to add that
he was an anatomist, not a mind reader. Henry Fielding and his
cronies were the men who set out to solve crimes of this nature,
and although he found himself increasingly drawn into this
murky arena of criminal deduction, he did not feel comfortable
in its glare.

Sir Stephen picked up a pencil and leaned back in his chair.
"And would I also be going too far if I were to ask you if you
had any idea as to this poor man's identity?"

This time Thomas was able to give an affirmative reply. "I
have an idea, sir, although it is subject to confirmation."

"Oh?"

"I believe the victim was a Matthew Bartlett, a botanical artist, recently returned from the expedition to Jamaica, sponsored by the Royal Society."

Sir Stephen arched a brow. "Do you indeed?" he said, leaning forward, as if his interest had suddenly been piqued even more. "And what makes you think that?"

"His shirt, sir. It was monogrammed with the initials M. B."

"Yes," the coroner drawled. "I noted that in your report, but is there anyone from the Royal Society who might be able to help you with the identification," he asked, adding, "despite the fact that there is no head?"

Thomas nodded. "Mr. Bartlett was known to Sir Joseph Banks."

Sir Stephen slammed the pencil down on his desk. "Well, there you have it!" he exclaimed. "A well-connected headless corpse!" He smirked at his own tasteless joke, then continued: "I shall write to Sir Joseph myself and ask him if he is willing to identify the body. I would not wish to release it for burial until we have some idea of who it is we are burying." He gave a neat smile. "You agree, Dr. Silkstone?"

Nodding slowly, Thomas eyed the coroner. The truth was that the postmortem had thrown up more questions about Matthew Bartlett and the Jamaican expedition than answers. If he was murdered, then the motive might have been the theft of Dr. Welton's journal. What could have been in it that was worth a man's life? The conundrums kept surfacing in his mind, whirling around on currents of doubt before being dragged down again into a quagmire of perplexity and confusion. It was high time, he told himself, that Sir Joseph Banks revealed to him the full picture. He would have it out with him as soon as he could.

"Of course, sir," he replied.

Word came the next day. Thomas was working in the laboratory. He had returned the corpse to its wooden box and dragged it outside in the courtyard where the freezing air ensured the process of putrefaction would be retarded. Before him, on his workbench, sat a mature aloe vera plant in a pot, its tubular flowers in full bloom. He had identified it both from Dr. Carruthers's knowledge and Mr. Bartlett's excellent sketches, which depicted the detail of the spiky plant with such consummate skill and accuracy.

The artist had even made a note underneath the drawing. It read: *Spent time in the hothouse where the resident physician employs native medicine to ease certain agues. He tells me aloe vera has many medicinal uses when applied as an unguent to rashes or wounds or when drunk to relieve a fever. In this respect it is particularly efficacious.*

Thomas sighed deeply. For such tidbits of information he was most grateful. They gave a tantalizing glimpse into what wonders Dr. Welton and his expedition must have uncovered, but in the absence of an authoritative medical contribution, his task was proving well-nigh impossible.

He did have access to Dr. Perrick's notes and observations, but they seemed to lack the detailed knowledge he felt necessary to record the specimens for posterity. Judging by the age of Perrick's wife, he believed he was a young man, perhaps only just received into the medical profession. He would, no doubt, have been content to allow his much respected father-in-law to shoulder the burden of recording the expedition's findings in his journal.

Thomas had just made a cut in the aloe plant's leaf to extract some of its curious sap when Mistress Finesilver brought him a message. It was from Sir Joseph Banks. He had received Sir Stephen's letter and consented to inspect the body and would welcome an opportunity to talk with him at his earliest convenience. Thomas began to clear away his instruments. The healing properties of the aloe vera plant would have to wait to be examined. Instead he grabbed his hat and coat and left the laboratory to make the necessary arrangements.

Chapter 25

The memorial service for Dr. Frederick Erasmus Welton, Fellow of the Royal Society, member of the Company of Surgeons, and respected physician, together with his assistant and son-in-law, Dr. John Perrick, was held at St. James's Church, Piccadilly. For a man of such eminence in his profession as Dr. Welton, Thomas was surprised to see so few people paying their respects. There were only around a dozen mourners aside from his close family members. There were no representatives from any of the major hospitals, no one from St. George's, or St. Bartholomew's or St. Thomas's. And from the Royal Society only Sir Joseph Banks was present.

Was Dr. Welton not liked in his professional circles? Had he done something to offend the medical establishment? Thomas glanced over to where Sir Joseph stood in a pew at the front of the congregation and remembered his words to him. "Play your cards right, Silkstone, and you will go far." Had Dr. Welton, by his words or by his deeds, offended those who could make or mar careers at a stroke of their pens, or a word from their tongues?

The service was a short, simple affair. Of course there were no coffins. Both men had been interred in the graveyard in Kingston. It was doubtful whether either widow would ever get to lay flowers on their respective husbands' graves, but a memorial stone in St. James's churchyard was planned.

There was little pomp and circumstance. Thomas had the impression that this was at the request of the two women. They sat in the front pew, both their faces obscured by black veils, united in their grief. He wondered if they thought it strange or insulting, or both, that Matthew Bartlett, as the only surviving member of the ill-fated expedition and a close colleague of the two doctors, had not made an appearance at the service. Of course they had no idea that he had gone missing, let alone been brutally murdered. He hoped it would remain that way for as long as possible to spare them the undoubted torment such news would bring. He had made plans for later that afternoon, arranging to meet with Sir Joseph at Somerset House. The headless corpse had been transported there and deposited in a well-ventilated stable. As soon as it had been identified it would be buried without delay.

The service over and the congregation dismissed, Thomas walked slowly down the aisle and out into the cold. Despite the chill, widows Welton and Perrick stood side by side, thanking well-wishers for their condolences. When it was Thomas's turn to give his sympathies, however, Mistress Perrick stepped aside, seemingly with her mother's approval.

"Dr. Silkstone," she said, the tone of her voice much lower than before. "I have something for you," she said in a half whisper. She delved into a black reticule she was carrying and brought out a bundle of what appeared to be letters.

"There is still no sign of my father's notebook?" she asked.

Thomas shook his head.

"Do you really believe it has been mislaid, Dr. Silkstone?"

It was not a question that Thomas had anticipated. He formed his lips into a smile and shrugged.

"It is missing, Mistress Perrick. Somewhere between Jamaica and London it has gone astray."

A gust of wind caught her veil and lifted it off her face for a moment. She looked serene and completely in command of her emotions. "That is why I thought these may help you, Dr. Silkstone," she said, holding the papers out to him. "My husband sent them from Jamaica."

Thomas shot her a puzzled look as she placed them in his

grasp. Quickly he scanned the closely written text. After a moment, he glanced up. "These are personal letters," he said.

She nodded. "But they also contain important information, Dr. Silkstone. You will find formulae for native physic in there; all sorts of intelligence that may be of value to you as a man of science." She remained calm and rational as she spoke.

Thomas shuffled the sheets and regarded her with a look of admiration. "I am most grateful to you, Mistress Perrick," he said. "These could prove an invaluable guide in my work."

It was only then that he detected her eyes moistening a little. "If that is so, then I am content, Dr. Silkstone," she told him, adding: "I do not want my husband to have died in vain."

Thomas's third meeting with Sir Joseph Banks was in great contrast to his first and second. Instead of the stately wood-paneled room, presided over by the great and the good of the scientific establishment, the men found themselves in a stable off the main courtyard of Somerset House. With their kerchiefs clamped over their mouths, they were staring at the sheet covering a corpse as it lay on a trestle table. A groom was in attendance.

Sir Joseph had already identified the soiled clothes as belonging to Matthew Bartlett. Now he was preparing himself to identify the body. He nodded to signify to the servant that he was ready and the cloth was pulled away to reveal the putrefying headless cadaver of a young man. Forcing himself to look at the grotesque sight, he turned away after no more than two seconds and the groom re-covered the corpse. Without a word he left the stable. Thomas followed immediately, filling his lungs with fresh air.

For a few moments Sir Joseph was silent, trying to compose himself, until finally he turned to Thomas.

"Yes," he said emphatically. "I am afraid I believe the body could be that of Matthew Bartlett."

Thomas felt a shiver course down his own spine. Until the last moment he had clung to the hope that this young man was a poor, unfortunate stranger who had fallen in with bad company, or been killed by a jealous rival in love.

The wind whipped 'round both men as they stood in the stableyard.

"May we talk, sir?" he asked

Sir Joseph fixed him with a solemn gaze. "I think we had better."

Thomas was led into Somerset House through a back entrance and shown into a smaller, more intimate room. Sir Joseph gestured him to sit in a chair by the hearth where a fire burned. It seemed to the doctor as though he had entered an inner sanctum, a private room where only the most trusted of Sir Joseph's associates were allowed to enter. He felt privileged.

Standing by the fireplace, Sir Joseph clasped his hands as if in prayer and stared into the fire, trying to frame his words, as if he were about to convey something quite momentous.

"I have not been entirely forthcoming with you, Dr. Silkstone," he began.

Thomas's first thought was that this was an understatement, but at least that problem would, hopefully, be rectified.

Sir Joseph continued: "I have not told you the real purpose behind Dr. Welton's mission on this expedition."

Thomas pressed his hands nervously onto his thighs and took a deep breath. *Now the truth will out,* he told himself.

"You have heard of the branched calalue plant?"

Thomas thought for a moment. He recalled one of Mr. Bartlett's sketches. For some reason, it was the only plant on the manifest that had been missing. He had been surprised to discover from the caption underneath that it was a species of *Solanum,* of the nightshade genus.

"Yes, sir," he replied.

"It was proposed that the expedition should, how shall I put it, explore the plant's potential." Sir Joseph put great emphasis on the last word, almost as if it were a euphemism.

Thomas frowned. "Potential?" he queried.

Sir Joseph looked uncomfortable. He cleared his throat. "There were . . . There are . . . ," he corrected himself, "great expectations of this plant."

"And Dr. Welton was to lead the party?" asked Thomas.

Sir Joseph's features tightened. "He was reluctant to agree to the commission."

"May I ask why?"

The great man's gaze veered away. "There are other interested parties," he told him in a low voice, as if he were afraid someone might overhear their conversation. Then, returning his regard to Thomas, he said, "Welton was aware of the plant's possibilities and wanted to put it to better use."

"What might that have been?" urged Thomas.

Shaking his head, Sir Joseph gazed into the fire once more. "He could see it had promise and that is how the rift occurred."

"Rift, sir?" Thomas was taken aback at such candor.

Suddenly Sir Joseph realized he had revealed more than he intended. "I cannot say more, Dr. Silkstone," he replied, adding: "I have said too much already and everything I have told you has been in complete confidence."

Thomas sensed that the door was closing once more. He had to strike before it was shut in his face again. "But what of Mr. Bartlett's murder, sir? And the missing journal? Are they connected with what you have just told me?"

The great man's features sharpened. "It is not your business, Dr. Silkstone. The Royal Society has employed you to catalogue the expedition's specimens, no more and no less. Please carry on with your work and leave any deeper investigations to others."

Sensing their discussion had drawn to an abrupt and wholly unsatisfactory close, Thomas rose. As he did so, Sir Joseph seemed to relent a little. He clicked his tongue. "If I tell you more, Silkstone, there are those who will accuse you of spying for your country, given our recent past." His mouth was pursed, as if he had just said something that was distasteful to him.

"I understand, sir," he assured Sir Joseph with a bow. He did not say he had no intention of complying with his wishes. His personal respect for Sir Joseph remained undiminished, but if the truth were to surface in this murky affair, he knew he would have to take personal control.

Making for the door, Sir Joseph following him, Thomas turned.

"One more thing, sir," he said, stopping in his tracks.

"Yes?"

"Did Matthew Bartlett have a frequent cough?"

Sir Joseph paused for a moment. "No," he said. "No, he did not. Why do you ask?"

Thomas shook his head, thinking of the dead man's badly damaged lungs. Forced to respond quickly he said, "Merely that I found a small tumor in the bronchioles, but it was obviously not big enough to cause irritation," he replied nonchalantly. Fortunately, Sir Joseph did not press him further.

Chapter 26

The slaves huddled around the hearth in the scullery. The hour was late and the dinner pots and plates had been washed and put away. The fires in the dining room and drawing room had been doused and the doors locked. Their duties done, Mistress Bradshaw had persuaded Mr. Mason to allow the Negroes the privilege of warming themselves because of the unusually cold weather. Some of the white servants were playing cards around the kitchen table. The maids were sewing or gossiping.

"Surely, Mr. Mason, you do not want any more of them dying?" the cook had argued, appealing to his practical nature rather than his humanity.

Venus had also put pressure on him. Being the housekeeper, she had her own room, with her own fire, but she always sided with Cook in trying to ease the slaves' burden. So they sat with glowing faces around the dying embers. They did not want to talk about how they had each arrived in slavery; how some of them were born into captivity, while others had endured the horrors of the journey from Africa. They had heard the stories so many times, of the wars and the Arab traders and the long treks to the coast. They knew of the families torn apart by the white men in their big ships. Only Homer, Hercules (the eldest), and Ezra, who was a skilled carpenter, remembered anything of their homelands. The others—Cato, Patience, and Phibbah—had been born into captivity, but they still seemed hungry for the stories, even though they had heard many of them before.

"My father was a fisherman," recalled Homer, looking into the flames. "We used to catch fish as big as a man in the lake. We never lacked food."

Hercules smiled and shrugged. "Until the Ashanti came and defeated us."

"And sold you to the white men," butted in Phibbah.

"That's right, child," continued Homer. "They took us to a castle and locked us in their dungeon, before loading us like cattle onto ships." He shook his head. "What I wouldn't give to go back home, to sit under the shade of a sweet dika tree, and watch the sun go down over Mount Afadjato."

Cato gave him an odd look. "Maybe you can."

"What you mean?"

He shrugged. "Why is it that we are still kept in chains? Do you not see our African brothers and sisters all around you in the street?" he asked.

"I see them," barked Hercules, "and I see them begging. I see them cold and without shoes on their feet."

"But at least their feet are free!" cried Cato. "At least they can run and not be chased and whipped!" He lifted his hands in a gesture of exasperation. "Do you not see? In England there are others like us who do not belong to a master. They are not property. They are human beings." He sank his hand into his breeches' pocket and pulled out a piece of paper. On it was large writing and a picture of a Negro man in chains. The others drew closer to inspect it.

"What is it?" asked Phibbah.

Cato brandished it like a silk handkerchief. "It is called a handbill and it is being passed 'round in some of the taverns."

Reaching into his pocket once more, he pulled out another two pieces of paper, exactly the same. Phibbah snatched one and inspected it.

"What does it say?" asked Homer. He could not read. None of them could.

"It calls for all slaves to be free," cried Cato.

"Who calls?" snapped Hercules, sounding a note of caution.

By now Cato's eyes were ablaze. "There is talk," he replied.

"What talk?" Homer challenged.

"There is a way for us to be free, back home, in Africa."

Homer snatched the paper and studied the drawing of one of their kind, on his knees, his manacled hands together in supplication as if begging for mercy.

"Where you get this?" he asked.

"Where our free black brothers meet, at an inn called the Crown." Cato's eyes were as bright as the Caribbean sun at noontide.

Phibbah had never seen him so animated. There was something odd in his manner; a fire that was burning inside him she had not encountered before. He had the zeal of a white preacher she sometimes saw in the market square, exhorting his audience to repent of their sins and turn to god, their white god. She saw him slide a sideways look at her, as if he realized that she knew something was about to happen, something big and frightening that might change their lives. His expression was that of an excited hound that had been digging in the dirt. What had he found? A bone of hope to chew upon, perhaps? He had discovered more than this trifling piece of paper with words on, surely? Did he dream of escape? She thought of her own plan. Should she tell him of the obeah in return for his secret? If he knew that, thanks to her, Mistress Carfax would be dead soon, then perhaps he would take her with him if he was going to break for freedom? She resolved to ask Cato the next time they were alone.

Venus slid through the silence of Samuel Carfax's bedroom, watching the mound beneath the blankets move up and down with each breath. Laying a cold hand on his shoulder, she stirred him with her touch. He opened his eyes, registered her face in the glimmer of the fire's embers, and smiled.

"I did not think you would come tonight," he told her softly. In the half-light she saw his naked head peeping out from the coverlet, smooth as a hard-boiled egg without its wig. Her touch moved him quickly into wakefulness and he turned onto his back. There was lust in his hands as he reached for one of the ribbons on her nightgown and began toying with it like a string on a lute.

She stayed his fingers and started undoing the ribbons herself. "Do I ever let you down?" she asked in a voice as smooth as velvet.

She did not tell him the reason for her lateness, that she was passing the scullery and had caught a fragment of conversation between the slaves that had held her attention. Such was her interest that it had caused her to stand silently with her ear to the door, listening to their talk for a full twenty minutes. She climbed into bed beside him and began warming her hands on his hot body.

"No," he replied as he felt her icy fingertips caress his thigh. "You never let me down."

Chapter 27

Mistress Finesilver woke Thomas with a message that morning. Through the fog of his returning consciousness he heard her say there was a carriage waiting to take him to the Carfax household.

"Who is ill?" he asked, pulling back his bedsheets.

"I do not know, sir," she replied, drawing the blind. "Only that it is urgent."

From the way the carriage clattered at high speed through the streets and along the river road, Thomas assumed some kind of terrible calamity had befallen the Carfaxes. Indeed, when the door was opened to him he heard a loud commotion coming from upstairs. He was therefore more than a little surprised to be ushered into the study, where he found Samuel Carfax seated at the desk, poring over some sort of ledger. He eased up his portly frame when Mason announced the doctor and strode over to greet him. As he did so, Thomas clearly heard a woman shouting, screaming even, and her cries were punctuated by a dog's howls. The noise was growing louder.

Thomas regarded Carfax quizzically, expecting some sort of explanation. When it came, it was not what he had anticipated. The plantation owner shrugged almost apologetically.

"My wife . . ." he began. "She . . ." He was not given the chance to finish his sentence. At that moment Cordelia Carfax burst into the room, carrying Fino under her arm.

"He's blind! My baby is blind!" she wailed, clutching the

whimpering canine. Her mouth was twisted and tears gushed down her cheeks as she thrust the animal into her husband's arms.

"Calm yourself, my dear," urged Carfax, suddenly landed with the distressed dog. He lifted it away from his torso, outstretching his arms, as if the creature were a bundle of foul-smelling rags. It was pawing pathetically at its flat muzzle.

Mistress Carfax, her face crumpled and puffy, leered at Thomas.

"Well, are you just going to stand there, Dr. Silkstone? Can you not see my dog is in anguish?"

Thomas stepped forward. Up until this moment, his only dealings with animals had been pegging them out for dissection, and with Franklin, his rat. He had never been asked to examine a sick dog before and was a little reticent to do so now.

"For pity's sake, take it, will you!" cried Carfax, anxious to be rid of the furry burden, plonking it into Thomas's arms.

Lifting the pug over to the hearth to take advantage of the light, the doctor could see that it was suffering badly. Its lids were closed and swollen and tears had gathered in the fur beneath its eyes. But it was its strong scent that struck Thomas. He sniffed at it and, much to his bewilderment, smelled roses.

"I need water," he called, but his order was lost in Mistress Carfax's shrieking. "Water, if you please," he repeated, only louder.

Heeding the request, Samuel Carfax tugged at the servant's bell.

Thomas pulled out a wad of gauze from his open case and began dabbing the creature's face. "I'd say that this little fellow has something caustic in his eyes," he said.

"Caustic?" echoed Mistress Carfax, tearing herself away from her husband's embrace. "Does that mean poison?"

"It could mean any manner of substance, madam," replied Thomas, as Samuel Carfax ordered a pitcher of water from Mason. "But from the smell of it, I surmise that substance is perfume."

Mistress Carfax gasped. "Perfume!" she repeated.

Thomas nodded. "Rosewater?"

Another gasp issued from the distressed woman as she thought of her silver scent bottle on her dressing table. "But how?" she asked.

Or rather who? thought Thomas. He said nothing of his suspicions, but instructed that the dog's eyes be regularly washed with cool, boiled water for the next few hours.

He left Cordelia Carfax billing and cooing over Fino, while Venus emerged to show him to his waiting carriage. Tall and poised, she led him into the hallway, where a footman waited with his topcoat. As he slipped his arm into a sleeve Thomas looked outside onto the back lawns. Squinting against the winter sunlight, his gaze snagged on what appeared to be two gravestones, side by side, at the bottom of the narrow plot.

He pointed to them. "Forgive me, those headstones, there?" he asked the housekeeper. "They belong to slaves?"

Venus also looked out. When she saw what Thomas was pointing at, she clicked her tongue as if chiding a white man's ignorance.

"Those belong to the missa's old dogs," she told him coolly. "Slaves do not have headstones, Dr. Silkstone."

As the carriage returned him home, Thomas pondered on the Carfax household and how it must be riven with hatred and mistrust. He had sluiced the dog's eyes and did not believe any lasting damage had been done, but someone had intended that the creature should be permanently blinded, presumably to wound Mistress Carfax indirectly. He suspected that the dog was the child she had never had—he was not aware of any offspring—and she lavished more love on it than on any human being, including her husband. Moreover, she treated her slaves worse than stray dogs. He had witnessed, with his own eyes, the woman's indifference to the death of the Negro boy and her anger when the girl had mourned so publicly. He'd wager that one of those poor, wretched slaves had poured perfume into the dog's eyes to vent their festering and impotent hatred of their mistress. Of course it was reprehensible to injure a defenseless creature, but it was a soft target, and its suffering was clearly felt vicariously by its owner.

So engrossed in his own thoughts was Thomas during the carriage ride back to Hollen Street that he became oblivious to all that was going on around him. In particular, he had no notion that he was being observed as he alighted outside his home. Two gentlemen sat inside another carriage parked opposite. They watched Thomas dismiss the driver and walk up the steps before instructing their own driver to move off.

Chapter 28

Josiah Dalrymple had business to conduct with Samuel Carfax. He duly arrived at the latter's villa at the appointed time, attended by his trusted slave Jeremiah. As his business was of a private nature, however, he told Jeremiah to wait downstairs in the servants' quarters, where he was duly dispatched by Mason the butler.

In the kitchen, Cook was standing by the range, stirring the stockpot. She turned, huffed, and said Jeremiah could sit and wait on the bench by the table. Mr. Roberts, mending a broken dish, however, had different ideas. As soon as the butler was out of sight he ordered Jeremiah stand.

"You!"

The slave looked up.

"There's no place for you black scum here." He spat the words as if they were poison.

Cook looked up, bobbed a glance at the slave, then at his tormentor.

"He'll do no harm here," she countered.

Angered by the cook's defense, Roberts stood his ground.

"I am not wanting to look at his dirty black face," he sneered, then turning to a confused Jeremiah, he barked: "Wait in the boot room." Heading for the door, he gestured to the slave to follow.

A few paces along the narrow passage, they came to another door. Roberts opened it.

"Get in," he ordered.

Jeremiah hesitated. It was not something he usually did when commanded by a white man, but, after a moment, he did as he was bade, walking into a tiny, dark room with only the smallest of windows to let in light. It was cold and smelled musty. The walls were lined with shelves for boots and hooks for riding crops and whips that he suspected were not used on horses at all. There were the familiar sticks, too, that had small paddles on the end that his master used to hit balls around for pleasure.

"You shall stay here until your master is ready for you," said Roberts, and with that he shut the door, locking it behind him.

Left alone in the murky darkness, Jeremiah walked over to the corner and sat himself down, rolling his body into a ball for warmth, and resting his head on his folded arms. This is how he must have fallen asleep, for it was how he found himself when he was wakened by the sound of the key in the lock. His head shot up to see a woman, swiftly followed by a man, as they blustered into the darkness of the room. He froze. They did not know he was there.

In the murky light he watched them move like shadow puppets, heard their panting, then their words.

"You should not have come here," said the woman.

"But we have business." The man lunged toward her, planting kisses on her neck. "Your lord and master is engaged upstairs."

"It is dangerous," she protested.

"You love the danger!" He laughed. "You have more for me?"

She pushed him away slightly. "There will be another very soon. A fine Coromantee male."

"Excellent," came the reply. Jeremiah heard the man's breathing thicken before he pushed the woman up against the wall. "My reputation is not the only thing that is growing."

The rustle of silk was heard and the grunting began. The woman let out an odd cry, somewhere twixt pleasure and pain, he a great roar. Then it was over and silence.

Jeremiah held his breath, willing them to leave as quickly as they had come, but in their exertions the couple must have knocked a shelf and a boot came tumbling down, narrowly missing him. As it clattered to the floor, he saw both their heads turn his way. Then the woman gasped.

"There's someone there!"

"What?"

The man instinctively grabbed the nearest weapon to hand, a golf stick, and launched himself into the darkness.

"A slave!" he cried, seeing the whites of Jeremiah's eyes, and he lifted the club to strike.

Jeremiah leapt up and headed for the open door, but before he could reach it, the man brought down the club on his back, striking him hard. A scream of pain tore through the darkness and he stumbled. His hands flew up to protect his head, but the man confronted him, raining another blow, this time on his skull. He felt the blood gush from a wound, but could see just enough to know that his attacker was about to strike again. Managing to scramble into the passage, he fled to the back door, shouldered it open and found himself outside. He staggered along a path and into the garden, leaving a trail of blood on the snow in his wake. There was a side gate. It was not locked. He glanced back. There were footsteps. He knew he could not return.

Later that night, in the solitary gloom of his own bedroom, Thomas began to read Dr. John Perrick's letters by candlelight. The small fire in his grate had long since died and he gathered the blankets from his bed and wrapped them around him. In the poor light he sat squinting at the closely written text of the correspondence between man and wife. He was not completely at ease doing so. He felt like a voyeur or an intruder. There were obviously passages which were of a private nature and he skimmed over these quickly. What was of the utmost interest were the excerpts that dealt with the adventures of the expedition members and at least he trusted that these, addressed as they were to his spouse, would not be as graphic as Dr. Welton's observations.

The letters did, indeed, prove a mine of helpful and intriguing information and threw up many pharmacological secrets, known only to the island's natives. With a journal open on his desk, Thomas made copious notes, adding his own deliberations every now and then. There were descriptions of various plants that were the basis of good physic. Aloe vera was mentioned prominently and, indeed, there was a recipe for the relief of fever which used it as the main ingredient, while garden balsam, it was said, was good for both colds and colic in babes.

Yet there were other, more sinister, entries, like Perrick's impression of Kingston on his arrival. *It pains me to say that I am glad you are not with me to see this port, my dear, for it is no place for a lady. Bewildered Negro men, women, and children, all with chains about their necks, are dispatched at markets to their owners as traders sell pots and pans in Spittle Fields.*

His candle now burned low, Thomas rubbed his strained eyes and decided to retire to his bed, although he knew he would not rest easy. Matthew Bartlett's murder had unsettled him and the mistreatment of their slaves by Carfax and his wife had disturbed him. These notes and letters opened the window even wider onto a world of savagery and inhumanity. It had always been there for him to see, but he had never taken the time to observe it. Now, like the botfly larva he had removed from the arm of Samuel Carfax, it was rearing its hideous head. Perhaps it was because he found it too terrible to contemplate that he had chosen to ignore it before. Now that it had made itself known to him, he could no longer brush it aside. He heard the watchman cry three o'clock before he finally fell asleep.

Chapter 29

The following day Thomas told himself would have to be devoted to working hard on the specimens. Forcing all thought of Matthew Bartlett's murder aside, he rose before dawn and concentrated his energies within his laboratory. The schedule he had set himself was slipping fast away. Since breakfast he had turned his attention to the snakes—there were four different species—and had ranged a number of large glass jars before him. The air turned sharp with preserving fluid as he poured at least two pints into each container, depending on the size of the specimen. By four o'clock, however, he found he had completely run out of the liquid.

He set off to visit the apothecary a few streets away to order some more and was almost at the end of Hollen Street when, in a pool of light cast by a streetlamp, he saw flakes of snow wafting overhead. Two chairmen stood by their sedan waiting for a fare, stamping their feet to keep warm. A carriage decamped its passengers and rumbled off into the distance. Three gentlemen on foot braced themselves against the northerly wind as they passed him. Their footfalls, crumping in the snow, had just receded when he heard the noise: a low moan, followed by a whimper. He stopped still and craned his head. There it was again. An injured dog, perhaps? Or a babe born of a street girl and left to die? He looked 'round. Something caught his eye on the steps that led to a basement nearby. He turned and squinted into the darkness. To his horror he could make out a hand, clawing at the street railings like a giant crab. Scooping up his cape and tucking it under his arm, he bent low. And there, in the blackness, he could see a man's face racked with pain.

Darting up, Thomas looked down the street once more toward the chairmen at their stand. Cupping his hands around his mouth he called out to them as loud as he could. "Over here. I need help!"

The men whirled 'round, saw Thomas's frantic waves, and hurried over.

Bending low once more, the doctor scrambled halfway down the basement steps to tend to the man. He could see he was barely conscious. Throwing off his cape, he was wrapping it around the patient to protect him from the cold just as the chairmen arrived.

"What goes on, sir?" called one of the men, frowning into the gloom.

"A man lies badly injured," replied Thomas, mopping a bleeding brow with his kerchief. "These wounds need treating straightaway. Help me, will you?"

The two men swapped shocked looks. This was way beyond their normal duties. Thomas read their faces.

"I will pay you double the fare," he snapped. "Just help me get him into the chair, will you?"

The injured man was broad and tall and did not come easily. With great difficulty the chairmen hauled him up out of the basement and onto the poorly lit walkway, where Thomas could at least discern his features to assess his injuries. But as soon as the men saw his face, both of them balked.

"A Negro!" cried one.

Ignoring their consternation, Thomas pulled away the folds of the cape to inspect the man's head as blood gushed from a wound. Wrapping his muffler around the skull, he managed to stem some of the flow, but he knew there was no time to waste. The Negro's eyes were now closed and his voice was stilled. He had lost consciousness.

"Hurry, men!" he shouted.

With little regard for their passenger, the chairmen bundled him into the sedan and within two minutes they were carrying the injured Negro through the front door at Hollen Street. Helen, answering the door, had screamed at the sight of the bloodied passenger, but soon the chairmen were laying him down on the chaise longue in the small downstairs drawing room as Thomas directed.

Dr. Carruthers pricked up his ears and came to the doorway. "What goes on?"

Thomas, putting coins into the callused palms of the chairmen, explained:

"A young Negro man has been viciously assaulted, sir. I found him with a severe head wound not two hundred yards away in the street."

Hearing the commotion, Mistress Finesilver also appeared at the doorway. The chairmen pushed past her, leaving muddy footprints in their wake.

"And what do you think you are doing, gentlemen?" she railed, hands on hips, as she surveyed the chaos in the small drawing room. A blue, bloodstained coat lay on the floor.

"I found a badly injured man in the street, mistress," explained Thomas, placing a cushion with the utmost care under his patient's head. "We could not take him upstairs."

"All this to-do!" she clucked, hurrying over to the stranger who lay unconscious on the good furniture. Her eyes widened in horror as she saw a cushion on the chaise longue spotted with blood. She snatched it away.

"Mind you take off his boots," she huffed as she drew closer to inspect the man's face. It was only then that she realized the identity of this unexpected houseguest and her hands flew up in shock. "A blackamoor!" she shrieked.

Thomas had anticipated her reaction, but refused to be drawn by it. "This man is my patient, Mistress Finesilver," he countered, "and will be here for at least the next few days. It would be most appreciated if you could fetch me warm water and my medical case."

The housekeeper's mouth opened to deliver a rejoinder, but closed again when she thought better of it. Instead her face set into a grimace, as if she had just sniffed a jug of sour milk in the pantry.

"Very well," she conceded and flounced out.

"His condition sounds serious," remarked Dr. Carruthers gravely.

"It is. He has lost consciousness," replied Thomas, peering at the man's head wound. "He is fortunate to have survived."

Thomas, squinting into the deep cut, touched the cranium lightly, pressing gently in search of cracks and bumps. The injuries were concentrated around the crown and left eye. The swelling and contusions around the latter were such that he feared for the man's sight. The injuries, he believed, had been inflicted by a blunt instrument. It seemed to him that he had been struck at least twice about the face and head.

There was worse to come. Loosening the young man's shirt at the neck, Thomas was shocked to see a silver collar, as if he were an animal. He had heard it was fashionable in some households where slaves were employed and now he knew it to be true.

Taking out his magnifying glass from his case that Mistress Finesilver had just grudgingly delivered, he peered more closely. It was as he thought. There were other, older marks around his wrists, too. They had been made not during this latest attack but, he suspected, sustained after manacles had cut into his flesh.

Gently examining the rest of the young man's body, Thomas could see it bore all the telltale signs of maltreatment. Apart from the bruises from the most recent attack, there were several scars. He ran his fingers over the lumpy tissue around the wrists. There was more around the ankles, too. The skin of his torso was stretched tight as a drum over ribs that looked so sharp he thought they would pierce through from the inside like needles. It was as if he were staring at a patchwork of abuse; a tapestry of torture and deprivation stitched on the body of a human being. It sickened him and he sighed deeply.

Straightening himself once more, he took a step back. Still gazing at his patient, he said, "This man is a slave."

Dr. Carruthers nodded sagely. "A runaway most like. Beaten by his master, I'll wager."

"We should call the constables," said Thomas firmly. He was surprised when his suggestion was met with derisory laughter.

"He is a slave, young fellow. He is tantamount to mere property under the law. He'll find no protection there!" came Carruthers's reply.

Thomas wondered at his mentor's cynicism. "Surely there is some recourse to the law?" he pressed, covering the young man with a blanket.

Dr. Carruthers thought for a moment. "There was a case, a few years ago, where a slave, by the name of Jonathan Strong, was cruelly beaten by his master. He was left for dead and cared for by a courageous clerk and his brother, a surgeon, but then seized back by his master two years later."

"What happened?"

"The master, a brute by all accounts, thinking he still owned the poor wretch, sold him back into slavery, to another rogue. But the clerk took the case to court and won the slave his freedom."

Thomas looked grave. "But I thought slavery was illegal under English law."

The old anatomist huffed. "Merchants from the Colonies are allowed to bring their slaves here and no one bats an eyelid," he chided, wagging his finger. He shook his head and said with a tone of resignation, "Surely you know that law and practice are two very different things, young fellow."

Thomas was forced to agree.

After stitching the slave's wound with catgut, Thomas applied sap from the aloe vera plant to the swollen areas of the face. The tissues surrounding the left eye were so distended they reminded him of a bruised plum. He knew the strange aloe gel contained healing properties and was glad to put it to the test to see if it could relieve the inflammation and swelling. The rest of the night he would spend propped up with pillows in a chair at his patient's side. The young man was still unconscious and, very worryingly, had developed a fever.

For the next two days, Thomas set aside his cataloguing in

the laboratory to make the wounded slave his priority. He tasked Helen to sit beside him for some of the time, while he returned to the laboratory to obtain more gel from the aloe plants or to make up some formula that Dr. Welton had recommended in his notes. Mixing aloe juice with coconut milk was, apparently, a well-known physic among the Maroons, known to bring down fevers, as well as being an excellent restorative. The regular application of the gel appeared to be working well on the head wound and the young man's fever seemed to be subsiding.

In the meantime, when it was his turn to sit at the slave's bedside, Thomas would read Dr. Welton's notes. He glanced through the various papers he had at his disposal, convinced that somewhere in those scant jottings and observations lay a clue as to why Bartlett was murdered. Picking up a random sheet written in Welton's hand his eyes were drawn to an account of a warning that had been issued to the expedition, by a seasoned plantation owner. It was the story of how the Maroons could be every bit as brutal as their erstwhile masters.

Over dinner, we were told the tale of a rebel leader who, with his men, raided an estate to the east of Kingston. Having tied the hands of the manager, by the name of Shaw, and plundered the house, they helped themselves to all his food and liquor as he watched on helpless. As he regarded them with great consternation, he suddenly realized that the leader, a man they called Plato, was known to him. The rebel had once been a house slave on his plantation and in his own service, so the manager pleaded for his life. "Do you not recall," he asked, "how, when you were only a child, I gave you morsels from my table? Remember this, and have pity on me." But the rebel replied: "You are right. You were my master and you did feed me. But do you also not recall what you did to my mother? You violated her before my very eyes, then when my father tried to

*stop you, you had him whipped until he died.
Now do you remember your own barbarity? You
do not deserve to draw breath. Saying this, he
took an ax and, ignoring Shaw's pleas, he held it
to his head and before his fellows, he chopped it
off to great applause. Not content with his death,
the rebels then skinned the man and used his flesh
as a floor mat.*

Thomas felt the nausea rise from his stomach as he read the last few lines of the page. A man's life, whether he was black or white, seemed to count for naught in this godforsaken colony, he told himself. He would force himself to read more of this sickening litany in the hope it may throw up some answers to the many questions he had. But for the moment he must concentrate on the work in hand. Earlier that evening he recalled how he had taken a wrench and prized off the lid of another crate; it had contained several small birds. He thought of the Weltons' parlor and of the doctor's own collections of exotica. How strange, he mused, that such beautiful creatures could be born out of such an evil place. The more he read of it, the more terrifying it seemed to become.

Chapter 30

Sir Theodisius stood warming his great frame by a roaring fire, the tails of his frockcoat raised so that his rump was exposed to the heat to maximum effect. Poor Dr. Carruthers, seated in a nearby armchair, felt himself eclipsed and hardly benefitted at all from the blaze.

"Ah, Thomas, dear chap!" said the Oxford coroner as the doctor walked into the room.

"How good it is to see you again, sir," Thomas said. In all the chaos and confusion of the previous few days he had forgotten a prior engagement with him while he was in London. He extended his hand. Sir Theodisius tugged at it heartily.

"Carruthers, here, tells me that you have encountered a spot of unpleasantness lately with a Negro."

Thomas arched a brow at the understatement. "You could say that, sir," he replied.

"And yet you find time to administer to animals now!" continued Sir Theodisius.

Thomas knew that he must be alluding to his treatment of Cordelia Carfax's dog, but he was puzzled as to how the coroner knew. His query must have shown in his face.

"I called in on Carfax on my way here. Wondered if he was up for another game of golf. It really is quite addictive," he reported cheerfully. "Said he best stay with his wife, who had taken to her bed with a most cruel fit of the gripes."

"Mistress Carfax is ill?" replied Thomas.

Sir Theodisius continued: "Rolling 'round like a loose barrel, she is, so when I told him you were my next port of call, he asked me to send for you."

Thomas frowned. His thoughts immediately turned to the plight of Cordelia Carfax's wretched dog that had been so maliciously blinded.

"Her condition sounds serious," he said. "I shall go to her immediately."

Sir Theodisius seemed a little taken aback. "But what of our luncheon?" he protested.

"Regrettably it will have to wait," Thomas told him, with an urgency that would brook no argument. Grabbing his medical case, he headed for the door.

The coroner, feeling a little aggrieved, had been hoping to enjoy a chop and some porter with Thomas at the very least. But as if he could read his guest's mind, Dr. Carruthers stepped into the breach.

"Not to worry, Sir Theodisius," he piped up. He lifted his head and sniffed the air. The smell of baking had wafted in on the current as Thomas opened the door. "I suspect Mistress Finesilver has just taken a venison pie from the oven," he said. "You will join me for luncheon, sir?"

Thomas arrived at the Carfax mansion less than an hour later. He had no evidence. He was simply following his instinct, but he had the direst suspicion that Cordelia Carfax could have been poisoned by one of her slaves.

As his carriage drew up, he saw Roberts hammering a notice onto the wooden gatepost outside the house. Alighting by the railings, he peered at the poster. It read *Runaway slave, answers to the name of Cato. Tall, broad, collared and branded S.C. Ten-guinea reward. Any information within.*

Thomas immediately thought of the young man lying injured in his own home. He did not recognize him as one of the household slaves. This runaway, this Cato, was just another among the many who came to England and took advantage of the law to make a break for freedom. The newspapers and coffeehouses of London were full of such notices.

Mason the butler led Thomas into a large bedchamber on the second floor. Cordelia Carfax lay in bed, groaning, while her anxious husband sat at her side. As soon as he saw Thomas he heaved himself up from his chair.

"Ah, Silkstone! I am glad you are here," he cried, beckoning him over.

Approaching the bed, Thomas could see that Mistress Carfax looked listless and her copper hair was plastered across her forehead with sweat. The small dog that had been in such distress earlier lay sleeping on the counterpane. Phibbah, the slave girl, the one who had been so distraught the other night, busied herself with a bowl near a table.

"How long has your wife been like this?" asked Thomas, turning his face away from the bed, out of the woman's earshot.

Carfax deliberated. "She was seized with violent gripes and vomits last night after dinner," he said in a low voice.

"And I can see that her fever is somewhat hectic," said Thomas.

For a moment he studied the woman's face. Her cheeks were as pale as milk.

Addressing her directly Thomas leaned closer and said, "I am sorry to see you unwell, Mistress Carfax."

The woman turned her head and eyed the young doctor. Even in her suffering, it was clear that she regarded him with disdain.

"What is he doing here, Samuel?" she snapped at her husband.

Carfax smiled awkwardly. "Dr. Silkstone wishes to help you, my dearest," he replied, bending low.

"Is there anything that your wife ate last night that might not have agreed with her?" asked Thomas.

Pausing to recall, Carfax said there was not. "Stewed carp, breast of pheasant," he replied.

"May I examine your wife's abdomen, sir?" Thomas asked innocently, but the plantation owner looked at him aghast, as if he had asked if he could make love to her.

"I should think not, sir!" he shot back. "It is clear my wife is sick and it is your place to ease her distress."

Thomas had, of course, encountered such reactions before. He was not entirely surprised by such ignorance.

Carfax held Thomas's gaze. "Well?" he said, impatiently. "What is wrong with her, man?"

The doctor squared up to him. "Without an examination I cannot be entirely sure, Mr. Carfax," he began. He had no intention of sharing his suspicions with him at the present time. "At the moment her life is not in danger," continued Thomas. "I prescribe plenty of boiled water with a little sugar in it to restore her strength. I will call again tomorrow to check on her progress."

At the news Carfax seemed disappointed that nothing more could be done for his wife. His shoulders visibly drooped.

"Very well, Dr. Silkstone," he said curtly, adding: "Venus will show you out."

Fino, seeing Carfax turn to leave, jumped off the bed and also headed for the door, pawing at it. It was then, as he eyed the dog, that Thomas noticed it: a small clod of what appeared to be soil on the floorboards. At first he dismissed it as mud carried in on outdoors boots, but then he lifted his gaze. A small object, he could not make out what, had been placed above the door lintel. He thought it strange, but said nothing. In a household such as this, he knew it wise to keep one's own counsel.

Once more Venus appeared at the door to escort Thomas out. She seemed even more aloof than before, as if her mind were far away. Downstairs, he paused on the front threshold and glanced over at the gatepost where the notice flapped in the wind.

"I see a household slave has run away," he said. He was thinking out loud rather than questioning Venus, but his words clearly galled her and she fixed him with a fiery glare.

"There are plenty of free Negroes begging on the streets of London, who would gladly give up their freedom for a meal or a coat, Dr. Silkstone," she replied. "The slaves here may be in bondage but at least they have a roof over their heads."

Thomas had not anticipated a response, let alone one so spirited.

"And you, Venus," he fired back. "Are you free to leave this household if you please?"

She opened her mouth to reply, but words failed her. Instead her expression betrayed a mixture of anger and regret that seemed to be tugging at her mind and staying her tongue. She simply gestured to the front steps and the drive, where the carriage awaited.

That night Thomas retrieved John Perrick's letters from a folder in the laboratory and went to read them by the slave's bedside. There was something that had been bothering him all day: the soil on the floor in Cordelia Carfax's chamber. Searching through the copious sheets, he had eventually found what he was looking for: the doctor's account of the sinister beliefs of the slaves.

By candlelight in his new patient's room he read: *There is a strange force that seizes some of the Negroes here called Obeah. It is practiced like a religion and the priest, for want of a better word, is apt to lay curses by collecting certain items, such as cats' paws, hair, teeth, and grave dirt, all relative to this kind of witchcraft, and placing them in a bag near the intended victim.*

Thomas looked up from the text and rubbed his eyes. He thought of the mysterious object above the door lintel. He did not need to see into it to guess what it contained. What's more, he would wager a great deal as to the person who had placed it there.

He returned to Perrick's letters. Now only a few remained unread. Dated just three days before the young doctor was reported to have taken ill, Thomas began reading one. After greetings to his wife and his excitement at the thought of the return voyage, Perrick went on to relate more scientific information. Halfway down the second sheet he wrote: *There is a plant, known as Maroon Weed, that is a rank poison known to the slaves for being able to dispatch intended victims either slowly or quickly. I spoke with another physician, whose Negro woman had intended to kill him with it. He was seized with violent gripings, vomited profusely, and was subjected to fevers and even convulsions. Realizing himself to be the victim of a poison, he sought help from another man of medicine, who prescribed the kernels of nhandiroba to be infused in wine and drunk frequently. This cured him in time.*

Looking up from the script into the darkness of his room, it struck him as soundly as if he had been dealt a blow across his cheek. Suddenly he knew exactly what ailed Cordelia Carfax, and it was what he feared. Seized with bellyache, feverish and vomiting, she had ingested something poisonous and it was most certainly neither stewed carp nor pheasant.

Thomas read on. *Another acquaintance told me that some slaves administer poison to their masters by putting powder under their thumbnail, so putting their thumb upon the cup or bowl they pass to their victim, they cunningly convey the poison; wherefore, any Negro with a long thumbnail is to be distrusted.*

It was then that it struck him. He pictured Phibbah, the slave girl, holding Cordelia Carfax's bowl of vomit in both hands, and he recalled most vividly the length of the nail on her right thumb.

Chapter 31

First light found Thomas in his laboratory. He had identified some leaves from a plant Mr. Bartlett captioned *Fevillea cordifolia,* apparently a popular herbal remedy among the Negroes. Also known as antidote cocoon, a small amount, according to Dr. Perrick, opened up the body and produced an appetite, whereas a large dose induced both stools and vomit. Infused with wine, the ground seeds of the plant could be given as an antidote to various poisons. So he had pounded the kernels and steeped them in wine for two hours, before straining the liquid.

As he worked, he battled with his own conscience. There was no question in his mind that Mistress Carfax was being poisoned, in all probability by one of the household slaves, the same one, perhaps, who tried to blind the dog. Yet if he informed Carfax of his suspicions, there would be no chance of justice for the accused. He simply hoped that this formula worked quickly and that Cordelia Carfax would be fully restored in a day or two. He poured the reddish liquid into a bottle and braved the snow once more.

If, as he suspected, Mistress Carfax was being poisoned by Phibbah, then the girl must not be allowed anywhere near her mistress. Yet if he told Carfax, she would be beaten to within an inch of her life and, most probably, hanged for attempted murder. He found himself torn between natural justice and his duty. He only hoped that the matron had not worsened overnight.

Cordelia Carfax remained weak and feverish but her abdominal pains seemed to have lessened and she had held down a cup of sweetened water. Heartened to find his patient in less pain, Thomas offered Venus the bottle of physic and instructed it be given at regular intervals until she was better.

The slave girl, Phibbah, was, once again, in the room, mending the fire. He moved closer to her, just to make sure that his memory was not playing tricks on him. He saw her place the poker back in the stand and focused his attention on her hand. He had not been imagining her thumbnail. It was inordinately long compared with her other nails. He resolved to speak with Venus.

As soon as Phibbah left the room, he turned to the housekeeper. "I think it best that you take sole charge of your mistress's care," he told her.

Venus's flawless complexion suddenly wrinkled. "Sir?"

She would not make this any easier for him, he could see that. "It is important that she be given the correct dose of the physic and I believe you are best able to do that," Thomas told her earnestly. He was looking at her intently, watching for a flicker of understanding, before he added: "You are more capable than Phibbah. Do you understand?"

Venus nodded, but in such a way that Thomas remained unsure as to whether she had taken his meaning.

She returned an odd, inscrutable look. "I understand, Dr. Silkstone," she replied.

It was early afternoon when the carriage dropped Thomas back in Hollen Street, but already the shadows were lengthening and the northerly wind blew stiffly down the narrow street. He turned to ascend the front steps of his house. As he did so, however, he happened to glance up and saw two gentlemen, dressed in sombre clothes, standing on the opposite side of the street looking at him. As their eyes met, one of them stepped backward into the shelter of a wall. The other quickly followed. Thomas faltered for a second. Should he ignore them and go into his house or should he cross the street and address them?

He decided on the former course of action. His unpleasant encounters with hooligans and cutpurses in this great city had taught him to look out for his own safety on the streets. He would not tempt fate again.

Striding upstairs, he went immediately to check on his patient. Between them, he and Helen had managed to stretcher the injured Negro, still unconscious, into the second floor guest room, much to Mistress Finesilver's displeasure. The temperature in the room was only a little more agreeable than the landing. The blinds had been left up all day and a fearful draft blew through a gap in the ill-fitting window. Helen had lit a fire in the grate, but it had not been properly tended. Thomas suspected that Mistress Finesilver had instructed the maid to enter the room only on her orders, and, judging by her sour manner toward their guest, that would not be often.

Edging closer to the bed Thomas heard his patient breathing, the air rattling in his chest. He checked his pulse. It was remarkably strong, and the fever seemed to have disappeared, giving him cause to believe he may recover consciousness. He did not have to wait long. His ministering seemed to have alerted the young man who, just as soon as Thomas had turned to open his case, suddenly let out a low groan.

Whirling 'round the doctor saw his patient's unharmed eyelid slowly open. It swiveled in its socket, taking in its new surroundings. Then, after a few moments, the young man's mouth tightened, not in a smile but in a look of fear. Bending low, Thomas quickly tried to reassure him.

"Do not worry," he soothed. "You have been badly hurt, but I am a surgeon. My name is Dr. Silkstone."

Thomas saw the young man push his legs away from him, as if to ease the act of sighing, which came next in a long and painful breath.

"Doc-tor Silk-stone," repeated the young man. He spoke as if each syllable stabbed his tongue like a dagger, but Thomas also detected a glimmer of recognition; as if his name was already known to him.

The doctor drew up a chair and carefully unwound the bandage that swathed the slave's head wound. Reaching for a candle, he inspected it closely. It was deep, but it seemed to be scabbing over. He would let the yellow crust continue to develop. There was a school of thought that propounded that scabs should not be allowed to form and should be knocked off. However, he was of the opinion that scabbing was a necessary part of the healing process to be encouraged.

"You are doing well," he told his patient. But he had wasted his breath. The young man's eyes were again closed. He had lost consciousness once more.

Returning down the stairs, Thomas heard the bell ring and arrived in the hallway in time to see Mistress Finesilver open the door, an arctic blast flooding inside as she did so.

Two men stood on the front step; both were equally tall, but the older one had a concave face and a large nose, whereas the other was younger and generally more rounded. They each wore heavy dark coats with expressions on their faces that were every bit as funereal.

"May I help you gentlemen?" asked Thomas before Mistress Finesilver could launch into her usual tirade. Dr. Silkstone should not be disturbed after the hour of eight o'clock unless their business was of an extremely urgent nature, she would say, although she never couched her meaning so delicately.

The taller man stepped forward a pace, whipping off his hat despite the cold, to reveal a gray wig. His face was angular and the chill had rendered his complexion as mottled as a map, all red blotches and blue veins.

"Dr. Silkstone?" he asked, giving a shallow bow.

"I am he," acknowledged Thomas.

"We should like to speak with you on a matter of great import," he began. His demeanor was intense, almost grave, but not threatening.

The doctor gestured the strangers inside. "The study, please," he said, ushering them toward the door. "I am afraid there is no fire in our drawing room."

Thomas introduced Dr. Carruthers, who had been dozing by the hearth, and bade them sit.

"What is it that I can do for you gentlemen?" he asked, seating himself opposite them.

Again, the taller man spoke. "Let me introduce ourselves, sir. This is Mr. Clarkson and I am Granville Sharp."

"Sharp?" repeated the old anatomist.

The man shot a glance at Dr. Carruthers. "I am known to you, sir?"

Carruthers chuckled and shifted in his chair excitedly. "Your reputation as a champion of the oppressed precedes you, sir, and I am most honored to welcome you into my home." Turning to Thomas he explained: "This, young fellow, is the gentleman who sponsored the case of the slave I was telling you about."

"Jonathan Strong?" queried Thomas.

"The very same!" exclaimed Carruthers excitedly.

Thomas smiled broadly. "Then you are indeed most welcome, sirs," he reiterated. "But how can we help you?"

Sharp nodded and leaned forward in his seat, as if he were about to impart a secret. "We are but a small group of men that finds slavery in all its forms to be against the law of both god and nature. We are therefore committed to work for its abolition."

Thomas nodded sympathetically. "An admirable ideal, gentlemen," he said. "And one that has my full support." Yet there was a slight catch in his voice. "How does this concern me?"

Sharp's brows knitted into a frown. "Forgive me if you believe we are intruding into your affairs, sir," he began. "But we have reason to believe that you have recently given quarter to a"—he fumbled for the appropriate word—"stranger."

Thomas suddenly tensed as he wondered how they knew he was harboring a runaway slave. He felt his heart beat faster and his mouth go dry.

Seeing the young doctor's reaction, Sharp responded by raising his hands. "It is true, sir. I confess we have been surveying your movements."

"My movements?" queried Thomas, growing increasingly alarmed.

The younger man intervened. "There is an inn, sir, the Crown, where Negroes gather. Our Quaker friends distribute pamphlets there and try to help them. That is how we heard, sir, of your charity, at the Carfax household."

"We only followed you to affirm our purpose," Sharp tried to assure him.

"And what might this purpose be, sir?" asked Thomas, warily.

The older man, after taking a deep breath, continued. "If you have shown charity to an injured stranger, sir, then we commend you, but I am afraid we also come to warn you."

Thomas cocked his head. "To warn me?" he repeated. "Against what, pray?"

Sharp and Clarkson exchanged nervous glances.

"It is not our way to disguise the truth, Dr. Silkstone. We believe in speaking plainly," the latter pointed out.

Thomas nodded. "That is a quality I much appreciate," he replied.

Clarkson pushed his spectacles up the bridge of his small nose. "We are here," he continued, "because we have heard of your reputation for good works, sir; and believe that you champion the poor and the vulnerable."

The doctor gave a flat smile. "I do what I can."

Sharp took up the running. "We also believe, Dr. Silkstone, that you are caring for a slave who has run away by the name of Jeremiah Taylor."

"And if I am, sir?"

Sharp took a deep breath. "If you are, sir, I am afraid you must know that it is not an end to the matter."

In his fireside chair Dr. Carruthers grunted. "I feared as much," he muttered, shaking his head.

Thomas shot a look at his mentor. What was it he had said? He had known he was taking a risk by caring for a slave. He knew he had to accept any consequences.

"Gentlemen, I am a surgeon and a physician. If I care for a

man it is because it is my duty to do so, regardless of whether he is free or a slave, white or black," he told them.

The bespectacled man nodded sympathetically. "We do understand that, sir, and we admire your compassion," he began.

Thomas detected a caveat. "But?"

Sharp resumed his warning. "But we are here to tell you that the slave's master will want him back," he said in a way that needled the doctor.

Thomas felt the anger swelling in his chest and he broke in suddenly. "Then the slave's master will have to deal with me first," he replied.

Clarkson's features tightened. "That is what we fear, Dr. Silkstone. By protecting the slave you are putting yourself at risk."

Thomas nodded. "I am aware of that, gentlemen," he replied, suppressing his mounting sense of outrage. "But that man upstairs was left for dead. If I had not found him, he would be buried by now. What right does one man, whoever he is, have to own another?"

At these words, Dr. Carruthers clapped his hands together. "Bravo, young fellow!" he exclaimed.

Sharp wore the wearied look of a seasoned campaigner. "Your sentiments are, indeed, admirable, sir, but the slave's master is looking for him. There are posters, leaflets . . . There is even a reward." He reached into his leather bag and pulled out a handbill offering ten guineas for the safe return of a slave known as Jeremiah.

Thomas studied the leaflet. It described the runaway as almost six feet tall and wearing a dark blue coat. It matched the description of the young Negro upstairs. He flung the paper down on a nearby table in disgust.

"If his master comes calling I shall deny all knowledge of this person, gentlemen," he said.

Sharp gave a wry smile. "I admire your principled stand, Dr. Silkstone. I am thankful that all Englishmen are born free, but those who are merely brought here from the Colonies deserve our protection, too, and I am afraid they do not get it. That is why we are trying to spread the word among them in taverns and coffeehouses and the like."

"And you do a marvelous job!" interjected Dr. Carruthers.

Sharp shrugged. "Thank you, sir. That may be so, but what I am saying, Dr. Silkstone, is if you should need to fight this case in the courts, then please feel free to contact me." With these words he rose, walked over to Thomas, and held out his calling card.

Thomas rose, too, and took it. "Thank you, Mr. Sharp," he said, looking first at the card, then at his guest. He knew he would be a valuable ally if, or when, the young slave's master came calling.

Chapter 32

White snow was falling on the white man's land. It was a sign, as if a sign were needed, thought Cato, that this was a place where he did not belong. His Coromantee name was Cudjoe. He had been born on a ship bound for Jamaica, but his mother had died shortly after his birth and his father had committed suicide, jumping overboard at the first opportunity rather than submit to the whip. At first he had been gifted to a white mistress who was kind to him, but as he grew, he seemed to lose the charm he had held and other, younger boys, slipped into his buckled shoes. He had worked in the Carfax household for fifteen years and now he had run away. It was not a decision he had taken lightly. Yes, there had been the odd beating at the hands of Mr. Roberts, the occasional withdrawal of food, but in general, his treatment, certainly compared with that of his fellows on the sugar plantations that he'd heard and seen, was bearable.

No, the reason he had slipped out of the back door of his master's house one night with the intention of never returning was because he had a plan. Under cover of darkness he had made his way to the Crown Inn. A new life, a free life in Africa awaited him. That is what was promised them on the pieces of paper handed out at the inn. Tonight he would be freed from bondage and liberated, forever.

The African brother with the gold tooth ushered him into a back room where the obeah-man sat on his mat, a goatskin draped around his bony shoulders. The room was dimly lit and all manner of strange creatures leered out at them from shelves: a squirrel monkey, its teeth bared, and a small crocodile, its jaws agape. A strange scent lingered on the smoky air and made Cato feel a little light-headed, as if he had drunk a quart of rum.

It was only when he was seated cross-legged on the floor that he saw the obeah-man's face, like half-eaten offal chewed by hungry dogs. A sound ushered from the old man's mouth that made him cock his head closer so as to understand what he was saying. He felt as nervous as a fledgling waiting on a window ledge before it took the first leap into flight. He leaned forward, eagerly anticipating the old man's instructions.

"You want be free?" he asked.

Cato nodded.

"Then drink this." He lifted a skull that sat by him; it looked like a human skull, and it was full of liquid.

"Then what?" he asked, almost breathless in anticipation.

"Then you sleep and when you wake . . ." The obeah-man's voice trailed off, taking Cato with him to a land of languor and plenty.

"I shall be free?"

The old man's tone suddenly sharpened. "You will be on a ship bound for Africa and when you wake you will be a free man."

Questions flew into Cato's mind like starlings swirling in winter twilight.

"A free man," he echoed. He reached for the skull, but the obeah-man swatted his hand as if he were a troublesome fly. The slave knew why and he delved into the pocket of his breeches. Pulling out a shiny sixpence, he laid it in front of him. He had found it in the master's pocket when his topcoat was put out for the laundry earlier in the month and kept it safe, knowing it might mean his salvation one day. Today was that day.

" 'Tis all I could find," he said apologetically.

The old man took it, laid it in his palm that quivered like a leaf, and with the other hand lifted it to the side of his mouth where a few blackened teeth remained. Biting into it, he seemed satisfied, and gave a reassuring nod before pushing the skull into the centre of the ring.

"Drink tonight and tomorrow freedom," he said, slamming down his palm on his thigh.

He began to chant. Through toothless gums his words were hard to follow, but Cato repeated what he said, then, tilting his head back, drank from the skull. The liquid inside tasted bitter and he shook his head as if trying to rid himself of the flavor that lingered on his tongue. After a few moments, however, it did not taste so bad after all; quite pleasant in fact. He asked for more and the obeah-man obliged.

In fact, Cato drank so much that when the old man told him to rise and drink the contents of a phial that he was offered, he did that, too. He even whirled himself 'round and 'round at his bidding, spinning wildly until he collapsed to the ground, clutching his belly. Within the hour, he was still.

Chapter 33

When Phibbah came to check on Cordelia Carfax the following morning, she found her mistress had worsened. As she opened the shutters, the thinnest shard of light appeared to pierce the woman's brain as if it were a spear. Even the sound of Phibbah's tread on the wooden floorboards sent her reeling. A low moan rumbled from her lips and her hands clutched her head.

The slave girl hurried over to the tangle of sheets and blankets and looked at her mistress more closely. She sniffed the acidic tang, then saw the vomit staining the white linen. Instinctively she curled her lip in disgust and her mistress caught her expression as she turned onto her back. She seemed too weak even to upbraid her. Her hair was stuck to her skull, and her skin was the color of porridge. From the filmy dampness on her forehead, Phibbah knew that Mistress Carfax was in the grip of some terrible ague.

Hearing his wife's moans, Samuel Carfax strode into the bedroom to find the girl standing by the bed, looking anxious and wringing her hands.

"What is the meaning of this?" he yelled, raising his voice above the din.

Phibbah spun on her heel. "Oh, sir!" she exclaimed, her face now contorted with worry. "The missa is taken real bad."

Carfax paced over to the bed, his expression one of annoyance rather than concern. How she needed to be always the centre of attention! Her senseless moans ranked her alongside the hysterical female slaves in his mind. He would have no truck with them and yet. . . . Leaning forward, he saw his wife's head moving from left to right and glimpsed her milk-white face before it was eclipsed by a pillow. She did not look well at all. Quite the opposite. He reached for her hand.

"My dearest," he whispered, bending low. " 'Tis I. 'Tis Samuel. Can you hear me?"

She grunted in reply. It was a sound that bubbled from her throat. He caught a whiff of the rancid smell on her breath, saw the stained sheets, and he, too, curled his lip in disgust.

Straightening himself, he saw Phibbah cowering on the other side of the bed. "Get this cleaned up, will you?" he shouted, grabbing hold of a sheet and tugging at it disdainfully.

"I shall call Silkstone again, my dear. He will see you right," he told his wife. There was pity in his words, but not in his eyes. He shot a glance at Phibbah. "Did I not tell you to change the sheets?" he yelled.

The slave jumped to his command and sprang forward toward the bed. Just as she did so, her mistress began convulsing once more. Lifting her head off the pillow, her eyes wide, she called out then retched. A stream of blackish vomit shot from her mouth, cascading over the bed linen and over the floor. Phibbah rushed to her mistress with a bowl, but it was too late. Her head sank back onto the pillows and her eyes closed.

Carfax and the slave exchanged glances once more. There was a strange glint in the master's eye that Phibbah could not read. He glowered at her for a moment, before storming out of the room and onto the landing. He was about to descend the stairs when he saw Venus through the half-open door to his own bedchamber. She was casting her critical eye over the room, seeing that it had been cleaned thoroughly, as she always did. Surfaces needed to be clear, sills free of mildew, linen smooth. On hearing footsteps, she turned to see her master. He blustered in and slammed the door behind him. His anger was palpable, and at the sight of him the features on Venus's normally serene face tensed a little.

"What is the meaning of this?" he hissed at her. His fists were balled at his sides. His eyes sharpened on her, yet she remained calm; her expression was impassive. Such indifference riled him. Her insolence lay barely concealed. There was derision in her manner; he detected the scorn of a woman who knew she could command him with her own body, the curve of her breasts, the silkiness of her thighs.

She curtsied. "I do not know what you mean, sir," she replied, looking at him squarely.

Her wanton impudence only served to inflame his passion. "You know damn well, you whore!" he growled, bringing his hand back and slapping her hard on the cheek as if he were swatting a mosquito. She reeled with the force, taking two steps back, but she did not fall. Nor did she rub her coffee-colored cheek even though it burned as brightly as if a brand had seared it. Instead she looked at him, but remained silent.

Carfax shocked himself with the ferocity of his attack. For a moment he stood still, catching his breath, until he turned and pointed. "Your mistress lies ill next door, spewing her guts out, and I know 'tis your doing."

Venus shook her head and her usual composure began to crack. A look of incomprehension scudded across her face. "I no understand, sir," she replied.

Carfax strode toward her. She could smell his smell; leather and tobacco, but still she stood her ground.

"This is your sorcery. Your slave magic, is it not?" He lunged at her body and grabbed the top of her stomacher, pulling her close to him, so that she felt his spittle splatter her skin.

"No," she gasped. "I know nothing."

He looked at her for another moment, as if trying to search behind her eyes, delving into her mind. Another tug on her bodice brought her even closer to him. "If my wife dies, I shall see to it that you are hanged for her murder, you hear me?" His grip was like a vise that squeezed the breath out of her lungs and pulled her whole body toward him. Thrusting his mouth against hers, he began biting her lips, and when she parted them to cry out in pain, he bit her tongue, too, as if his hunger was driving him mad. His ferocity lasted only two or three seconds and he pulled away as quickly as he had lunged, his eyes suddenly wide with horror. Blood smeared Venus's face. With his forefinger he traced the slash of scarlet that streaked her cheek from her mouth toward her left ear. His touch was suddenly tender and his grasp loosened.

"I cannot have a suspicious death around my neck if I am to stand for Parliament," he said firmly. He eased his hold even more. "You understand?"

She nodded and he opened his clenched fist, letting her step backward. Wiping her face with the back of her hand, she juddered slightly as she saw the blood from her bitten lip.

"I am glad you do," he said, his tone suddenly softening. Straightening his waistcoat that had ridden up in his exertions, he nodded, as if he had just concluded a business transaction. "There must be no scandal," he repeated to himself as much as to Venus and he made for the door.

As soon as she was sure that the master had returned downstairs to his study, Venus picked up the hand mirror from the chest of drawers and inspected her lips. There was a purple slit on the bottom, which was slightly swollen. Licking her handkerchief, she dabbed the wound gently, wiping away a smear of blood. No one must know of her humiliation. A canker, she would say if anyone drew attention to it. The English climate did not suit her skin.

Her composure restored, she entered Mistress Carfax's bedroom. Phibbah was wrestling with a bundle of foul-smelling sheets. Remaining by the door, she surveyed the scene: Mistress Carfax covered in an eiderdown, barely able to move, the bowl of rancid liquid, Phibbah flustered and incompetent.

"Where is Patience?" she asked suddenly, making the girl jump.

Wheeling 'round toward the door, Phibbah, the bundled sheets now under one arm, registered surprise at Venus's presence. She sketched a curtsy. "Patience downstairs, missa," she replied quickly. "She sent me to clear up sick."

Venus nodded, seemingly satisfied with the girl's answer, but her gaze began to wander. Her eyes roamed the room, first to the fireplace, then to the dressing table, then to the floor. Phibbah, thinking she could resume her duties, took a few steps toward the door.

"Not so fast," said Venus, raising her hand coolly.

Phibbah frowned. Her mouth opened in silent protest, but she knew better than to question Venus.

"Where is it?" asked the housekeeper, keeping her voice low so as not to wake her mistress.

Phibbah shook her head. "Please?" She blinked nervously.

"Where is the obeah bag?" Venus's voice was as calm as a summer's day. "It has to be in here somewhere." Her eyes remained darting high and low. She glided over to the fireplace, where a sickly blaze spluttered. She ran her hand under the mantelshelf. With the poker she jabbed under the fire hood and up the chimney breast.

"It is in this room. I know it."

Phibbah's eyes betrayed her as they darted involuntarily to the lintel. Venus followed them and sashayed over to the door.

"No!" screamed Phibbah, but it was too late.

Venus reached up and felt the coarse fabric of the lumpy bag. Pulling it down, she fixed Phibbah with a knowing stare and held it triumphantly aloft.

The girl was squirming, like a maggot on a fishhook. She kept throwing glances over to the bed to see if her mistress stirred. Thankfully Cordelia Carfax seemed oblivious to the drama that was playing out in her bedroom.

"Please, Venus," begged Phibbah. "Give it to me." The girl lurched forward, trying to snatch the bag, but Venus, who was considerably taller, simply extended her arm and held it high above her head, out of her reach.

"So, what have we here?" Venus asked softly, when she had assured herself that the girl would not try and retrieve the bag. Loosening the drawstring, she delved inside. First she pulled out the ball of hair, followed by the pig's tail, then the nail clippings and the kersey band. The grave dirt was sticking to her own hands. Suddenly she lifted them, cupping them, her palms held upward. She shook her head as she looked up at Phibbah, then, in a sharp, lurching movement, grabbed the girl's right hand to inspect it. Grasping her thumb, she noted that the nail was exceptionally long, then scowling, she flung down the hand with such force that she almost broke the girl's wrist.

"You are very foolish," she chided her. "Why you want her dead?" She jerked a look over to the bed.

The slave's eyes glistened with reproach as she rubbed her injured hand. She began to snivel. "She kill my baby. She try to kill me."

A strange smile floated across Venus's cut lips. "You stupid girl," she told her softly. Her tone would have been the same had she been complimenting Phibbah on her stitching or her cleaning. It was steady, unhurried, patronizing. She shot her a quick look of disdain before drawing tight the strings around the bag's mouth. Then, cupping it in her hand, she flung it onto the fire and it flared into a cone of flame.

Phibbah screamed and ran toward the grate, but the hessian of the bag was well ablaze. She shot back at the bed, as if expecting to see her mistress writhing in agony as the imprint of her soul went up in flames. But there was no sound other than the hissing and fizzing of the bag as it was consumed by the fire in the hearth.

In the refuge of his own laboratory, Thomas sat staring into the dying embers of the fire. He was pondering on Sir Joseph Banks's disclosure about the purpose behind the mission to Jamaica. There was something that troubled him deeply about their last meeting, something that told him the great man was still holding back. He was convinced that somewhere in this tangle of secrecy and intrigue lay vital clues as to who may have killed the young artist.

He strode over to his desk and pulled out from a drawer a folio containing several of Matthew Bartlett's sketches and began leafing through them until he came to the drawing of the branched calalue. He walked over to the wall and tacked the sketch onto a wooden board that hung there. Taking a few paces back, he studied it. The tropical herb, with its long-stemmed, egg-shaped leaves, and small white flowers, looked innocuous enough, yet, in all probability, it would possess the same properties as its European relative, the deadly nightshade. It was beautiful, but lethal if taken in sufficient quantities. Yet Dr. Welton, from what he could glean from Sir Joseph, also had faith in its narcotic powers.

Glancing over to the bookshelf, he resolved to discover exactly what was known of the plant's power. He strode over to consult one of the many tomes, seeking out an ancient volume belonging to Dr. Carruthers that listed all known herbs and their properties. He soon found it and, blowing the grime from its cover, he leafed through its well-worn pages. He quickly came to the page with the heading *Solanum nigrum.* Yet, instead of answering his questions, the entry in the pharmacopeia only served to disturb him. With mounting unease he read: *Also known as Pretty Morel, an herb sacred to Hekate, one of the Titans, who holds the keys to the Underworld. Often associated with lunar magick or works related to death, and in witchcraft.*

Thomas slammed the book shut, sending clouds of dust billowing into the air. "Witchcraft," he murmured, his thoughts darting back to one of John Perrick's letters that had mentioned what he called a *"kind of witchcraft."* What was it called, he asked himself. Obeah. Yes, that was it. Obeah, a form of religion practiced by the Negroes.

Rushing over to his desk, he rifled through his drawers once more and pulled out the sheaf of Perrick's letters from a leather wallet. There remained only two or three that he had not read. He scanned one of them quickly, then another, until he came to the fourth page. Moving over to a lamp, his eyes widened as he read Perrick's words. *There are those whom slaves hold in high regard called obeah-men. They practice witchcraft or sorcery using narcotic potions, made with the juice of a herb (Calalue or species of* Solanum*). The ingestion of such potions will induce a trance or profound sleep that can last for several hours, depending on its strength. The guileful spectators are thus convinced that these priests possess the power to resurrect the dead.*

Thomas was trying to digest the significance of what he had just read when he heard the door open and a voice call his name.

"Thomas! Are you there?"

It was Dr. Carruthers. He waved his stick through the doorway to gauge its width before he came over the threshold.

Thomas leapt to his feet. He had completely forgotten the time and had been due to read the day's news from *The Gazeteer and New Daily Advertiser* to his mentor.

"Forgive me, sir. I was distracted," he said, Perrick's letter rustling in his hand.

"So you have been reading the notes and letters again," Dr. Carruthers said with a chuckle. "I am sure they are much more interesting than the usual obituaries." The fact that Thomas did not reply to this good-humored observation spoke volumes. "You have found something, dear boy?" he pressed.

Thomas looked grave. "Indeed I have, sir," he said solemnly.

"And you will share it with me." It was a statement rather than a question from Carruthers as he perched himself on a stool.

Thomas raked his hands through his hair and took a deep breath. "I believe I have uncovered the real reason behind the expedition to Jamaica, sir," he began.

The old anatomist raised an eyebrow. "Have you, by Jove?"

Walking over to his mentor, still clutching Perrick's letters, Thomas sat by him. "I have, sir, and it is a sinister one."

Carruthers leaned close to Thomas. "You have my undivided attention."

"As you know, Sir Joseph told me that the aim of the expedition was to investigate a plant with great medicinal properties."

"The branched calalue," butted in Carruthers. "An atropine, related to belladonna."

"Indeed," said Thomas. "I was told that Dr. Welton was investigating its narcotic properties. Yet according to what I have just read in Dr. Perrick's letter, African slaves consider it to have magical properties, too."

"Magical?" repeated the old anatomist.

"Their priests mix its juice with other herbs and when it is drunk during an elaborate ritual the victim dies shortly after—or so it seems. The following day, the dead body is brought before the crowd once more and, after more ritual and another dose of potion, he rises."

"Extraordinary," remarked Carruthers.

Thomas shook his head. "But there is more, sir. According to Dr. Perrick, not only does this seemingly give the power over life and death to the priest, or obeah-man, as he is called, but the victim never fully recovers. He becomes incapable of his own thoughts. He is rendered completely compliant to the will of the priest, or whoever gives him orders."

Thomas allowed his words to hang in the air for a moment, so that Carruthers could fully understand their implication.

The old anatomist was unusually silent at first, as he considered what he had just learned. "And such a power could be put to wider use," he said finally.

Thomas nodded. "There you have it, sir." He thought of the customs man, leading Matthew Bartlett away from the *Elizabeth*. "There might be those who are anxious to exploit this potion, or physic, call it what you will."

Carruthers shook his head in disbelief. What he had just been told was quite momentous. "Slaves would never again revolt against their masters," he ventured.

"Nor prisoners of war rebel against their captors," added Thomas.

"Whole armies could be recruited."

"And would never mutiny."

Both men were silent for the next few moments, pondering on the enormity of what they had just considered. The possibilities of such a powerful potion were limitless.

Dr. Carruthers broke the silence. "You believe Matthew Bartlett might have been killed for this formula? You think it was written in Welton's journal?"

Thomas thought of unscrupulous traders and even government agents who might use the formula to their advantage. "There are many who would wish to get their hands on it," he replied.

The old anatomist sighed deeply. "Do you think that Mr. Bartlett would have known of the journal's significance when he slipped it into his satchel?"

Thomas nodded. "I fear so," he said, adding: "And I believe someone else did, too."

Carruthers cocked his head, noting the timbre of his protégé's voice. He sensed he had an idea. "You have someone in mind?"

"The last time I was with Sir Joseph, he inadvertently mentioned a rift," replied Thomas, shuffling his papers.

"A rift? Between whom? Welton and Perrick? Welton and himself?" asked Carruthers brusquely.

"Or perhaps someone else?" replied Thomas, opening the wallet and returning the letters to it.

The thought had taken root in his head. Perhaps this rift, this disagreement, this dispute, could be at the heart of the matter. Perhaps whoever had cause to quarrel with Dr. Welton may have found cause to murder Matthew Bartlett for the journal and gain control over this powerful potion. It seemed a feasible hypothesis. The question was, who?

Chapter 34

It was Mistress Finesilver's custom to go to market on alternate weekdays and, it being the Wednesday before Christmas Day, she thought it the perfect opportunity to execute her plan. Accordingly, as soon as Helen had cleared the breakfast dishes from the doctors' table, she made ready.

The maid, stacking the plates at the sink, studied her mistress as she eased her chapped hands into her gloves. Jane Finesilver was always a nervy woman, yet that morning she seemed particularly on edge, shifting all about her and clucking.

"What are you staring at, girl?" she asked tetchily. Of course she knew very well. The maid was wondering why her mistress was wearing her blue cape with the fur trim that usually only came out for Sunday worship. "A woman of my standing has to look her best at all times," she snapped, as if arguing with some unseen challenger.

Helen said nothing but averted her gaze and returned to the eggy plates. Knowing her mistress as she did, there would be accusations of insolence or tardiness, or both, if she did not carry on with her duties efficiently.

"And besides," the housekeeper continued, "my other cape is growing shabby." She raised her eyes to the ceiling. "And on what those two gentlemen pay me, it'll be a good few years before I can afford another one."

Mistress Finesilver was clearly in no mood to brook arguments, or questions. At the end of her peevish speech, she gave an odd sort of grunt to show that she had said her piece, before picking up a pannier from the table.

"I may be a little longer than usual. I have many things to buy for the festivities," she told Helen. She paused for a second on the kitchen steps, as if mentally ticking off an imaginary list of tasks. "You can see to the goose while I'm gone. Pluck, dress, and stuff it," she added, glancing at the forlorn carcass hanging near the back door. Happy that the servant would be usefully engaged for the next two hours at least, she flounced up the remainder of the steps and out of the house.

Helen stayed at the sink for the next ten minutes, keen to dabble her hands in the water warmed by the copper. It was not until she turned 'round that she saw that the provisions list was still on the kitchen table. Wiping her damp hands on her apron, she peered at it, written in Mistress Finesilver's spidery hand. How annoyed would her mistress be when she discovered she had left her list? Helen could not read herself, but she did not have to. Even she could see that there were only five items written on the paper.

Out on the main street the snow did not seem to have dissuaded people from going about their daily business. A carriage clattered along the cobbles, the horses' shoed hooves swishing over the slushy roads. Errand boys skittered about, clutching packages tight to their bodies. A tailor and his assistant carried a bolt of cloth into a nearby house. All was normal. Life went on. And yet Jane Finesilver felt so different, as if all this was about to change. A seed of doubt sowed itself in her stomach. She paused and took out of her small purse a piece of paper on which was written an address: the George Coffee House in Chancery Lane.

She had come to the decision the previous night. The house was silent. The doctors and Helen were abed. The fire in the study was all but ashes and she was just making her final rounds, checking bolts and shutters, when her candle had illuminated a small leaflet of some sort that had been left on the table in the study. Her curiosity aroused, she walked over to it, bent down, and squinted at it. She read it once, then again, then rocked back with wide eyes and a sharp intake of breath. Pausing to consider what she had just gleaned from the flyer, she looked at it again, even more intently, as if memorizing its words. In her own room, a few minutes later, it was this memory that she committed to paper in the form of an address. And it was to this address that she now proceeded.

Sometimes her pace was assured, hurried even. At other times, she slowed, mulling over the consequences of her actions. She loitered outside a milliner's on the Strand and pictured herself wearing a new bonnet at Easter. She paid more attention to what fashionable women were wearing, even though admittedly not many had braved the elements that morning. The gold straw picture hat with blue silk and lace trim took her fancy. A large, handwritten card beside it drew attention to the fact that this was what the Queen of France, Marie Antoinette, would be wearing in the spring (she did not think to question how a London milliner would know), and blue was a popular color. How drab and dull she felt. She may have been widowed a good twenty years ago, but she still had womanly wants and needs. New fripperies, a fashionable titfer, surely this was not too much to ask for a woman of her station?

Taking a deep breath, she turned up Chancery Lane, looking out for the sign of the coffeehouse overhead. The narrow street was crowded with men in black, the lawyers and barristers who habituated this part of London, like nesting rooks. Some huddled in doorways out of the wind, others moved quickly, purposefully, their heads down and bodies bent.

A few more paces and the George loomed in front of her. She stopped abruptly outside the door and a man who had been walking behind her mistakenly barged into her left arm.

"Watch what you're doing!" he barked.

She jolted forward, her nerve momentarily rattled, but taking a deep breath, she composed herself and focused on the door once more.

Inside it was dark, but warm. The smoke from dozens of pipes filled the air, catching her throat, and the sickly smell of ale stung her nostrils. This was a man's world. It was no place for a woman like her. She felt men's eyes boring into her, like worms into an apple, as she walked toward the bar. They leered at her, jeered, made lewd remarks as she ran their gauntlet toward the bartender. Could they not see that she was a respectable woman? Did she not look clean and tidy? Was it not obvious that she was not of the streets? Perhaps her blue cape with its fur trim made her appear shabby. The thought of a reward strengthened her resolve.

"Good day, sir!" she called to the burly man behind the bar. Opening her bag once more, she brought out the piece of paper, unfolded it, and, holding it at arm's length, where her focus was best, she read what was written. "I am looking for a gentleman who has lost his slave," she told him.

The barman leered at her. He did not take her seriously.

"Have you, my word?" he mocked.

Unfazed, she continued. "I believe I will find him here," she said firmly, without appreciating his tone.

The barman flipped a cloth over his shoulder and lowered his elbow onto the counter, leaning forward confidentially. "Then you are in luck," he told her in a half whisper.

"I am?" replied Mistress Finesilver, half shocked, half relieved.

The man straightened himself. "You'll find Mr. Dalrymple over there," he said, pointing a fat finger into one of the dark recesses of the inn, on the other side of a roaring fire. "A gentleman with a red jacket."

Feeling a little more at ease, Mistress Finesilver jutted out her chin and pointed herself in the direction of the barman's gesture. It was easy to spot a man in a red jacket in among all the black. It was more plum-colored than red, she thought to herself, but she was relieved to find that its wearer had the appearance of a real gentleman, who obviously took great care with his dress. He sat in a corner, talking business with a rougher sort of man, he seemed to her, whose face was as pitted as a peach stone.

Mistress Finesilver cleared her throat. "Begging your pardon, sir," she said, giving a shallow curtsy. "Are you looking for a slave that has run away?"

Dalrymple looked up from his conversation and frowned. "Who wishes to know?"

The housekeeper felt suddenly very exposed, as if telling this stranger her name would be the same as opening her cape to him and showing him her bodice. She crossed her hands in front of her stomacher.

"I have information, sir," she told him. "About a slave."

Dalrymple inclined his head. "You do, eh?" he said, lifting a brow. "Then perhaps you would care to take a seat."

She saw him nudge the ruffian, who pulled out the chair next to him, and she sat down, smoothing her skirts self-consciously.

"Leave us, Rake," he barked at the pock-marked man, who duly obliged.

With her, the gentleman's tone was soft. He lifted his lips into a smile. "So you know where my slave is, do you, mistress?"

The housekeeper nodded and slid a coquettish look toward her inquisitor. "That I do, sir, if he wears a midnight blue coat with silver brocade."

Dalrymple smirked and leaned back in his chair.

"That sounds like Jeremiah," he said, eyeing her thoughtfully as he pushed his tongue into the side of his cheek so that his face bulged for a moment. The sight of it made the housekeeper feel even more uncomfortable. He leaned forward quickly.

"So where might this black knave be?"

Mistress Finesilver caught a whiff of rum on his breath as he came closer and drew back a little. "He is at my master's house, sir," she replied, still holding her cards close to her chest.

A look of exasperation scudded across the gentleman's smooth face. "Do we really need to play games, mistress? You are obviously a woman of some accomplishments."

Mistress Finesilver was not used to such flattery. Young Dr. Silkstone sometimes complimented her on her cooking, but by and large she felt her efforts went unappreciated.

" 'Tis not right that I should be asked to wait on him hand and foot while he lies in his sickbed."

"So the slave is unwell?"

"Beaten up he was. Not that I know aught about it. But he

will soon be well enough to walk and that's why I came. He needs to be back with his master."

"How very right you are, Mistress . . ."

She felt easier in his company now. This gentleman would be a man of his word, she told herself.

"Mistress Finesilver, sir," she volunteered.

"And the house?" he pressed.

"In Hollen Street. Number thirty-four," she told him, adding: "The home of Doctors Carruthers and Silkstone."

"Silkstone, eh?" he echoed, as if the name were familiar to him. "I am most grateful to you, Mistress Finesilver."

"And is now the time for you to show that gratitude, sir?" she asked, suddenly feeling emboldened. "Your advertisement said that you are offering a reward of ten guineas."

"Of course," said the gentleman, delving into his pocket and bringing out his purse. He shook it and five coins rolled out and spun on the table. She watched them dizzy around and drop, as if mesmerized by them, before she shot him a puzzled look when she realized how many guineas there were.

"This is but half," she said indignantly. She could not hide the contempt in her voice.

"And the rest when he is captured, dear lady," assured the gentleman.

Mistress Finesilver tried to stifle the sigh she felt bursting in her chest. Her new hat would have to wait a little while longer.

"When I have my slave firmly back in chains, mistress, then you shall have your money. And not before."

Chapter 35

The ax cut hard and clean and Richard let out a squeal of delight as the sturdy log was severed from its trunk with a dead thud. Nicholas Lupton, his face red from exertion and his eyes streaming with the cold, wiped away tears with the back of his gloved hand. The child flapped his arms, dancing around the fallen oak branch. Lupton's gaze followed him and he chuckled.

"Come, help me lift this onto the sleigh," he instructed.

Since the excursion onto the frozen lake two weeks ago, the boy had been Lupton's regular companion. Despite, or perhaps because of, another heavy fall of snow, the young earl had insisted on accompanying the estate manager on his rounds. Naturally this had caused problems. In some places the drifts came up to the child's head and he took cold very quickly, so Lovelock, the groom, and the ploughman had rigged up a contraption that enabled the sleigh to be dragged along behind a horse. Snuggled beneath a cover of fox fur, the boy had relished being a passenger in his very own winter carriage and was frequently heard laughing as the sleigh rounded a corner or bridged a bump on the track.

Lydia had registered her initial concern, fretting that Richard's arm was still delicate, or that his vulnerable chest might become weaker still in the freezing cold. Such objections were, however, quickly overcome. Mr. Lupton, ever jovial and energetic, joined in with his young master's enthusiasm. The suggestion to foray into the woods for the yule log that Christmas Eve had come from him. It was a long-held tradition in the region that each household should burn a special log in the hearth on the eve before Christmas Day. Some said it would ensure the luck of the house from one year to the next, others that it offered protection against witchcraft. Whatever the reason for such a custom, the suggestion was met with unbridled glee from the boy. Lydia had no choice but to agree.

Once the log was secure and his young passenger was tucked safely on the sleigh, Lupton mounted his horse and they set off back to the hall. It was a twenty-minute journey and he took it upon himself to teach Richard the words and tune to another, very appropriate, carol.

"The holly and the ivy," he began, and the boy followed suit, learning quickly, so that by the time the horse and sleigh came to a halt in front of the house, the two of them were singing in unison.

Lydia had been watching for them at the drawing room window and ventured onto the steps to greet them.

"Mamma, we have the yule log," yelled Richard breathlessly, scrambling off the sleigh and pointing at the large slice of oak branch. Jacob Lovelock and his son Will appeared to carry the log inside.

"It is very fine," remarked Lydia as the child ran up to her.

Lupton was smiling at Lydia as he approached up the steps. It was the smile of an equal and it unsettled her a little. "Shall the men put the log on the fire now," he asked, adding a moment later than he should have, "your ladyship?"

Nodding, she lifted the corners of her mouth in a careful smile. Her eyes must not stay on his face a moment longer than was seemly, she told herself.

Switching her attention to Richard, she said: "Come, you must get warm." She then took him by the hand and led him toward the door.

Boots and coats were soon jettisoned and Lupton was asked to join mother and son a few minutes later in the drawing room around the hearth. The large fire basket was laid with kindling and the yule log was placed ceremoniously at its centre.

For the past week the household had been in a flurry of activity. Every room, even in the servants' quarters, was decorated with holly and ivy. Swathes of dark green leaves were festooned across the mantelpiece and blood-red berries blazed out from arrangements on tables and sills. There were more candles than usual, too, ranged high and low on every available surface.

"Would you do us the honor, Mr. Lupton?" asked Lydia, holding out a box containing a shard from last year's log. She had preserved it according to custom. Striking a flint, the estate manager lit a spill and held it to the burned wood. The flame licked at it until it took hold and Richard let out a whoop of excitement as the blazing shard was laid upon the log. Lupton performed his duty with great merriment, even reciting a ditty before he lit the kindling.

"With last year's brand, I spark the new block, and ask that sweet luck may light our way," he declared.

As he said the words, he shot Lydia a look so joyful and so full of hope that her heart leapt in her chest. She felt herself wanting to take his hands and dance around the room with him. Had they been alone, she may well have been that rash. As it was, Richard was the one to reach up and clasp her waist, demanding to hug her. She bent low and took his hands in hers.

"Hot chocolate!" she cried. "Let us have hot chocolate."

Her suggestion was greeted with mirthful cheers and, without thinking, Lupton reached out and pulled the bell cord by the fireplace. The sudden tinkling cut through the laughter like a knife. Both Lydia and Lupton froze in the moment as they realized what he had done.

"Forgive me," he said, shaking his head as if waking from a dream. "I forgot myself."

Embarrassed, Lydia smiled and looked away from the hearth. Her face was tingling and she brushed her hand against her own cheek, feeling the heat rise from her skin. She was not sure whether it was the fire's glow or her own discomfiture that caused her to blush.

"Think nothing of it, Mr. Lupton," she replied, turning her attention to Richard. She fussed about the boy, exaggerating her gestures in a show of enforced mirth, which only served to fuel the unease. The awkwardness persisted, so that when Hannah appeared, she could sense a certain tension hanging in the air.

Lydia let out a little laugh. "Three cups of hot chocolate, if you please," she blurted as soon as she saw the maid. Hannah curtsied and was heading for the door, when, remembering some previously forgotten question, she turned.

"Begging pardon, your ladyship," she began. "But Mistress Firebrace would be obliged to know if you be requiring a bough of mistletoe hanging in the hall?"

Lupton and Lydia exchanged glances. It was as if they both pictured amorous lovers stealing a kiss under its green clusters. Every kiss beneath meant a pearly berry fresh plucked from its curved leaves.

Lydia turned to the maid. "No, Hannah," she said emphatically. "There will be no mistletoe this year."

Chapter 36

Thomas found Jeremiah Taylor sitting up in bed that morning when he came to check on his dressings. Helen had already plumped his pillows and crumbs were all that remained on a plate on the bedside table. His patient even managed to curl one corner of his mouth into a smile.

"You seem in better spirits today, Jeremiah," remarked the doctor as he carefully unfurled the bandage about the slave's head.

The attempted smile soon vanished.

"Sir, you know my name?"

Thomas thought of Messrs. Sharp and Clarkson and the handbill advertising a reward for his capture.

"It matters not," he shrugged.

Once more Thomas examined the area around the socket and saw that it was scabbing over well. The swelling seemed to have lessened and the eye was slightly open. "Your wound is making good progress," he said after a moment.

Yet the news did not seem to please the slave. His shoulders slumped, and he let out a small sigh. "Does that mean I will have to leave soon, Dr. Silkstone?" he asked. There was a note of resignation in his voice.

Thomas stepped back to study his patient. He looked so vulnerable, lying on the bed, still too weak to walk. The visit from the two campaigners the previous evening had left an indelible impression on him. How easy it would be, he thought to himself, for Jeremiah's owner to come bursting in and snatch him, dragging him off down the stairs and into a waiting carriage. What was even more outrageous in his mind was the thought that the law of the land would sanction such violence. In England a slave was mere chattel, a piece of property to be used and abused as the owner saw fit.

"You are welcome here for as long as it takes to see you restored to your former self," reiterated Thomas, patting Jeremiah gently on the shoulder.

His patient looked up at him with a doleful expression. "And what then, sir? I go back to my massa? He will be looking for me."

Thomas frowned. "Surely you do not wish to return to the man who almost killed you?"

The slave's swollen face could make no show of emotion, but his voice became urgent. "My massa did not do this!" he said almost indignantly, pointing to his head.

Thomas was puzzled. "Then who . . . ?"

"I do not know who," said Jeremiah.

Thomas seated himself on the chair beside the bed. He realized he had broken his own rule; he should never assume anything. Anxious to know more, he asked, "Can you remember what happened?"

The slave silently composed his thoughts, as if searching for memories inside the recesses of his battered brain. "My massa had business with Mr. Carfax."

"Samuel Carfax?" Thomas shot forward, frowning.

"Yes, sir."

Thomas did not comment further, but wondered if the connection was a coincidence. "Carry on," he urged.

"He sent me downstairs to wait for him in the kitchen. But a man, he was mean, he told me to wait in another place." Thomas instantly thought of Roberts. "He locked me in a room and then a man and a woman come and they—" He broke off, his gaze lowering.

"What happened?" pressed Thomas.

"They talk."

"What did they say?"

"She say he should not come, but he say they have business."

"What sort of business?"

"She say she will have another fine Coromantee for him soon."

"A slave?" Thomas struggled to understand what he was being told.

"A fine one, she say."

"And then . . . ?"

"Then he had her against the wall and a boot fell from the shelf and then they saw me."

"And it was then that he hit you?"

"Yes."

"With what?"

"A stick for golf?"

Thomas's eyes widened. "That would certainly explain the seriousness of your injury," he said. "Can you describe the woman?"

"It was dark. I no see well."

"The man?"

"He big, tall, and . . ." The slave paused, reliving the moment he had seen his attacker in silhouette.

"Yes?"

"His nose was squashed, like a fighter's."

"A broken nose," said Thomas incredulously. "Are you sure?"

"Yes, sir, I see'd him side on afore I ran out the door."

Thomas took a deep breath, marshalling his thoughts. He knew exactly where he needed to go next.

Thomas arrived at the late Dr. Welton's townhouse to find a carriage waiting in the snow-banked street. One footman was helping Mistress Welton inside, while another was assisting the driver to load boxes and chests. Mistress Perrick, dressed in a hooded woolen cloak, stood on the doorstep instructing her housekeeper. She turned when she heard footsteps.

"Forgive me, Mistress Perrick," Thomas greeted her, bowing and removing his tricorn. "I wondered if we might speak?"

The young widow's eyes shot sideways toward the waiting carriage.

"This is a most inconvenient time, Dr. Silkstone," she said. "My mother and I are about to leave town for a few days."

Thomas nodded sympathetically. "So I see, and I apologize for the intrusion, but I come on a matter of the utmost import."

She gave a barely discernible sigh and nodded.

"Very well, but please be quick," she said, leading him over the threshold. "So how can I be of assistance, sir?" she asked him curtly, as soon as they entered the upstairs drawing room.

Her mien seemed completely changed from their previous encounters. Gone were the dark shadows of grief that circled her eyes and her complexion was blooming, even though she still wore her mourning clothes. She gave no invitation for Thomas to sit.

"I have found your letters invaluable, Mistress Perrick," Thomas began.

She frowned. "Is that what you have come to tell me, sir? Could your thanks not have been committed to paper and sent to me?"

Thomas felt chastised. He knew he had to be brief. He came to the point. "I have recently spoken with Sir Joseph Banks," he continued. "He told me about some sort of rift during the planning stages of the expedition."

She shot an angry look at him. "Why should that concern you, Dr. Silkstone?"

He had not wanted to, but Thomas knew he would have to break the news of Matthew Bartlett's murder to her. "I am afraid, Mistress Perrick, that it concerns me because Mr. Bartlett has been found."

She pulled back. "Found? What do you mean, found?"

Thomas looked grave. "I fear he was murdered."

"Murdered!" The word escaped her mouth in a cry. "No! Who . . . ? Why?" She paced across the room to the window and looked out at the waiting carriage.

Thomas did not follow her. "I believe he was killed for your father's journal," he told her. "I am convinced it contains information that could be dangerous in the wrong hands. That is why it is important I know everything if I am to uncover those behind the murder," he pleaded.

Thomas could see the young widow's shoulders rise as she took a deep breath, then slump before she turned from the window to face him.

"Then I think you should know, Dr. Silkstone, that my husband was not originally chosen for the Jamaican expedition."

"No?" This was, indeed, a revelation to Thomas.

"My father asked him just two months before he was due to sail."

"Why might that have been?"

She took another deep breath and her whole body seemed to judder. "There was another doctor who had been nominated by the Royal Society to go with him, but my father was deeply unhappy; so much so that he refused to work with him."

Thomas's expression registered surprise. "And do you know the name of this other doctor, madam?"

She frowned and looked about her as if searching for inspiration. "I believe it was Blizzard or . . ."

"Izzard?" suggested Thomas.

"Izzard! You are right!" she said. She pivoted 'round, her eyes wide. "You know him, Dr. Silkstone?"

Thomas was shocked. He had his suspicions concerning Izzard. He very much wanted to know how he obtained so many uncorrupted Negro corpses for dissection and had intended to probe him at some point. Now he would be asking him about Matthew Bartlett's murder. Thomas's mind flashed back to the operating theatre and the Negro woman's corpse. The memory of his public humiliation by the surgeon when he forced him to make the first cut still rankled.

"Indeed I do," nodded Thomas. He did not elaborate. "Do you know why your father refused to work with Mr. Izzard?"

She shook her blond head. "All I know is that my husband filled his place at short notice." Suddenly her voice cracked, and she produced a handkerchief to dab her eyes.

Thomas moved nearer. "I am most grateful to you, Mistress Perrick," he said. "What you have just told me could prove very helpful."

She nodded and he could see her eyes grow glassy once more. "If that is so, then I am glad, Dr. Silkstone," she told him, adding: "As I said before, I do not want my husband to have died in vain."

He wanted to tell her that it was also his great wish that her husband's work and that of the expedition was not entirely lost, and that without Dr. Welton's journal the whole mission might be a wasted endeavor, but he did not. Instead he bade her a good journey.

"You said you are leaving for the country?" he said, as she made for the door.

She turned back. "Yes, we have a modest house," she replied.

"In West Wycombe?" ventured Thomas.

For a moment Mistress Perrick looked shocked, until Thomas threw a look over to where the painting of the golden ball hung in its gilded frame.

"Yes, West Wycombe," she replied. "You know it?"

Thomas gave a wry smile. "I have passed many hours there," he said vaguely.

She did not press him further. She appeared in too much of a hurry and with a nod she led Thomas into the hallway. It was clear from her reaction she wished the place mentioned no more.

Chapter 37

The operating theatre at the Brewer Street School of Anatomy was packed full of students, all eager to see Mr. Hubert Izzard perform an autopsy. Banked in rows that looked down upon a dissecting table at the centre, they were given an excellent view of the spectacle about to unfold before their eyes. Since Thomas's unpleasant encounter with the surgeon, Izzard's fame had spread. He was the anatomist who could provide his pupils not just with arms or legs, not just with moldy, putrefied corpses, but with whole, entire, newly dead cadavers, their flesh so fresh it was barely cold to the touch. What was more, their supply seemed regular; not one a month, which by any standards would have been considered excellent, but one a week. No one queried this frequency. Nor the fact that all the dead were Negroes. No one, that is, except Thomas.

Sitting anonymously, surrounded by men only a few years younger than he, he blended in well with the audience that now waited in hushed awe as Hubert Izzard held his scalpel poised over another young Negro.

"A fine Coromantee," he pronounced.

Thomas felt his heart miss a beat. Were those not the exact words used by Jeremiah's mystery woman? The man who beat him with a golf club was, he said, big and tall and with a flat nose. Any doubt that Thomas may have held dissipated. He watched the anatomist make the first cut and bile rose in his throat. He was not only looking at a man implicated in

Matthew Bartlett's murder, but also, it seemed, in the commissioning of slaves' corpses to order.

In a theatrical style, and wearing a flamboyant yellow frock-coat, Izzard incised with panache. He flourished his knife as if it were a conductor's baton and seemed to take a macabre delight in his work, cutting off digits and distributing them among his stunned audience. No respect was shown for the dead and indeed, it appeared to Thomas, very little deference to the anatomist's profession, reducing it to that of a showman or a mountebank.

As he watched this gruesome sideshow, he was reminded of Dr. Carruthers's experiences in the sugar islands all those years ago. Although he never said much, Thomas assumed they involved the ill treatment of slaves. He knew from both Dr. Carruthers and from Dr. Perrick's letters that many physicians condoned the barbarous trade, meeting ships at port after the gruelling Middle Passage and selecting the fittest slaves to work in the cane fields. Many of the Africans would be half-dead after the privations of the voyage; the same number would have died already. Some surgeons were even known to conduct experiments on hapless Negroes, with no thought for their suffering, in the name of medicine.

At the end of his macabre charade, Izzard took a bow and his grateful students applauded him. As his assistants disposed of the corpse and the theatre gradually emptied, Thomas stayed behind. He watched until the surgeon had sloughed his hands of the bloody detritus of a dissection, the water in the large bowl turning red, before he stepped down from the rows of seats.

"Mr. Izzard," he called.

The surgeon looked up smiling, expecting to be accosted by an intense student eager to heap adulation on him. Instead the sight of Thomas wiped the grin from his face.

"Silkstone," he grunted, drying his hands on a cloth. "It is gratifying that you think I can teach you more."

Thomas nodded and smiled. "Yes, and I am hoping you can enlighten me even further, sir," he began.

Izzard puffed out his chest, allowing himself to be flattered.

"I will do what I can to help you," he replied, flinging the wet towel on the table.

The beadle was scooping up the corpse's entrails into a bucket a few feet away.

"Perhaps we could go somewhere private," suggested Thomas.

"My office?" Izzard flapped a still-damp hand toward a door on the other side of the operating theatre.

The room was large and low-ceilinged and formed part of the building's attic. Its walls were lined with display cases crammed full of exotic specimens: the skeletons of small mammals, reptiles, and shells.

Thomas surveyed them from his seat, letting his gaze travel around the shelves. "You have some impressive souvenirs, sir," he began. "That conch shell is from Jamaica, if I'm not mistaken. You spent time on the island, I believe, sir."

Izzard looked at him quizzically. "How did you know I was there, Silkstone?" he asked.

"Dr. Carruthers sends his regards," Thomas said, with a wry smile.

Izzard subconsciously stroked his flattened nose and, unsure of the young doctor's motive, grunted. "That was a while ago now," he conceded, his gaze scanning his collection.

"You obviously look back at your sojourn with fondness," said Thomas.

A self-satisfied grin planted itself on Izzard's face. He leaned back in his chair. "Indeed I do, Dr. Silkstone."

"So much so that you wanted to return there, I believe?" asked Thomas.

Izzard bridled at the suggestion. His head jerked up and he fixed Thomas with a glower. "What is this about, Silkstone? Why are you here?"

The doctor cut to the chase. "I am here, sir, because I have some questions about the Royal Society's recent expedition to the island."

Izzard puckered his mouth. "What of it?"

"I believe you were originally selected to accompany Dr. Welton, but that he objected to you joining him. May I ask you on what grounds?"

The surgeon's features suddenly gathered themselves into a scowl.

"Who told you that?" he snapped. Thomas remained silent, allowing Izzard to simmer. "I am not sure what you are insinuating, Silkstone, but I do not like your tone."

Thomas knew it would be difficult to tease out information from this arrogant man without confronting him directly. He decided to tread more warily.

"I did not mean to offend, sir, but the expedition's last remaining member has been found murdered, and I am sure you understand that questions must be asked of all those with any connection to the venture."

Izzard eyed Thomas for a moment. "And you have taken it upon yourself to ask them?" Thomas felt his tone was patronizing.

"I feel it my duty, sir," he replied. "I am cataloguing the collections and am therefore deeply involved in the whole affair."

"The murder is the talk of the clubs and salons, Silkstone," Izzard conceded. "If it gets out that 'twas I who was originally nominated to go, there will be even more, and of a slanderous nature."

"So you will answer my questions?"

Izzard shook his head and his lips flickered into a smile, but his eyes remained cold. "Come, come, Silkstone. We are men of science. Let us speak frankly. Perhaps it is you who can tell me what you know?"

Thomas sensed that a trap was being laid. He would be cautious. "I know that there seems to have been a disagreement between you and Dr. Welton over the nature of your mission."

Izzard cleared his throat and arched his brow. "You have been speaking with Sir Joseph?"

Thomas nodded. "I have, sir."

"Then you know that our brief was to bring back the formula for a most potent physic that appeared to give its administrator the power over life and death." He gave a wry smile.

"There were certain admirals and generals in whose hands such a weapon could prove most advantageous."

"And you objected to this?" Thomas did not understand where Izzard was taking him.

The tall man slapped the desk. "Good god, no, Silkstone! I am a patriot. Not a traitor. I could understand that if word got out of this there would be some lily-livered Whigs who might object. John Wilkes would have a rant and protest that such a potion could enslave all our enemies. Well, in my book, sir, that would be an excellent thing." His face was reddening with excitement. "To me, you Americans will always be disobedient colonists, sir," he cried, adding: "And I'd like nothing more than to see George Washington in chains!" His eyes widened at the prospect.

Ignoring the jibes, Thomas remained confused. "So why, if you backed the mission whole-heartedly, did Dr. Welton replace you?" he pressed.

"Petty jealousy? A clash of personalities? Your guess, Silkstone, is as good as mine. All I know is that my chances of membership in the Royal Society have greatly diminished and that I've lost a fortune in fees." He coughed out the words in exasperation.

That, thought Thomas, would explain why the anatomist had embarked on another route to his own aggrandizement; building up his reputation among both peers and students and being rewarded with packed audiences who paid handsomely for the privilege of watching him perform dissections.

"So you attract students with a plentiful supply of the most magnificent corpses to make ends meet." Thomas's suggestion clearly rankled.

For a moment Izzard seemed wounded. "Good god, Silkstone, they're Negroes!" he barked.

Thomas nodded and, thinking of the damning words of Dr. Carruthers, held his nerve. "Yes, and judging from your behavior, you regard them as barely human," he said.

Izzard shot back. "How else is mankind to progress unless we push the boundaries of medicine?"

"I agree," conceded Thomas, then leaning forward, he added: "But do you not find it strange that when men are paid handsomely to rob graves for scarce corpses, there is suddenly such a copious supply of dead Negroes?"

Izzard slammed his fist down on the desk. "God's wounds, Silkstone. You sound like one of those benighted Quakers, intent on abolishing the trade. These Africans are goods, commodities to be used and traded and, yes, experimented upon, if you will. That's how I see them and I am most certainly not alone in my views."

"But Dr. Welton did not agree with your stance?" asked Thomas, wondering if the men's personalities were at the root of the quarrel.

"Welton was a sentimental fool. He thought Negro lives were worth saving!" thundered Izzard.

"So that is how you justify dissecting such perfect corpses?"

Izzard narrowed his eyes and leaned closer toward Thomas. "My sin, if I have one, Silkstone, is one of omission."

Thomas nodded in agreement. "You do not bother to ask how your specimens have died. You just take delivery of them." He did little to hide the contempt he felt.

Izzard bobbed his head. "Precisely."

"And you see nothing wrong in that?"

"Come, come, Silkstone. Name me a white man charged with the murder of a Negro!"

His challenge was greeted with silence. Thomas knew that a slave's life was of little consequence to him except in monetary terms. He could not give him an answer—he knew there had been no such prosecutions—and his silence brought their interview to an end.

Rising from his desk, Izzard told him: "If that is all, then I would ask that you leave my office, now, Silkstone. As it is I have said too much, especially to you as a former enemy of the Crown."

Thomas could see that he had touched a raw nerve, but he had barely begun his questioning. Yet he had little choice but to do as he was bidden.

"As you wish, sir," he conceded.

As he headed for the door, Thomas turned. "Am I right in thinking you know Samuel Carfax?"

Izzard frowned. "Yes. What of it?"

"And his wife, Cordelia?"

Thomas saw the anatomist's face twitch and redden. After a moment he said, "I am acquainted with Mistress Carfax and her husband, socially, but I do not see that it is any of your business."

Thomas remained calm. "I was hoping we gentlemen might all be able to play a round of golf sometime soon," he said. "I have it on good authority that you are most proficient at wielding a club, sir."

Izzard's eyes widened, but he kept his own counsel. He did not wish to incriminate himself, so instead he managed to nod his head. There was no need for Thomas to stay any longer.

Chapter 38

Silently Phibbah slipped out of the house unseen. It was not difficult. The white servants were either helping Mistress Bradshaw prepare the Christmas feast or adding fresh-cut branches of holly to the displays of greenery. There was a general liveliness and gaiety in the household. Perhaps it was because the mistress lay in her sickbed, still stricken and unable to control and shout and order. Although she was no longer dosing her, the missa remained held in the poison's sway. Even Mr. Roberts was mellow that evening. He had broken open a cask of ale in the cellar and was helping himself when he thought no one was looking.

There were rumors among the servants, of course. There always were. Belowstairs was a melting pot of gossip and insinuation, seasoned with liberal helpings of disloyalty. That American doctor had looked grave, they said. He had shaken his head. Someone even mentioned poison. Someone even mentioned obeah. But Mr. Carfax had instructed Mason to proceed with the dinner as usual. Everything had to run smoothly, even if, under the surface, a storm was brewing.

Out on the street, the darkness wrapped around Phibbah like a quilt. It protected her from being recognized, or called to question. Once more her shawl was her disguise as she teetered on borrowed pattens through the slushy streets.

"Nine o'clock on Christmas Eve!" called the watchman as the church bells struck.

The main streets were almost deserted. All the shopkeepers had long put up their shutters. There were bands of apprentices who'd been let out for the evening. Some linked arms and sang songs as they meandered drunkenly along. Phibbah avoided their sort, walking in the shadows, even though the mud on the road sucked at her feet.

Moments later she found herself once more at the Crown. Through the fog of smoke from dozens of pipes, she saw a few heads turn when she walked in. At least she was among her own kind now. They would not spit at her as she passed. She could lift her gaze and look them in the eye without fear of being whipped for effrontery.

There was the man with the brightly colored bird again and the man with the ship on his head. A smile found its way onto Phibbah's lips, but there was something amiss. There was no music. Not much laughter. There was a low hum of conversation, but many of the patrons were clustered around two white men, who sat on settles. She had never seen white men at the inn before. How did they get here? Who let them in? Now she found herself feeling affronted. What right did these whites have to enter the black man's domain? She drew closer for a better look. Her Negro brothers seemed to be listening intently as the older man, the cheeks of his thin face sucked in, spoke to them. Now and again he raised his finger and pointed at a leaflet he held in his spindly hand. His companion, much younger than he and with hair as red as rusting iron, was nodding enthusiastically. They did not appear to be threatening, but talked in soft, low voices.

Phibbah turned to Goldtooth. He had been eyeing her reaction to the white men from behind the bar. As she pulled the shawl away from her head, he recognized her instantly and beckoned her toward the low door. A shudder of remembered horror ran through her body as, once more, she was shown into the room where the obeah-man held sway.

The same damp, earthy smell assailed her nostrils and from out of the shadows she felt the strange creatures fix their dead stares on her; the snake, the monkey's head, the puffer fish. The chickens still scratched and clucked in the corner and the old man still sat at a table in the centre of the room, all of them conspirators in this macabre theatre.

This time the obeah-man's head was not bowed, as if he had no need to hide his hideousness from her any longer. In the candlelight his twisted features still repulsed her, still made the nausea rise in her throat, but her terror had cooled. Her fear no longer boiled inside her; now it was only simmering.

The old man peeled back his lips in a sort of greeting, but Phibbah did not return a smile. Instead she forced herself to look at him squarely. But just as the breath was filling her lungs to speak, the obeah-man butted in first.

"Your missa not dead yet," he told her. His words were framed not as a question, but as fact.

Phibbah froze. It was as if he had reached into her mind and plucked at her thoughts. He let out a cackle, a sound like one of the hens, and brought a clenched hand up to the table. Shaking his fist, he made a rattling noise, then opened his fingers to send several jagged teeth tumbling like dice across the wooden surface.

"They tell me what happen." His voice was hoarse and his breath rasped in his chest.

Phibbah considered the teeth for a moment; creamy white, some sharp as daggers, others plump like pillows. Were they animal or human? She was not sure.

"You know the obeah bag was burned?"

The old man nodded his grisly head. "I know," he replied with the calm self-assurance of a seer.

Phibbah suddenly jolted forward, as if some unseen force had grabbed her and pulled her toward the old man. Resting her small breasts on the table, she fixed him with terrified eyes and her mouth contorted into a fearful scowl.

"What will happen?" she implored him. "What will happen to the magic?"

The obeah-man tilted his head thoughtfully and drew the scattered teeth toward him with his gnarled hand. Cupping them in his fist, he shook them once more, before throwing them onto the table. For a moment he was silent, studying the pattern they made, reading them as a scholar reads a book.

Phibbah looked on, too afraid to breathe. She felt the magic in the room, as if she were being wrapped in its great black cloak. Her eyes were wide in wonder and awe.

Finally the obeah-man said to her, "You have the power."

She swallowed hard, but dared not blink lest the magic disappear. "I have the power?" she repeated, a tremble snagging on her voice. "I no understand."

The old man lifted his hand up to his chest and palmed it to his heart. "The obeah is still with you. It come from inside," he replied.

Still Phibbah frowned. "Inside?" she echoed.

The obeah-man shook his head and lifted his half-eaten lips into a shapeless smile. "Your freedom comes from in here." Again he touched his heart.

"Freedom," she repeated. It was a word she hardly ever heard; a concept she could barely even dream of. Her mind suddenly flashed back to Cato, the night before he had gone missing, when his eyes were wild with excitement and he had spoken of the white men, the good white men, with their pamphlets and their talk of freedom. She caught her breath and held her thoughts for a moment before sharing them.

"The white men outside," she began, raising her hand and motioning behind her. "Why are they . . . ?"

The obeah-man cut her short, slicing through her words with a wag of his finger.

"The white men mean well," he told her. "They promise freedom, but they cannot deliver it."

Phibbah gathered her thoughts that lay scattered like the teeth before her on the table. Is that what had happened to Cato? Had the white men promised him freedom? She recalled how he talked of seeing his homeland that night; how his words had left his mouth like music. But then a shadow suddenly loomed across her vision. Where was he now? She imagined him on a ship bound for Africa, but when she searched the obeah-man's face, she knew that she was wrong. Any dreams that Cato had nourished had been fleeting. He had been cresting a wave that had broken and dissipated so far away from the shore. She suddenly realized he had been betrayed.

The obeah-man remained holding her gaze. "You know what you must do," he told her. He punched his chest lightly with his fist. "You know in here," he said. And as he spoke, a flapping, whirling sound suddenly filled her ears and she saw feathers like snowflakes drift in front of her eyes. A loud gasp escaped from her throat as she looked up and saw a single white dove rise from behind the obeah-man and fly up to one of the rafters above her head.

A weight seemed to be lifted from her shoulders and a sudden surge of confidence washed over her. A way ahead opened up to her. She nodded to the old man. "I know," she said.

Chapter 39

Thomas found Jeremiah lolling in a high-backed chair, beside the glowing embers of a small fire. A blanket was draped across his knees and it was clear he had been dozing before the creak of the opening door had aroused him. He sat bolt upright, as if he had been caught doing something he should not have been.

" 'Tis I. Dr. Silkstone," Thomas reassured the slave as he advanced toward him in the half light. Both the young man's eyes were now open and there was a fear in them that the doctor wished he could ease. No balm could soothe away the years of mistreatment, that much he knew. " 'Tis good to see you sitting up," he remarked.

Jeremiah nodded. "I grow stronger, sir," he replied. He managed to form the words well and did not wince with pain as he spoke, noted Thomas.

The doctor was about to take his patient's pulse when there came a loud knock at the door, followed by a violent tugging of the doorbell. Both men shot an anxious glance at each other, but Thomas tried to make light of the sudden intrusion.

"Revelers, or mummers!" he suggested. " 'Tis Christmas Eve," he added, heading for the door.

Standing on the landing, looking directly over the bannisters, he saw Mistress Finesilver open the front door to two men; one uncouth and burly as a baboon, while the other, in his plum-colored coat, appeared to be a gentleman. Thomas did not like the look of them. There was something in their manner. Something was wrong. Yet instead of asking the men how she could help them and the purpose of their visit, Mistress Finesilver mumbled a few words, then simply stood aside. The men brushed past her and headed up the stairs.

Thomas rushed down to meet them on the first floor landing. "What is the meaning of this?" he asked breathlessly. He could see them more clearly now and from the look on their faces, they had not come on a social visit. The ruffian, his face pitted as orange peel, sneered at him and pulled back his coat to reveal a leather cosh hanging at his belt. Squaring up to Thomas, he stuck out his belly and put his hands on his hips.

"I'll handle this, Rake," came the gentleman's voice. It was calm, but authoritative. He set foot on the landing and faced Thomas.

Events were moving quickly. The blood began pounding in the young doctor's ears. He needed his wits about him. Strangers were trespassing into his home and he suspected Jeremiah was the reason. The runaway was in danger.

"Who are you to come barging into my house like this, sir?" Thomas cried.

The gentleman's chin jutted out, as if he felt he had every right to be there. "My name is Josiah Dalrymple and I am here to take back what is rightfully mine," he barked.

Thomas would not be bullied. "You are trespassing, sir, and I would have you leave my house before I call the constables."

The gentleman fixed him with a stare so close, his breath wreathed the young doctor's face.

"Constables, eh? 'Tis you who should be arrested for stealing another man's property!" he cried.

Thomas narrowed his eyes. He had guessed as much. "Property? And what might that be?" he asked mockingly, trying to play for time.

"You have my slave, sir, and I am come to take him back." The intruder was intent. Shoving Thomas aside with his shoulder, he pushed past him and into Jeremiah's room. His henchman followed suit.

"You cannot go in there!" protested Thomas, leaping up the stairs after them. But it was too late. The door was wrenched open and the men burst in. At first sight it appeared the room was empty. The bed was made and, much to Thomas's surprise, the chair had been vacated. It was the whimpering that gave the slave away. He was huddled in the corner, his arms crossed over his head. "No, massa. Please, no," he whined.

Thomas rushed to his side to protect him. Standing in front of Jeremiah, shielding him from his master, he squared up to the men.

"You have no business here. Get out, will you!" he cried, pointing to the door. But his words fell on deaf ears. Dalrymple signaled to Rake to fetch Jeremiah and he lunged toward the terrified man, hooking his arm around the slave's.

"No!" cried Thomas, trying to shove the ruffian away, but Rake landed him a punch to the jaw, sending him flying across the room and onto the bed.

Jeremiah was hauled up and Rake produced a thick chain. His hands reached up to the slave's throat, probing for the collar.

"You'll not find it," yelled Thomas, heaving himself up from the bed. "It has been removed." He had taken a pair of surgical pliers to the heinous band when the young man was still unconscious.

Rake dragged Jeremiah out onto the landing, howling like a dog. At the top of the stairs they paused for a moment.

"Hurry, man!" ordered Dalrymple.

Rake kicked the slave in the ribs and started to drag him down the stairs. Thomas, still recovering from the punch, ran after him onto the landing and grabbed hold of the thug by the shoulder, but he was just swatted away. The slave half scrambled, half fell down the flights of stairs, until he, Rake, and finally Dalrymple reached the hallway. Mistress Finesilver had been watching and waiting anxiously all the while at the bottom. She had been joined by Dr. Carruthers, who wondered at the commotion.

"Will someone tell me what is going on?" he bellowed, trying to make himself heard above the general furor. The front door had remained open, so the slavers' getaway would be easy.

"Stop them, for god's sake!" shrieked Thomas as he headed down the stairs, but Mistress Finesilver remained impassive.

The disturbance was so great that it could be heard on the street and the night watchman had been alerted by anxious neighbors.

"What be the meaning of this?" he yelled, holding his lantern aloft on the front steps.

Thomas seized the initiative. "These men entered my property in order to rob me and kidnap my manservant, sir," he explained breathlessly. He pointed to Dalrymple and Rake.

The watchman narrowed his eyes. He was not the sharpest of men, but he could smell a rat. He saw Jeremiah, bandaged and crouching by the door, and he saw Rake with his cosh. It was his duty to help a man protect his own home and Dr. Silkstone and Dr. Carruthers were known to him as decent, upright gentlemen. It was clear that the two men before him were scoundrels who had entered the property uninvited.

"I suggest you scarper afore the constables come," the night watchman told them in no uncertain terms.

Dalrymple snarled like a wounded hound. He turned to Thomas. "You have my slave, sir, and I will get him back."

Thomas was not intimidated. "You come like a thief in the night, sir," he replied. "If you want your slave back you'll have to fight for him in court."

"Oh, I will!" hissed Dalrymple, and with that he and his lackey climbed into their waiting carriage and sped off into the night. Thomas slammed the door behind him, then tilted his head back and leaned his body against it like a buttress. He knew the fight for Jeremiah's freedom would not be easy.

Chapter 40

For the first time in six years Lady Lydia Farrell was enjoying Christmas Day. Richard was with her and his excitement was infectious. She had risen early and when he opened his eyes she had been there to wish him joy. Kissing him on the forehead, she had felt herself surely the most fortunate woman in the world. To think that last Christmas she could only have the vaguest of hopes that he might still be alive, let alone be able to hold him and hear him call her "Mamma."

After breakfast they attended a service at St. Swithin's. The new vicar, the Reverend Unsworth, had given a passable sermon, even though Richard was not the only one who found it on the dull side. Sir Theodisius, newly back from his London sojourn, had joined them in their pew, together with Lady Pettigrew. The coroner had proceeded, in a most irreverent way, to distract Richard with tricks he learned during his days in the Royal Navy using lengths of string.

Afterward, Sir Theodisius and his wife accompanied Lydia and Richard back to Boughton Hall to enjoy the festivities. Snow still covered the landscape, but there had not been a fresh fall for almost a week, so that roads and tracks were less difficult to negotiate. Mr. Lupton had ordered a party of men to clear the drive and they had banked the snow high on either side, making it passable to traffic.

Mistress Claddingbowl's sterling efforts in the kitchen paid off. Richard had eaten heartily and Sir Theodisius pronounced her roast turkey the most tender he had ever tasted. The coroner's enthusiasm was, no doubt, fuelled by the excellent wines that Howard had chosen to accompany the many courses. He had been eager to wash down as many mouthfuls as he could with a good vintage.

It was toward the end of the meal, after plum pudding, when Sir Theodisius was wiping the corners of his mouth with his napkin, that Lydia noticed that his gaiety was giving way to reflection. She sensed he was becoming a little morose.

"I would like to propose a toast," he said suddenly, his face ruddy with wine.

Lady Pettigrew, sitting opposite him, fussed. "Oh, really, Sir Theo. Any excuse!" she scolded.

The coroner had already taken it upon himself to propose a toast to both Lydia and Richard, so the former was a little puzzled. She shot a quizzical look at Lady Pettigrew, who was watching her portly husband disapprovingly.

Unable to lift himself up from his chair without the greatest of difficulty, Sir Theodisius merely called for his glass to be charged with white burgundy and raised it. "Let us drink to the man who should be here," he said, giving a nod to the empty seat at the head of the table. "Let us hope that he will one day take his rightful place." His eyes suddenly moistened and his words slurred. "Let us drink to Dr. Thomas Silkstone, as fine an anatomist, and as devoted a husband and father as one could wish for," he said finally.

Embarrassed and not a little shocked by Sir Theodisius's sudden outburst, Lydia raised her own glass. "To Dr. Silkstone," she mouthed. The coroner's words had reminded her of a nagging pain that she was trying to ignore. The toast simply brought back the sense of longing that she was working so hard to dispel. They soon retired to the drawing room where a huge fire blazed and at its centre was the yule log.

"A very fine specimen!" quipped Sir Theodisius, pointing to the log ablaze in the grate.

Lydia settled herself on a sofa. Richard climbed up to be at her side and she put her arm around him. "Indeed," she replied. "Richard helped choose it." She squeezed him to her.

"With Mr. Lupton," Richard piped up.

"Ah, Lupton. Your new estate manager, I believe," said Sir Theodisius to Lydia, easing himself gently down onto the sofa opposite.

At the mention of his name, Richard suddenly became very animated. Tugging at Lydia's sleeve, he said, "Mamma, can Mr. Lupton come and play with us this afternoon?"

Lydia shot an uneasy look across the room at her guests.

"Mr. Lupton is a favorite companion of Richard's," she explained.

"So I see!" replied Sir Theodisius, slapping his ample thigh. "And what sort of mischief do you get up to, sir?" he asked the young earl with a wink.

The child paused. "We have been playing in the snow. Mr. Lupton built me a sleigh."

Sir Theodisius leaned back, rocking with laughter. "Well, well. There's a novelty," he said. "He sounds like a good egg, this Mr. Lupton."

"He is not an egg, sir. He is a gentleman," countered Richard seriously, making the coroner guffaw even louder.

Lydia, however, remained uneasy. "Surely you would like to show our guests your drawings, my sweet?" she asked, although her tone was more of a direction than a question.

"But what about some games!?" interjected the coroner.

"Games?" asked Richard excitedly.

Sir Theodisius waved his fat hands in the air. "Blind man's buff or hunt the slipper?" he suggested.

Lydia slipped a sideways glance at Richard. She knew he would never have heard of such games, but their exotic names made them fanciful and full of promise. The boy jumped down from the sofa and grabbed her hand.

"Please, can Mr. Lupton join in, Mamma? Please?"

An awkward smile pursed Lydia's lips. "It is most unusual, dear . . ."

Sir Theodisius came to her rescue. "Oh, let the man come! 'Tis Christmas!" chuckled the coroner.

Lydia nodded. After all, she would be entertaining the servants in the ballroom later on that day. Social convention might frown on an estate manager being invited into the higher echelons, but hers was hardly a conventional family. She glanced at Lady Pettigrew for approval and was given it with a sly nod of her head.

"Please, Mamma!" pleaded Richard, jumping up and down.

"Very well, then. We shall ask Howard to send word down to Plover's Lake," she said. "We shall invite Mr. Lupton to join us."

Christmas dinner at Hollen Street was a subdued affair. The goose was fatty, the beef tough as boot leather, and the claret decidedly acidic.

"Tastes more like vinegar," commented Dr. Carruthers, his tongue flapping disapprovingly inside his mouth. Thomas did not disagree and shot a look at Mistress Finesilver, whose face had been equally sour since the previous evening.

Jeremiah Taylor lay in bed upstairs, resting after his ordeal. He had not sustained any new physical injuries—Thomas had made sure of that—but mentally he was in a poor way. He remained in a state of high anxiety, despite the fact that he had downed a dose of laudanum. Fearing the return of his erstwhile master, he had begged not to be left alone, so Helen had been tasked to sit with him until the Christmas meal had been eaten.

Thomas waited until Mistress Finesilver was out of the room to discuss Jeremiah's predicament. She had made no secret of the fact that she disapproved of the slave's presence in the household, and, it seemed, had betrayed him to his former master. How else would Dalrymple have known that he had given him refuge? He knew he would have to deal with her betrayal soon enough, but for the moment he was forced to rely on her service. Discretion was paramount.

Dr. Carruthers banged his knife handle on the table. "You showed the varlets!" he cried approvingly, referring to the previous day's escapade.

"Indeed," replied Thomas. "But my only fear is that next time they will succeed."

"You are thinking of moving the runaway?"

Thomas nodded. "The only question is where. I do not believe he is safe in London. We need to find him somewhere well away from here."

"And I'll wager I know where that place might be," ventured Dr. Carruthers, smiling to himself. "I am sure he will be most welcome."

Dressed in his green brocade jacket and knitted silk breeches, the estate manager walked into the drawing room with a confident air. Sir Theodisius eyed him with great interest, following him as he bowed to Lydia, with all the self-assurance of a master.

The young earl greeted Nicholas Lupton as if he were his long-lost father. Running to him with outstretched arms, he hugged his legs, nearly knocking him off balance.

"Sir! Please mind yourself!" scolded Eliza, who had been tasked to keep the young earl under control. Lydia darted him a disapproving look, surprised by her son's outburst of affection.

Yet the smile did not leave Lupton's lips. "And a happy Christmas to you, too, young sir!" he cried, rubbing his hands over the child's mop of curls in a familiar manner.

"Sir Theodisius and Lady Pettigrew, may I present to you Mr. Nicholas Lupton, Boughton's estate manager," said Lydia, her smile once more restored.

Lupton gave a deep bow. "I am most honored," he said, a wide grin planted firmly on his face.

Lady Pettigrew flapped her fan girlishly, while Sir Theodisius fixed him with a quizzical glare.

"Surely not one of the Yorkshire Luptons?" he asked.

Lupton paused for a moment, as if caught unawares. "I do not believe so, sir," he answered circumspectly.

"Ah! Of course not!" he exclaimed, changing the subject. "It seems your services are in demand, sir," he said, watching the young earl sidle up once more.

"Can we play, Mr. Lupton? Can we play?" Richard was tugging at his frockcoat.

"Richard, behave yourself, or Eliza will have to take you upstairs," Lydia scolded, raising her voice and immediately hating herself for doing so. The child's bottom lip began to tremble.

Lupton threw back his blond head and laughed. " 'Tis no matter, your ladyship," he told her, holding out his hand to Richard. "I should be honored to play with my young master!" He bent low to address the child. "What'll it be, sir? Charades? Hunt the slipper?"

A state of high excitement pervaded the room for the next hour or so, as Mr. Lupton took on the role of master of ceremonies and suggested games and diversions to amuse and involve both young and those not so young. He even showed himself to be an excellent musician, when he sat at the fortepiano and played a medley of seasonal songs.

Outside, night was closing in and Hannah entered the drawing room to close the blinds and mend the fire.

"Is there anything you need, your ladyship?" she asked her mistress.

Lydia was aware that the question was a leading one. It was the custom on Christmas Day for the servants to enjoy their own feast once all their other duties had been performed. They would gather 'round the large table to eat their roast joints and a goose and even a pheasant or two. There would be sweetmeats, too. And some of them would definitely wake up with sore heads the next morning. She would join them a little later.

"We can take care of ourselves for the next hour or so," she replied.

Just as Hannah was about to take her leave, however, the front doorbell was rung loudly and insistently. Lydia, her face flushed by wine and the heat of the room, shot a glance first at Lupton, then at Sir Theodisius.

"Who on earth could that be?" she asked, frowning, as the bell continued to ring.

Lupton, still seated at the fortepiano, shrugged and smiled.

"Wassailers from the village most like, m'lady," he replied nonchalantly. "The maid will see to them," he added, glancing at Hannah.

The party settled back into its rhythm once more until less than a minute later, an anxious-looking Hannah reappeared at the doorway.

"Begging pardon, your ladyship," she began. "But there is a messenger needs to speak with you urgent."

The color drained instantly from Lydia's cheeks. Nodding her head, she took a deep breath, as if steeling herself to receive bad news.

"I will come," she said.

Lupton made to follow her, but she lifted her hand. "Please, Mr. Lupton. I shall go alone."

Standing in the hallway was a rider, his face purple with the cold, his arms hugging his body.

"Get this man a hot drink," Lydia instructed Hannah as soon as she saw the horseman shivering by the fireplace. "Well? You have a message?"

The messenger bent double in a bow and when he rose she could see his stubble was flecked white with frost. No one would brave riding through the biting cold on Christmas Day unless their news was of the utmost importance.

"You are Lady Lydia Farrell?"

"I am," replied Lydia, her back held straight as a die.

"I am come from Banbury, from Draycott House," said the messenger.

Draycott was the home of Sir Montagu Malthus, a family friend, a formidable lawyer, and godfather to Lydia's late brother. It was he who had made young Richard a ward of court, with the condition that Lydia and Thomas never marry.

"Sir Montagu!" she cried. "What is wrong?"

"I am sent by Mr. Fothergill," began the messenger, his voice rasping. Lydia recalled the stooped little clerk, who had made her sign the legal documents presented by the court. "I am to tell you that Sir Montagu has taken gravely ill, your ladyship. You are to expect the worst."

Chapter 41

The day after Christmas Day Thomas kept his appointment to check on Mistress Carfax's progress. He was gladdened to see that she was sitting up in bed, her copper hair covered by a large cap, drinking thin gruel. She did not smile when she saw him enter the room.

"I hope your pain has lessened, madam," said Thomas, setting down his case.

"I am feeling stronger," she acknowledged. She slipped him an odd look, as if testing him. "Do you know what caused my upset, Dr. Silkstone?" she asked.

Thomas reached for his case, turning his head away from hers. He did not want to betray himself with a look. "I daresay something you ate, Mistress Carfax," he replied.

"Or drank?"

Away from her stare, he rolled his eyes. It was clear she suspected one of the slaves had been poisoning her.

"Perhaps," he replied, twitching his lips into a smile. "But you seem to be well on the road to recovery, and that is what matters."

Venus knocked and entered as Thomas set down another bottle of the antidote on the dressing table. From the look of his patient, the remedy seemed to be working well.

"I have brought more physic," he told Mistress Carfax. "You will need to take it for at least another week," he instructed.

"Very well," she replied, nodding her head. "Venus will show you out."

The housekeeper led Thomas across the landing, but just as he was passing the staircase that led to the attic, he heard a terrible moaning sound. He stopped dead.

"Phibbah?" he asked knowingly.

Venus took a deep breath. "Yes, sir."

"I shall see her," he said.

Venus shook her head. "No, sir. The missa say . . ."

Thomas fixed her with a stare. "Your mistress need not know," he replied and he began to climb the stairs, the moans growing louder with each tread.

In the garret room Thomas found the slave lying listless on a pallet on the rush-strewn floor, a filthy blanket covering her.

"How long has she been like this?" he asked Venus, feeling the girl's pulse.

"She took bad last night, sir," replied the housekeeper, standing at his side.

At the sound of Thomas's voice, Phibbah's lids opened slowly, as if acknowledging his presence. "Are you in pain?" he asked gently.

Her cracked lips mouthed a feeble reply. "Yes."

Thomas rose to face Venus. "She has vomited?"

"Yes, sir."

"And she has belly cramps?"

"Yes, sir."

"You must keep her warm. Another blanket, perhaps," suggested Thomas. "And see that she has small beer to drink."

Venus curtsied. "I shall do as you say, sir," she replied.

Thomas was puzzled. The girl's symptoms were consistent with Mistress Carfax's. It occurred to him, as he studied her pained face, that perhaps poison was not to blame for these mysterious bouts of illness. After all, she was the one he suspected of dosing her mistress with the deadly weed. Perhaps his diagnosis had been misguided, Thomas thought to himself. Perhaps there was some sort of ague, unknown to him, that was affecting the women. He found himself confused.

"Inform me if her condition worsens," he instructed Venus as he picked up his case. Just as he did so, he saw the corner of a piece of printed paper peeping out from under the sick girl's pallet. He wondered why one who could not read might be secreting it. Snatching a look 'round, he saw Venus was distracted. Quickly he swept it up and dropped it into his bag.

"Remember, call me if she grows worse," he told Venus as he brushed past her and out of the room. He doubted very much that she would.

As soon as she was sure Thomas had left the building, Venus returned to the garret to find Phibbah bleating faintly and lying doubled up on her side. Calmly she walked over to the girl and knelt down beside her. Looking into her face, she could see that her time was near. Her cheeks were hollow and her eyes sunken. She touched her hand. It was as cold as the frosted windowpane. No extra blanket had been forthcoming. No water had wetted her lips.

"I no die?" Phibbah's voice was as brittle as a cane stalk.

Venus stroked her forehead, as a mother would her drowsy child's, then said: "She knows."

For a moment Phibbah's moans were silent. "Who?" she asked, aware of the answer full well.

"The missa knows you tried to kill her," she said softly, lifting her hand and inspecting the slave's long thumbnail. "You are very foolish, child."

Phibbah let out a feeble cry. "What she say?"

Venus studied the girl as beads of sweat studded her brow, then tilted her head as if she were about to sing a lullaby to a sick child.

"She say I got to kill you."

Chapter 42

The carriage was returning Thomas home via White Hall, running parallel with the Thames. Blowing on the window-pane, the doctor's hot breath melted a large patch of crystals big enough for him to view the river in all its chaotic splendor. For more than two weeks the Thames had held ships, both large and small, in its frozen grip. Not a brigantine nor a barque, not a lighter nor a launch had been able to dock or set sail. Marooned like beached whales, wherries and square riggers alike remained imprisoned, unable to move in or out of port.

The *Elizabeth* would still be there, he told himself, probably laden with new cargo, but still held captive. Like his own investigation into Matthew Bartlett's murder, time had frozen around it. If that was so, then perhaps some clues remained on board, too. It occurred to him that the dead artist's belongings might still be in his cabin, unless his family, if indeed he had any, had claimed them.

Leaning out of his carriage window, he instructed the driver to go over Westminster Bridge and to deliver him to Hope Wharf. As far as his eye could see, hundreds of masts stood like trees, some tall, some like broken stumps. The northerly wind was whistling downriver, jangling rigging ropes, playing them as if they were the strings of a giant's harp. The music was strange and haunting.

The weather did, however, offer some advantages. A new

route had opened up to the few sailors that were retained. Now as well as being able to cross from shore to shore over the many ships that moored cheek by jowl across the river, they could maneuver their way over the river's glassy surface. Sometimes they skated. Others built sledges that slid over the ice to transport small quantities of goods. Enterprising merchants had set up stalls to serve the new prisoners; hot gingerbread and roasted chestnuts were always popular. Such distractions helped dispel the frustration that the harsh weather brought in its wake.

Thomas surveyed the scene for a few moments, watching men crawl up the masts like insects. Others scrubbed the decks, but on the quayside there was less activity. The watermen were idle, their small craft held in the jaws of the ice. Ships were full of cargo—bales of wool, kegs of beer, casks of wine—ready and loaded for their voyages to far-off climes, but prevented from leaving by the coldest winter in living memory.

It was as he hoped. The *Elizabeth* was one such ship. He boarded her and found Captain McCoy poring over his charts in his cabin.

"Ah, Silkstone, you bring news?" he said, walking forward with his hand extended. "I heard that a body was found. It is . . ." The captain's tongue cleaved to his mouth.

"It has been identified as Mr. Bartlett," replied Thomas with a nod.

"Och! 'Tis a shocking business," said the captain, shaking his head. "Who would do such a thing?"

Thomas sighed deeply. "That is what I am here to try and find out, Captain McCoy."

"So you are working for the Admiralty?" he asked, gesturing to a chair and seating himself at his desk.

Thomas looked puzzled. "The Admiralty? Why should that be?"

McCoy flapped his hands. "Two officers were here a couple of days ago. They said that the expedition was their business and claimed jurisdiction." The captain seemed resigned. "I didn't argue."

Thomas leaned forward as he recalled Sir Joseph's warning to him to stay out of any investigation. "What did they want?" he asked.

"They came for Mr. Bartlett's personal effects," replied the captain.

Thomas bit his lip. They had beaten him to it. "And you gave them to them?"

McCoy let out a laugh. "That was the thing, Dr. Silkstone. There was nothing to give."

"What do you mean?"

"All the lad had was a small chest and it was empty."

"Empty?"

"Aye. There was nothing in it at all," replied the captain, both bushy brows raised. "No letters from home, no comb, not even a change of clothes."

Chapter 43

Thomas sat at his desk in his laboratory. The notes made at his last postmortem were before him, splayed across the surface like giant playing cards. He had reread them at least a dozen times and each time they raised more questions than they answered.

The household had long since retired, and the embers of his fire were dying down. Outside in the street, an occasional carriage swished by and the odd dog barked. Franklin the rat, always more energetic at night, had been let out of his cage and scuttled around the room.

From his drawer Thomas took out a clean sheet of paper and, dipping his quill into his inkpot, he began to write:

The Principles of Investigating a Crime
at Its Place of Discovery

1. *A corpse should always, if possible and practical, be left in situ until relevant authorities arrive. It should not be touched or interfered with in any way.*

2. *All articles surrounding the corpse or found nearby are to be collected and used as possible evidence in the solving of the crime. These may*

> *include any type of material left at the scene, or*
> *the result of contact between two surfaces,*
> *such as shoes and the soil, or fibers on*
> *garments.*

3. *The circumstances in which the corpse was dis-*
   covered must be ascertained. These factors in-
   clude the weather, the hour of the day, whether
   light or dark . . .

Thomas paused, then resumed writing. . . .

> *whether, in the case of a corpse discovered in a*
> *dock, river or in the sea, if the tide was high or*
> *low on that occasion.*

He set down his quill and walked over to his bookshelf. Scanning the many volumes, his eye settled on the current almanac. He took it off the shelf and leafed through it until he came to the lunar calculations for the month of December. The headless body had been tied to the pier during a spring tide, when the full moon was approximately aligned with the sun and the earth, causing greater ebbs and flows than usual. Perhaps, thought Thomas, it was the murderer's intention that the corpse be discovered sooner rather than later.

Seating himself once more, he reread his notes. He studied his second point once more, then searched for Sir Stephen Gandy's initial letter, commissioning him to carry out the postmortem. *The corpse was tied to the pier.* But with what? A length of rope, a chain? Such evidence was surely crucial to any investigation.

At that moment, he suddenly became aware of a noise behind him. He turned to see Franklin on the bookshelf above his head, scuttling over the tops of various volumes, and was reminded how, after Lydia's husband had been found hanged in his cell, the rat's instincts had pointed him to the murderer. He resolved to return to Sir Stephen's office first thing tomorrow and find out what happened to the ligature, whatever its nature or origin, that had secured the headless corpse to the pier. It may prove vital in his investigation.

Sir Stephen Gandy had agreed to see Thomas at short notice. The coroner was standing by the hearth, holding his hands to the fire, when he entered. He turned and acknowledged the doctor's presence, somewhat grudgingly, it seemed.

"So, Silkstone, you have more to tell me, I hope, about how this Mr. Bartlett came to be found in such an unfortunate state in the Thames?" His manner, thought Thomas, seemed rather brusque and glib, as he paced to and fro in front of the fire, his hands now clasped behind his back. He did not invite Thomas to sit.

"Actually, it is my intention to ask a question of you, sir."

"Oh?" The coroner arched a brow.

Thomas cleared his throat. "You mentioned that the victim was tied to a pier when he was found, but you did not say how."

"What of it?" The coroner's mood grew sourer by the second.

"I wondered if I may see it, sir, if it is still available, whatever it was."

"And you think this will help track down the perpetrator of this crime?"

"It may or it may not. 'Tis hard to say without having seen it."

Sir Stephen's lips pursed into a grimace. "Very well, Silkstone. If you think 'twill help." Ringing a bell on his desk, he summoned his clerk, then instructed him to fetch all documents relating to the murder of Matthew Bartlett.

"I am a busy man, Silkstone," he muttered as he strode over to his desk and sat down.

Thomas gave a stilted bow. "I appreciate your time, sir," he said, as the clerk returned with a leather wallet and laid it before the coroner. Opening it, Sir Stephen pulled out a long cloth strap and held it up. "This is what secured the corpse, although how it proves anything is beyond me," he snapped.

Thomas smiled as he was handed the item. Clutching it in his fist, he knew instantly that this new piece of evidence could prove key in his search for Matthew Bartlett's killer. His heart was pounding fast, but he willed himself to remain calm in front of the coroner.

"I am most obliged to you, sir," said Thomas, placing the strap in his medical case. "I am sure it will be of use," he added, before making a low bow and taking his leave.

Back at Hollen Street, Thomas found Dr. Carruthers cradling a brandy in the study.

"Ah! You are in a hurry to tell me something, young fellow," said the old anatomist, having listened to the pace at which Thomas had walked through the hallway and into the room.

Thomas, slightly breathless with both exertion and excitement, acknowledged that he was, indeed, in a hurry.

Opening his case, he took out the cloth strap and placed it in the old man's free hand.

"What have we here?" asked his mentor, placing his brandy glass on the side table so that he could concentrate on what had just been placed in his palm.

His first reaction was one of disgust. "The stink tells me it has been in water. The Thames most like."

Thomas smiled, but resisted the urge to reveal any more as he watched the old man run his gnarled old fingers along the ligature. When he came to an end, he felt its frayed edges and discovered telltale holes had been made in the cloth.

After only a few seconds, Carruthers nodded. "No mystery about this, young fellow. 'Tis a tourniquet strap."

Thomas retrieved it and inspected the length of cloth once more. "I believe it is, for use with a screw tourniquet, if I'm not mistaken," he said, inspecting the holes in the cloth where a buckle would have been attached. He pictured how, before an amputation, the belt was pulled tight around the limb above the wound, with the screw over the main artery. He had used one many times himself, turning the screw to compress the artery and, in so doing, aiming to deaden the main nerves, thus helping to numb the pain.

"Now will you tell me what this is all about?" asked Carruthers, with an air of impatience.

Thomas, still holding the tourniquet tight between his two hands, looked up.

"It reaffirms my theory that Mr. Bartlett was not murdered by a bunch of cutthroats but by a man of medicine, a surgeon or an anatomist most like. The decapitation itself, and now this. If I'm not very much mistaken, I'll wager this tourniquet came from Hubert Izzard's anatomy school."

Carruthers shook his head. "I would not give you long odds on that one, young fellow."

Thomas watched his mentor's expression. It had suddenly become very grave. He knew him well enough to realize when something was troubling him; the way his forehead puckered and his mouth drooped.

"What is it, sir?" asked Thomas, drawing up a small chair to sit beside his mentor.

Carruthers thought for a moment, as if framing a painful memory in his mind's eye.

"Sir?" pressed Thomas.

The old man turned his head toward his protégé. "I have not been totally honest with you, young fellow," he began.

His words jerked Thomas upright. He had never heard such an admission from his mentor before. He knew him to be straight as a die. He frowned. "Not honest?"

Carruthers smiled and shook his head. "I have never lied to you, but perhaps I should have told you the whole truth about Izzard before."

Thomas shot back. "I suspect that man's hand in all of this, sir, but if you have any evidence . . ."

Carruthers raised a finger. "What testimony I shall give you is only regarding the man's character," he insisted. "I did not tell you before, because I did not want his vile past to color your own judgment. You must be impartial in your search for the truth. You, of all people, young fellow, know that."

Thomas knew Carruthers to be right. The evidence, in all

things, must speak for itself. Whatever his mentor was about to say must corroborate, not convict. "That I do, sir," he replied.

The old anatomist took a deep breath and reached for his half full glass of brandy. "My story," he said, "is of how Izzard's nose was broken."

"You have known him long?"

Carruthers nodded slowly. "His father was the surgeon who employed me in Jamaica."

"I see," nodded Thomas, suddenly understanding his mentor's reticence on the subject. "So how did he break his nose?" he urged, unsure as to where the trail might lead.

Carruthers's shoulders heaved in a great sigh. "He was but sixteen when he was found raping a slave woman by her husband. In his rage, the man punched the braggart in the face. The Negro was sentenced to death, and Izzard watched him as he was strung up with a hook through his ribs." The old anatomist gulped back his brandy. "It took three days for the wretch to die, and during that time Izzard taunted him till he drew his last breath. I shall never forget the man's piteous cries."

Thomas remained silent for a moment, his head bowed, picturing the scene.

"You understand why I did not tell you before?" asked Carruthers.

"I do, sir," nodded Thomas. "I would break his nose a second time," he said between clenched teeth.

"Such was his contempt for the slaves, even when he was barely a man," continued Carruthers. "His father was little better, praising his son's actions."

"And that is when you resigned?"

The old anatomist nodded. "I could not stand the barbarity of it. I left for England the following week."

"And after all these years, Izzard still shows his contempt for Negroes," mused Thomas. "So you believe he is having them killed to order, sir?"

Thomas's gaze switched back to his mentor. A single tear was running down Carruthers's cheek and he wiped it away with the back of his hand. "I think not, young fellow," he said, shaking his head.

Thomas thought of Izzard as a young man, taunting the dying Negro. It was the behavior of a bully, but perhaps not of a killer. "Because he is too much of a coward?" he ventured.

"Precisely," came the reply. "I do not believe he is a murderer, but he may well be doing business with someone who is."

Chapter 44

At the country seat of Draycott House, the men were gathered at the far end of Sir Montagu Malthus's bedchamber. There were three of them, two physicians and a surgeon, and they huddled like vultures eyeing a dying animal. Sir Montagu had taken to his bed on Christmas Day when the pain in his leg had become too much to bear. His knee, calf, and foot were now hideously swollen and the skin on his leg had turned an ugly speckled brown.

Like all good physicians, Doctors Brotherton and Biglow had tried to alleviate their patient's discomfort by adding to it. Leeches had been applied in clusters to suck out the excess fluid. They had even endeavored to bleed his offending leg, although this had proved a dangerous undertaking, as Sir Montagu kept lashing out at whoever tried to make an incision.

There was, they had concluded, no other course of action but to call upon expert advice. Mr. Percival Parker, a surgeon of good repute, had been drafted in from Oxford. He had examined the patient and agreed with the physicians that Sir Montagu was suffering from a popliteal aneurysm in his left leg. It was so large, he observed, that it was distending two hamstrings. If the condition did not kill him outright, he told them, Sir Montagu could spend the rest of his days in crazed agony. There seemed little choice. Amputation was the preferred course, but a highly risky one nonetheless. It was this decision the men were discussing in such reverent tones when Lydia was shown into Sir Montagu's chamber.

The blinds had been half drawn, so that the room was in shadow. Shapes were blurred; the men of medicine in the corner were silhouettes. In the semidarkness sounds were magnified—the creak of the floorboards as she made her way toward the bed, the ticking of the mantel clock marking time, the rasping of Sir Montagu's breath.

The patient's pain was being kept at bay with regular doses of laudanum and it therefore took him a while to realize Lydia's presence. She sat down at his bedside and, for a moment, studied his furrowed forehead, dotted with drops of sweat. Agony was written on his face as clearly as if it had been in ink.

This was the man, she reflected, who was depriving her of her happiness; keeping her and her beloved Thomas apart. His death might even lead the Court of Chancery to reconsider the conditions of the wardship placed on Richard which meant they could never marry. Yet seeing him like this, so fragile and sick, her heart felt heavy. He had been such a good friend and ally to both her father and her mother; the man they had entrusted to be her brother's godfather, and, after her own father's death, her own self-appointed unofficial guardian. He had watched her grow from a baby into a young woman. He had seen her trials and tribulations and even added to them, yet still she felt a strange closeness to him, as if he were her own flesh and blood.

"Sir Montagu, 'tis I. 'Tis Lydia," she said softly, scooping up his hand in hers. It was icy cold to the touch.

Slowly he stretched open his eyes from beneath hooded lids and looked up at the ceiling.

"I am here, sir," said Lydia.

Turning his head a little he focused on her face with a filmy stare. It was a while before he recognized her, but when he did, the corners of his mouth turned up.

"My dear, how good of you to come," he croaked. He raised a hand slowly and pointed at the huddle of men in the corner of his room. "I have had to endure their poking and prodding too long."

On hearing their patient's words, the physicians looked toward the bed and all gave odd, stilted bows to Lydia. She acknowledged them awkwardly with a tilt of her head and her thoughts flashed to Thomas. How different he was from these men in this profession that fawned and prevaricated and acted according to a patient's purse. Full of their own self-importance, they seemed to do more harm than good to those most in need of help.

Sir Montagu raised his hand once more and beckoned with a hooked finger. Lydia leaned closer. "They want to cut off my leg," he told her. She felt the blood drain from her face.

"To amputate?" she murmured. The unexpected news churned up her stomach. She was fully aware of the implications.

Sir Montagu gave a little nod. "They may as well string me up from a tree and leave me to die," he said, his voice suddenly gathering strength. "You hear that?" he shouted contemptuously to the men.

The physicians turned in unison to see their patient flapping a hand at them in a derisory manner. "Look at them!" he cried. "Bunch of quacks and mountebanks. They'll not be having my leg. Not even after I'm dead and gone," he scowled.

Lydia shot the men a discomfited look. "I am sure they are only trying to do what is best for you, sir," she told him gently, even though she knew he was unlikely to survive surgery.

Hearing the timbre of resignation in her voice, Sir Montagu grabbed hold of her arm suddenly.

"Do not let them cut off my leg. They must not," he begged.

Lydia felt pity well up inside her as she regarded Sir Montagu. For the first time in her life she could see that he was afraid. The light of terror shone in his eyes as clear as day. She looked down at her hand. He was squeezing her fingers so hard that she had to stifle a cry of pain before she tried to pull them free.

"There has to be another way," he said, releasing her from his grasp.

Lydia took a deep breath as she studied his pained expression. The clock on the mantel struck three. "I believe there may be," she said, quietly at first, so that Sir Montagu told her to speak up.

"What did you say, child?"

"There may be another way," she repeated, only louder. It can be the only way, she told herself.

Chapter 45

The following day, early, Thomas found himself outside Granville Sharp's residence in Fulham. He wished to relay in person what Jeremiah Taylor had told him about his attacker. Perhaps, even more importantly, he would tell him how the slave's testimony might prove invaluable in tracking down the suppliers of Negro corpses used for Hubert Izzard's famed dissections. Thomas feared he had, quite by fortune, uncovered a heinous racket that murdered Negro slaves to order. To his certain knowledge, Hubert Izzard had dissected at least six such corpses over the last three months. His were not the first suspicions aroused. When a justice of the peace had thought to inquire why so many Negroes had died in London, Izzard had replied it was simply down to the cold. "Their bodies are not used to our freezing winters," he had said, and the justice was satisfied. No further questions were asked.

Convinced that the answer to so many of these pressing queries could be found at the Crown Inn, Thomas was about to enlist the help of Mr. Sharp, who had offered his assistance when he heard of Jeremiah Taylor's plight. He recalled his words: he felt it his duty to protect those who, in a foreign land, could not help themselves.

The reformer, his head buried in some lofty tome, looked up at the sound of the knock and the creaking door and welcomed Thomas warmly into his study.

"I heard of your recent intruder, Dr. Silkstone," he said, his eyes bright as new pins. Word had spread quickly of Dalrymple's attempt to recapture his slave.

"News travels fast," replied Thomas, settling himself on a chair.

"Bad news even faster," came the response. Sharp paused and stroked his long chin as if he had a beard. "So you wish me to act for your Jeremiah Taylor?"

Thomas nodded. "I would be most grateful. I fear that this Mr. Dalrymple will try anything, fair means or foul, to re-enslave the young man."

Sharp nodded sagely. "Have no fear, Dr. Silkstone. The time is ripe to question the law, and, indeed, to clarify it."

Thomas smiled. "I have great faith in you, sir," he said, adding: "but first I would like you to help me with another grave matter that seems to be affecting the Negro slaves of London."

Sharp leaned forward, his long fingers tented. "What is that, pray?"

Thomas looked deeply troubled as he told Sharp his suspicions about the number of dissections of Negroes Hubert Izzard was undertaking; he spoke of their state of preservation and of Jeremiah Taylor's testimony.

"So you fear that Izzard's Negroes are not all dying of natural causes?" asked Sharp finally. He tilted his thin face sympathetically, but his expression was slightly pained.

Thomas nodded and eagerly awaited a reply. When it came it was not altogether positive.

"This is most interesting and I do not doubt what you say is true, Dr. Silkstone, but we need proof," Sharp told him. "And besides, a judge will hardly believe the word of a Negro against a white man."

Thomas smiled wryly. "I am aware of that, and that is the reason for my visit, Mr. Sharp," he replied. "I wish you to accompany me to the place where I believe we will find proof that somehow these slaves are being lured to their deaths." He reached into his pocket and flourished the small handbill, retrieved from under Phibbah's pallet, in the air.

"These are being distributed by Quakers at an inn frequented by Negroes," he said, pressing the bill into Sharp's hand.

Scanning it, the campaigner nodded. "I have seen such a pamphlet before."

Thomas thought of the runaway Cato. "It is my suspicion," he said, "that at least one slave, but possibly up to a dozen, have been lured to this place and promised their freedom, never to be seen again."

Sharp's eyes widened. "And you think they are murdered to furnish this anatomist with corpses?"

"That is my belief, sir, but I hope to be proved wrong."

Sharp looked troubled and stroked his long chin once more. " 'Tis dangerous ground, Silkstone, not to be trodden alone."

Thomas's face lit up. "Then I may count on your assistance, sir?"

"That you may," acceded Sharp, with a gracious nod of his head. "And what is the name of this inn?" he added.

"The Crown, off the Strand," replied Thomas. "I think that is where we must begin our investigations."

When Samuel Carfax called in to see his wife that morning he found her sitting up in bed, her frizz of copper hair peeping out from a freshly laundered cap. She appeared much restored after her ordeal. Patience sat darning by her side. Fino was lying on the counterpane, yet still the air was heavy with ill-concealed acrimony.

"It is good to see you looking so much better, my sweet," he told her, pecking her lightly on the cheek.

At first she made no reply. Her eyes followed him as he drew up a chair at her bedside. When he settled himself a sneer tugged at her lips.

"I know you do not mean that," she smirked.

Patience shot a shocked expression at her master. He countered it with a command. "Leave us," he ordered the slave, and she scurried out of the room, quick as a mouse.

Carfax leaned close to her. The whites of her eyes, he noticed, were still yellowish in hue. "What did you mean by that, my dear?" he said, smiling, although his teeth were clenched.

"You know very well, Samuel. My death would not have suited your plans. That is the only reason you wanted me alive." Her voice was measured, as if she was giving a household order.

At the sound of her wounding words the plantation owner leaned back and withdrew his head into his neck, like a turtle. "You are not yourself, my dear," he murmured.

"Oh, but I am," countered his wife. The dog, sensing her angry tone, rose from the bed and jumped to the floor. "Your plans to buy a rotten borough would have been set back if 'twas found your wife had been murdered. Your so-called friends would avoid you, cross to the other side of the street when they saw you. There would be a stop on all your meetings and dinners and rounds of golf. All the machinations that are necessary for your plans would have ground to a halt." Flecks of spit were hurled from her mouth, landing on her husband.

Taking out his kerchief, Carfax dabbed his face. " 'Tis true I must avoid scandal, my dear," he acknowledged.

"Scandal? Ha!" she cried. "So that is what my death would have meant to you: a scandal to harm your chances of buying a seat in Parliament!" Her arms flew out in a gesture of exasperation. A lavender bag had been left to scent her pillows and she picked it up and hurled it at her husband. "Get out of my sight," she screamed. The well-aimed bag hit his cheek and he flinched.

Rising slowly, his shoulders drooping, Carfax turned toward the door, but his wife's insults still followed him.

"Go to your mulatto whore! Go to her and find comfort between her thighs!" she yelled. " 'Twould not surprise me if 'twas she who put the girl up to poisoning me so she could have you all to herself!" she screamed. The exertion of the outburst took its toll, and she collapsed back onto her pillows, surrendering herself to a flood of tears.

Thomas and Sharp reconvened later that day before their foray to the Crown. They were about to enter an alien place, peopled by foreigners from the other side of the world, some of whom worshipped fantastical gods. As white men, they had no right to be there. Yet they would enter as friends, with good intentions. Thomas hoped their intrusion would not be misconstrued.

Their carriage dropped them at the neck of the narrow alleyway that led to the inn. Scores of pairs of eyes were trained on the anatomist and his companion as they ducked down through the low door and into the candle glow of the tavern.

It took only a few seconds for silence to descend on the throng once they realized there were strangers—white strangers—in their midst. The banter hushed, the fiddle player stilled his fingers, and even the parrot stopped squawking for a moment.

Thomas scanned the room, but after a second or two, the tavern hum began to rise once more as customers resumed their talk and picked up their tankards. Feeling as self-conscious as a schoolboy, the young doctor flattened his mouth into a smile and followed Sharp to the bar.

Reaching into his pocket, Thomas pulled out the handbill and placed it on the counter. The Negro with a front tooth of gold stood at the pump, eyeing them suspiciously.

"Good evening," Thomas began. "We were hoping we might speak with some of your patrons about this." He pointed at the piece of paper.

Goldtooth glanced at the pamphlet and grimaced. "I see'd it," he replied, a look of slight reproach settling on his face. "The white Quaker men give them out."

Thomas had not intended to alarm. "We mean no harm. We would very much like to talk to someone who is interested in the cause."

Goldtooth suddenly let out a mocking laugh. His metallic incisor glinted in the candlelight. "You talk of abolition, sir?" He was chuckling as he plonked a tankard on the bar.

Sharp frowned. "My friend has said something amusing?"

Goldtooth leaned forward on the counter, as if about to impart a confidence. "Slavery will only be abolished the day all men's skins are the same color, sir," he said. And with that he threw his head back and broke into a hearty laugh.

For a moment Thomas felt foolish. He was white, comfortable. He answered to no one except his Maker. What did he know of the Negro's yoke? He had left his homeland of his own free will in pursuit of scientific knowledge, but these people here, these downtrodden pedlars and hawkers, these former soldiers and former slaves, had never been given choices. Their lot had been predestined. Acknowledging his naïveté with a nod of his head and a sigh, he said: "You are right. We cannot begin to understand what it is like to spend your life in chains. But we can still enjoy a tankard of ale." Thomas put a shilling on the counter.

Still Goldtooth remained unimpressed. He moved to a shelf behind him and gathered another clutch of pot handles between his fingers. "My advice to you, sirs," he drawled, pulling at the pump once more, "is to go home and sit by your big fire and eat your big dinner. We can look out for our own kind."

Thomas arched a brow and persisted. "From what I've heard many of your kind are dying in this cold. Am I right?"

The Negro shrugged. "The English winter always claims black lives," he replied, his eyes swiveling to the low door behind him. And with that, he turned his back on the men and made busy with a barrel.

Such an unhelpful reception came as no great surprise to either Thomas or Sharp, but undeterred, they took up their tankards and toasted each other. Rounding away from the bar, Thomas held his pot up to his lips. "He knows something," he whispered.

Sharp nodded. "You are talking to someone who understands these people, Dr. Silkstone," came the wry reply. "We need to know what goes on behind that door."

Not wishing to remain a moment longer than they had to in this foreign place of black faces and broken lives, Thomas and Sharp drank quickly and walked out into the night once more.

The cold hit them both in the face as surely as if it were a fist. Underfoot the cobbles were glassed over with frozen rainwater. They trod carefully along the alley, passed broken kegs and piles of rotting rubbish. Sharp, a good deal older than Thomas, struggled with the uneven ground and put out his arm to steady himself now and again.

Turning a corner, they saw the faint glow of a candle spreading from a low window. Both men swapped glances and, without uttering a word, moved closer. They peered inside. It took them both a while before they could make out the strange shapes of the snakes hanging from the rafters, the bunches of herbs, the skulls on the shelves.

"Obeah," whispered Thomas. "It is their magic," he said, recalling the dark world evoked in one of Dr. Perrick's letters to his wife.

Remaining transfixed at the window, they saw something or someone stir. In the shadows they caught a glimpse of an old man, hobbling across the room, a staff in his hand.

"The obeah-man. A priest," said Thomas.

They watched him pull a bottle from the shelf with his gnarled hand and pour its contents into a glass phial.

"Some sort of narcotic?" whispered Sharp, hardly able to believe his eyes.

"Perhaps," replied Thomas.

They watched the old man as he carefully wiped the lip of the bottle and slid it across the table.

"There is someone else with him," whispered Sharp.

From out of the shadows a hand appeared to take the phial. It belonged to a woman. At that moment, they heard footsteps approaching. Sharp signaled to Thomas to leave the alleyway via a different route. They hurried on, not daring to look behind them, until they reached the main street.

Feeling safer under the glow of a streetlamp, Sharp paused to catch his breath. "What have we uncovered?" he panted.

Thomas shook his head. "All I know, sir, is that the answer lies in that bottle," he replied.

The letter was waiting on the salver on the hall table on Thomas's return from the inn. He recognized Lydia's handwriting immediately and smiled. Her weekly missives always brought him great joy. The latest one had arrived on Christmas Eve, so he was a little puzzled as to why she should put her quill to paper again so soon. Even so, the prospect of reading her news gladdened him.

Dr. Carruthers had long retired to bed as Thomas, a candle held aloft, made his way up the stairs to his room. Inside it was cold. The fire had been left to dwindle, but he would be able to read by the light of its glow. He opened his case and reached for a scalpel to slice the seal. Immediately he was struck by the brevity of the letter—a few paragraphs in her hurried hand. The address was Draycott House, Sir Montagu Malthus's residence. It was dated three days previously.

With mounting concern he read:

> My Dearest Thomas,
>
> I write to tell you that Sir Montagu is ill. He suffers from a terrible swelling and his surgeon has recommended the amputation of his left leg. You, my love, of all people know how dangerous such an operation could prove, and so I am imploring you to come and attend him with a view to examining him and prescribing an alternative treatment. He is willing to undergo such an examination at your hands and hopes any enmity between you can be set aside.
>
> I understand that this places a huge burden on your shoulders, but I would ask you, for my sake, to look favorably upon my request. Sir Montagu grows worse by the day, so your earliest attendance, should you choose to accept the task, would be most appreciated.
>
> I shall return to Boughton Hall tomorrow and will await there for your reply.
>
> Your ever-loving
> Lydia

The irony of Lydia's request was not lost on Thomas. She was asking him to treat a man whose death might open the way for their marriage; a man who loathed and despised him and who had gone to great lengths to ensure that his happiness was unattainable. But there was no question as to whether or not he would accede to Lydia's plea. He was a physician and surgeon first and foremost, a disciple of Hippocrates and a healer of the sick. It was his sacred duty to impart his wisdom freely, irrespective of race, creed, color, whether a patient be free or a slave, whether he be friend or, as in Sir Montagu's case, a sworn foe.

He began to pack his surgical instruments. From Lydia's description the swelling might well be a popliteal aneurysm. There was an operation that he had seen performed with a degree of success by a surgeon of great skill. The only problem was that the surgeon was John Hunter, a man of undoubted genius, but whose obsessive nature made him ruthless in his pursuit of knowledge. Thomas had encountered him a few months ago in London and his cruel treatment of Charles Byrne, known as the Irish Giant, had left an indelible stain on his character in Thomas's eyes. Hunter was a man he could not trust. He would have to tackle the perilous procedure on his own.

As for the strange goings-on at the Crown Inn and his investigation into Matthew Bartlett's murder, these most pressing matters would, regrettably, have to wait. Lydia's request must take priority over everything else. He would make haste to Sir Montagu's residence without further delay.

Chapter 46

By the time Mistress Finesilver inquired of Dr. Carruthers as to the whereabouts of Dr. Silkstone and "the slave," as she insisted on calling Jeremiah Taylor, both of them were already on the road to Oxford.

The old anatomist, halfway through a slice of toast and marmalade, wiped his mouth with his napkin.

"I am sure I am not privy to Dr. Silkstone's movements," he told her with a chuckle.

Thomas had confided in his mentor early that morning. He knew that it was only a matter of time before Dalrymple would revisit them and try to take back his slave by force and, with Mistress Finesilver as his accomplice, he might well succeed.

Pouring tea into the old anatomist's dish, the housekeeper's eyes narrowed. She'd sensed something was afoot when she had discovered the young doctor's shaving brush and alum stick were missing. A quick foray into his clothes chest, together with the sight of the slave's empty bed, confirmed her suspicions. The doctor and his black friend had taken flight. The dream of owning her blue hat with its gold lace trim had slipped away from her and she set the teapot down with such a force that Dr. Carruthers's dish rattled on its saucer.

The journey to Boughton took two days. Leaving Hollen Street before first light, they had been on the road for four hours before Thomas thought it safe to stop. He had hired a cab to take them out of London as far as Beaconsfield, from whence they had taken the coach to Oxford. Jeremiah was traveling as his manservant so as not to arouse suspicion. It had been agreed that he would be much safer at Boughton Hall than in London.

Less than five miles north of the city the landscape had changed into a frozen wilderness. Snow carpeted the fields, rivers were glassy ribbons, and although the roads were passable with care, the icy ruts and gouges proved formidable obstacles from time to time.

Jeremiah remained subdued, sleeping most of the way. Thomas had swathed him in blankets so that his head, in particular, had been cushioned against the buffets of the carriage as it rattled and swayed over the country roads. The thick leather curtains in the coach had provided scant protection from the cold, so Thomas's face and feet were still numbed. Yet the sight of the chapel spire on the Boughton estate set his pulse racing and he managed a broad smile.

"We are here, Jeremiah," he announced. He glanced over to his patient, who opened his eyes at the sound of Thomas's voice. Blinking away the fog of sleep, he sat up slowly. Thomas had cleared away a large circle of misted glass, so that Jeremiah could see the chapel up ahead.

"In a few moments we shall be warm and safe, Jeremiah," muttered Thomas, as much to himself as to his patient. "Warm and safe." It was Will Lovelock, the young groom, who spotted the carriage first and alerted the rest of the household. Lydia, who had been on tenterhooks since sending Thomas the letter, rushed downstairs in time to see the carriage arrive.

As soon as he saw Lydia standing on the steps waiting to greet him, any discomfort Thomas felt melted away. Ignoring the stiffness in his joints and the bruises he had sustained after his journey, he bounded up the steps and clasped her by both hands. Holding them tight for a few seconds, he gazed into her eyes for the first time in months. He found the look she returned reassuring.

"But you must be frozen!" she exclaimed. "Come inside. There is hot soup waiting!"

Thomas hesitated to follow. "I am not alone," he told her. Lydia's brow furrowed. "Not alone?"

Letting her grasp fall, Thomas returned to the carriage and, proffering his hand, led out a slightly bewildered Jeremiah Taylor. As he guided him up the hall steps, a look of alarm darted across Lydia's face when she saw that the stranger's head was swathed in a bandage. Thomas presented Jeremiah to her and the slave managed a shallow bow.

"This, Lady Farrell, is Jeremiah, and we would ask you . . ." Thomas suddenly checked himself. "I would ask you that he stay here for a few days."

The confused look on Lydia's face suddenly dissipated. "He is your valet, yes?"

The doctor was supporting the young man, clasping him 'round his waist, as his legs bowed under his own meagre weight.

Thomas teetered as the slave shifted awkwardly. "I will explain everything," he told her, "just as soon as we are inside."

"Of course," she replied and she turned quickly, leading her guests into the warmth of the entrance hall where a fire blazed in the grate.

Howard the butler swiftly assessed the situation. A room had been prepared for Dr. Silkstone, but not for his manservant. Orders were given. Suitable accommodation was found in the servants' quarters. Mistress Claddingbowl, the cook, was informed of the arrival and food was prepared. Within a few minutes the flurry of excitement had died down and calm had been restored to the hall.

Lydia was forced to wait until Howard had poured Thomas a brandy and left the drawing room before she could start her interrogation. Planting herself next to him on the sofa where he sat warming himself, she began.

"Tell me, what on earth is going on?" Her voice was brimming with curiosity as she clutched hold of his arm. "That blackamoor is no more your manservant than I am! Something is afoot and I have a right to know."

Thomas nodded. "Of course you do!" he protested. "It is just that we must be discreet." He lowered his voice. "Jeremiah Taylor is a slave who was beaten to within an inch of his life. He managed to escape, but his master wants him back and has already tried to recapture him."

Lydia looked shocked at the prospect. "To recapture him by force? But surely the law of England does not permit that?"

Thomas saw her concern. "The law has little regard for runaway slaves and their owners even less. They regard them as their property. There is scant regard for their welfare."

She nodded. "Then he is most welcome to stay here for as long as he chooses," she replied. "We can find work for him when he is fully recovered. I shall inform Mr. Lupton."

"Mr. Lupton?" repeated Thomas.

"The new estate manager."

The doctor could not hide his surprise and his brow arched involuntarily. In her letters she had not mentioned she had replaced Gabriel Lawson. His death in the summer had left the post vacant. Thomas had thought that Lydia might have consulted with him before she had appointed someone to the position. She had always valued his opinion before. It suddenly occurred to him that perhaps their enforced separation meant that the distance between them was growing.

He nodded, yet at the same time detected a certain awkwardness in her manner, as if she were holding something back from him.

"I am glad you have found a new man," he told her. "He is proving efficient in his post?"

"Yes. Most. Mr. Lupton has many ideas," she replied coolly. Her mouth worked itself into a smile. She was careful not to be too gushing in her praise.

News of Thomas's arrival spread as quickly as spilled buttermilk across the estate at Boughton. The young groom had told the shepherd, who had told his father, who had told the miller, who had told the dairy maid, and so it went on. Dr. Silkstone was back, and he had brought a blackamoor with him.

Sitting by the fire at Plover's House later that evening Nicholas Lupton was eager to find out more.

"So, Mistress Fox," he began, addressing his housekeeper, "there are visitors at the hall, I believe." He was filling his pipe at the time.

Mistress Fox, always keen to pass on scraps of gossip as if they were bones to dogs, set down her master's rum toddy with a gleam in her eye. "Yes, sir," she replied. "Dr. Silkstone has returned."

Lupton nodded. "The famous Dr. Silkstone, the American colonist once betrothed to Lady Lydia, if I am not mistaken." There was a hint of sarcasm in his tone, as if he were standing at the village pump, dishing out scandal.

It made Mistress Fox more wary of him. She straightened her neck. "Dr. Silkstone is a man of good standing, sir, with a reputation for being a fine surgeon."

Lupton sucked on his pipe and a curl of smoke rose into the air. "So I hear. I believe he will visit the late Lord Crick's godfather."

Mistress Fox narrowed her eyes slightly. Her master seemed very well informed about her ladyship's relationships for a man who had only been in his post for little over a month. "I believe so, sir," she replied, bobbing a quick curtsy and making for the door.

"Oh, and Mistress Fox," Lupton called her back. "One more thing. Did Dr. Silkstone travel alone?" He had heard the rumor, but needed it confirmed.

The housekeeper clamped her mouth shut, as if to staunch the flow of words, but she could not stop her natural inclinations for long. After a moment she replied, "I believe he was traveling with a Negro, sir."

"A Negro?" Lupton raised both brows.

"Yes. You don't see many of that sort 'round here, unless they be at fairs or shows," she mused, her eyes suddenly bright. "Some say he's a runaway slave."

"Do they indeed?" Lupton drew on his pipe once more, content to listen to the woman's prattle.

"Yes, sir, that he was beaten then rescued by Dr. Silkstone.

'Tis just the sort of thing the good doctor would do, him having a heart of gold," she told him in a flurry of breathless excitement. " 'Tis only a pity that that ogre will not let them marry."

"You speak of Sir Montagu Malthus?"

Mistress Fox checked herself for speaking out of turn. "You know him, sir?" she asked awkwardly.

"You may speak freely. He is of no consequence to me," came Lupton's reply.

Reassured, the housekeeper glowered into the grate at the very thought of the lawyer who stood in the way of her mistress's happiness. "As mean a man as you'll ever find, sir, and that's no lie."

"So it sounds," said Lupton, with a nod. "This Dr. Silkstone is obviously a man of great reputation here at Boughton," he said finally. "I hope I shall have the pleasure of making his acquaintance."

Thomas lay in his bedchamber at the hall, his body rigid with anticipation awaiting Lydia's coming. Each footstep, each low whisper, each door shutting on the landing, caused his heart to leap. It was after midnight when his own door opened and she stood for a moment, holding her candle. Leaping up, he took it from her and in the darkness found her mouth. But she was quick to push him away.

"My love," she whispered, "not tonight. I need you to hold me."

In a second Thomas's ardor fell away, as if someone had taken his breath from him. But in the half light he saw Lydia smile at him and he felt reassured.

"Of course," he said softly, taking her by the hand and leading her into his bed. She lay her head on his shoulder and he stroked her chestnut hair. It had been so long since he had felt its silkiness against his skin and smelled her scent of lemon.

Neither of them spoke a word. Thomas longed to, but he recognized there was healing in the silence. In the candlelight, he studied her hand, palmed against his naked chest, her delicate fingers and her neat nails. For now this was all he could ask for and, for now, it was more than he could have hoped barely three months ago. He did not care that they had broken a court order; no one would ever know. No piece of parchment could tell them that they should forever be apart. He would not give up hope. He watched the candle as it guttered and fizzed and was suddenly gone, leaving the entire room in darkness. Now the only sound he could hear was Lydia's breath as it gradually slowed and deepened and she fell fast asleep.

Chapter 47

Lydia insisted on accompanying Thomas on the journey to Draycott House. Normally it would take three hours, but the condition of the roads lengthened it, so frequently did the carriage become mired in the slushy ruts. They sat side by side, a fur throw covering their knees, with Eliza opposite them. They talked more as friends, not lovers. They spoke of Richard and of the estate and of Thomas's cataloguing work in London, but on their enforced separation there was a tacit silence. Thomas knew that Lydia had engaged a lawyer to seek a review of their case by the Court of Chancery, but he could not talk of it in front of the maid. If there had been progress, he knew she would have mentioned it. There was so much he wanted to say and yet his tongue felt constrained by Lydia's manner, as well as by Eliza's presence. As soon as he saw that the maid had dozed off, he reached for Lydia under the throw; he plaited his fingers through hers and felt the warmth of her palms on his cool hand.

"I have missed you more than I can say," he said softly. But as soon as he had uttered the words, he realized they were lost amid the clatter of the horses' hooves and the rattle of the carriage. He wondered if he should repeat them but when he glanced up at her and saw she was looking out of the window, he thought better of it. Instead he turned his thoughts to Sir Montagu and the prospect of performing a pioneering and dangerous operation on his old adversary.

* * *

Arriving in the early afternoon, Lydia was immediately shown into Sir Montagu's chamber. Thomas was asked to wait downstairs. The room was still in semidarkness and one of the physicians took her gently to one side as soon as she entered.

"He has been asking for you, your ladyship," said Dr. Brotherton, in reverent tones. "We have sedated him, but he cannot continue like this indefinitely."

Lydia nodded. "I am come with Dr. Silkstone, as I said I would," she replied.

The physician's lips moved in a smile, but his eyes were full of resentment. It was evident he did not care for any outside intervention.

"He has asked to speak with you, Dr. Brotherton," she told him.

She waited until the physician had left the room before walking over to where Sir Montagu lay. Pain seemed to have shrunk his body. He looked like a pale rag that had been wrung out and his breathing seemed labored. Sitting by his side, she took hold of his hand and he opened his eyes. She noted they seemed to have sunk further back into his head, like pools of cloudy water.

As soon as he recognized her, he let out a shallow yelp.

"My dear, I am so glad you are here," he whispered, his breath rasping.

She stroked his forehead. "Dr. Silkstone is come, too, sir," she replied softly. "He will examine you and make you well again."

Sir Montagu grunted. She was not sure if he was deriding Thomas, or if he was thankful for his arrival.

"I need to tell you something," he said, squeezing Lydia's hand as tightly as a sick man could. "Something important."

Lydia felt her heart jump. Perhaps the thought of his impending death had made him relent. Perhaps he would lift the court order that prevented her from marrying Thomas. She had not dared to dream of such a moment. Ever since, less than six months ago, he had shown her the huge scroll, covered in Latin script, and told her that Richard was a ward of court, her vision of the future had seemed without hope.

"Yes, sir," she said, leaning closer so that she could feel his breath on her cheek.

"I am dying, Lydia," he said, looking up at her with listless eyes.

She gripped his hand tighter. "No, sir. Dr. Silkstone will save you. I know he will."

He closed his hooded lids for a moment, then opened them once more and fixed her with a strange look. His eyes were welling up, so that a tear spilled over and ran down his cheek. "I am dying," he reiterated, suddenly finding more strength, "and I need to tell you something. Something I have kept hidden for many years."

Lydia suddenly felt her nerves tighten. His words sounded weighty and ominous. "I am listening," she said softly. "I am listening."

Thomas donned his leather apron and laid out his personal set of knives on the bureau. If all went according to plan he would only need to use one. He left the bone saw in its case. There would be no need of it, he told himself.

They had brought a table up from the kitchen and set it beside the window so there was a good supply of natural light. Dr. Felix Fairweather, familiar to Sir Montagu, had been summoned from Brandwick and had agreed to assist the other physicians should it be deemed necessary. While he had a previous association with the patient, he came more out of curiosity than respect for Thomas as a surgeon. Sir Montagu's groom and footman had been tasked to hold their master firm.

The patient's senses had already been dulled by a shot of brandy mixed with laudanum, so that he offered no resistance as they carried him onto the table. A cloth gag was placed between his teeth to muffle his cries.

Thomas did not allow himself to look into Sir Montagu's face. All his feelings toward him must be put to one side. He dared not let his own emotions cloud his judgment. His focus was the left leg that lay dappled and distended in front of him. It was his alpha and his omega. In that moment, there was nothing else. He lifted the scalpel, saw the muscle tense, and leaned over to deliver the first cut.

The incision, about five inches long, was made swiftly along the inner, lower part of the thigh. Sir Montagu let out a muted whine and flinched, but the men held him steady and, undeterred, Thomas exposed the bulbous section of the artery, the size of a pigeon's egg, as it throbbed in the leg. Seizing it in his left hand, he separated it from the membrane and the vein, so that he held the swollen crimson tube in between his thumb and his forefinger.

The footman's face turned a shade of pale gray and he swayed a little. The groom saw him waver and nodded at the bed. The footman staggered away from the table and sat down, his head bowed.

"Probe," Thomas called to Dr. Fairweather, holding out his bloodied hand. The physician, whose attention had been drawn away by the fainting footman, looked blankly at Thomas.

"Probe," he repeated, this time louder.

Fairweather seemed vexed. He dithered, his hand hovering over three or four instruments before he lifted the appropriate one and gave it to Thomas. Seconds had been lost, valuable seconds, but soon Thomas was passing a silver needle threaded with a thick ligature under the artery.

Sir Montagu gave a sharp yelp each time the thread was tied, but the groom kept his body steady.

"This will block it off," Thomas explained, tying the catgut tightly at the lower end.

The pulsation in the bulging mass stopped immediately but the blood was pumping with such force that there was still a danger the artery might burst. It spattered the nearby wall and sprayed the coverlet on the bed.

"We will lose him," blurted Fairweather. His hands began to shake and he sent the probe clattering to the floor.

Ignoring the physician, Thomas worked as deftly as a lace maker, tying another thread two inches away from the first, finishing the knot less tightly. Above this second one he made a third, securing it more loosely, followed by a fourth. Sir Montagu expelled another longer moan, but the groom was now joined by the footman once more and together the men held their patient firm.

Next Thomas pulled the threads to the outside and separated them, before securing the edges of the wound. It was only then that he became conscious of breathing again. He sucked in deeply and looked at Dr. Fairweather, his cheek spattered with blood. The whole procedure had been completed in less than five minutes and yet they had seemed among the longest five minutes of his life. Each second had seemed magnified, elongated, and held aloft, but at the end of it he felt exhilarated and triumphant.

"Shall you dress the wound, Dr. Fairweather?" Thomas asked. He was eager to give the physician a chance to redeem himself. Such displays of nerves were usually confined to sophomores, who were new to surgery. He had not expected to see such edginess in a physician of many years' standing, even though the operating theatre was not his usual domain.

Taking a step back, Thomas let Fairweather inspect the wound. He still seemed aloof and strangely tense.

"Leave the threads out. I shall remove those later," Thomas instructed.

Walking over to his case, he took out a jar of aloe vera gel. "Smear this along the wound, too, if you will. It contains healing properties," he told the physician.

Fairweather nodded and, taking the pot, began to coat the laceration in the greenish gel.

Thomas walked up to the other end of the table and motioned to the men to stand aside. Leaning over, he saw that Sir Montagu's eyes were half open and his features were more relaxed. Gently he removed the gag and smiled.

"It is done, sir," he said, a note of victory sounding in his voice.

His patient licked his lips. "And I am alive," he replied weakly.

Wiping his bloody hands on a towel, Thomas felt his patient's pulse. It was steady.

"You are, indeed, alive, sir, and I believe the operation was a success."

Sir Montagu grunted and touched his surgeon's hand. "Then I am much indebted to you, Dr. Silkstone," he said.

As soon as Lydia heard footsteps on the landing she rushed into the hallway. She had been pacing the floor in the drawing room, wringing her hands, mouthing prayers, while the operation had been in progress. She had dreaded hearing Sir Montagu's cries, but feared the silence, too. He had obviously thought he would die on the operating table. He did not have the faith in Thomas that most men of medicine did. Why else would he have told her? Why else would he have divulged the secret that had been kept hidden for twenty-five years? She had not wanted to tell Thomas before the procedure. One slip of the scalpel, one artery severed in a split second. It would have made his burden even greater, almost intolerable.

Now, as she saw Thomas descend the stairs, she looked for signs in his manner. He appeared calm. She tried to read the expression on his face as he lifted his gaze. It was inscrutable, but it did not take long before she allowed herself to smile.

"All is well, m'lady," he announced as he reached the bottom of the stairs.

"Thank god!" she cried, hurrying toward him. Her inclination was to bury her head in his shoulder and to tell him that she had never doubted him, but Dr. Fairweather was following close behind.

"How fares Sir Montagu?" she asked anxiously, her eyes darting from one man to the other.

Thomas nodded. "It was a difficult procedure, but the swelling has gone down and I believe he is out of imminent danger."

Lydia's small frame heaved visibly with relief. "I am most grateful to you," she said, looking at Thomas. "And to you, Dr. Fairweather," she added.

The older physician shrugged and shot a sheepish glance at Thomas. "I was only a bystander, your ladyship. Dr. Silkstone must take full credit," he told her in a show of uncustomary modesty.

"May I see Sir Montagu?" asked Lydia.

The two men exchanged looks. "He is resting now," Thomas told her.

"And that is what I must do, too," butted in Fairweather. "I have had quite enough for one day," he murmured under his breath and, bowing graciously to Lydia, he left the room, so that she and Thomas were alone at last.

Lydia walked forward and Thomas reached out for her hands. Drawing her close to him, he breathed in her perfume, trying to dispel the metallic reek that enveloped him. She felt so slight and delicate in his arms as she buried her head on his shoulder.

"Thank you," she whispered.

" 'Tis too soon for thanks. The next few hours will be critical," he told her.

She pressed his chest with the palms of her hands so that she could look him in the eyes. "And we will spend those hours together?"

He smiled and kissed her tenderly on her forehead. "If you will allow it."

"I would not have it any other way," she replied. "But first I need to tell you something." Her smile suddenly disappeared to be replaced by the look of one who has solemn news to impart. "We need to sit," she told him.

As she led Thomas by the hand to the window seat, there was a knock. Howard's head appeared 'round the door.

"Mr. Parker is here, your ladyship. He wishes to speak with Dr. Silkstone," he said.

Thomas sighed. "The surgeon," he explained. "He intended to watch the operation, but was delayed. Forgive me. I must go to him."

Lydia nodded. "Of course," she said. "What I have to tell you will wait."

Chapter 48

A slice of first light cut through a gap in the drapes, nudging Thomas from a disrupted night's sleep. He had spent the last six hours in a chair by Sir Montagu's bed, propped up with pillows and a coverlet to keep out the cold. There had been a slight possibility that his patient could hemorrhage, in which case quick action would be imperative. As it was, Sir Montagu seemed to have spent a more restful night than his surgeon.

Thomas rose slowly and stretched his stiff limbs, extending his arms wide and rolling his head around, before lifting each leg to aid circulation. Despite his care not to make a sound, Sir Montagu opened his eyelids and called out.

"Silkstone," he cawed, his great arm flapping against the bedsheet.

The doctor leaned over. "Sir, how do you feel this morning?" he asked, taking his wrist and checking his pulse against the ticking of his pocket watch.

"The pain is lessened," he replied, lifting his head slightly from the pillow to look at his leg. "It is still there?" he asked, momentary panic seizing his voice.

Thomas nodded. "It is, indeed, sir. I did not amputate, and in a few days you should be able to walk."

His patient grunted and fell back onto his pillows. "Silkstone," he called once more. The doctor bent low again. "Thank you," said Sir Montagu, his hooded eyes wide with gratitude. He clasped Thomas's hand in a rare and almost unheard-of show of appreciation. "Thank you."

By ten o'clock, washed and packed, Thomas had joined Lydia for breakfast in the morning room. Its dimensions were not too grand, but the fact that the servants still hovered by the sideboard meant that they could not talk freely unless they lowered their voices.

"Your patient seemed in remarkably good spirits," said Lydia, her voice slightly stilted, as she sipped a dish of tea. She had already called in on Sir Montagu to bid him farewell and had found him sitting up in bed eating porridge.

"Yes," agreed Thomas. "I am very pleased with his progress." Doctors Brotherton and Biglow had excused themselves, both citing urgent cases that needed their attention, so the lawyer's care had been left in the hands of Dr. Fairweather. Despite the physician's poor showing as an assistant at the operating table, Thomas was confident in his ability to administer to Sir Montagu over the next few days until he could return himself in person.

Seated opposite Lydia at the small, round table, he smiled as a plate of eggs and bacon was set before him. This was what he relished; this was what he so missed: the domesticity of it all, of being able to look at the face of the woman he loved over the breakfast table each morning and to discuss their plans for the coming day. And in this setting, in this moment, he dared to dream. A great rush of warmth suddenly engulfed him.

"Do you think . . . ?" he began. She returned his gaze with a look that so captivated him, it made him forget what he was about to say. She cleared her throat pointedly and he sharpened his eye on her once more. "You were going to tell me something when the other surgeon arrived yesterday."

He noted the expression of surprise on her face. Slowly she lowered her dish into its saucer, as if trying to play for time, before she met his gaze once more.

"I have reason to believe that Sir Montagu might relent," she told him.

Thomas's eyes opened wide and, without thinking, he grasped

her hand. Her head darted toward a servant and he withdrew it immediately.

"What gives you cause?" he urged, trying to suppress his excitement.

Lydia straightened her back and leaned forward slightly. Her voice lowered to a whisper. "He told me how very grateful he was to you," she murmured.

Thomas seemed a little disappointed. "And no more?"

Lydia's lips quivered. "Now is not the time," she told him, glancing at the servant who approached to clear her tea bowl. "I will tell you presently," she added with an intriguing smile.

The return journey proved almost as treacherous as the outgoing. Eliza joined Thomas and Lydia and together they were jounced around bends and jostled over rutted tracks until Boughton's boundary finally came into view.

The young anatomist remained tense throughout. Although the surgery on Sir Montagu had gone as well as he could have anticipated, his mind was still deeply troubled by events in London. He had made little progress with the cataloguing of the specimens and was no closer to finding Matthew Bartlett's murderer.

A few minutes later and the carriage was rattling through the gates at the southeastern corner of the estate, near Plover's Lake. Looking out of the window, Lydia spied Nicholas Lupton on his horse as he rode down the track from his house to meet the main drive through the estate. As he pulled up to allow the party to pass, Lydia knocked on the ceiling with a stick to signal the driver to halt.

"What goes on?" asked a puzzled Thomas.

"I want you to meet the new estate manager," replied Lydia, grabbing the handle on the carriage window to open it. She put her head out and signaled. Lupton urged his horse nearer until he had drawn level.

"Good morning, Mr. Lupton," greeted Lydia cheerfully.

Lupton doffed his hat. "Good morning, your ladyship," he replied with a smile.

Thomas leaned forward in his seat. He did not understand why Lydia felt it necessary to introduce them, let alone at this particular juncture.

"Dr. Thomas Silkstone, I would like you to meet Mr. Nicholas Lupton, Boughton's new estate manager," said Lydia proudly.

Thomas managed a thin smile, but Lupton went further.

"I am honored to meet you, sir. I have heard so much about you."

Thomas acknowledged the greeting with a considered nod. "You must not believe everything you hear, sir," he replied. There was an awkward pause as Lupton considered how to react, until Thomas came to his aid. "I hope you are settling in well, Mr. Lupton," he said.

Lupton nodded and slithered a sideways smile toward Lydia.

"Her ladyship has made me feel most at home at Boughton," he said.

Thomas noted the manner in which the estate manager looked at her and the way that Lydia returned his look. He detected a certain intimacy between them and he was not comfortable with what he saw. It seemed as if some invisible electric current sparked between them and it was surely the reason why Lydia's ardor toward him had cooled. Nevertheless he nodded politely, masking his discomfort, and within a moment or two the carriage had set off once more, back to the hall.

Richard ran to greet his mother as soon as he saw her coming up the steps, despite Nurse Pring's protests. He buried his face in Lydia's skirts and she held him close.

"Yes, I am back, my sweet, and I bring a dear friend with me," she said.

The boy looked over to Thomas, his eyes traveling up and down his body.

"You remember Dr. Silkstone? He helped make your arm better?"

Thomas bent low and smiled. "Hello, Richard," he greeted. "How you have grown!"

Yet still the child remained looking quizzically, until finally he shook his head. "No, Mamma. I don't recall him," he replied, then taking Lydia's hand, he asked: "Can I go riding with Mr. Lupton today?"

The slight was unintentional, but Thomas found it deeply wounding. He had been absent a long time. Too long. Worse still, it seemed that this estate manager, this Mr. Lupton, had slipped into his shoes. He had wormed his way certainly into the young earl's affections, and perhaps Lydia's, too.

Before she replied to her son, Lydia shot Thomas a chastened look that also seemed to contain an apology, but it was too late. Upstairs in his room, he made up his mind. He would return to London later that day.

Chapter 49

Phibbah had lingered seven days before she gave up the fight. A few hours before she expired, Patience found the girl delirious with fever, shouting out all manner of obscenities and curses and claiming there was an obeah on her. She spoke of a great black bird swooping down, pecking at her eyes, and she jerked and jolted her body to avoid its attack. Her own arms flapped wildly and, no matter how she tried, Patience could not calm her. She had called Venus, who had managed to pour some medicine down her gullet. Within a few minutes she was calm. Within a few more, she was dead.

They covered her body in a bedsheet and Venus ordered that it be left on the floor of the garret until Mr. Roberts could deal with it. Then she went to inform her mistress. Entering Cordelia Carfax's chamber, she found her standing by her window, looking out onto the gardens.

"Phibbah is dead, missa," she said, bowing her head as she curtsied.

Without turning from the window, Cordelia Carfax was silent for a moment. A victory had been scored; a small one, granted, but a victory nonetheless. "Good," she finally replied. "Make the necessary arrangements."

Thomas returned to Hollen Street two days later, exhausted after his arduous trip back from Oxfordshire. He was looking forward to sleeping in his own bed and seeing Dr. Carruthers once more. Perhaps he was imagining it, but it felt a good deal less wintry in London. Most of the snow was gone and the wind had lessened. Thoughts of resuming his cataloguing and taking up the reins once again in the search for Matthew Bartlett's murderer flew around in his head like the pigeons at St. Paul's. They were present, but for the moment they could wait until he had settled back in. He had certainly not anticipated what happened next.

As he stepped out of the carriage to walk over to the front stairs of his home, he felt someone tap him on the shoulder. He turned to see a man, small and round, dressed in the black garb of the legal profession, standing beside him.

"Dr. Silkstone?" he asked, his face as void of expression as a blank piece of parchment.

"Yes," replied Thomas, with the uncertainty of a man taken by surprise.

"Dr. Thomas Silkstone?"

"I am he."

Moving forward a pace, the man brought his arm up. He was holding a scroll in his hand and touched Thomas with it lightly on the shoulder.

"Then, sir, I serve you with this summons to appear before the Westminster magistrate, charged with the kidnap of the slave Jeremiah Taylor, property of one Mr. Josiah Dalrymple, resident of Jamaica."

For a moment Thomas simply stared at the scroll as it rested on his shoulder. He then lifted his gaze to the little man, who remained motionless, like some strange automaton. Finally he reached up for it and with a fervor that registered shock on the little man's hitherto blank face, he snatched the summons from him with a smile.

"I am most grateful to the court and to your good self, sir," said Thomas, bowing his head graciously.

The court official, his expression now altered to reveal his surprise at this defendant's reaction, returned the bow. It was not often that he came across one so grateful for his visit.

"I bid you good day, sir," he said, turning and walking off down the street.

"A good day, yes," repeated Thomas to himself, opening his front door. So, the gauntlet had been thrown down and he had picked it up with relish. The opportunity was great, but so, too, was the legal challenge. Here was his chance to clarify the law of England, to establish a right to freedom of all slaves on English soil once and for all. He would visit Granville Sharp at the very next opportunity.

At Hubert Izzard's anatomy school that evening all was quiet. The students had left, the beadle had mopped the floor clean of blood and discharged all the entrails and soft tissues into the street drain. So now the anatomist found himself alone in his office awaiting the next delivery for tomorrow's public dissection. It came on time.

As soon as the porter had laid it on the table in the theatre and been paid for his pains, Izzard casually lifted the hessian. A pubescent Negro girl, he noted. He drew the sackcloth back further to inspect the breasts. Interesting, he thought to himself, for a girl so painfully thin, how many small pimples dotted the area around her nipples. He counted a dozen in the areola. A smile hovered on his lips. Could it be that the girl was either pregnant or recently so? The answer to his question came swiftly and without a cut being made. He had not realized it at first, but this time the corpse had come accompanied.

Cordelia Carfax had been watching him and now emerged from the doorway, swathed in a cloak. Pulling down her hood, she revealed an expression of smugness on her face, like a cat that had snagged a mouse, and was now depositing it at its master's feet.

Izzard's eyes widened at the sight of her. "Cordelia! But you should not be here!" he blurted, flinging the hessian back over the corpse and striding over to her. Arms enfolding her, he tried to turn her away from the cadaver, but she ignored him, pushing him aside. Eagerly she made her way over to the dissecting table.

"This one is special," she told him, her footsteps quickening as she approached. For a moment she paused, considering the cloth-covered mound, her eyes sharp as hooks. Then she stepped forward and, touching the hessian lightly, she said: "This one was bearing the child that I could never give my husband. This one tried to kill me." Snatching at the covering, she peeled it back once more and allowed herself a moment to gloat. As she studied the cadaver, her eyes lit up. She said nothing, but turned to Izzard with a strange smile on her face, as if she was relishing a triumph. Her victory was complete.

Chapter 50

"**D**alrymple is taking me to court!" cried Thomas, brandishing the writ he had been served only a few hours before.

Granville Sharp, not a man to express his emotions in such a demonstrable way, nodded but showed no more sentiment. "That is good news," he replied. He was sitting reading a folio as Thomas strode into his study. "It is high time the law was clarified. Please sit, Dr. Silkstone."

The young anatomist's head was reeling. It was crammed with facts that Dr. Carruthers had imparted about a famous case just ten years previously, involving a very similar situation, when an American slave named James Somersett escaped from his master while visiting England.

"The court found in his favor. I have precedence on my side, do I not, Mr. Sharp?" said Thomas, settling himself by the fire.

Sharp rose and, walking over to a brandy decanter on a small table nearby, poured out a large glass. He was not a qualified lawyer, but was well-versed in the vagaries of the law, having brought cases on behalf of the disadvantaged in society.

"Many hailed the ruling as a victory for freedom," he conceded, handing Thomas the glass, "but Lord Justice Mansfield's judgment did not expressly say that slaves become free when they set foot on English soil."

Thomas thought for a moment, then took a large gulp of brandy. "So I will have a real fight on my hands?"

Sharp shrugged. "I am afraid so, Dr. Silkstone. Mansfield's judgment is silent as to what a slave's status is in England."

Shaking his head, Thomas realized that his enthusiasm for his summons might be misplaced. In his mind's eye he saw the Carfax household and the cruelty and the machinations that blighted its every turn. He drained his glass and set it down with a dull thud on the table.

"But that still does not mean they can be murdered to order. English law does protect them on that score, surely?" he said, rising.

"Indeed, but . . ." Sharp was confused by Thomas's sudden change of direction.

"Then I suggest we pay another visit to the Crown Inn," he replied. "I am convinced that there lies the key to why so many have appeared on Hubert Izzard's dissecting table."

They waited until eleven o'clock, then took Sharp's carriage to the inn. It was shortly after midnight when they were deposited nearby. This time the campaigner had brought with him a young whippet of a boy. "My messenger," he announced. "In case we need to call the constables." He smiled reassuringly, but his foresight only served to unsettle Thomas.

Not wishing to draw attention to themselves, they walked a hundred yards or so to the alley. The doors of the inn were locked and they crept past them and stationed themselves by the small window once more.

The obeah-man was there again. He sat cross-legged in front of the fire, eating what looked like bread and cheese. The boy, meanwhile, set to work on the lock at the side entrance. It did not take him long to pick it, and soon he was opening the door into a passageway. At its end lay the obeah-man's lair.

When he heard the door creak open on its hinges, the old man lifted his head, then let out a muffled cry as he saw Thomas and Sharp walk in. In the half light they could see his face more clearly now, and, noting their shocked expressions, he seemed to be ashamed of himself and held up his hands to cover his face.

"We mean you no harm, sir," Thomas said calmly. "We would ask you some questions."

Scrambling awkwardly to his feet, the obeah-man appeared to concur and Thomas and Sharp drew closer, but then he suddenly snatched the snake from around his scrawny neck, and pointed it at them.

"You die!" he grunted, as the snake's tongue shot toward Sharp's face.

Undeterred, Thomas stepped forward and grabbed the serpent with his bare hands.

"Silkstone!" called Sharp, horrified.

Holding the creature close to his own face, Thomas inspected it as, obviously angered, it hissed at him.

"There is no need to fear, Mr. Sharp," he said. "I recognize this creature from the expedition's specimens brought back from Jamaica. It is neither venomous nor a constrictor. At the very most it will give you a harmless nip."

Thomas flung the snake to the ground and it slithered off into the shadows, sending the chickens squawking and flapping into a frenzy.

"So tell us, old man, what do you do with the slaves who come to you looking for freedom?" asked Thomas. He was advancing on the priest so that he was forced to slump onto his chair.

Narrowing his eyes, he seemed confused by the question. He shook his head. "I no kill slaves," he protested. "They go sleep, then wake up free." His tongue flapped inside his mouth and a spool of saliva hung down.

Sharp frowned crossly. "He talks gibberish, Silkstone."

Thomas raised a hand. "Perhaps not," he replied calmly.

Bending down so that he faced the man in all his hideousness, he said, "Where do they wake up free?"

The obeah-man tittered. "In Africa, of course," he said, nodding his head.

"What? The man's a demented idiot!" cried Sharp, but Thomas silenced him.

"It may not be as mad a notion as it sounds," he told him, wagging his finger. "The Quakers talk of freedom and to many of the slaves that is synonymous with their homeland." He looked about the cobweb-covered shelves. "What do you give them, old man, these slaves who would be free?"

The obeah-man hobbled over to the large glass jar that took pride of place on his shelf and heaved it down. Thomas moved forward and prized off the lid. Bending over the jar's neck, he sniffed at the contents, then delved into it, pulling out a handful of leaves. Holding them to the light, he inspected them closely, then began to shake his head. The distinctive leaves were familiar to him.

"What is it, Silkstone?" asked Sharp anxiously.

"If I am not very much mistaken, sir, these are from the branched calalue, a poisonous plant that seems to kill anyone who drinks it. In reality, however, it only slows down all the vital organs so that those who drink it have the appearance of being dead."

A look of concern scudded across Sharp's face. "And then?"

"And then they are given an antidote that seemingly brings them back to life."

"How do you know this?"

"This is the physic that Dr. Welton called the Lazarus potion. It can raise the dead." He turned to the obeah-man. "Is that not right, my friend?"

The old man lifted his half-chewed lip into a smile.

"Yeah. Yeah!" He nodded.

"Only in these cases, I am afraid no antidote is ever administered and the victims are dispatched, still alive, to be cut up on the dissecting table for profit."

"No!" shouted the old man, shaking his head vigorously. "No true!"

"I am afraid it is," came a voice in the doorway.

"Venus?" called Thomas, squinting into the darkness on the other side of the room.

"Yes, Dr. Silkstone. It is me," she replied, gliding into the pool of candlelight.

"You know this woman?" asked Sharp.

"She is a slave and housekeeper to a plantation owner," Thomas explained. He turned back to Venus and fixed her with a stare. "So you are the one."

"I do not understand!" snapped Sharp.

Thomas, keeping his eyes on Venus, began to enlighten his friend. "I knew in all of this there had to be someone the slaves would trust; a go-between who would convince them that the obeah-man's potion could somehow liberate them; that if they drank it they would wake up free."

Venus stepped forward, her composure suddenly deserting her. "I had no choice. I was forced."

"Who forced you, Venus? Who is behind all of this? Samuel Carfax, is it not?" He had seen master and housekeeper exchange furtive looks in the bedchamber when they thought he was not looking. He was certain she was his mistress as well as his slave.

Venus shook her head. "It is my missa."

Thomas frowned. "Mistress Carfax?" He found the thought so shocking that he let out an involuntary laugh. Then, after a moment's reflection, he recalled Jeremiah's account of the man and woman in the boot room. Izzard and Cordelia Carfax were lovers? If that was the case, it was all beginning to make sense, although he still could not fathom the housekeeper's role in all this. "So you would betray your own kind for her?" he pressed.

She shook her head despondently. "She promised me my freedom if I helped her."

"So you began where the Quakers left off, dangling liberty in front of any slave willing to listen?" Thomas brought a handbill from his pocket. "You knew that some of them would fall into the trap. That they would think they would escape to freedom, when all the while you knew they were going to their deaths?" As his anger mounted, so his voice grew louder. "How many died? Three, four, half a dozen?"

She shook her head. "I did not want to . . . I . . ." Her eyes were brimming with tears.

"You were trapped." Thomas made her excuse for her. "Is that it?" He recalled their conversation on the stairway a few weeks back and he realized he had no right to judge a woman in her position. He neither wanted nor needed a response. Instead he changed tack. "But your master knew nothing of this?"

She choked back her tears and straightened her long neck. "I hate my master as much as I hate her," she hissed.

Her logic made sense to Thomas. Hatred was an understandable reaction to her treatment. She had allowed herself to be used by Cordelia Carfax, although it did not excuse her actions. Thomas thought of the little Negro child.

"You killed Ebele?"

Venus shook her head. "I tried to save him, Dr. Silkstone, but he was weak."

Thomas held her gaze for a moment. "So you dispatched his body for dissection anyway?" He shook his head as he spoke. How sad it was, he thought, that those who were abused in life so often repeated the crimes that had been committed against their own person. She herself had been treated as less than human and that was how, given authority, she treated others.

She shrugged. "What should a white man care about one black child slave?" she asked.

"There are those of us who care most deeply," replied Thomas, resenting her remark and throwing a glance at Sharp.

He saw her mouth tighten as she lifted her head. "I care, too, Dr. Silkstone. That is why I am here. I care about Phibbah."

"Phibbah?" echoed Thomas. He thought of the girl whose simmering resentment had led her to try and poison her mistress. "What of her?"

"She dead, Dr. Silkstone," she told him, as calmly as if she were telling the time.

"How?" Thomas flashed a look of horror at the housekeeper. "You killed her?"

Venus's jaw worked uncomfortably. "She was a fool, believing in all this, thinking that obeah could kill the missa," she said, opening her arms and looking about her at the obeah-man's paraphernalia. "She was carrying the massa's child and the missa made her lose it."

"And now she lies dead by your hand?" Thomas asked incredulously.

The housekeeper lifted her gaze. "She no dead, Dr. Silkstone."

"What?"

"She only seem dead. The poison I gave her did not kill her."

"She remains alive?"

"That is why I am here. The obeah-man say he can raise her with the antidote. I want to save her from the knife man, otherwise she will be cut at first light tomorrow morning."

"The Lazarus potion," murmured Thomas.

"What?" snapped Sharp.

"The potion I was telling you about, that seems to have the power to raise the dead." He flashed a look back at Venus. "Where have they taken Phibbah?"

"To Mr. Izzard's anatomy school."

"I knew it!" Thomas shot a glance at Sharp. "This is how Izzard gets his corpses."

Chapter 51

Phibbah did not know if she was alive or dead. All she sensed was confusion and fear. A strange fog had settled in her head, dulling all her senses. There had been no vision, no dream, no encounter with her ancestors as she had imagined in death. There was no color, no music. Only darkness and silence. Then it occurred to her. What if she was dead and had been buried? Buried alongside the white people in the graveyard where she had collected her grave dirt. Sealed in their coffins and watched over by the women with wings, there was no escape for them. Perhaps she was now trapped, too.

A terror took hold of her guts and churned them about at the very thought. A pounding thumped inside her head, setting her teeth on edge. And now the fog was lifting. The blackness shifted and shapes began to appear in her head. At first she did not dare open her eyes. She was terrified that all she would see would be the blackness of the earth, that she would be lying entombed. She shivered. It was cold, as cold as the grave. Yet upon her forehead she could feel pricks of sweat. There was the coarseness of the hessian against her skin, too. She inhaled. The air was sharp, but not earthy. It whiffed of something strange and pungent like the missa's smelling salts. Trying to fill her lungs, she felt them tighten, as if an iron brace had been clamped around her ribs. She sniffed the air and thought she caught the scent of blood, a faint note of it that underlay everything else. It left a sickly taste in her gullet that unnerved her.

As the fog dispersed it drifted from her ears. Sounds were no longer muffled, but clear—strange creaks, as if from timber. From somewhere nearby came a sudden clank, followed by footsteps, then voices.

The noises made her stir. One by one she began trying to move her fingers, trying to coax her sluggish blood back to life. But she could not. Next she tried twitching her toes, but they refused her bidding. She tried to gulp down another lungful of air, but found that her chest still resisted her, as if there were hard, flat stones pressing down on her breasts. She was alive, yet she could barely move.

Slowly, fearfully, she tried raising her lids, as if they were windows opening onto a day that promised either death or deliverance. They unlatched themselves and she blinked. There was daylight, a checkered pattern that imprinted itself on wooden boards through a large pane up high. Light, not earth. She willed her drunken eyes to still in their sockets. Through a blurry haze she could make out rows of wooden benches. Perhaps she was on board a ship. Perhaps Cato had come and rescued her from her sickbed and she was bound for Africa. The sounds she had heard were the familiar creak of the mast and the feet of sailors on the upper decks as they made the vessel ready to cast off and set sail. That was what the obeah-man had tried to tell her. He had said she would know in her heart what path she should take and now she was on her way. That was it! They would leave the freezing, gray waters of England and make for the clear warm seas that washed the white beaches of Africa and all the stories she had heard and all the dreams she had dreamed would be real.

Phibbah's heart leapt at the very thought of it and she felt a great surge of joy pulse through her body, making her try and lift her head for the first time. But she could not. Instead she heard a voice, followed by another, oddly familiar, and then she felt a great tug across her torso that robbed her of her breath, followed by a stab of pain. A sharp cry escaped from her lips and she tried to bring her arms up, but they would not move. She tried lifting her legs, but they refused to obey.

Gasping for breath, she gulped the metallic air that now flooded her nostrils and mouth and terror seized her. She began trying to lash out. But she could not. There was a hurricane in the back of her throat that came rushing forth in a deafening torrent before another stab of pain silenced her.

They waited, all four of them, in the obeah-man's room for the rest of the night. The old man had given Thomas a phial that, he swore, contained the antidote for the poison. According to the old man, if its entire contents were poured into Phibbah's mouth, she would, within the hour, come alive again. Thomas recalled Sir Joseph Banks's account of the potion. He had shown faith in it and now so must he, despite his misgivings.

Time had hung slow and heavy and had given Thomas space to reflect. He mused on the small glass bottle he cradled in his hands. The amber liquid held therein looked so innocuous, yet it was so powerful. Could it be that Matthew Bartlett was murdered for its formula when this ugly old toad of a man knew it all along? Surely Cordelia Carfax's hand was not behind the brutal killing of the artist, too? The more he thought about it, the more disturbed he became and the more convinced he was that he was no nearer to finding out who killed Matthew Bartlett, or, for that matter, why.

Finally the night watchman called seven o'clock. It was still dark, but it was imperative that Thomas, Sharp, and Venus reach the anatomy school as soon as it opened if they were to save Phibbah.

The streets of London were waking to another cold day as the coach made its way to Brewer Street. They arrived just in time to find the night porter unlocking the door of the anatomy school for the beadle. Thomas accosted him.

"Sir, my name is Dr. Silkstone and this is my associate, Mr. Sharp. We would speak with Mr. Izzard on a most urgent matter. May we come in?"

The beadle, hunched and advancing in years, glanced beyond them to Venus, who waited in silence behind. He eyed both men suspiciously.

"A physician, you say?"

"Yes, and a fellow anatomist."

The beadle sighed heavily. "Very well," he conceded, gesturing the three of them inside. "Up the stairs," he told them. "Mr. Izzard will be in before eight o'clock."

It was a relief to hear that the anatomist had not yet arrived. It was so cold that Phibbah's body would no doubt have been stored upstairs overnight in readiness for the morning lecture. They waited on the landing so that the beadle could open the appropriate door for them. Choosing a key from his belt, he inserted it in the lock and pushed. The door opened onto the lecture theatre and there, to everyone's surprise, was Hubert Izzard. Seated on the front row, he cut a solitary figure, his head in his hands. He glanced up at the sound of footsteps, then shuddered as he took a deep breath.

"Sir, you are early. These gentlemen asked to wait for you," the beadle called across the room, shuffling toward the anatomist.

The old man's remarks seemed not to register. As Thomas drew nearer he could see there was a strange expression on Izzard's face, a wild, haunted look. His eyes were wide but unseeing and his lips were loose and pale. What was more, his skin was deathly white against the dried red blood on his yellow jacket.

Thomas glanced over to the dissecting table in the centre of the floor. There was a body on it, covered with blood-stained sacking. A sticky puddle of blood had congealed on the floor. A look of horror crossed Thomas's face and his eyes met with Izzard's.

From near the table came a cry. Venus had just thrown back the cover.

"Phibbah!" she gasped, her eyes wide with terror.

Granville Sharp had rushed over to her. Now he turned away to retch.

"She was alive, was she not?" said Thomas, drawing beside Izzard.

He returned his gaze and nodded slowly. "She asked . . ."

Thomas broke in. "You mean Cordelia Carfax?"

"Yes," he said, nodding slowly. "She asked me to cut the body in front of her. I had no intention of doing so. I wanted to save the girl for my students. But she said she admired my skill and wanted to watch." His eyes began to fill with tears. "I told her it was no sight for a lady."

"So you refused?"

"Of course, but she insisted and when I declined, she took the scalpel from me and made the first cut herself."

A terrible sound flew from Venus's mouth and she tugged at her hair.

"Tell me what happened." Thomas remained outwardly calm, despite a knot tightening in his stomach.

"She plunged the blade into the heart and the girl's eyes shot open." Izzard's body began to shake. "I begged her to stop. I tried to take the knife from her but she kept stabbing her, screaming all the time, until the girl was dead." His trembling turned to sobs and he dropped his head into his hands once more. "Oh god, Silkstone!" he wailed.

Granville Sharp could not hide his revulsion. "We must find this woman, immediately," he said, his face drained white. "Where is she now?"

Izzard shook his head. "You need look no further," he said, his voice juddering. "She is over there." He pointed to the far row of the lecture theatre, to what looked like a crumpled heap of rags. It was only when Thomas moved closer that he could see a syrupy pool of blood on the floor. But it was only when he was nearer still that he saw the familiar face of Cordelia Carfax, as she lay on her back, sprawled across a bench, a long blade embedded in her own heart. He shot a questioning look back at Izzard, whose watery eyes were now fixed on him.

"I tried to stop her," he muttered, shaking his head. "She killed herself."

Chapter 52

Sir Stephen Gandy had wasted little time in requesting a post-mortem on Cordelia Carfax. Thomas had no choice but to agree, so once again, he was faced with the prospect of performing an autopsy on someone he had known in life.

In the laboratory, Dr. Carruthers stationed himself by his side, as much for moral support as for professional input. There was important work to be done. Had Cordelia Carfax turned the knife on herself after killing Phibbah, as Izzard testified, or had he, her lover, stabbed her himself? A man's life hung, almost literally, in the balance. The gallows awaited Hubert Izzard if he had murdered Cordelia Carfax and on Thomas's shoulders lay the burden of proof.

Try as he might, however, the anatomist found it almost impossible to look on the corpse without recalling the look on Phibbah's face when he had found her dead earlier that morning. Her eyes, still open, almost bulged from their sockets, and horror had etched itself on her features.

Standing over Cordelia Carfax's naked torso, he was only glad that Dr. Carruthers could not see his hand tremble as he examined the knife wound. The blade remained in her chest—often a sign of a self-inflicted wound, he noted. It had entered between the third and fourth ribs, two inches to the left of the sternum at an acute angle upward from the subcostal region. Again, this was, in his understanding, another indicator of suicide. He shared his thoughts with his mentor from time to time, and received reassuring nods and grunts. There was only one fatal wound, he observed, which had been made when her chest was already exposed and not via her garment. This was often a feature of suicides, in his experience. They would often expose the proposed area of their self-inflicted wound.

"So was her heart black?" queried Carruthers, lifting his stick and tapping it on the stone flags. It was as if he had sensed the tension in the air and sought to break it with a quip.

Thomas allowed himself to smile. "Many would be surprised that it was not," he replied.

"And you have checked the hands?" asked the old anatomist. Thomas had. They were bloodied, but bore no defensive wounds, as might be expected in the case of an attack.

"I believe she took her own life, sir," Thomas concluded, straightening his aching back.

Dr. Carruthers nodded. "From what you have said, I concur."

"And Hubert Izzard is in the clear," replied Thomas. For the time being at least, he thought.

The drapes were drawn at the Carfax mansion, and casements shut, despite the turn in the weather. Even from the outside it seemed that the whole house was in mourning. Inside, it was the same story.

Thomas was shown into a hallway devoid of furniture. Gone were the grand paintings, and the marble busts had been covered with white sheets. Only Fino the dog seemed eager to greet him in the hallway with a frantic barking, thinking perhaps his mistress had returned.

He found Samuel Carfax in his study, staring out of the window onto the gardens. His normally jocular aura had dissipated to be replaced by a look of despair. His habitually ruddy complexion was pale and under his eyes were great bags. His large head seemed to have sunk even further between his shoulders. For a moment after Thomas was announced he did not move, as if trying to determine in his own mind how he should address him. Eventually he turned and looked at the doctor blankly.

"She's gone," he said. It was as if Carfax was thinking aloud rather than addressing his visitor. "She has left me."

Thomas thought of Cordelia Carfax's corpse now lying in the mortuary, bloated and darkening, awaiting the grisly fate reserved for those who took their own lives. She would be accorded the same fate as all her slaves. There would be no headstone for her, either, no marks made in stone to testify to a life well lived, no carved prayers or kind words from a loving husband, no women with wings to watch over her.

"My condolences, sir," said Thomas, his voice subdued. That was the reason for his visit. He had delivered his postmortem report to Sir Stephen's office and knew it would not be easy for Samuel Carfax to face the truth. His wife had led a double life. Not only had she been conducting an affair with one of his acquaintances, she had secretly trafficked the corpses of at least half a dozen slaves, selling them for a tidy profit to her lover. Some of them had even been murdered to order, but her last crime, the vicious stabbing of Phibbah, was the most horrific of all. Nevertheless their marriage had been a long, if not a happy, one and his wife's suicide would have compounded his intense distress. "You will miss Mistress Carfax greatly," he added, immediately realizing he sounded glib.

Carfax's reaction to his words came swiftly. He shrugged his great shoulders and shook his head, glowering at Thomas in disbelief. "I speak of Venus, Silkstone. Venus is gone."

Thomas could not hide his shock. He was lost for words and when they did come into his mind, he thought it best to remain silent. He would only allow Samuel Carfax to explain himself if he so wished. In his hand Thomas noticed the estate owner was holding something like a small coin. He turned it 'round and 'round, flipping it between his fingers, studying it now and again.

"She said she wanted her freedom, you see, Silkstone," he mumbled eventually, tossing the roundel disdainfully onto the desk. Thomas caught a glimpse of it as it scudded across the surface and landed nearer to him. It was a token against slavery, the sort that the Quakers distributed in the Crown Inn. He thought of Venus, tall and poised and proud, yet all the while hiding a hatred and contempt for both her master and mistress that had seared itself into her psyche as surely as the brand on Phibbah's flesh. Her attitude had at first surprised him when he had spoken briefly to her about Cato's disappearance. She seemed ambivalent to freedom; not content, yet not craving an escape.

"And you let her go?" asked Thomas gently.

Carfax snorted, as if he found Thomas's question vaguely amusing.

"I have no longer the will to fight, Silkstone. I am a broken man. I have lost my wife, my reputation, and any ambitions I had for a career in politics."

He picked up the roundel from the desk once more. Squinting at it, he read the inscription: "Am I not a woman and a sister?" and let out an odd laugh. "So she is now free and I have become a slave to my own folly. The irony of it, eh, Silkstone? The irony."

Lydia took advantage of the spring thaw to drive the dogcart down to Plover's Lake and to call in at Mr. Lupton's residence. Most of the snow had melted, leaving green shoots in its wake. She had even seen some primroses in bloom in the hedgerows. Hearing the clatter of the cart, the housekeeper came out to greet her.

"Will you have Mr. Lupton come and see me today, Mistress Fox?" Lydia asked her, adding: "I am most anxious to speak with him."

With the warmer weather, she wanted to revive the plans for draining the marsh land. The housekeeper, however, looked perplexed and began fidgeting, smoothing her apron with her plump fingers.

"What is it, Mistress Fox?" asked Lydia, seeing the woman's disquiet.

She shook her head. "I am most anxious to see him too, m'lady," she replied. "But he is gone."

"Gone?"

"Yes, m'lady. He took off early this morning, without so much as a by your leave. Didn't touch his breakfast." The woman twisted her apron.

"I am sure he will be back by nightfall," Lydia said, smiling.

But her words did nothing to allay the housekeeper's fears. "That's the thing, you see, m'lady. It looks like he won't be coming back."

"What do you mean?" Lydia snapped.

"Taken all his things, he has. All his bags and his trunk have gone. A carrier called for them, m'lady."

Lydia's forehead was suddenly furrowed by a frown.

"I see," she said slowly. "I am sure he will return presently," she tried to reassure her. She gave the housekeeper a polite smile to disguise her own surprise, then with a flap of the reins she urged on her horse.

In Draycott House, Sir Montagu Malthus was also relishing the sunshine that had been so noticeable by its absence throughout the coldest winter he could remember. The warm rays streamed through his bedroom window and added to his already cheerful mood. Only four days had elapsed since the operation on his aneurysm, but his recovery was astounding his erstwhile surgeon.

"I have to confess I am most impressed by Dr. Silkstone's ingenuity," murmured Mr. Parker as he inspected the leg. The scar was approximately six inches long and from it protruded intermittent lengths of thread, yet already the flesh was knitting and there seemed no sign of infection.

"I fear it takes little to impress you, Parker," sniffed Sir Montagu, easing himself up onto his elbows. "You'll tell me next that Fairweather is a passable physician."

The surgeon looked quite shocked. He was used to hearing physicians maligned by members of his own chirurgical profession, but not by patients and certainly not to his face. Personally he did not rate Fairweather, either. His knowledge was sketchy and his judgment was often, in his opinion, very poor. Nevertheless he felt compelled to spring to the defense of a fellow medical man. He cleared his throat.

"I believe he acted admirably during your surgery, sir," he countered.

Sir Montagu let out a derisory laugh. "Admirably, you say?" he repeated. "I expect he told you that!"

Mr. Parker cocked his head to one side and was reluctantly forced to admit that, yes, he had heard the phrase from Fairweather's own lips.

Sir Montagu, his hooded eyes returned to their piercing alertness, fixed the surgeon with an unnerving stare. "I may have been semiconscious when that American upstart, Silkstone, cut open my leg, but I was compos mentis enough to know that Fairweather went to pieces at the sight of this bloody limb." He pointed to his leg as Parker bent low to re-cover the wound. "I fear that the country physician let himself down very badly during his foray into chirurgical practice," he snarled, "and I do not intend to let him off lightly."

Chapter 53

The preliminary hearing of *Dalrymple versus Silkstone* was scheduled to be heard before the local magistrate at nine o'clock in the morning. Thomas had been given little time to prepare for the case, but had put his trust in Granville Sharp, whom he knew to be as good an ally as any man could have. Traveling as Sir Theodisius's manservant, Jeremiah Taylor had arrived back in London from Boughton Hall the previous day and had been offered accommodation at Sharp's Fulham residence.

The hearing was held in a small, cramped room that afforded little space between the players of the drama and served only to intensify the enmity between the two sides in the case. Sir Theodisius found the conditions particularly constricting, his cumbersome frame having to support itself on two wooden chairs.

The magistrate, a Mr. Burrill, was curmudgeonly and suffered, Thomas suspected, from asthma. He wheezed between each sentence and the stuffiness of the room seemed to compound his breathing problems. He sat behind a desk at the top end of the room, flanked by tables at which the two opponents were seated. By them sat their own counsel.

A clerk read the charge. Thomas was accused of stealing Jeremiah Taylor, the property of Josiah Dalrymple, and forcibly imprisoning him. The judge was told that on the afternoon of December 22, Taylor had gone missing from the residence of Mr. Samuel Carfax, where Dalrymple was visiting on business.

Acting on information received, the slave was later found at 34 Hollen Street, the home of Dr. Thomas Silkstone, "a citizen of the United States of America," the clerk helpfully pointed out. The Negro had been severely beaten. When asked to hand over Jeremiah, however, Dr. Silkstone had refused and challenged Mr. Dalrymple to fight him for the slave in court. Josiah Dalrymple's lawyer was a dishevelled young man who went by the name of Fitzroy. His experience was obviously very limited, as he told the magistrate, with the misplaced smugness that came with the arrogance of his youth, that it was a straightforward case that could be dealt with swiftly.

"I would remind you, or perhaps in your situation tell you, for the first time, Mr. Fitzroy, that there is no such thing as a straightforward case," wheezed Mr. Burrill.

Duly admonished, the young man sat down. Dalrymple glowered at him. He wore the angry expression of a man who realized, perhaps too late, that his barrister should not have persuaded him to accept this underling in order to save his services for the courtroom proper.

"So, Dr. Silkstone." Mr. Burrill turned to Thomas, who now stood. "I see you have a most learned friend." He nodded to Sharp, who returned the greeting. "What have you to say for yourself?"

The young doctor, although he could feel his guts churning inside, looked outwardly calm. Dressed in his smartest fustian coat and wearing, uncustomarily for him, a wig, he summoned all his composure, just as he would before performing surgery.

"Your honor, I am afraid the picture of events that has been painted is entirely spurious. The truth of the matter is I came across Jeremiah badly injured in the street. Had I left him there he would most surely have died in a few hours. As a doctor the Hippocratic oath binds me to care for the sick, so I did my duty and took him into my house. It soon emerged, however, that my patient was a slave from the branding on his chest and the collar around his neck."

Thomas paused for effect, allowing his gaze to roam 'round the stuffy room, giving Mr. Burrill a moment to ponder his words. He resumed: "Once he was conscious, he expressed a desire to escape his slave bonds. As I understand the law in England, sir, slavery is not permitted, as established in the case of James Somersett." He glanced to his right, deferring to Sharp, who sat listening intently. "I therefore believed myself acting in accordance with the laws of this fine land. I neither stole, nor kidnapped Jeremiah. He was free to leave my house at any time, but he chose not to return to captivity."

Mr. Burrill raised both brows, so that his wig lifted, too. "You would make a good lawyer as well as an anatomist, Dr. Silkstone," he complimented. He coughed into a kerchief, then proceeded. "So you would wish to call character witnesses, I believe?"

Thomas nodded. "I wish that Jeremiah Taylor give you his version of events first, sir."

"You may proceed," nodded the magistrate.

Jeremiah Taylor, looking fine in a dark green coat loaned by Granville Sharp and a high stock, stood up to speak. His nerves were plain for all to see. His hands shook and his voice was faltering when he confirmed his name. In answer to the magistrate's questions, he told him he had belonged to Mr. Dalrymple for ten years and lived on his sugar plantation near Kingston. Sometimes his master beat him, or withheld his meals.

"And that is why you ran away?" asked Mr. Burrill.

Jeremiah locked eyes with Thomas, then shook his head. "No, sir."

"Then why, pray?"

The slave tensed. His forehead suddenly glistened. "Because I heard something I was not supposed to, sir," came the reply.

The magistrate leaned forward. "And what might that have been?"

Jeremiah proceeded to tell Burrill how he had been locked in the boot room and how a man and woman had entered and spoken in low voices about dead Negroes, and that he hadn't understood what they were talking about but was afraid.

"What happened next?" pressed the magistrate.

"A boot fell off a shelf and then they saw me, and the man,

he beat me with a big stick, but I escaped, sir. I ran and I ran, even though my head hurt and there was a lot of blood."

"And where did you run?"

Jeremiah turned and fixed his eye on Thomas. "I wanted to find Dr. Silkstone."

The doctor was taken aback. This was the first time Jeremiah had mentioned that he knew of him prior to the attack and had been purposely seeking him out. Up until now Thomas had believed it was by sheer good fortune that he had found the injured slave.

"Why Dr. Silkstone, pray?"

"Because I heard he help sick slaves."

The magistrate leaned back in his seat. "Is this true, Dr. Silkstone?"

Thomas stood. "I attended the sugar planter Mr. Samuel Carfax at his home and found that one of his slaves, a child, had died without receiving any medical attention. I therefore offered my services free of charge should any more slaves fall sick, sir."

The magistrate arched a brow. "How very noble of you," he wheezed. He turned back to Jeremiah Taylor. "And you were treated by Dr. Silkstone?"

The slave nodded. "He save my life, sir, but when my master came looking for me, I did not want to go back with him. I want to be free man, sir."

"It is not your choice," mumbled Dalrymple under his breath.

Mr. Burrill coughed once more. "That is all," he told Jeremiah. "Do you have any other witnesses who can testify to your good character, Dr. Silkstone?"

Unsure of himself, Thomas looked questioningly at Granville Sharp, who nodded.

"I believe so, sir," he replied.

"Well then, where are they?" asked the magistrate, his head swiveling around the small room. "I can see no one else." Dalrymple snorted at the jibe, but as he did so, a second clerk appeared in the doorway. Standing behind him was a tall, distinguished-looking gentleman. It was Sir Joseph Banks.

The great man held his audience under his spell. He spoke eloquently of Thomas's many talents. He was, he said, a man of judgment and reason, who would never knowingly flout the laws of England, despite being an American citizen. He told Mr. Burrill how Thomas had been appointed to the prestigious position of keeper of the collections following the Jamaican expedition, and how his professionalism in all matters was unimpeachable.

Obviously honored that the president of the Royal Society should grace the hearing, Mr. Burrill had no choice but to dismiss the case against Thomas, even though he was already minded to do so before Sir Joseph's appearance. Dalrymple's charges, he opined, were ludicrous and would not stand up in a higher court. Somersett's case set the precedent for any English court to abide by the wishes of a slave to remain a free man while he stayed in this country.

Addressing Dalrymple, who had sat with a face like thunder throughout, the magistrate directed: "I order, sir, that you manumit Jeremiah Taylor and make a deposition to that effect."

Mr. Burrill then brought the proceedings to a close, walking out of the stuffy room, wheezing and puffing as he did so, desperate for a breath of fresh air.

The rest of the courtroom followed. Once outside, Thomas thanked Sir Joseph, Mr. Sharp, and Jeremiah most profusely.

"I am very much obliged to you all," he said.

"Nonsense," replied Sir Joseph. "The charges were a complete fabrication."

"So both of you are free men," remarked Sharp, lifting the corner of his mouth in a rare show of mirth. Turning to Jeremiah, he said, "Nothing would give me greater pleasure than to draw up that deposition and give it to your former owner."

The party broke up. Sharp took Jeremiah with him back to Fulham and Thomas was about to hail a carriage to Hollen Street, when Sir Joseph indicated he wanted a word. Thomas suspected the nature of the conversation and he braced himself for a chastisement.

"Matthew Bartlett," said Sir Joseph, drawing up beside the doctor.

"Sir?" replied Thomas disingenuously.

"Come, come, Silkstone," he said, as they continued to walk down the lane toward the main thoroughfare. "My spies tell me you have been rooting, despite my strict instructions to leave the matter to me."

Sir Joseph's words made Thomas wonder just how much the great man knew of his activities regarding the artist's murder. Nevertheless he did not anticipate what next came.

"All my inquiries have drawn a blank," he told Thomas, pausing to study his reaction. His voice barely hid a plea. "Have you fared any better?"

Thomas suppressed a smile. "I will revisit my postmortem notes, sir, to see if there is anything I might have missed."

Sir Joseph nodded. "You are a good man, Silkstone," he said. "Let's keep this between us, shall we?"

The young Earl Crick was decidedly bored. For the past two days Eliza had sought diversions for him, from playing with his tin soldiers to drawing. Lydia had even tried, unsuccessfully, to teach him to play draughts, but all he really wanted to do was frolic outside with Mr. Lupton.

"When will he be back, Mamma?" he would ask at every opportunity.

Lydia only wished she knew. All that she had been told by Mistress Fox, who was admittedly not the most reliable of sources, was that her master had taken off most suddenly. Standing by her study window, she looked out over the lawn. The snow was all but gone. The wind had changed direction and the mercury was rising. There were daffodil shoots in the shrubbery and the mere thought of spring brought a smile to her face.

What was more, she had heard word that the Treaty of Paris had been ratified by the Congress of the Confederation in Maryland. This meant that America and Britain were no longer at war. Thomas could no longer be termed an enemy of England. Another obstacle to their union had been lifted. She thought of him on his last visit. She had been deliberately distant with him, shielding herself from her inevitable despair at the prospect of the ban on their union never being lifted. He had not given up hope. She could tell that from his gestures, the way he had declared his love for her though she had pretended not to hear. She loathed herself for such seeming callousness, yet she felt she was acting in both their best interests.

Perhaps now, however, was the right time for her to pen her letter to him. Sir Montagu was making remarkable progress and had sent her word of his quickly improving condition only that morning. The news had lifted her spirits and given her fresh hope.

Turning to her desk, she picked up his letter and read it for the second, or was it the third time? *My condition is transformed,* he wrote. He had even, he reported, put pressure on the offending leg and managed a few steps. In fact, such was the rate of his recovery, that he had issued an invitation. It would, he told her, give him the greatest of pleasure if he might join her for what he described as *a celebratory dinner in honor of that most skilled and revered of surgeons, Dr. Thomas Silkstone.* She read the line again. They were words that she never thought to read from the pen of the man who had hitherto done everything in his power to vilify Thomas.

Why such a change of heart? Why would the man who was preventing their marriage make such a grand gesture unless it was designed to engender a reconciliation? It had to be, she convinced herself. He wanted a rapprochement. When everyone else had failed him in his hour of need, Thomas had saved his life. Thomas was his saviour. He had proved himself not only a superlative surgeon but a fitting consort, too. After years of hostility toward her beloved, Sir Montagu Malthus had relented.

She settled herself at her desk and dipped her pen into the inkpot. This would not be an easy letter to write. There would be several drafts, of that she was certain, but she needed to make a start. She was not entirely sure how she would couch her momentous news. Perhaps it was best to start with Sir Montagu's invitation and her suspicion that he may well, in the very near future, quash his objections to their union. Only after relating such conjecture would she be able to deliver her reasoning that explained the underlying cause for such a volte-face; the news that had come like a bolt from the heavens to her. Sir Montagu had told her when he thought he was dying, when he thought he only had a matter of hours to live. The fact that he survived surgery changed nothing. What he had told her could never be untold. What he had told her changed everything, forever.

Chapter 54

Naturally Thomas felt relief that Dalrymple had been forced to drop all charges against him. Yet the case was just one link in a chain that made him feel ensnared. The past few days had been lost to him in a whirlwind of tragedy and acrimony that left in their wake a deep disquiet. Matthew Bartlett's murder remained unresolved and the distance between himself and Lydia had widened, not only physically but emotionally, too.

Seeking solace in his laboratory, he surveyed the unopened crates and the barrels of specimens that remained untouched. No doubt they all contained treasures; fantastical insects and reptiles, miraculous plants that could cure any manner of ills, vicious fish with teeth as sharp as razors. Yet he found he had little appetite for the knowledge contained in the vessels. He had accepted Sir Joseph's commission with relish. This was his chance to discover, to explore, to shine. That was before he had uncovered the world that was home to these most exotic collections, before he had devoted even a few seconds of his thoughts to the barbarity of slavery. He felt guilty and he felt wretched.

Hearing a noise coming from the corner of the room, he saw Franklin, scrabbling at his latch, frantically trying to open his cage. His efforts brought a smile to Thomas's face. He strode over and opened the door so that the creature bolted out and scuttled across the workbench. As he did so he began to lick the neck of a bottle that had been standing there, untouched and unnoticed for the past few days. On the night of the deaths of Phibbah and Cordelia Carfax, Thomas had returned home late. He never had the chance to give Phibbah the antidote from the obeah-man and the bottle remained corked and neglected. He had deposited the miraculous medicine unthinkingly on the work surface. There it had remained, but Franklin, in his exuberance, had sniffed it out and now managed to knock it over, dislodging the cork and spilling thick amber liquid across the bench.

"No!" cried Thomas, rushing over to right the fallen bottle. Only half its contents remained and Franklin was lapping up the rest. Fearing it might harm him, Thomas swept the rat away and locked him back in his cage.

"What goes on here?" asked Dr. Carruthers, tapping his way into the laboratory and hearing the commotion.

Thomas, mindful that he had not yet analyzed the bottle's contents, had grabbed a spoon and was desperately trying to rescue some of the spilled liquid.

"Franklin," he explained. "He has upset a bottle of physic."

Nostrils flared, the old anatomist paused for a moment and sniffed. "I detect honey," he declared, moving toward the workbench.

Thomas frowned. "Honey? But this is the antidote for the *Solanum nigrum*. This is the physic that can restore and revive," he insisted. "This is the Lazarus potion that Dr. Welton talked about." He had fully intended to examine it before, but had been distracted by events.

Dr. Carruthers, sensing his protégé's prickly mood, came up with a suggestion. "Now is surely as good a time as any to analyze it, young fellow."

Thomas, the sticky bottle in his hand, concurred. "I am sorry, sir. I did not mean to sound abrupt. You are right. I shall set to work on it immediately."

Setting a flask on the table, he poured out a small quantity of preserving fluid and an equal amount of the liquid into it. A little golden globule formed almost immediately, while the rest of the solution turned slightly milky.

"Well?" asked Dr. Carruthers impatiently.

"You are right, sir," said Thomas. "There is honey in this mixture, but that is not the sole ingredient."

"The litmus test?"

"Yes," replied Thomas, reaching for a solution of litmus from the shelf. Dipping a strip of filter paper into the liquid, he transferred it to the physic. The answer took only seconds to emerge. The blue strip turned red.

"So we have some sort of acid," said Thomas, inspecting the paper.

"Acid, you say?" mused Dr. Carruthers. "Let me have another sniff."

Thomas passed over the flask and the old anatomist wafted it under his nose.

"Vinegar!" he cried. "Test for vinegar."

Thomas sniffed the solution again. Yes, he could also detect a hint of what could be vinegar.

This time he fetched pearl ash from a jar and added the fine white crystals to a flask containing water. Waiting until the powder had settled, he poured in a small quantity of the physic. The reaction was immediate and dramatic. The solution bubbled then rose foaming over the sides of the flask.

Hearing the fizzing sound, Dr. Carruthers clapped his hands. "There you have it!" he exclaimed.

Thomas shook his head. "Honey and vinegar," he muttered. "This miraculous medicine that can raise the dead is nothing but honey and vinegar." Stunned, unable to laugh or cry, he fell back on a stool. The Royal Society had been duped. Men had died in the pursuit of this potion and yet it was all a sham. The quest to bring back the formula to restore life after death was based on nothing but superstition, lies, and manipulation. There was no medical foundation for the antidote, for this Lazarus potion, at all.

"Come, come!" Dr. Carruthers slapped Thomas on the back. "At least you can now prove that all this obeah is just stuff and nonsense."

The young doctor looked at his mentor. "You are right. I

must notify Sir Joseph as soon as possible," he said. He should have felt relief that he had so easily disproved the existence of an all-powerful potion that could take life away and give it back, bending the mind in the process. Of course more tests would be needed to show that the formula was nothing but a ruse, a terrible deceit in order to hold an enslaved people in awe of a few powerful priests, but the initial evidence seemed irrefutable and the deception so simple, that he blamed himself in part for allowing himself to be hoodwinked. His healthy skepticism seemed to have deserted him and everyone else associated with this project. So much so, that they had even murdered for it.

Thomas corked the bottle containing the remainder of the potion and put it high on a shelf, out of harm's way.

"Come, sir," he said, slipping his arm into Carruthers's. "I think we have discovered enough for one day."

That evening after dinner both doctors retired, as usual, to the study. Mistress Finesilver was mending the fire. Since the episode with Jeremiah Taylor she had remained remarkably subdued. Not that she had confessed to her betrayal of the slave to his master, but she was aware that her loyalty was now doubted by both Dr. Carruthers and Thomas. Suspicion did not sit easily on either man's shoulders and Thomas had wondered, once or twice, if he should confront her with the accusation that she had gone to Dalrymple, but he thought it best to let sleeping dogs lie, for the time being at least.

Mistress Finesilver was much changed, too, since the incident when Dalrymple burst into the house. Whereas before she had never been afraid to voice her normally negative opinions, she now held her tongue. Her responses to various questions were always muted and there was a general malaise that hung about her person like a bad smell. After she had dusted the hearth of coal splinters and moved away from the fire, she curtsied as usual.

Thomas managed a smile. "Thank you, Mistress Finesilver, that will be all."

Instead of leaving the room, however, the housekeeper remained rooted to the spot. Her mouth worked awkwardly and Thomas realized something was wrong.

"Is there something bothering you, Mistress Finesilver?" he asked, settling himself down in front of the fire.

Her eyes were sliding all over the room and she was rubbing her hands, not to warm them, but to ease her own nerves.

"Yes sir, there is," she replied, her voice resonating with uncustomary meekness.

Dr. Carruthers arched his brow. "Then please tell us, do," he said.

The housekeeper took a deep breath. " 'Twas me who betrayed the slave to his master, sirs," she blurted. "There was a reward and the devil tempted me with a blue hat with a gold lace trim." As she spoke, her lips began to quiver and the tears welled up in her small eyes and spilled over onto her cheeks.

Thomas was silent for a moment, then nodded slowly. Watching the woman sniveling so wretchedly, he decided best to put her out of her misery.

"We know that it was you, Mistress Finesilver."

Her head darted up. "You knew?" She wiped away her tears with the back of her hand.

"Who else but you, my dear lady?" replied Dr. Carruthers, his expression, for once, quite stony.

"And you said nothing?" she protested, almost indignant that she had been allowed to go unpunished.

"What good would that have done?" asked Thomas. "Besides, Mr. Taylor is now a free man, so the matter has ended well."

"But I betrayed him, sir!" She stepped forward, her hands clasped, almost in supplication.

Thomas was bemused. "And so you ask for punishment?"

The housekeeper shook her head. "I ask to make amends, sir." Delving into her apron pocket she pulled out a bag that jangled with coins. She held it up and once more her lips began to tremble. "These are my eight pieces of silver," she croaked.

"This is my reward for betraying the slave." She handed the bag to Thomas.

Pouring out the coins onto his palm, he counted five guineas. "You are giving these to us?" he asked.

Mistress Finesilver shook her head. "I wish them to be given to Jeremiah. Now that he's free, he'll have need of the money," she said, her voice suddenly gaining strength. "Seeing how that poor blackamoor suffered, got me to thinking. 'Tis not right for one man to belong to another and to be so cruelly abused," she said. She shrugged her shoulders, then added: "Besides, I would not have felt right wearing such a hat knowing the misery I have caused to both the slave and to you, Dr. Silkstone."

Thomas returned the coins to the sack. "You have done a good thing, Mistress Finesilver," he told her.

"Aye," Dr. Carruthers concurred.

"I shall see that Jeremiah gets these monies and we'll say no more about the matter," he said, nodding his head emphatically.

The housekeeper curtsied once more, exhaling loudly. "I am most obliged to you, gentlemen," she said, and she left the room, her step seeming considerably lighter than before.

Dr. Carruthers waited until he heard the door shut before he said, "Well, well. That was a turn up for the books, young fellow! Perhaps some good has come out of this ghastly business after all."

Thomas paused before he replied. "Perhaps so," he reflected with a note of hesitation in his voice. Until he had resolved the question of Matthew Bartlett's murder, he could not consider the matter closed.

Chapter 55

Sir Joseph Banks stood on the terrace of Somerset House looking out onto the Thames. The stretch of river was even busier than normal as ships that had been held captive by the ice for weeks tried to maneuver their way out of port. Thomas joined him.

"A fine sight, Silkstone," pronounced the great man, his large hands flat on the top of the stone balustrade. His coat flapped gently in the stiff breeze. "Discovery, trade, commerce: the bedrock of the British nation."

Thomas wanted to venture that slavery should be added to the list, but he did not. He had come to talk about the murder of Matthew Bartlett and was in no mood for polemics. Late into the night he had been reading his postmortem notes. They had thrown up even more unanswered questions and it was these that he now wished to place before Sir Joseph.

A footman hovered nearby on the terrace. Their conversation could be overheard.

"So," said Sir Joseph, "you have, no doubt, come to update me on your progress with the cataloguing, Silkstone." His gaze remained on the river. It was evident that he was being cautious.

"I have to admit I have been distracted, sir, as you know," Thomas replied, phrasing his reply carefully.

Sir Joseph's shoulders rose and he let out a snort. "Men like you do not allow themselves to be distracted, Silkstone," he barked, "unless there is very good reason." He turned and took

Thomas by the arm, leading him away from the footman, walking him along the terrace and out of earshot.

Thomas tensed. "I believe murder is reason enough," he replied, keeping his voice low.

The great man suddenly jutted out his chin. "I told you not to meddle, Silkstone," he said, switching his eyes to the river once more, "but I am glad you did. The Admiralty seems to have drawn a blank. What news have you?"

Thomas took a deep breath. "I could not help but give the matter a great deal of thought, sir, and there are certain things that do not make sense." He had tried to rein in his anxiety, willing his tongue to slow down and his words to sound more measured, but his disquiet was plainly evident.

Sir Joseph threw a glance backward to ensure their conversation was not being overheard.

"Very well, Silkstone. You may have your say."

Thomas took a deep breath. "You see, sir, I know."

Sir Joseph's head jerked up, as if tugged by an invisible rope. Thomas saved him the embarrassment of having to further interrogate him with an explanation.

"I know about the extraordinary powers of the branched calalue and how there are those who would seek to exploit them to the advantage of slave owners and the military alike," he told him.

Sir Joseph made no attempt to deny the truth of Thomas's words. "How did you find out?" he asked.

"Perrick's widow entrusted me with the letters her husband sent from Jamaica."

Sir Joseph's nostrils flared. "I saw her with you at the memorial service," he said with a nod.

Thomas could see that, although Sir Joseph was angry, he was prepared to listen to what he had to say. "The letters spoke of obeah and the hold it has over the enslaved peoples, and, as I feared, Mr. Bartlett's murder appears directly linked to the contents of Dr. Welton's journal."

Sir Joseph shrugged and shook his head. "I never actually doubted that myself, Silkstone. Perhaps I should have told you the whole truth before. I rated you highly, but even so, it seems

I underestimated you. I had to be careful, because of the relationship between our two countries." He cleared his throat a little and began to walk further along the terrace. "Tell me what else you know."

Thomas turned and drew alongside, the wind now sharp against his face. He began by recalling how the previous evening he had been reading *The Gazeteer and New Daily Advertiser* to Dr. Carruthers as usual. "I saw, sir, that on the same day as Mr. Bartlett's body was found, there was also a spring tide. The river went out much farther than usual."

"What are you saying, Silkstone?"

"I am wondering, sir, whether it might be possible that the murderer wanted Mr. Bartlett's body to be discovered."

Sir Joseph's brow buckled. "Why would they want that?"

The young anatomist shook his head. "I cannot answer that, sir. But I do know that whoever killed Mr. Bartlett did so on a false pretext."

Sir Joseph stopped in his tracks. "A false pretext? Explain yourself, Silkstone," he snapped, before he began walking again.

"I managed to obtain a small quantity of this miraculous formula, said by an obeah-man to contain the restorative powers that Dr. Welton was investigating," Thomas began.

Sir Joseph's eyes opened wide. "In London?"

"Yes, sir, from a priest who practiced his black art from an inn."

"And?"

"I discovered it is a mixture of honey and vinegar."

"What?"

"Honey and vinegar," repeated Thomas, his words struggling against the wind.

Sir Joseph's shoulders slumped and his head shook in disbelief. "But that cannot be," he said breathlessly.

"I am afraid so, sir. There is no miraculous formula, no herb that can bring men back to life from death and subjugate their wills, no Lazarus plant."

Thomas saw Sir Joseph's color drain from his face as he hit the rail of the balustrade in anger. "Then this has all been a waste, of time, of money and"—he drew a deep breath—"of life. The mission was cursed from the very outset."

Thomas had to agree. "I am sorry to be the bearer of such news."

Sir Joseph lifted his gaze and looked him in the eye. "You have done a great service, Silkstone. You questioned. That is what all men of science do. They must question and they must experiment until they have an answer." He turned to look out over the river.

"But sometimes that answer is not what we wanted to hear, sir," added Thomas.

"How true," came the forlorn reply.

Aware that Sir Joseph needed time to recover from his revelations, Thomas backed away.

"If I can be of further assistance, sir . . ." he said.

Sir Joseph was still reeling. "What? No, Silkstone. That will be all."

Thomas's departure was acknowledged with a nod. It was clear that the great man had much on his mind, not least how he was going to explain to the members of the Royal Society that their most recent expedition was founded on a false premise. They had allowed themselves to fall victim to the propaganda of obeah and shown themselves to be gullible in the extreme. They were men of great learning and intellect, yet, just like Phibbah the hapless slave girl, they had fallen under the spell of a destructive myth.

When Thomas arrived home he heard laughter coming from the dining room. There he found Sir Theodisius Pettigrew tucking into one of Mistress Finesilver's famous venison pies. Dr. Carruthers was with him, his face almost the color of the claret he was imbibing.

"Sir Theodisius. How good to see you, sir!" greeted Thomas, walking over to the coroner wearing a wide smile. He had last had contact with him at the court hearing, but had been unable to hear all his news from Oxfordshire. "You will have much to relate, I am sure," he said, seating himself at the table.

The coroner wiped his chin with his napkin. "Veritably I do!" he replied, "but first and foremost I am a messenger for Lady Lydia." He delved into his pocket and brought out a letter. "Her ladyship was most anxious that I give this to you in person," he said. The way he winked led him to believe the missive contained good news.

Using a table knife to break the seal, Thomas begged to be excused while he read the letter at the table. He smiled as he saw the familiar script and he scanned the single sheet quickly.

"Her ladyship says that Sir Montagu is much better in himself, growing stronger every day, and he has asked her to host a dinner at Boughton in my honor!" he said, unable to hide his excitement.

"That is most excellent news!" said Dr. Carruthers, clapping his hands.

Thomas's head bobbed low once more to read a few more words, then rose again. "It seems she believes he may be going to give his blessing to our union!"

In truth Thomas was reading between the lines of Lydia's letter. What she had in fact written was that Sir Montagu had told her a secret that, she believed, "could be used to our advantage," as she put it.

"Then let us a drink a toast to you and her ladyship," declared Dr. Carruthers.

Thomas charged all their glasses with claret.

"May both of you enjoy the happiness you truly deserve together," cried Sir Theodisius. "To Dr. Thomas Silkstone and Lady Lydia Farrell. Here's hoping you both prosper."

Glasses clinked and wine was drunk, and order was soon restored at the table. Mistress Finesilver entered with a large slice of pie and some boiled potatoes that she had kept warm for Thomas. She set down the plate before him with a self-conscious twitch of her lips.

"I am most grateful to you, Mistress Finesilver," he told her with a smile. He reached for the salt cellar. "So what other news do you have for us, sir?" he asked the coroner, seasoning his pie.

Sir Theodisius leaned forward conspiratorially. "Upon my

word, I have plenty," he began. "It concerns that estate manager chap, Lupton."

Thomas set down the cellar with a thud.

"I take it you did not approve of him, young fellow," remarked Dr. Carruthers with a wry smile.

Thomas was rapidly losing his appetite. "I found his manner very"—he sought the appropriate word—"impertinent," he said finally.

"Pah!" exclaimed Carruthers. "We shall make an Englishman of you yet!"

"Pray continue," Thomas urged.

Sir Theodisius emptied his mouth, let out a faint belch, and began again. "I recognized the name and quizzed him when I met him. But he said he had no knowledge of the branch of the family I had in mind."

"And which branch was that?" interrupted Carruthers.

The coroner slapped his palms on the table. "Only the Earls of Farley."

Thomas pushed his plate away from him. "I knew it," he growled between his teeth. "I knew there was something about him that could not be trusted."

" 'Tis true he seemed to have ideas above his station," agreed Sir Theodisius.

Dr. Carruthers shook his head. "But what, in the name of Zeus, was he doing at Boughton, working as an estate manager?"

Sir Theodisius nodded and slapped the table once more. "That is precisely what I wanted to know," he said. "So I made discreet inquiries."

"And?" asked Thomas.

" 'Twas not hard to find that he himself is the Right Honorable Nicholas Lupton."

Thomas flew up from the table. "He has designs on Lydia!" he cried, throwing his napkin down in disgust.

Sir Theodisius nodded, but laid his hand gently on Thomas's arm, encouraging him to be seated once more.

"I am afraid, Thomas, that you are absolutely right. Lupton's father is an associate of Sir Montagu Malthus, and I bet the old devil was trying to make a match with her ladyship."

Thomas's anger could not be assuaged. Rising from the table, he excused himself. "I must go and see this Lupton and have it out with him once and for all," he told his friends in a rare show of anger.

"Not so fast!" cried Sir Theodisius, his hand rising in the air. "It would pay you to hear the rest of my tale."

Thomas, about to open the door, turned. "There is more?"

"If you were to leave for Boughton now, you would not find Lupton there."

"What do you mean?"

The coroner shook his head. "He has left, taken all his belongings, and disappeared without a word."

Thomas frowned. "And he did not inform her ladyship?"

" 'Twould seem not."

Pausing on the threshold for a moment, as if weighing up his options, Thomas suddenly turned.

"What will you do, young fellow?" asked Dr. Carruthers.

"There is only one thing to do," he replied, with the certainty of a man whose future happiness teetered on a cliff edge. "I must go to Lady Lydia right away."

Chapter 56

"You wished to see me, sir?" Dr. Fairweather bowed low in front of Sir Montagu, who sat in a chair by the window, his bandaged leg stretched in front of him, supported on a footstool. The physician was surprised to find him out of bed and looking so robust. Mr. Parker, the surgeon, had been the only medical man Sir Montagu had permitted to examine him since the operation. Fairweather had no idea why.

The lawyer remained staring out of the window, not even turning to acknowledge his physician's presence. Instead the latter stood awkwardly, shifting from one foot to the other, now and again throwing a glance out over the gardens that were bathed in warm sunshine.

"Sir?" he said finally, angling his body into a position that he hoped might be within Sir Montagu's eye line.

After a few more awkward seconds the lawyer did turn to look at him.

"Is that you, Fairweather?" he asked, his head cocked to one side.

At first the physician feared his patient had perhaps taken too much laudanum.

"It is, sir," he replied.

Sir Montagu nodded. "I had trouble recognizing you, you see."

Fairweather frowned. There is something seriously amiss, he told himself.

He edged forward. "Perhaps if I come closer, sir?" he ventured.

Sir Montagu's eyes narrowed. "No, even that is no better, Fairweather," he said.

"Sir?" The doctor remained puzzled.

His patient shook his head. "You see, even if you were under my very nose, you would still have as much respect from me as I do for that ant." He pointed to an insect on the windowsill and promptly reached out and squashed it with his thumb. "Yes, that is how much respect I have for you, Fairweather, after your behavior the other day."

The physician's head juddered, as if he was trying to shake away a bad dream. "But . . . but sir!" he bleated. "I . . . I . . . do not understand."

Sir Montagu shook his head. "From your manner I can tell you do, Fairweather. You are flustered. You are faltering, just as you did when you thought I would die on the operating table."

The physician dropped his gaze and bowed his head as if reliving the moment he abandoned all his years of training and nearly swooned at the sight of so much blood.

"I let myself down," he acknowledged quietly.

"You did, indeed, and some would say your reputation is at stake."

Fairweather's head shot up. He looked at Sir Montagu, whose piercing gaze was digging into his mind just as surely as if it were a surgeon's probe. He took a step nearer his tormentor.

"You would not . . . please, sir. You would not tell . . ."

Sir Montagu shrugged his great shoulders. He had the demeanor of a crow about to feast on carrion. "That is up to you, dear Fairweather. Entirely up to you."

Chapter 57

The golden dome of St. Lawrence's Church loomed up above the coach as it trundled into West Wycombe. Seeing the magnificent structure on top of the ridge brought the recent past flooding back to Thomas. The village did not hold happy memories for him. Nevertheless it was a convenient staging post for his journey to Boughton. That night he would stay at the George and Dragon before resuming his trip the following day.

Leaving his bags at the inn, he decided to seek out the Weltons' house. He walked down the main street of the village on his way to he knew not where. All he could remember of the cottage in the painting was that it was probably Tudor, with its obvious beams and pitched roof. There were pink rambling roses around the door, too, although at this time of year they would not be evident. A stiff northerly wind funnelled itself down the main street, setting the shop signs creaking. He held on to his hat.

All he knew for certain was that the cottage would be to the west of the village because the golden ball could be seen on the ridge behind it. That was how he took his bearings and that is how he found himself leaving the ribbon of higgledy-piggledy houses and in open countryside.

Walking past the wall of West Wycombe Park, toward the church, it was the first house he came to; the painting had done it justice. It was quaint with its exposed beams, but not particularly handsome, and the garden, deprived of its summer roses, looked rather forlorn and bedraggled.

Up the front path he strode, rehearsing his address to the widows Welton and Perrick as he went. He would tell them he was passing by chance, which was almost true, that he wished to see how they fared, which, too, was true. Only after such pleasantries had been exchanged and he had, hopefully, been invited inside, would he be able to ask the myriad of questions that still plagued him.

He seized the knocker and rapped three times. No reply. He tried again a few seconds later. Still silence from within. He looked about him. There were no signs of life; no milk pails or muddy boots, no dogs barking, no chickens; no baskets; none of the ordinary, everyday signs of life associated with a village dwelling.

He decided to venture further. Skirting 'round the front of the house, he found himself in a large, unkempt garden, the damp grass brushing his ankles. A few paces away there was another small building. Once a barn or perhaps a stable, it seemed to have been altered so that it now had the appearance of a single-storeyed dwelling with a high pitched roof and large windows that were at odds with its original design. Peering inside, he was shocked to see a young man hunched over a microscope, and drawing on a sketchpad.

Cupping his hands against the glare, he saw the whole space had been turned into some kind of laboratory. There was a re-tort, several flasks and beakers, and shelves containing various jars that one might see in an apothecary's. Another shelf, opposite a large window, was occupied by dozens of pots containing green plants. He told himself he must have the wrong house. This could not possibly be where Mistresses Welton and Perrick were staying. He had made a mistake. He had resolved to return to the inn immediately when suddenly a voice came from behind.

"May I help you, sir?"

Thomas pivoted 'round to see a gentleman. His head was wigless, showing his thinning white hair, and the lines of his tanned face betrayed his advanced years. His eyes were an intense blue, and he had about him an odd familiarity that Thomas could not quite place.

"Forgive me, sir," he said, taken completely off guard. "I did not think there was anyone about. I . . ."

It was then, when his tongue was on the cusp of a word and his mind on an apology, that the memory returned to him, the striking portrait above the Weltons' mantelpiece. Could it be that he was staring at none other than Dr. Frederick Welton? Had he not succumbed to the yellow fever after all? Thomas's expression must have betrayed the fact that he knew the man's identity, yet Welton seemed unfazed. Instead, as the doctor floundered in a mire of embarrassment and bewilderment, the elderly man threw him a lifeline.

"Dr. Silkstone, is it not?" he asked.

Thomas's eyes widened in surprise. "How . . . ?"

"My daughter, Henrietta, told me that you might pay a visit," he said, smiling. "I am delighted to meet you, sir," he added, holding out his hand.

Thomas, still reeling from the shock of discovering him alive, shook Dr. Welton's hand, almost expecting to wake from a dream as he did so.

"I have heard much about you, Silkstone," he said, opening the low door to the laboratory. "Please, I bid you come in."

Inside, the room was much bigger than Thomas's first impression. The ceiling was high and there were skylights on either side of the roof's pitch that allowed light to flood in. At one end of the room was a large range, where a fire roared in an oven, and in its centre a rectangular table. In the corner was the young man Thomas had seen through the window. Looking up from his work, he scrambled from his chair with the clamor of a child caught stealing.

Welton raised a hand. "Calm yourself, Matthew. This is Dr. Silkstone," he said. The young man, his face serious and his dark brows joined across his forehead, gave a shallow bow.

Thomas looked bewildered. "Matthew Bartlett?"

"The very same," replied Welton.

"But . . . ?" Thomas shook his head in disbelief. "So your deaths were a charade?" he said, not knowing whether to be angry or relieved. "And what of Dr. Perrick?"

Welton bit his lip. "Tragically my son-in-law did fall victim to the yellow fever," he replied. "But if you will allow me to explain . . ." He offered Thomas a chair.

"Yes," said Thomas, his mind so full of questions that he had to will himself to remain silent. "There is much I would like to know."

Matthew Bartlett joined them as they sat at the table. He brought with him three glasses and a bottle of wine, which Welton poured out.

"I will start with an apology," Welton began, dispensing the claret. "I am sorry you had to be dragged into all this wretched business, but you were our only hope. And now you are here, we must make huge demands of you as a fellow scientist and, I believe, as a man of great humanity." He slid a full glass toward Thomas.

"I am most eager to be enlightened," he replied, anxious to be guided through this mystery that was about to be laid before him.

"Like you, Dr. Silkstone, I was summoned to see Sir Joseph Banks at the Royal Society." Welton was staring at the red liquid in the glass, like some Gypsy peers into a crystal ball. "He told me my mission was highly sensitive and was at the behest of some well-connected military personnel, although he did not mention any names."

Thomas arched a brow. Already his suspicions were aroused.

Welton continued: "I was to go to Jamaica and seek out the ingredients for a potion that could, it was said, raise the dead." Welton's lips curled into a sneer. "Naturally I was skeptical. I thought it ridiculous, impossible. But Sir Joseph insisted that there were reports that the slaves' magic men had knowledge of a plant that had this power. He told me the expedition was an opportunity for me to crown my career. It would be," he said, momentarily searching for the phrase, " 'a very prestigious feather in my cap.' " He fingered the stem of his wine glass as he recalled what happened next. "I accepted the task and details were discussed, but it was soon after that I began to see what troubled waters lay before me."

"How so?" asked Thomas.

Welton darted a look at Matthew Bartlett, as if he were about to embark on the telling of a revelation that would be new to him, too. He lowered his voice, like a man who suspects someone might be lurking in the shadows, listening to his account.

"I was visited late at night by two gentlemen saying they were agents of His Majesty's government. They wore Admiralty uniforms. They told me that the juice from the herb I was to seek out could be put to excellent use. It would provide, they said, the answer to the plantation revolts in the West Indies. If I could find out the formula for this obeah potion, then all slaves could be treated with it and kept under control." Welton shook his head. "You see, when the victim is supposedly resurrected, then their mind is said to be altered, so that they obey all commands."

Thomas was listening fascinated to what Welton was telling him. It was just as he suspected. "They would diminish the slaves' powers of thought, so that they would do their masters' bidding without question," he said, nodding his head.

Welton gulped his wine, as if to give himself more courage. "But there is more, Silkstone. These agents also told me the formula could be used against Britain's enemies, too. Captured soldiers would be made to drink this cursed potion and die, only to reawaken as slaves of their enemy. The French, they said, would be begging for mercy."

Thomas also sipped his wine, but anxiety soured it on his tongue. There were some Englishmen who would like to dose his fellow Americans, too.

"How did you respond?"

Welton looked resigned, his mouth drooping at the corners. "What could I say? I was being made privy to the realm's secrets. If I betrayed them at this stage, then I could be accused of treason and locked in the Tower! I was in too deep to refuse."

"Did you go to Sir Joseph?"

Welton shook his head. "He was not aware, I am convinced of it. These agents made me swear not to tell a living soul of the purpose of our mission, apart from . . ."

Thomas tensed. "Yes?"

"Hubert Izzard."

"I see," said Thomas, nodding. "He was to accompany you on the trip?"

"Yes, and he was to share in the secret."

"So what did you do next?"

"I agonized. That night was my Gethsemane. I knew of Izzard's reputation from his time in the West Indies; I knew of his sheer ruthlessness and cruelty. And I knew that he would jump at the chance to aggrandize his own worth. I had been trapped and I had to find a way out."

"So you hatched this elaborate plan?"

Welton shunted his glass over to Bartlett, so that he could recharge it.

"Yes. I managed to persuade Sir Joseph that Izzard was the wrong man for the job. I said his health was poor and I could not run the risk of taking him on the expedition."

"And you proposed your son-in-law in his stead?"

"That is so, a decision I now regret," he said, sipping more wine. "But I knew I could trust John. Bartlett here," he said, throwing the young artist a nod, "had worked for me before and I knew I could rely on him, too."

"So you set sail, embarked on the expedition, then what happened, sir?" asked Thomas.

Welton shook his head reflectively. "We saw hell, Dr. Silkstone," he replied. "We sought out these demented obeah-men with the knowledge of this plant and we watched them ritually poison their victims. Women and children were murdered in front of our eyes and then supposedly resurrected before a huge crowd. When they reawakened, usually the next day, their whole demeanor was changed. They looked blank. They had lost the power of speech. They could only obey."

Thomas's eyes were wide with amazement. "So what the agents said was true. This potion did have the power they said it did?"

Again, Welton shook his head wearily. "Like most religions, obeah worked on the principle of coercion, Dr. Silkstone. Its creed was intimidation and its mantra obedience. The obeah priests whipped up mass hysteria. Their victims were not really dead, but their internal organs were slowed, so that it *seemed* they were. There was no magic antidote that woke them. It was the effect of the original poison wearing off that damaged the brain."

Thomas nodded. "Honey and vinegar," he mumbled.

"What?" said Welton.

"I analyzed a phial of liquid that an obeah-man was passing off as an antidote in a tavern in London. I found it to be simply honey and vinegar, sir," Thomas replied.

Welton's eyes suddenly sharpened and he smiled. "So now we even have proof that this whole expedition was based on a lie." He patted Thomas's arm as a sign of his gratitude.

"But how did you fake your own death?" pressed the young doctor. "What about the return journey?"

Welton smiled at Matthew Bartlett. "That was the easy part. My late son-in-law was able to pronounce me dead in Kingston and make all the arrangements for my burial. White men die in their hundreds out there. My death meant just another grave to dig. I laid low for a week or so, changed my identity, then boarded a ship for England. John sadly did not. He died, as you may be aware, the day the *Elizabeth* was due to return to London, ironically from the yellow fever."

Thomas switched his gaze to the young artist. "And Mr. Bartlett's murder? I assume the customs officer was a stooge?"

Welton's shoulders lifted as he exhaled through his nose. "Yes. And the satchel in the Thames was obviously a decoy. The body, too."

"Whose body was it?" Thomas interrupted.

"It is easy to obtain a corpse, Silkstone, when your associates are anatomists, as you surely know. He was an unfortunate, whose body ended up on the dissecting table."

"And you wanted it to be discovered?"

"Indeed, yes."

"And you knew I would be called upon to conduct a post-mortem?"

"Right again." Welton gave a smug smile. "You are the only anatomist with the appropriate skills in the Westminster jurisdiction."

"But what about your notes? This mysterious journal that was supposed to contain the formula?" Thomas's look flitted from one man to the other and back.

Welton leaned back in his chair and, plunging his hand into his coat pocket, he brought out a leather-bound notebook. "I think you refer to this, Dr. Silkstone," he said, putting the volume on the table and stroking it lovingly. "I call it The Book of Lazarus. I keep it with me at all times."

Thomas stared at it. It looked like so many other notebooks he had bought himself for a crown at stationers' shops in London and Oxford, and yet John Perrick had died for this one. He touched it lightly, half expecting something to happen, he knew not what. He shook his head and frowned.

"But there is no accursed Lazarus potion," he said. "Why is this so precious?"

Welton's lips twitched out a smile. "Oh, but there is a Lazarus formula, Dr. Silkstone. The *Solanum nigrum,* the same plant that the obeah-man uses to poison, can also be used for good. It may not raise the dead, but it can make a patient appear dead so that they feel no pain, and are unaware of their suffering for a short period of time."

Suddenly it was as if Welton had lit a candle in the darkness. "So you would use the herb in surgery," said Thomas. "For amputations, lithotomies, and the like?"

Welton nodded and picked up the notebook. "Indeed, Silkstone. There is, in here, the basic formula for a strong sedative that causes insentience. It can be used to alleviate so much dread and fear and suffering in a patient. It will assist surgeons and reduce the risk of hemorrhage."

Thomas could not hide his delight at this possible breakthrough. "But this is, indeed, wonderful news, sir. So you are conducting experiments here?" He lifted his head and looked about the room once more. Welton rose from the table and walked over to one of the plant pots on a shelf near the window.

"The branched calalue?" asked Thomas.

Welton nodded. "It has similar properties to the mandrake root," he said, fingering the leaves. Thomas recalled that mandrake was used in Pliny's days as a relaxant, a piece of the root being given to the patient to chew before undergoing surgery. "Only I have found it to be much more effective. I have already used it on animals. I dosed a cat, cut it open, stitched it up, and within a day or two it was catching mice again!"

Thomas had noticed a cat dozing by the fire when he first entered. He switched his gaze to it and Welton acknowledged him. "The very same," he said.

For once Thomas found it difficult to process the information he had just gleaned. That such encouraging breakthroughs could come out of such tragedy was a rare occurrence in his experience. He found himself both saddened and yet delighted by such an outcome.

Welton returned to the table. "So now you know, Silkstone," he said, seating himself once more.

Thomas nodded and studied the doctor thoughtfully for a moment. It was only then that it occurred to him he had sentenced himself to living a lie. He was Dr. Frederick Welton, the brave doctor and explorer who had died in the service of his country. If he ever resurrected himself he would be vilified by the establishment. Any work he published would have to be under an alias, or through another collaborator. He had sacrificed his own career and reputation for a greater cause. Yet he was now free to pursue his own research. In some ways, mused Thomas, he had broken his bonds.

"You can be sure your secret is safe with me, sir," he said, looking Welton in the eye. "I shall not say a word, but I do look forward to the day when I can use the formula to anaesthetize my own patients before I operate on them."

Welton nodded. "So do I, Silkstone. So do I."

The three men drained the bottle between them as the afternoon light faded. It was the clatter of hooves that alerted them to the arrival of the ladies.

"My wife and daughter have been visiting," Welton said as he went to open the door. Turning to look out of the window, Thomas saw the two women whom he had last seen wearing widows' weeds stepping down from the carriage.

"My dears, we have a visitor," Welton called to them as he stood in the doorway.

Thomas watched them both look up and make their way over to the laboratory. As they came closer he could see their expressions tense, unsure as to who might be waiting for them.

"A visitor?" he heard Henrietta say to her father. He knew that her subterfuge would make her wary of him. He wondered at her cunning.

As soon as the two women saw Thomas, the anxious look on their faces tightened even further. Unsure as to how their deceit would be received, they remained guarded until Welton spoke.

"Henrietta said you would come. Did you not?" he cried, a wide smile on his face. He watched his daughter walk toward Thomas.

"I did indeed, Papa," she said, her gaze fixed on the young doctor.

The features that Thomas had last seen bleached by grief now seemed to be more colorful and softer. Mindful, however, that she had, indeed, suffered bereavement, Thomas bowed and smiled gently at her.

"Your father has told me the whole story, Mistress Perrick. Your husband was, indeed, a brave man."

Acknowledging his words with a slight nod, she allowed herself a smile. "And you are a most tenacious one, Dr. Silkstone," she replied. "Our confidence in your powers of deduction was not misplaced."

Thomas thought of Perrick's letters, the satchel in the river, the corpse tethered to the pier, Welton's portrait, the painting of West Wycombe; they were all clues designed to bring him to this very laboratory; all clues that led him to this new truth. Yet still he remained puzzled.

"But why did you not tell me directly and be done with all this secrecy?" he asked.

Welton gave a slight shrug. "With John's death, I was forced to rethink my plans. He was vital in my scheme and I knew it would be hard to find someone to replace him. I had no idea whom we could trust. If we had told Sir Joseph of our proposals it would have placed him in an impossible position."

The situation was becoming clearer to Thomas. "So you put me to the test?"

Welton paused for a second, unsure as to whether the anatomist's tone was one of approbation. "I knew of your repute; of your intelligence and understanding: of your compassion, too. I feared the recent enmity between our two countries might also color your judgment, but in the end I was sure you would understand." He paused, watching anxiously for Thomas's reaction. "Perhaps I have been too presumptuous." A sense of doubt had crept into the learned man's words.

Thomas did little to dispel it. He remained silent. He had been exploited. His own professional reputation had been put in jeopardy and yet he could not escape the sense that he was honored to be chosen. A stranger was entrusting him with a momentous secret because he knew of his reputation not only as an outstanding anatomist and surgeon, but also as a man of good character and sound judgment, a man of integrity. He nodded and a smile finally spread across his face.

"I am glad I proved worthy of your trust, sir," he replied.

For the second time in as many days Sir Montagu Malthus summoned Dr. Felix Fairweather to his chamber. On this occasion they were not alone. Sir Montagu's clerk, Gilbert Fothergill, was skulking at the desk by the window where his master was seated and, to the physician's surprise, fully dressed.

"But sir, you look much restored," remarked Fairweather with a smile.

Sir Montagu, who had not so much as looked up when the physician had been announced by the butler, merely shook his head. His eyes remained fixed on a document.

"No thanks to you," he muttered.

Fairweather darted Fothergill a nervous glance. He did not wish to be humiliated in front of a clerk.

"You wished to see me, sir," he said, endeavoring to sound assured.

"Indeed," came the reply. "I have a job for you."

Unable to disguise his relief, Fairweather allowed his features to gather into a smile. It was, however, premature.

"Come closer," Sir Montagu beckoned. His tone sounded ominous and his hooked fingers drummed impatiently.

With his heart working its way up to his mouth, Fairweather did as he was bid. He approached and followed the lawyer's finger to the document that was on his desk.

"Sign here, will you?" Sir Montagu commanded.

Frowning, the physician peered at the paper, then taking out a pair of spectacles from his pocket, he read the text. After a moment or two he straightened himself and snatched his glasses from his nose. Looking at Sir Montagu with an expression of complete horror, he protested: "But sir, this is . . ." His voice became lost in his own sense of outrage.

"I know what it is, Fairweather. Now sign it."

Fothergill stepped forward with a pen.

"Sign it," insisted Sir Montagu, through clenched teeth, "or I shall see to it that you never practice medicine again."

S ir Montagu arrived unannounced at Boughton Hall with all his usual rich man's bluster. And, as usual, the household was sent into a flurry.

Lydia, checking her hair in a mirror held by Eliza, was fretful.

"Is his lordship clean? What is he wearing?" She feared that Richard might be scrabbling about in the garden dirt or up a tree, although since Mr. Lupton's departure, he had remained relatively subdued. No one had seen hide or hair of the estate manager and Lydia was none too pleased about his sudden disappearance.

"His lordship is in his day clothes, but looks quite respectable," answered the maid, trying to remain calm. She knew how these impromptu visits from Sir Montagu had put her mistress so ill at ease on a number of previous occasions.

Taking a deep breath, Lydia walked to the front doors that were flung wide open in order to greet her guest. Her studied smile turned to a look of shock, however, when she saw that Sir Montagu was accompanied not just by Dr. Fairweather, but also by her errant estate manager, Nicholas Lupton.

"Sir, you honor us with your presence," she said, greeting Sir Montagu as he reached the top of the front steps. She wanted to say that he was not expected until later on in the week when Thomas would be there. She wanted to ask him what on earth Dr. Fairweather and Nicholas Lupton were doing in his company, but her good manners dictated otherwise.

"And of course you know Dr. Fairweather and Mr. Lupton, my dear," he said, flapping his long arm toward the two men who now stood beside him.

Lydia's voice wavered. "Yes, I do . . . I . . ."

Sir Montagu cut her short.

"You always make me feel most welcome, my dear," he replied, sweeping his way past her into the entrance hall.

Lydia cast a disapproving look at Lupton, whose mouth remained set in a strange sort of sneer, and accompanied the mismatched party through the hallway and into the drawing room.

Fairweather and Lupton settled themselves on chairs behind the sofa where Sir Montagu spread his tall frame. Lydia sat on a sofa opposite him and asked Howard to bring tea. But Sir Montagu shook his head.

"I would prefer it if we were not disturbed, my dear," he told her in front of the butler.

Lydia's smile shriveled. "As you wish, sir," she replied and she waved Howard out of the room.

"I shall come to the point quickly," Sir Montagu began as soon as the door was shut. "You are acquainted with Mr. Lupton here?"

Lydia frowned. "Of course I am, sir. He departed from my employ only last week and took off without so much as a farewell." Her anger had resurfaced.

"Calm yourself, my dear," said the lawyer, switching his gaze to Dr. Fairweather, seated to his right. "You see. There is distinct agitation there," he mumbled, only his pitch was sufficiently loud so that Lydia could hear his words.

"Sir, I . . ." She opened her mouth to protest, but Sir Montagu's large palm presented itself to her.

"Please listen to what I am about to say," he told her, adopting the tone of a tutor.

"You see, my dear, Mr. Lupton was actually in my employ, too."

Lydia felt her jaw drop in amazement. She looked askance first at Sir Montagu, then at Lupton, who sat impassively to his left.

"I'm afraid I don't . . ." Her words remained stuck in her mouth, yet she managed to direct her glower at the former estate manager.

"Mr. Lupton's full title is the Right Honorable Nicholas Henry Pierpoint Lupton, the second son of the fourth Earl of Farley."

Lydia felt her breath judder inside her chest.

Sir Montagu continued: "I sent him both to spy on you and to seduce you." His delivery was unembellished, doing nothing to disguise his utterly brazen motives. "You see, my dear, I know it all. I know that Silkstone broke his court order by coming here and that you lay with him again, going against Chancery's express orders. And you know what that means." His tone had suddenly become threatening and he glared at her.

Lydia's eyes widened and she shot up from her seat. "No!" she shouted at Lupton. She marched over to him and in a fit of rage slapped her erstwhile estate manager on the cheek. "How dare you?!" she cried. "I treated you well. You wormed your way into my son's affections and this is how I am repaid?" She flew over to the window and looked out, her fists clenched, leaving Lupton to rub his reddened cheek.

"You see, Fairweather," said Sir Montagu. "Another demonstration of her irascibility."

Lydia pivoted. "What is this? What are you saying? What are you trying to do?" Her anger had turned to tears. Her eyes were watery and her cheeks flushed. Suddenly she hurried over to Sir Montagu and sat by his side.

Taking his hand in hers she said, "Do you not remember what you told me when you were ill, when you thought you were going to die?" She smiled through her tears, willing him to divulge the secret they shared. "Surely we can tell everyone now, can we not?"

Sir Montagu looked at her, his great brows meeting in a frown.

"What are you saying, dear Lydia?"

"Tell them," she urged him. "Tell them what you told me,

please!" She tugged at his hand, but he pulled it away from her. "Tell them I am your daughter, sir!" she cried.

"There we have it. She is mad, Fairweather! Hysterical!" exclaimed Sir Montagu, pointing at Lydia, kneeling at his feet. "You have seen it with your own eyes. This is precisely the kind of madness I was telling you about. The poor child is not only violent, she is also deluded."

Fairweather, remaining solemn throughout the exchange, now nodded.

"I see your fears, sir," he said slowly. "A case of hysteria, I would say, brought on by a voracious sexual appetite."

Lydia's head shot from one man to the other. "What?" she gasped. "What are you saying?"

"What Dr. Fairweather is saying, my dear, is that you are mentally unstable."

Lydia shot to her feet. "You have no right . . . you cannot . . . I . . ." Her anguish was tying her tongue so that her words were held captive.

"I am afraid we have no choice," said Sir Montagu, rising from his seat. The other men did likewise.

"No choice but to do what?" pleaded Lydia, suddenly finding her voice.

"You have broken the terms of the court order by seeing Silkstone and your mental faculties are most gravely impaired. I have no choice but to have you committed for your own safety and that of your son," he told her.

Her breath snagged in her throat. "Richard!" she said, then, when it dawned on her what the lawyer was saying, she repeated it in a scream: "Ri . . . chard!"

Lupton and Fairweather stepped forward and, grasping her firmly by both arms, Sir Montagu read out an official document to her. She did not hear his words as they buffeted the air with their cruel insinuations. She was struggling and crying out and when Howard came to see the cause of the commotion, he found her being dragged toward the door.

"Sir, please tell me what is going on?" he cried to Sir Montagu.

The lawyer brandished the legal document and placed it in Howard's hands.

"You can tell Dr. Silkstone, when he comes to call, that we have taken her ladyship away for her own good."

Howard looked horrified. "But sir . . ." he protested. "Where, sir? Where are you taking her ladyship?" But his pleas went unanswered as his voice was drowned out by Lydia's screams that splintered through the hall and out into the open air.

The coach for Oxford left at first light. Thomas had spent an enjoyable evening in the company of Dr. Welton and his family. The veil of secrecy that had lain over the whole expedition had been lifted and Thomas had heard tales of the remarkable creatures encountered and the extraordinary adventures the men had experienced. Dr. Welton had even given him a sheaf of his own notes detailing various specimens to assist Thomas in his cataloguing.

Even though it was still winter, the countryside, as Thomas looked out of the coach window, seemed to be waking from its long sleep. The snow on the hilltops had entirely disappeared and in the poplar trees that lined the riverbank, the birds were nesting.

Leaving the coach at Oxford, Thomas hired a carriage to take him out to Boughton. It was late afternoon before he finally saw the needle of the chapel and allowed himself to feel he was at journey's end. The carriage set him down in front of the house as usual and Will Lovelock sprang from nowhere to help with the baggage.

"Will! Good to see you!" Thomas greeted him. The boy managed a weak smile but no more.

Striding up the steps, two at a time, Thomas half expected the doors to be thrown open at any moment. Howard answered his ring.

"Dr. Silkstone," said the butler. His face betrayed his surprise.

"Is all well, Howard? Where is her ladyship?" Thomas walked in, taking his gloves off as he spoke, glancing at each of the doors that led from the hallway, anticipating one to open suddenly. He pivoted on his heel. "And the young master, where is he, Howard?"

The butler's expression checked Thomas's exuberance.

"Oh sir, I cannot begin to tell you . . ."

"What has happened? Where are they? Tell me, man, for god's sake." He was growing more anxious and impatient with each passing second.

Howard set his face, drained of all its color, to meet Thomas's square on.

"Sir Montagu was here yesterday, sir."

Thomas looked puzzled. He was not due until later in the week. "Go on."

"He came with Mr. Lupton and Dr. Fairweather."

At the mention of Lupton's name Thomas's expression changed from anxiety to rage. "I knew he was Malthus's lackey!" he cried. "What did they do? Where have they taken her?"

"Sir Montagu brought with him papers," said Howard, trying to remain composed.

"What sort of papers?"

"These sort, sir," said Eliza, emerging from a doorway. She had been watching the exchange through the half-closed door and hurried out to hand Thomas a scroll of parchment. He could tell from her eyes that she had been crying.

"They said she was mad, sir," she blurted. "They have taken her away, and the young master, too." The maid began to sob again and Howard motioned her to leave.

"What does she mean, Howard? Where have they taken her?"

Howard, himself fighting back the tears, cleared his throat. "Sir Montagu took his lordship back with him to Draycott House, but her ladyship . . ."

"Well? What have they done with her, for god's sake?" Thomas could not suppress his impatience. Suddenly he felt the air, full of recriminations and doubt, stifle his breath and close in on him.

The butler steeled himself to deliver the rest of his news, as if it was too awful for him to speak. His mouth opened, but no words came forth.

"Where?" urged Thomas once more, grabbing hold of the butler's arm.

"Oh, sir," he wailed, unable to rein in his anguish any longer. "They have taken her to Bedlam."

Postscript

In 1783 a lobby group was formed by six Quakers to campaign against slavery. Four years later it had grown into the Society for Effecting the Abolition of the Slave Trade. By the end of the eighteenth century public opinion was swinging in favor of the abolition movement in Great Britain. Thanks to the largely forgotten efforts of Granville Sharp and, more famously, William Wilberforce, the Slave Trade Act was passed in 1807. While the slave trade was abolished in the British Empire, slavery itself was not actually outlawed until 1833.

Granville Sharp went on to campaign for worldwide abolition and was behind the plan to settle freed slaves from North America and the Caribbean in the territory of Sierra Leone, West Africa. The aptly named Freetown was its capital.

The scourge of slavery continues to this day. At a conservative estimate, the campaign group Free the Slaves puts the number of modern-day slaves, i.e., "People held against their will, forced to work and paid nothing," at between 21 and 30 million globally.

Glossary

Chapter 1

magic man: There are several contemporary accounts of this ritual. One of them comes from Stephen Fuller (1716–1808), who was the British agent on Jamaica. Matthew Lewis also produced an account in *The Journal of a residence among the negroes in the West Indies,* written between 1815 and 1817.

Maroons: Escaped slaves in the West Indies. The word comes from the Spanish *cimarron,* meaning fugitive.

Obeah: There seem to be several ways to write this, including Obi or Obia; its definition is a folk religion of African origin that uses the tradition of sorcery.

myal: A form of an African religion.

conch shell: Used by slaves either as a musical instrument or to sound an alarm.

branched calalue: The herb, a member of the *Solanum* genus (possibly black nightshade, *Solanum nigrum*), was known to have high concentrations of the hallucinogens atropine and scopolamine.

bloody flux: Now known as amoebic dysentery, this was one of the most lethal diseases that could break out aboard a ship.

Royal Society: This learned society for science was founded in 1660.

yellow fever: The disease, spread by mosquitoes, affected mainly those of European origin.

Chapter 2

Brewer Street: The school of the famous anatomist Dr. William Hunter was in neighboring Great Windmill Street, Soho, London.

The Anatomy of the Human Gravid Uterus: Published in 1774, this was a remarkable book, featuring engravings by Rymsdyk, which were modeled on Leonardo Da Vinci's sketches.

Monsieur Desnoues: French physician Guillaume Desnoues (or Denoue) created very lifelike wax anatomical models in breach of medical ethics. These were displayed in London and Paris and proved extremely popular until his death in 1735.

drinking concoctions: Many enslaved women chose to abort their fetuses by taking herbal potions.

Rousseau: The French philosopher's treatise, *The Social Contract,* published in 1762, helped inspire political reforms or revolutions in Europe, especially in France, and arguably in America.

Chapter 3

as cold a November: The winter of 1783–84 was one of the coldest on record, and the River Thames froze over for a time. Some experts attribute the severity of the weather to the effect of the Laki fissure eruption in Iceland in June of 1783.

Coromantee: Derived from the name of the Ghanaian coastal town Kormantse, the terms "Coromantins," "Coromanti," or "Kormantine" were also used as the English names given to Akan slaves from the Gold Coast or modern-day Ghana.

Ashanti: A nation and ethnic group, also known as Asante, living mainly in Ghana and Ivory Coast. European slavers regarded them as the most warlike tribe.

Mansu: The great slave market where Gold Coast Negroes were sold to Europeans.

a hat modeled on a ship: Joseph Johnson was a London beggar, famous for his "ship" hat. His story appeared in *Vagabondiana, or anecdotes of mendicant wanderers,* printed in 1817.

Lord Mayor's edict: In 1731, black people were banned from taking up a trade, a law which led many into poverty.

yaws: A neglected, and potentially disfiguring, tropical disease still prevalent in several tropical countries that affects the skin, cartilage, and bone.

Ob: Or Oub, was the name of the royal serpent and oracle worshipped by some Africans.

Chapter 4

Somerset House: Built in 1775, this famous London building was home to the Navy Board, as well as the Royal Academy of Arts, the Society of Antiquaries, and the Royal Society.

Endeavour: HMS *Endeavour* first set sail for Australia and New Zealand in 1769.

Captain Cook: Captain James Cook was killed in 1779 by Hawaiians during his third exploratory voyage in the Pacific.

the Great Fogg: For several weeks during the summer of 1783, a dry fog covered the eastern half of England and some of northern Europe, blocking out the sun and causing many respiratory diseases in livestock and humans.

Treaty of Paris: Signed on September 3, 1783, the treaty ended the American War of Independence with Britain, but was not ratified until January 14 the following year.

Daniel Solander: A Swedish naturalist and friend of Sir Joseph Banks, who accompanied him on several expeditions.

Sydney Parkinson: The artist employed by Sir Joseph Banks to accompany him on James Cook's first voyage to the Pacific in 1768. He produced thousands of drawings, but died of dysentery before returning home.

the Lizard: A peninsula in Cornwall, near the most southerly point of the British mainland.

Chapter 6

Court of Chancery: The Court of England and Wales that had responsibility for wards of court and lunatics.

caves in West Wycombe: Known as the Hellfire Caves, they were excavated from an old quarry by Sir Francis Dashwood in the 1750s.

Chapter 7

red coral: This was believed to prevent hemorrhaging.

the purchase of slaves: According to the eighteenth-century explorer John Atkins, "the Commanders, with their Surgeons (as skilled in the Choice of Slaves) attend the whole time on shore, where they purchase, in what they call a fair open Market." Source: http://www.nhm.ac.uk/resources-rx/files/chapter-6-resistance-19110.pdf

Chapter 9

how would the dead eat? The famous physician and naturalist Hans Sloane observed in 1688 that at funerals some Africans threw "Rum and Victuals into their Graves, to serve them in the other world. Sometimes they bury it in gourds, at other times spill it on the Graves."

Source: http://www.nhm.ac.uk/resources-rx/files/chapter-6-resistance-19110.pdf

cages over the graves: Mortsafes.

Chapter 10

Oxford Street: Sophie von la Roche, a German visitor to London in 1786, wrote of fashionable Oxford Street: "First one passes a watchmaker's, then a silk or fan store, now a silversmith's, a china or glass shop."

Blackheath Golf Club: The first official golfing club in Great Britain, it was also a London meeting place for several slave traders and plantation owners.

The round was enjoyable enough: The club's first course consisted of just five holes on Blackheath itself, with three circuits, i.e., 15 holes, constituting a round.

Chapter 11

Legal Quays: The area known as Billingsgate on the south side of the City of London was where all imported cargoes had to be delivered for inspection and assessment by Customs Officers.

Pool of London: The name given to the original Port of London on the Thames, which ran alongside the Tower of London.

Scuffle-Hunters, River Pirates: Gangs operated in the Port of London, frequently stealing cargo from ships and quays. One estimate put the merchants' losses at £500,000 a year, including 2 percent of all sugar imported.

tide waiter: An official who checked boats coming into the Thames to ensure goods were not sold on the way to the Legal Quays for a tax-free profit.

Gravesend: In 1782, the first customs house in the town, Whitehall Place, was built opposite the present Customs House to house tide waiters, who had previously been based at the port's inns.

lighter: A masted barge used for transporting goods to and from larger ships to port.

Black Loyalists: Between April and November 1783, those slaves who fought for the British in the American War of Independence were given their freedom and evacuated. As well as coming to London, many went to Nova Scotia. Their names are recorded in *The Book of Negroes*.

Ebele: An Igbo name, meaning mercy.

Sambo: A common name given to African slaves by their white masters. In 1736, a young, dark-skinned cabin boy or slave known as Sambo was buried in a field near Overton, Lancashire.

Igbo: An ethnic group of southeastern Nigeria.

Chapter 12

Kew Gardens: The Royal Botanic Gardens at Kew, near London, were founded in 1759 in what was formerly Kew Park. George III improved the gardens, helped by Sir Joseph Banks.

Chapter 13

a trained one: According to papers belonging to a Liverpool merchant and slave trader, male slaves were fetching £40 each in 1772.

Hibiscus elatus: Jamaica's national tree.

Chapter 14

image of a Negro man: Several slave owners incorporated images of slaves on their crests. John Hawkins, the famous explorer, for example, was proud of the source of his wealth. His crest bears the image of an African in bondage.

larva of the botfly: The botfly lives mainly in South America, although it is also found in Jamaica, but only the larvae of *Dermatobia hominis* will live in humans.

bridle: An appalling instrument of torture designed to dig into the tongue so that the wearer had to remain silent, these were not confined to slaves, but to ordinary women, too, when it was called a scold's bridle or "the branks." Although not widely employed in the eighteenth century, the last reported use was in 1856 in Lancashire.

Chapter 15

some Negroes: The naturalist and physician Sir Hans Sloane observed: "The Negroes from some Countries think they return to their own Country when they die in Jamaica, and therefore regard death but little, imagining they shall change their condition, by that means from servile to free, and so for this reason often cut their own Throats." He visited Jamaica in 1688 and later published two volumes of his experiences.
Source: http://www.nhm.ac.uk/resources-rx/files/chapter-6-resistance-19110.pdf

Chapter 16

first snows: According to contemporary accounts, the winter of 1783–84 was one of the coldest in living memory.

Chapter 17

"God Rest Ye Merry Gentlemen": The carol was first published in 1760.

Chapter 18

Sir Joseph's famous herbarium: Sir Joseph Banks collected thousands of specimens during his voyage on HMS *Endeavour*. Many of the 30,000 plant specimens were pressed on sheets and can be seen today in London's Natural History Museum.

Dr. Grainger: James Grainger was a Scottish doctor who, in 1764, published *Essay on the more common West-India Diseases*. It was the first work devoted to the diseases and treatment of slaves in the Caribbean.

sufferance wharf: Where cargo can be inspected by customs and excise authorities.

Graviora manent: The English translation is "heavier things remain," or "the worst is yet to come."

Chapter 19

golden dome: The famous ball has sat on top of St. Lawrence's church tower in West Wycombe since 1761 and can be seen for miles around.

Chapter 20

pomade: Mashed apples were a common ingredient in this scented ointment that was often used on the hair and scalp.

Chapter 21

lime wash: A traditional plaster wash for covering exterior walls. Color pigments were often added.

freeze over: The River Thames at London froze over several times during the seventeenth and eighteenth centuries during what is known as the "Little Ice Age."

spring tide: Not a tide during springtime, these exceptionally high tides occur during the full and new moon.

mud larks: Mainly children, they would scavenge the shoreline at low tide for anything of value.

Execution Dock: Located on the shore at Wapping, this was the place of execution for those pirates, smugglers, and mutineers condemned to die by the Admiralty Courts. It was last used in 1830.

Chapter 22

bur: A prickly husk of a seed or fruit.

Chapter 23

livor mortis: A purple discoloration of the skin that occurs after death when blood collects and sets in the lower parts of the body.

parenchyma: The functional parts of an organ in the body.

phthisis: An archaic term for consumption or tuberculosis.

Chapter 24

Wapping or Deptford: The currents of the Thames tended to wash bodies to these locations.

Henry Fielding: Together with his younger half-brother John, he helped found the Bow Street Runners, in 1749, described by some as London's first police force.

hothouse: A slave hospital.

Chapter 25

Solanum: A large genus of flowering plants.

Chapter 26

dika tree: Indigenous to West Africa, the tree can grow to 40 meters and produces a fruit.

Mount Afadjato: The highest mountain in Ghana.

Chapter 28

Bewildered Negro men, women, and children: This description is adapted from John Atkins, *A Voyage to Guinea, Brazil, and the West Indies,* published in 1737: "This is a Rule always observed, to keep the Males apart from the Women and Children, to handcuff the former . . ."

Spittle Fields: An area of London, now called Spitalfields, where there has been a market since 1638.

Chapter 29

Jonathan Strong: A young black slave from Barbados who had been beaten by his master and abandoned. He recovered, but a few years later was recaptured and sold to a planter. A legal challenge followed and Strong regained his freedom. He died five years later.

Over dinner, we were told: This account of brutality is inspired by John Gabriel Stedman's *Narrative of Five Years' Expedition against the Revolted Negroes of Surinam* (1796). It became an abolitionist publication.
Source: http://www.nhm.ac.uk/resources-rx/files/chapter-6-resistance-19110.pdf

Chapter 30

Maroon weed: The naturalist and physician Henry Barham described the well-known use of savanna flower (*Echites umbellata,* commonly called Maroon weed) as a poison in Jamaica in 1710: "It is too well known, and it is pity that ever the negro or Indian slaves should know it, being so rank a poison: I saw two drams of the expressed juice given to a dog, which killed him in eight minutes time . . ."
Source: http://www.nhm.ac.uk/resources-rx/files/chapter-6-resistance-19110.pdf

I spoke with another physician: This fictional excerpt is inspired by another account by Henry Barham of his experience with Maroon weed.
Source: http://www.nhm.ac.uk/resources-rx/files/chapter-6-resistance-19110.pdf

thumbnail: Barham wrote that some slaves scooped up poison under their thumbnail, and, "after they drink to those they intend to poison, they put their thumb upon the bowl, and so cunningly convey the poison; wherefore, when we see a negro with a long thumb-nail, he is to be mistrusted."
Source: http://www.nhm.ac.uk/resources-rx/files/chapter-6-resistance-19110.pdf

Chapter 31

Fevillea cordifolia: Natural historian Patrick Browne wrote of *Fevillea cordifolia*, also known as antidote cocoon, in 1756: "The kernels are extremely bitter, and frequently infused in spirits for the use of the negroes: a small quantity of this liquor opens the body and provokes an appetite, but a larger dose works both by stool and vomit. It is frequently taken to clear the tube, when there is any suspicion of poison, and, often, on other occasions."
Source: http://www.nhm.ac.uk/resources-rx/files/chapter-6-resistance-19110.pdf

Mr. Clarkson: Thomas Clarkson (1760–1846) was an English abolitionist and a leading campaigner against the slave trade in the British Empire. He helped found the Society for Effecting the Abolition of the Slave Trade and to achieve the passing of the Slave Trade Act of 1807, which ended British trade in slaves. In his later years Clarkson campaigned for the abolition of slavery worldwide.

Sharp: Granville Sharp (1735–1813) was one of the first English campaigners for the abolition of the slave trade. His involvement in the Jonathan Strong case led him to study English law, which he declared to be "injurious to natural rights."

Our Quaker friends: In 1783 an informal group of six Quakers presented a petition containing over three hundred signatures against the slave trade to Parliament.

Chapter 33

There are those whom slaves: This excerpt is based on an account in a book written in 1800 called *Obi; Or, The History of Three-Fingered Jack,* by William Earle, and inspired by the story of an escaped slave called Jack Mansong, who practiced obeah.

Chapter 34

George Coffee House in Chancery Lane: Anyone interested in an advertisement offering a fourteen-year-old Negro slave boy for £25 was asked to apply to this coffee house in 1756.

Chapter 35

Yule log: For centuries it was customary to burn such a log in the fireplace at Christmas. The tradition dates back at least three hundred years.

Chapter 36

West Wycombe: A historic village, now largely owned by the National Trust, and home to West Wycombe Park, a Palladian mansion, the Hellfire Caves, and St. Lawrence's Church, with its famous golden ball.

Chapter 37

Middle Passage: The voyage of slave trading ships from the west coast of Africa across the Atlantic. It was the longest, hardest, and most horrific part of the journey.

John Wilkes: One of the most colorful and controversial figures of the eighteenth century, best known for his prominent political career and eventful personal life.

murder of a Negro: In 1811, Arthur William Hodge became the first West Indian slave owner to be executed for the murder of a slave considered his property.

Chapter 39

mummer: An actor and entertainer who is usually part of a troupe of fellow actors who travel from place to place.

Chapter 40

blind man's buff: The children's game dates back to at least the sixteenth century.

hunt the slipper: The game is described as a primeval pastime in Oliver Goldsmith's 1776 novel *The Vicar of Wakefield.*

wassailers: A group of men who visited homes to enact an ancient ritual to wish good cheer to residents.

Chapter 42

frozen grip: The winter of 1783–84 was one of the most severe on record in England. Many modern experts attribute this to the effect of the eruption of the Laki fissure in Iceland, which sent millions of tons of ash into the atmosphere, blocking out the sun.

Chapter 43

almanac: The London Almanack for Year of Christ 1783 was published by the London Stationers' Company.

screw tourniquet: Also known as a Petit tourniquet, after its inventor Jean-Louis Petit (1674–1750), this was used to stop excessive bleeding during amputation.

wretch: In his 1774 account of the brutal treatment of slaves in the Dutch colony of Surinam, the Scottish-Dutch soldier John Gabriel Stedman described how a slave was suspended to a gallows by means of a hook through his ribs and left to die. His subsequent book was illustrated by the famous artist William Blake and caused an outcry against slavery in Britain.

Chapter 44

popliteal aneurysm: A large swelling in the artery behind the knee. A London surgeon, named Wilmer, wrote in 1779 that "there is not, that I know, a single case upon record where that operation has succeeded." The famous surgeon Percivall Pott (1714–1788) advocated amputation as being the best treatment for popliteal aneurysms that were causing severe pain.

Chapter 45

rotten borough: A small constituency in the United Kingdom with only a few voters that could be used by a patron to gain a seat in the House of Commons.

John Hunter: A Scottish surgeon and anatomist, born in 1728, and often regarded as the father of modern surgery.

Charles Byrne: An eight-foot-tall Irishman who exhibited himself in London in 1782–83.

Chapter 47

incision: This fictional account of surgery on a popliteal aneurysm was inspired by observations made by an Italian surgeon, Paolo Assalani, who was present when John Hunter first successfully performed the operation on a coachman in 1785. The account is featured in Wendy Moore's *The Knife Man.*

Chapter 49

clarify the law of England: During a lengthy court case in 1772, the slave James Somersett was freed by the judge, Lord Mansfield, on the grounds that slavery was so "odious" that the benefit of doubt must prevail on Somersett's behalf, although, in practice, the law remained ambiguous.

pregnant: Small bumps around the nipples, called Montgomery's tubercles, appear during pregnancy and remain afterward.

Chapter 50

James Somersett: See Chapter 49.

carrying the massa's child: Sexual abuse was endemic between enslaved women and their enslavers. The Rev. William Smith's account, written in the early eighteenth century, is one illustration. He wrote of a Negro woman giving birth to both a black child and one of mixed race, pointing out: "Her Husband had carnal knowledge of her, just before he went out to his work, and as soon as he was gone, the White Overseer went to the Hut, and had the like carnal knowledge."
Source: http://www.nhm.ac.uk/resources-rx/files/chapter-6-resistance-19110.pdf

Chapter 52

self-inflicted wound: Studies show many suicides choose an exposed area of flesh to stab, so their clothing is not damaged.

roundel: In 1787 the renowned potter and reformer Josiah Wedgwood produced medallions bearing the famous inscription *Am I not a man and a brother.* The inscription *Am I not a woman and a sister* did not appear until 1828.

Chapter 53

Congress of the Confederation in Maryland: The Congress ratified the Treaty of Paris on January 14, 1784, in the Senate Chamber of the Maryland State House, formally ending the Revolutionary War.

Chapter 54

litmus test: Robert Boyle (1627–1691) discovered that litmus paper turns bluish-green when in contact with alkalis.

Chapter 57

George and Dragon: An early-eighteenth-century coaching inn, still a hotel to this day. A secret tunnel is rumored to run between the hotel and the famous Hellfire Caves. The ghost of a serving girl, who was found dead in the caves, is said to haunt the inn.

West Wycombe Park: The ancestral home of the Dashwood family is open to the public and provides the setting for several period films and television series, including *Little Dorrit* and *The Duchess.*

lithotomies: The surgical procedure to remove stones from hollow organs.

mandrake: Pliny the Elder describes how the root was used by ancient surgeons as an anesthetic.

Chapter 58

Bedlam: The full name of the famous hospital for the mentally ill is Bethlehem Royal Hospital, but from the fourteenth century it was often referred to as Bedlam.